To the Reader

First and foremost, I would like to thank you for opening this book. It really means a lot to me.

Secondly, I am not a native speaker of English, and although I tried to do my best to make this book readable and even artistic at times, I am not sure there will not be anything to grate on your ear. Please bear with it and forgive me for it. The reason why I still decided to use English is obvious, however, struggling with a foreign language was the least difficult thing in the process of writing.

And, finally, some of my personal thoughts. I came up with the idea of this book more than five years ago, and I initially planned to make it so exaggerated that I could hardly imagine anyone who would believe it. But as time went by, all those things which seemed unbelievable, suddenly became part of our everyday reality, and somehow, I feel that there is more of them to come. Before they do, I would like to capture this moment, to reflect on it and maybe it will help to deal with the situation and remain cold-headed when the whole world is going to pieces. Even if some of the ideas seem primitive, they might be a good ground for further reflection.

And a disclaimer. This story is fictional and does not depict any actual people places or events.

Doors opening

To the future or to the past, to a time when thought is free, when men are different from one another and do not live alone — to a time when truth exists and what is done cannot be undone: From the age of uniformity, from the age of solitude, from the age of Big Brother, from the age of doublethink — greetings!
George Orwell, 1984

To Alexei Navalny, the prisoner who knows all about freedom

Prologue. 2036

Long, cold and uncomfortable corridor with gray shabby walls, which are covered with faded pictures of butterflies, rabbits, balloons and something else, hardly visible in the all-consuming darkness. A lonely silhouette of a boy with downcast eyes is placed right in the middle of the corridor. It looks like he's been crying because his eyes are red and watery, but now he's just standing there, and the door closes behind him, and the walls are closing too, and there is no way to escape, so there's no point in crying anymore. The boy is holding tight to his two dearest belongings – a stuffed toy elephant and a large book in a thick cover. In front of him there are two women, one of which is measuring him with a long worn-out gaze as if trying to figure out something in her mind. At last, she speaks, coldly and firmly:

"You're Borya Arsenyev, right? Come closer, Borya. We've been expecting you," then she turns to her colleague, apparently a nurse. "Lyudmila Ivanovna, please, take Borya's things from him," and then to Borya again. "You are not allowed to have any personal belongings here."

The nurse makes two confident steps towards the boy and rips the elephant and the book out of his hands. The other woman nods approvingly, gives both of them a final meaningless stare and walks away, her steps echoing coldly against the walls of the corridor. After she disappears in the darkness, Lyudmila Ivanovna grabs Borya's hand and drags him up to the door of the dormitory.

"Here, Borya, time to sleep. Go in. Quiet, don't wake the others up. Your bed is the second one on the left, you see it? The empty one."

She opens the door and pushes him inside. The second bed on the left is covered with a spiky brown blanket, on top of which there is a grey knobby pillow without a case. The dormitory is lit by a greenish night light, which illuminates the beds, the blankets, and the heads of the other children – round and short-haired, as if copied one from another. Borya sits down on the blanket and keeps still for a few minutes, observing the surroundings, until he is finally taken down by weariness. Realizing there's nothing left to do, he falls on the blanket and buries himself in the pillow which smells of dirt and someone's tears. He doesn't want to sleep, he doesn't want to cry, he doesn't want anything but to dissolve in this pillow, die under the spiky blanket or just vanish in the green light. He wants to forget that he has just lost everything, including his treasured toys, and all those things holding his life together are gone now, gone for good. And also, he wants a drink of water, but he doesn't know who and how to ask for it. His mouth is dry, and so are his eyes, which are tired of crying and seeing things a six-year-old boy is not supposed to see.

Suddenly Borya hears a sound of the door opening and after it some quiet hostile steps approaching his bed. He squeezes himself deep into the pillow, ignoring its filthy fetor and tries not to move. The steps are getting closer, and now he can feel someone's hand tapping gently on his shoulder and then pushing something under his head. He is still afraid to move and holds his breath, which has already soaked up the dirt from the pillow. The steps are fading gradually, and finally he hears the door closing behind them, and the dormitory sinks back into silence. He opens his eyes and looks down. Beside his bed there is a small cup of water with a picture of an elephant making a funny fountain out of its trunk. Borya starts drinking insatiably and when the cup is empty, looks at it for a while, and a faint smile lights up his face. He likes elephants. They are big and strong, just like his… no, he doesn't remember. Then he gets his hand under the pillow and fishes out his book – the one that they took away in the corridor. It was brought back by someone who might be his new friend. On its front page there is a note, written in familiar firm handwriting – "For Boris, to learn to read. Your Grampy." Borya touches the letters gently, closes the book and puts it back under his pillow, which for a while has stopped being so disgusting. He is now ready to let his thoughts go and to sink into heavy sleep full of fearful dreams, which have occupied his shortly cut head for long years. Lyudmila Ivanovna, watching the boy from the dormitory window, makes sure that he is asleep and then goes away with a despondent sigh, leaving his fate to the enveloping darkness.

Bears went to the hike
A-riding on a bike.
Then came Tom-the-Cat,
Back-to-front he sat.
Spry mosquitoes drifted by
In a big balloon on high.
Lobsters looked like shrimps
On a dog that limps.
Wolves were mounted on a horse.
Lions drove in cars, of course.
Hares in pairs
Crammed in a tram.
Toad rode on a broom...
What a merry bunch!
Gingernuts they munch.

"What a nice little boy," says the darkness. "Sleep tight, my dear, as you have a long way ahead of you. I hope that you'll make it, as I have plans for you. Big plans for a little boy. I'll be here, and you'll meet me later. Much later, when you're old enough to go on my altar."

Chapter 1. 2060

1

Boris woke up to the chipper sound of morning alarm which was supposed to instantly throw all combatants out of their beds. While the others were quickly getting dressed and rushing to the washing room, he could take his time. Today was a special day for him, and the rules of the army didn't work on him anymore. It was quite chilly in the barracks, but that was not the sort of cold which had dominated here throughout the winter, exhausting the soldiers more than campaigns and marches. That cold seemed to have soaked into the walls and the beds, into every object that it had touched, but despite all its efforts, spring was finally there, bringing in the sun and the joy of renovation. Boris was especially waiting for this spring. Having spent several weeks in hospital after being injured in a battle, he felt low and completely devastated, like a helpless child. To his relief, with the first rays of spring sun, life was gradually returning into his injured body, and his melancholy was bit by bit going away.

Boris managed to get out of his bed almost at once, quickly put on his uniform and stood to attention when Colonel Petrenko entered the barracks. He knew why the Colonel was there and felt a bit sad to say goodbye to him.

"Ready?" asked Petrenko cheerly.

"Yes, sir! Sergeant Boris Arsenyev ready to transfer to reserve!"

"Haven't changed your mind, have you, Arsenyev?"

"No way, Colonel!"

"Listen to me, Arsenyev," Petrenko seated himself on the bed and invited Boris to sit next to him. "How long have I known you? Fifteen years or so? I remember how you got here, green and frightened, like a tiny little sparrow. Raised you from the cradle, so to say. And that's what I think. You're not gonna find a good life in the rear. It's so different from what you're used to. You got a family?"

"No way, sir, I'm an orphan. I don't remember my family. Grew up in the Center of Patriotic Education for Boys. I think I've told you already."

"Okay-okay. I know. Happy with your new accommodation?"

"Yes, sir. Thanks for your help, sir. I know it was hard to arrange it for me – soldiers don't often get free rooms from the State nowadays."

"It's your flat, anyway. When you got to the orphanage, it went to the city authorities, and they granted it to new people. I don't know who they are, and I don't know if they are happy to have you as a neighbor, but I heard they freed up a room for you, the smallest one, of course, but considering it's in the capital, almost in the center, this fact makes you quite an eligible bachelor. But don't jump into marriage, Arsenyev, that's the worst thing to do now."

"I wasn't going to. I have to find my way in life first," Boris felt a trifle uneasy discussing such matters with a superior.

"Good," nodded Petrenko. "So, back to where you belong then, right? Maybe you'll even find something from your childhood there. A picture, or a toy you used to like. Of course, all the things from your flat have long been utilized, but if I were you, I'd try my luck in some nice hiding place. Maybe it will help you remember your past. A man without a past is like a tree without roots. He can't grow, I mean."

Petrenko had this funny habit of trying to be philosophical at times, and he must have thought he sounded sublime, but no one else thought the same. Worse than his philosophical outpourings was only his sense of humor translated in unfunny jokes as old as this world.

The Colonel paused. "Anyways, Arsenyev, you are a good soldier. The Center of Patriotic Education knows its business, they only send the best ones to us. If not for your wound, I'd never let you go. You're brave and devoted, and the army needs such combatants. The rear is not for you, Sergeant. You'll have to learn to live there, with your boldness, but without arms, without anyone to direct you. How're you going to make your living, I wonder?"

"I think I'll start with learning. Studying graphics. It's been sort of my childhood dream to draw holograms. I used to draw in the Center, but it wasn't encouraged there. They said it wouldn't have helped if foreign agents had attacked us. 'What would you do?' they asked. "Show them your scrabble?" And now I can try to learn. I can draw whatever you want – broadcasts, window wallpaper, advertisements, you name it."

"Broadcasts…" the Colonel seemed to be lost in thought. "Drawing is good, I guess… We all kinda think these things are useless, a piece of crap. People will watch a broadcast and forget about it straight away. But there's more to it. Everything depends on what you tell them, how much soul you put into it. And you think right thoughts, Arsenyev, and people listen to you. People listen to me, too, by the way, but I can't draw. My job is to lead and to command. So let me do it for you for the last time. Sergeant Arsenyev, internal number 152-AH1021, at my command!

Attention! By the Order 94-11CH you are transferred to reserve starting from today, the 21st of April year 2060!"

"Yes, sir!"

"At ease! Oh, I almost forgot! I've got a present for you, Sergeant," Colonel Petrenko went into his pocket and took out a rectangular object made of black shiny plastic with a small screen on top. It was not more than ten by fifteen centimeters and lay quite comfortably on his palm. "It's not a real present because it's my duty to give it to you, but I was actually the one who chose the model."

"Is it a broadcaster?" guessed Boris.

"Right. All citizens are obliged to have one. They usually buy it when they're fifteen, and they might use one broadcaster for the family if they live together. However, you must always have one registered for yourself, keep it charged and turned on because if your broadcaster is offline for more than twenty-four hours, you'll be in trouble. Do you know how it works?"

"Yes… In general terms…"

"So, first you have to register it. Put your finger on the screen for it to read your fingerprint. And let it scan your retina, too. No, no, roll these eyes back, it will do it automatically, just try not to blink for a couple of seconds."

The broadcaster turned on, and Boris pressed his thumb on its screen.

"Biometrical data registered," confirmed the device.

"Good," nodded the Colonel. "It will take some time for the artificial intelligence to get used to your voice, but it will, eventually. Now say your name and internal number."

"Boris Arsenyev, internal number 152-AH1021."

"The device is registered to Boris Arsenyev, internal number 152-AH1021," announced the machine. "Connecting to network… Successful. Retrieving data… Successful. Updating… Successful. Setup finished. The device is ready to use. Enjoy your day!"

"Now," continued Petrenko, "when you enter the city, it will connect to the National Network Assistant Katyusha. It will control the broadcaster and do whatever you ask it. The screen here has a built-in projector. It will show all national channels and display information on your request. And take good care of the device, if it gets damaged, you'll have to report it to the authorities and wait for several weeks to get it replaced. Got it?"

"Yes, sir! Thank you, sir!"

"No problem. This thing also keeps names and internal numbers of other citizens. You just tell it to store the details and later you'll be able to contact the person. It will retrieve the number from its memory and sent the message you dictate to it. I've stored mine because you never know what might happen to you out there. If you have any problem on your way to the capital, just let me know, okay?"

"I promise I'll send a message when I get… home." Boris said this word and it sounded very unnatural, as if pronounced by someone else.

"It's up to you. I'll probably be… I'll probably be too busy to reply. What else?... You can keep your army satnav; it'll guide you to the destination. And the most important thing," the Colonel handed him a small black card. "This is your micropass. It's already registered to you. It opens the doors in the city, but only those which are stated in your route list. I've approved your movement, and the route list will automatically go into your broadcaster. Now swipe the micropass against the screen to activate it."

Boris did.

"Micropass activated," said the machine.

"You can go now, Sergeant Arsenyev. I've done everything I could. For you, and for… Never mind. So, are you sure you don't remember your family?"

"No, sir, I don't, sir!"

"Go then. Good luck. Good goddamn luck to you!"

Boris saluted the Colonel for the last time and watched him walk away from the barracks, and a strange but familiar feeling of loss rose from the inside, went down his injured spine and settled in his heart. However, there was no time to grieve. He had to pack his things and go, or he'd be late for his train. The new life welcomed him with a light breeze and sparkling cloudless sky.

Boris's military unit was located in the middle of the country, about 300 kilometers from the capital. It was an old tradition to call all military locations 'the frontline', although the real frontline was more than 50 kilometers further to the south. Most of the time the combatants of Boris's unit were occupied with studying and developing military equipment, drawing maps, checking and replacing broken and outdated facilities and other routine, which seemed unimportant, but needed to be done for the benefit of the State. Boris was very fortunate to get a place here right after graduating from the Center of Patriotic Education, because most of his peers, as he knew, were transferred to the rear to ensure the safety of civilians. Terrorists and foreign agents aimed their attacks mostly at cities and towns where common people were locked inside their homes, terrified by constant enemy raids. Cities were just as dangerous as scenes of the fighting, so Boris wasn't expecting a quiet life there. Nevertheless, he was happy to make this change. He didn't mind serving the State, but he wanted to try something different, something he'd always dreamt of. He let the streamers of sun lick his clean-shaven face and the tender wind of spring patted him gently on his shortly cut hair.

The way to the station was familiar to Boris, but still it somehow felt weird to walk it at a normal pace, not marching to the Officers' commands. The path was narrow and winding, chaotically blocked by puddles filled with sticky dirt, which were willing to catch his shoes and the bottom of his pants into their viscous prison. Boris was so afraid to miss his train that he ignored the condition of his clothes and hurried towards the station. There was not a single person on the way, only a couple of self-registration points, demanding him to swipe his micropass and give his name and internal number. When he was about halfway through his journey, he was stopped by a human military patrol, which consisted of two Officers, whom he'd never met before. One of them was quite young, not more than eighteen, and another one looked the same age as Boris. They checked his biometry twice, tested his micropass on their equipment, questioned him about his starting and destination points, and all the stopovers that he was going to make between them. The interrogation took about fifteen minutes, and finally they let him go, although their faces showed that they still weren't convinced.

Boris felt extremely nervous about being late for the train, but when he got to the station, he found out that he was more than an hour early and sighed with relief. The platform was empty, and he felt a bit alarmed because he wasn't used to be all alone, especially in an unfamiliar place. Apart from that, his backpack seemed too small and light and didn't provide any sense of security at all. An electric train departed from the station once in 24 hours and it was supposed to take Boris to a hub, from which he would catch another one, heading for the capital.

A self-registration point refused to let him to the departure zone although he swiped his micropass and gave his name and internal number several times. "Your transport is leaving in… 57 minutes. Please wait. The access to the departure zone will be granted in… 26 minutes… 14 seconds," informed the mechanical voice. Boris was starting to get annoyed and, ignoring the desperate squeaking of the machine, went straight to the platform and sat on the old, cracked asphalt. The patrolling drone appeared in less than ten minutes, and Boris noted to himself that it was followed by an advanced model of self-isolator, 185-SB004, equipped with hypno-rays and paralyzing gas. It politely asked him to identify himself and after he had done so, opened the doors cordially and informed that "Citizen Boris Arsenyev, internal number 152-AH1021, has been made aware of the necessity to leave the departure zone at 13 hours and 3 minutes. The order of the Government Committee of Migration Control was ignored. The violation implies a penalty of five hundred thousand GKB, paid immediately, or a 24-hour immobilization." The choice was obvious. Immobilization was out of the question, especially since the train departed in less than 40 minutes. Boris had received a neat compensation for his service, which was supposed to have arrived on his account, so he swiped his finger on the self-isolator's sensor, waited for the payment confirmation and finally left the runway only to return in less than 15 minutes.

It was not so easy to get to the capital. Every 20 kilometers all passengers were required to undergo a self-registration procedure and at some points they were subject to biomaterial analyses. After 24 hours, exhausted and starving, Boris entered the doors of the Capital's Station number 3 of the Citizens' Reception and Distribution. The hall was almost empty with only a few people dressed in black standing in front of self-redirection points. Even though there was no queue, Boris had to wait another 30 minutes to be granted the permission to exit, but only after receiving a package with self-camouflaging means: a black hat, a black mask and black silicone gloves. They looked so ugly that his first thought was to tuck them deep into his backpack, but then he remembered his encounter with the self-isolator at the station and changed his mind.

Anyway, he was used to wearing uniform and it never seemed to bother him at all.

There were three public transport routes through the city, and only one of them went close to the area that he needed. A self-driving tram with blinded windows was empty and extremely stuffy, which at first made Boris claustrophobic and a bit panicky. There was nowhere to sit down, so he accommodated himself on the floor, close to the doors, and put his backpack between his legs. The car went slowly, swinging from side to side and rattling its worn-out motor desperately, while the mechanical voice announced the stops and informed the absent passengers of the importance of following the security regulations. Boris counted the stops and prayed that the tram didn't break down half-way, because it would have taken him another two or three hours to wait for the next one. He was so hypnotized by the stiffness and the swinging that he nearly fell asleep, woken up by "Next stop is… 5th Unity Lane. Please swipe your micropass on the controller before you leave the transport. Warning: according to the Order of the Government Committee of Migration Control, all attempts of unauthorized displacement will be suppressed." That was his stop, and Boris quickly picked up his backpack and jumped to his feet, impatient for the doors to open and reveal his new place of dwelling.

However, it was not the end of the journey. The stop was about 2500 meters from his house, and there was no other option than to walk through empty streets, generously furnished with self-registration points, under the scrutiny of all-seeing patrolling drones. The army satnav was old and half-broken and would not show the correct way to the destination, making Boris meaninglessly wander the streets of the capital. At times, especially when he took a wrong turning, self-registrators warned him about it with loud disaffected signals, reminding of penalties for violating the rules. Having grown up in the public orphanage and then having served in the army for fifteen years, Boris had already got used to obeying the orders and being under permanent control, but this time it seemed so hard and senseless. The machines were cold, dead-hearted and aggressive, as if their whole mechanical world was revolting against him.

As Boris had expected, the city contained more war than the frontline. Houses, leaning against each other, were crying with fading plaster on their walls; roads, ruined by mutilated asphalt, were covered with cracked mouths of hollows, which had caught some pieces of inelaborate city trash. But what scared him most was silence – dead and desperate silence, which plunged into the ears and tore the eardrums apart, more violently than military grenades and bombs. The city made everything broken – machines, people, the scenery – all of those seemed unnatural, unexplainable, alien. Even the time was wrong. It was absorbed in the crumbly damp walls, it got stuck in attics, basements and narrow gateways, it lost itself in wires, hanging from rusty pillars – and seemed to come to a stand. It was impossible to tell whether he'd been roaming there an hour or a century, it was all the same, and nothing in this world could make the time break free from the deadlock where it had voluntarily painted itself. And only the sky, looking cautiously from behind the iron-plated roofs, suspiciously smooth and irrelevantly blue, reminded that the world had more colors than light and dark grey. The city smelled of rotten bricks and unsettled spring.

Boris was feeling increasingly anxious, and his only desire was to finally reach his new place of dwelling and sleep until he completely forgets the shock of the past twenty-four hours. But the houses looked all the same and almost locked him between their cold shabby walls. Passing for the fifth time on the same dead street, Boris lost his nerve, stopped and started looking around, trying to find whatever could help him get out of this nightmare. He didn't know how long he would have to stand like this, being vigilantly gazed by mobile self-registrators, when suddenly something caught his eye. His memory responded to some tiny part of the landscape and made him examine the surroundings more closely.

Opposite him, just across the road, he spotted a hill, sparkling with withered grass left from last year, topped with colorful rubbish. The place was quite regular for the city, but, at the same time, it had a meaning, something that made it special, or even homey. It looked like a piece of his earlier life, a place where they used to go with someone, a relative maybe, maybe even with his grandfather, to play, to sit on the ground and watch the world go by, or just hang around and chat about nothing. They could probably look at the clouds and follow the flight of starlings up in the sky, they could feel the smell of freshly cut grass in summer and chill out eating chips, which were sold in the nearby stall. And sometimes grandfather let him browse funny comics on his old phone with a broken screen, and they would laugh like crazy at those simple pictures. His grandfather. He was sure he didn't remember him. He must forget again, or something bad would happen to him and to… Boris tried to kick the uninvited memories out of his head, but they just kept pushing their way through his thoughts, like a big hulking tank.

There they are, sitting on the grass and someone asks little Borya tenderly, yet seriously.

"So, tell me, chubs, when you grow up, what're you going to be?"

"I think, Grampy, I think I'm gonna be a scientist. I'll invent things – all sort of things, whatever I want. And when it bores me, I'll be an artist, I guess."

"An artist?" Grampy raises his eyebrows in unnatural surprise. "And what are you going to draw, young man?"

"Elephant!"

"An elephant?" Grampy seems even more surprised. "With a trunk?"

"Sure! With two trunks! No, with a hungried trunks!" Borya bursts out laughing and Granddad notices that one of his front teeth has finally come out, and it makes the boy look so touching and helpless.

"One hundred, Borya, say 'one hundred trunks.'"

"You remember we went sledging here in winter?" Borya doesn't like to be corrected and changes the subject. "Are we going again?"

"Of course, we are. And this time we'll take Nastya, too."
Borya frowns.

"We'd better not, Grampy. She's always crying. She'll ruin all the fun. Just you and me, okay?"

"Deal! Just you and me. Our small team."

"And is winter coming soon?"

"Not so soon, chubs. Summer ends, after it there is autumn, and finally comes winter. Just wait. Oh, I've got an idea! Let's get you a bike, chubby! A big bike for a big boy."

"I dunno… Maybe… Maybe you could get me an elephant? A real elephant? They're big and funny, and I can keep one in our room, instead of the piano. No one plays it, anyway. Like you read me in our book: 'And an elephant all-a-shake sat on hedgehog by mistake!'"

Borya laughs again and demonstrates how the elephant landed on the hedgehog. "There were bears on a bike there, remember? The bears rode it, I know, but I'd still prefer an elephant. Will you read the 'Cock-the Roach to me at bed today?"

"Why not, chubs. I like it, too. Or maybe you want to learn to read yourself? Homeschooling is good, but I'm not sure you read enough with your mum. Do you want me to teach you?"

"Not really. I guess it's sort of boring. You know what, Grampy, I'd better learn to draw. You'll grow old soon and you'll maybe forget how we went sledging here. You know what I'll do? I'll come to visit you and I'll draw us together on the snow. You'll look at the picture and tell me if I'm a good artist or not, okay? And how do I draw snow? Is it just white? It isn't, I think it's like… like… mac… nac… nacreous?"

"Promise me you'll come to visit me, Boris," Grampy's voice is low and somewhat tragic. "Promise me you'll draw the elephant, and the snow, and you and me together. I'll be waiting for you, Boris, anytime…"

Boris shook his head and looked away from the hill.

"I promise you, old rat, I promise to forget you, I almost have, and you just… You just wouldn't stop! You keep visiting me in my nightmares, again and again, with your frozen eyes and your bloody twisted leg! I don't need to come and talk to you to know for sure that I'll make a good artist, even though your rotten blood is still running through my veins. Nothing will stop me. Do you hear me, traitor? I'll soon cross you out of my mind forever, and my memory isn't so good, as you probably know. And if you ever dare to disturb me, I'll kill you again. That's what I promise. With these bare hands of mine!"

"You ok, lad?" Boris gave a start. The voice quite obviously belonged to a human, not a controlling machine, which was even more frightening. "Lost something?"

"No, I'm fine. Just thinking."

He turned around and saw a young man, probably of his age, or even younger, dressed in a black coat and rubber boots. He also had all the self-camouflaging items, but his mask was moved to his chin, so Boris could see his entire face. The guy measured him with a long stare.

"If I were you, I wouldn't 'ang around too long. This rubbish is kinda toxic, in case you didn't know. So, tell me, lad, you from 'ere? 'aven't seen you before, 'ave I."

"Yes, I'm from here. Sorry, I haven't got time," Boris wanted to get rid of the strange guy and started looking around as if he was really in a hurry.

"That's ok. I'm from 'ere too."

"I see. But aren't all citizens supposed to stay home? Locked down?"

"Not me, mate. I'm a factory worker."

"Factory worker?"

"You dumb or what? Or fell from the Moon? Factory worker, lad, we work outside and provide you with food and supplies, got it now?"

"So, you can travel around without… route lists?"

"Yes and no, mate. We're taken to and from work by buses. Self-driven ones, of course. They get us straight 'ome and we shouldn't wander around 'ere. It's kinda illegal. But I've got business today. I'm Joseph, by the way, and you?"

"Joseph? Strange name, I'd say."

"I know. My folks took it from a book. You know, books, things to read?"

"Never heard of them. Well, I'm Boris."

"Great. Boris – a name for a champion. Are you a 'ome person, Boris? What do you do?"

"I'm an artist."

"I bet you are. You're all artists, or programmers, or composers. You white- 'anded are all the same. Deadbeats. Never 'eld nothin' 'eavier than a spoon in your 'ands. Wait. You look too fit for a homebody. They're normally a bit squabby 'coz they don't exercise much. You know what? You're good and strong, as I see. I can take you to my factory. I can talk to people. Whad'ya say, lad? Wanna work with me?"

It sounded so strange that Boris couldn't come up with an answer at once. He stood there, with his hands in his pockets, trying to figure out how to escape quickly and without raising suspicion. Just finish this silly conversation and get home.

"Thanks, buddy, but I'm fine where I am."

"I'm chuffed for you then, mate."

Boris suddenly noticed that the guy's coat was unnaturally bulging as if he was hiding something inside it.

"What have you got there?" he wondered.

"Shhhh, mate, you're not supposed to know! That's none of your business!"

"Something prohibited?"

"Yes and no again. If I show you, you promise not to tell anyone?"

Boris looked around to see if there was a self-registrator or something he could report to in case he found out that the man turned out to be a felon. He already regretted being so stupidly curious and asking questions that had no relation to him.

"I promise. I guess…"

The guy unzipped the top of his coat, and Boris saw two green eyes blinking at the daylight.

"What's that? Is it a…? How's it called? 'Then came Tom-the-Cat, Back-to-front he sat'," he suddenly remembered these words from his book and a picture of a cat riding a tiny bike.

"The daft ball of fat, mate, that's what it is, innit? Picked it up just before meeting you and that was the business, I told you about. Thought that they'd all been eaten by rats, but this one's quite alive."

"Can you keep it?"

"Dunno. What does it feed on? Mice? Anyways, I'd better be off. I'm bloody starving, mate. Gonna get some scran and then put my feet up and watch the 'broadie'. You sure you don't wanna go to factory?"

"I am, but thanks for offering. See you when I see you then, I suppose?"

"Quite fair. Ta-da, lad, stay safe."

When Joseph walked away, Boris felt relieved. He knew that he had to make just one little effort and strain his memory, which turned out to be more reliable than his satnav. The hill was there, on the left, which meant that his house should be very close. He noticed the spot where they used to cross the road with his mother, and she held his and his sister's hands tight because the traffic at those times was rather busy. After that they would stop near the stalls where ruddy, overly cheerful saleswomen sold various knick-knack, which was extremely attractive to kids. Toys, bubble blowers, cards with characters from the children's TV network Fidgy Freckles, and even sets of felt pens of acid colors – a longed-for dream of little Borya. His mother used to hold his hand even tighter not to let him stare at those treasures, because she was probably sorry she didn't have the money to buy anything from there.

The place of the stalls was now occupied by a heap of scrap metal with a tint of corrosion and mold, but it was still recognizable. The house should be just a stone's throw away, and Boris speeded across the road, paying no attention to the signals of a self-registrator, jumped over a pile of stinky rubbish, kicked away a rat that tried to block his way and immediately stepped into some thick brown goo. All of this didn't matter. The new life awaited him, where he would surely become a good artist and draw an elephant with one hungried trunks on the macreous snow.

2

The block of flats had only one entrance with the door that wouldn't close and was roughly attached to the hinges in the doorway, ready to come off them at any moment. The lift was expectedly broken, to be more exact, it was missing completely, and its shaft gaped between the stairs like a gullet of some huge prehistoric animal. Boris looked at it suspiciously, wondering if the lift had been there when he was a child. He was almost sure it had because he remembered its clatter every time someone was using it. He could almost hear the sound, and suddenly a wave of cold sweat enveloped him from head to toes. "Run and hide! Run and hide! Run and hide!" rattled the missing lift, and some unsettling feeling caught Boris by his throat and made it almost impossible for him to breathe. He leapfrogged to the fifth floor in less than a minute. The darkness of the hall was torn apart by the dim glow coming from red diodes, attached above each flat door. These red lights meant that the doors were blocked and will open only upon special request to those who had a necessary authorization. The same diodes were placed on the opposite sides signifying that the flat was safe from the inside. Boris searched his pocket and for the hundredth time pulled out his micropass, which he had received from Colonel Petrenko. He swiped it on the lock of Flat 42 and waited for its reaction. "The micropass is not registered for access to these premises. Please use another micropass. Two attempts left." The mechanical voice was accompanied by an alarm signal which sounded so loud that Boris almost jumped out of his shoes. "Two attempts and then what?" he thought. "Penalty? Immobilization? Self-liquidation?" He remembered the words of Colonel Petrenko and now they made more sense than ever. What if this hostile world would never take back its prodigal son, who had left it twenty-four years ago? What if he would never get used to life in the rear? What if he'd be standing here at the blocked door, trying vainly to get in, until a self-isolator arrived to immobilize him till the end of his life? He swiped the micropass again.

"This micropass is authorized to enter the premises," the machine suddenly informed. "Door will be unblocked for ten seconds. Warning: according to the Order of the Government Committee of Migration Control, all unauthorized attempts to leave the premises during the unblocking will be suppressed. Starting the countdown. Nine..." Boris didn't wait until it said "eight" and swiftly broke into his new old apartment. The light diode went red again behind his back.

It turned out that his hustle behind the door had jolted other residents of the flat. An elderly lady with a garish kerchief upon her grey hair stuck her head from one of the rooms and, just in front of her, an old man in shabby sweatpants and an inappropriately solemn white shirt with a missing button was squinting at him with a mixture of curiosity and distrust. Boris was not prepared for such a warm welcome and gabbled whatever he could think of first: "Citizen Boris Arsenyev, transferred to reserve on the 21st of April 2060 has arrived at the place of permanent deployment!" The old man assumed a dignified air and approached Boris.

"So, you are Arsenyev, aren't you?" he said as if he hadn't heard the salutation. "The rightful heir of the flat. I'm Yegor Semenovich Mikhailov, if you please, and over there is my wife, Juliana Pavlovna, also Mikhailova, quite coincidentally. Welcome home, citizen Boris Arsenyev! Have you disinfected yourself?"

Before he could answer, the elderly lady rushed to Boris with a disinfecting lamp and sprayed him with something from a large plastic bottle. It looked like plain water, but surely enough possessed strong antimicrobial powers. After making some mysterious movements with the lamp and sprinkling Boris's clothes with the disinfector, Juliana Pavlovna stepped back behind her husband.

"So… Where can I accommodate myself?" asked Boris shifting from one foot to the other.

"Don't you remember?" Yegor Semenovich looked surprised. "It's supposed to be your home, isn't it? Your former home, I mean."

"No… No, I don't remember. I was too small, I guess," answered Boris.

"The door on the left, sonny," Juliana Pavlovna said kindly. "We've left you some furniture, you know, a table, a sofa and a couple of chairs. Not much, but that's all we have for now. I'm so sorry there's nothing to treat you to. Our grocery sets have already been delivered but you should order one for yourself tomorrow. I'll show you later if you don't mind."

Boris thanked the hostess and opened the door of his room. He was not sure whether he was hungry or not, but he was definitely tired. So tired that he threw himself on the sofa, which quivered under his body and momentarily bit his ribs with its sharp protruding springs. He could sleep now, and no morning alarm would ever wake him up. Overwhelmed by the bitter reality of his new life, he dozed off at once, although it was only about six o'clock in the evening.

3

The first thing which the next morning brought Boris was unbearable pain in his back, irradiating throughout his body. The wound had responded to the long journey and uncomfortable sleeping position, and he had to lie still for a while before he could make himself get up. After pain came another horseman of apocalypse – hunger. Boris couldn't remember when exactly he had eaten up all the feed he'd kept in his backpack, but that must have been even before he'd arrived in the city. He had to find something to chew up on right now, and he made a few staggering steps towards the door. His pain was still there, although it had already begun to cease, as if absconding before the next battle. Comparing to the dormitory of the Center of Patriotic Education and the barracks in the army, Boris's new room looked tiny and miserable. There were only five steps from one wall to the opposite, but even these steps were difficult to make due to the shabby old-fashioned furniture, which was too cumbersome and bulky for such small space. A couch with deranged springs, yielding spasmodically after each movement, an unsteady wooden table with some uncleanable sticky stains, a crooked chair and a wardrobe without one door. It all belonged to him now, and he was happy because it was still better than nothing. At least the squares of the linoleum, which covered the floor, were even and enjoyable to look at.

The flat smelled of unwashed floor and greasy linens. It was strange, but Boris couldn't recognize it at all. He tried to imagine himself here, as a child, and finally some vague recollections started to shine through the mist of the past. The large bedroom had been occupied by his mother, father, sister and himself, and the smaller one, the one where he was staying now, belonged to his grandfather. But that was all he could remember, as if his memory had been completely deleted and all the earlier events had been cleared out by someone, maybe even by himself. Boris had a feeling that his grandfather's room had always been closed, and the children were rarely permitted to go in. However, he could recall himself at some point, hiding under the grandfather's sofa, but he couldn't figure out what for. Ironically, the room was now all his, and other people would have to knock at the door, like he'd done as a kid, to get permission to go inside.

It was completely logical to start looking for food in the kitchen, but before going there, Boris turned in the bathroom, where he found out that there was no water to flush the toilet. Feeling a bit uneasy, he tried to clean up after himself and then quietly proceeded to the point of his destination. First thing he saw was a large window, disguised by cheap animated wallpaper, which showed three dull landscapes. The view of a winter forest was followed by a garden with blooming apple trees and finally it displayed a picture of a mountain spring. Then the three-image loop started again. The air conditioner occupied the top right corner of the window, and it blew out some gusts of cool air at regular intervals. Boris was staring at the wallpaper trying to make out whether he liked it or not, when Juliana Pavlovna entered the kitchen.

"Up already, sonny?" she asked. Her voice seemed to have lost all yesterday's shyness and sounded soft and soothing. "Don't worry about the toilet, dear, we only flush when we get water, which is barely two hours in the morning and two hours in the evening. But you know what they say, your own waste smells of roses," she laughed warmly, like all old people do.

"Thank you," Boris said gratefully. "Excuse me, ma'am, where can I find something to eat here?"

The old woman livened up.

"Over here, sonny, you're just in time. We must make our orders before ten o'clock, otherwise they won't get into today's delivery."

She led Boris to a small square door on the outer wall, above which there was a screen with some pictures on it.

"This is our self-provision point. You choose a grocery set every morning and it's delivered in the evening. All houses have different delivery schedule, and it changes every year or two. Ours is from five to seven in the evening. There are mainly three sets available: number one, two and three. We usually order set number three, and once a week number two. Our money allowance isn't so generous these days," she clarified embarrassedly.

"So, it means that the third one is the cheapest?"

"Yes, but it's also quite poor. Nothing to eat, really. Here, let me show you. It's all on the screen."

The screen displayed various images, which made Boris's mouth water. When you pressed on an image, the familiar mechanical voice began reading its description, and Juliana Pavlovna commented on each of them, as if they were her good friends or close relatives.

"Grocery set number three," uttered the voice. "Contents for April 24, 2060. Main menu. Bread classified as standard, three slices."

Juliana Pavlovna pressed on the screen to pause the description. "100 grams of bread," she explained. "It was called 'third grade' some time ago, but now they changed the name, so it's 'standard'. Made from, I guess, tailings or something. Then goes artificial butter spread, look."

"Vegetable fats spread," confirmed the voice. "With butter flavor."

"It'll make your bread quite edible. It really has a taste of butter, too acrid maybe, so don't hold it in your mouth for too long.

Also, there must be cereal – the source of carbohydrates, let's see what they've put today."

"Hand-picked pearl barley processed and exfoliated," said the machine.

"Oh, pearl barley…" Juliana Pavlovna looked upset. "Not your day today, sonny, I'm sorry. No, it's not that bad, but it can be a bit cloggy and sometimes it tastes moldy. Corn is better, but my favorite is rice. It's perfect for soup, especially if you put butter spread in it after it's cooked. I make great soup, you know, very rich and delicious. And of course, meat. It's always the same, and I'm not sure what poultry it comes from."

The mechanical voice agreed with her. "Chop meat of mechanical deboning. Classified as standard."

"I put it in soup, too," continued Juliana Pavlovna. "But first you should make sure you've plucked all feathers out. And eat it with bread to make it more wholesome, that's my advice. There is also dried fruit, but be careful with them, they're not so clean. I usually soak them first, when I have enough water, of course. You'll see how much dirt comes out. Sometimes they have worms, very small and harmless, so it's ok. Another source of protein for us, that's what I call them. It's better to stew the fruit first, but there is always a chance that the drink will come out too sour because we haven't been getting any sweetener recently. It used to come with every grocery set, but now, for some reason, it doesn't. So, finally, tea drink. Tasteless, but clean – Yegor Semenovich loves it. And for breakfast, let us see… It's bread again, omelet powder, beetroot chips, condensed cranberry yogurt and oh my God, biscuits! I can't believe it, biscuits from set number two! I bet they're a bit rancid, they'd never put fresh cookies in set three, but it's no big deal, we're not some aristocrats, anyway. Ah, almost forgot, vitamin supplement. A capsule of vitamin D for the morning and a packet of group B vitamins for dinner. Don't forget that they turn on the cooker for two hours in the morning from 8 till 10 and for 2 hours in the evening, from 5 till 7. There are two burners, one is ours, and the other one will be yours, of course. Poor boy, you look so scared!" Juliana Pavlovna smiled. "Don't you worry, dear, I'm here to teach you everything," and she patted him on his shoulder, so softly that it felt like his mother's cuddle.

Boris spent another ten minutes pressing on the screen, still lost and confused. The only thing he knew for sure was that he was starving and would eat anything, and even artificial butter spread looked extremely palatable. He finally decided not to squander his money and ordered set number three. He was informed that the payment was successful and noted sadly that it would be delivered only in seven hours.

His reflections were interrupted by a loud shout of Yegor Semenovich, which came from inside his room:

"Come here, old girl, quick! Pravdin is speaking!"

Juliana Pavlovna gasped, put aside a piece of old cloth that she was using to wipe the table and hurriedly shuffled into her room. Boris thought it was essential for him to listen to the President's speech and went into his den too.

His broadcaster had already connected to the National Network, and Katyusha Assistant had been loaded. The screen was projecting a hologram of a governmental building, topped with the flag of the Commonwealth State. He heard the familiar abrupt chords of the National Anthem and stood to attention, like he had always done in the army. The image changed. Now there was a massive wooden table with small flags on each side and a broad-shouldered man with round face and sharp perceptive eyes was sitting on a high-backed chair. He was wearing a dark-blue suit and a blue tie, and all his figure seemed so straight and proportional that it was hard to believe it belonged to a real person. The President was looking keenly and solemnly right at Boris, and he was instantly hypnotized by this look, so trustworthy and reliable.

"Your attention please! You will now hear the address of the President of the Commonwealth State, Victor Vasilyevich Pravdin!"

Pravdin cleared his throat and began his speech. While he was speaking, his face seemed to be torn apart by a sharp line of his thin lips.

"Dear fellow citizens! My devoted friends! As you all know, our country is preparing for

the most important celebration in our calendar – the Great Liberation Day. I know that the time must be very hard for all of you. The time, when we are attacked from the east and from the west, when the constant threat from our endless enemies does not allow us to live, work and raise our children peacefully. Every day our courageous army men arrest hundreds of foreign agents who are trying to sneak into our towns and cities and destroy them from inside. Every night our military planes draw the teeth of dozens of bombers ready to drop shells and capsules with poison on our houses. And every day, you, common citizens, fight these criminals, whom I can't even call humans. You do it even without noticing. Yes, dear friends, you must keep your homes disguised at all times, and your doors are permanently blocked for the enemy; you sometimes do not have enough food supplies and for some periods your houses are cut off from water and electricity. But, fellow citizens, this is the spirit of the Great Liberation – to be strong and patient, and the State will provide you with everything you might need for a happy and worthy life. As the popularly elected president, I swear to you: no one will ever be able to break our strong spirit, which we have inherited from our glorious forefathers. Just like they fought for our land, we will fight today and tomorrow until the last foe is destroyed!

We have celebrated dozens of victories so far, and our state is getting stronger with every battle won. Our mission, as a country, is to guard and to protect the whole world from evil, which lies deep in the land of our geographical neighbors and keeps spreading further, making its way on the ground and on the sea, regardless of our efforts. What is more, it settles in the minds of those who are too weak to resist it, and if we discontinue our standoff, it will seize the planet in no time. That is why, my dear friends, we must go on fighting until the Black Plague is defeated and eliminated completely. And please don't doubt our victory, because good always wins over evil. You just need to be patient and committed to the ideals of our State – freedom, unity and truth.

And now I would like to announce the decrees that I have recently adopted. Firstly, all through the Great Liberation Day, the doors of your houses will be unblocked, and all of you will be able to celebrate this day together with your close ones. The exit and return schedule will be available on the National Information Portal. Secondly, I have decided just before the holiday to award all of you with an extra grocery set number two. Spend this day at your family table remembering our forefathers, who could not afford such a feast. Please do not forget that the Liberation is our common goal and only united we can stand and make this country a perfect place for everyone.”

The President finished his speech, and the final sound of fanfares was followed by Juliana Pavlovna’s gasp: “Isn’t he our savior! Our mentor! Our heart and soul!”

“Brilliant. Absolutely brilliant, no more and no less,” concluded Yegor Semenovich.

Boris sat down. For him the President was not only an anonymous symbol of power, but a big brother, a close friend, ready to fight back-to-back with him, to come to the aid at any difficult situation. This feeling of unity rooted in his childhood, and he could even trace it back to the earliest days in the orphanage. Boris was adopted in the Center of Patriotic Education just about a year after Pravdin had been first elected President and all kids had to study his biography, with constantly added new facts and details. Every evening, the supervisors seated the children of every group on low wobbly chairs (Boris always used to get the lowest and the wobbliest) and demonstrated printed self-prepared pictures with scenes from the President’s life, reading the approved texts from brochures and accompanying them with their own comments.

“When our future President was a little boy,” Natalia Yevgenyevna began in smarmy voice, “he saw some naughty children trying to take away a favorite toy from a baby (Misha, stop picking your nose!) Vitya Pravdin couldn’t ignore this outrageous behavior and despite of the fact that the naughty boys were bigger and stronger than him, he attacked them, and he beat all of them, even those who had sticks and slingshots! (Zahar, what did I say about standing up? Go to your place, quickly!) He knew that the power was in his hands, the power of good, the power of truth, and all bad people would flee when facing his courage and boldness. And now, when our country is under the threat of terrorists and foreign agents, he alone can come to our rescue, so that they never take away what belongs to us. (Borya, don’t you swing on your chair! You’ll have broken all our furniture by the time you leave the Center! – Ma’am, why can’t Pravdin come and repair the chairs? Isn’t he strong enough? – Stop laughing, you silly children! Fedor, if you ask any more questions, I’ll put you in the corner for the rest of the day! Why? Because, that’s why! Shut your mouth, sit straight, hands on your knees, now!) And so, you, children, should realize that you are living in the happiest and the most secure time in the history of our country. And every day you should thank Victor Vasilyevich Pravdin for it. When the rest of the world is agonizing with wars and conflicts, when millions of kids like you, and their parents, are dying under the foot of the Black Plague, we all are protected by the forces of our almighty President." (Ma'am, Sasha spat in my drink at lunchtime. Will Pravdin beat him too?)

When all children of the Commonwealth State reached the age of ten, they had to join the National Youth Organization. The procedure was relatively new at that time, untried and untested, and the only thing that was clear about it was that membership wasn't granted automatically. The candidate had to pass an improvised exam, the results of which influenced their grade, represented by the color of the armband they received. The armband had to be worn on one's right arm to symbolize that everything its owner did was for the sake of the State. Blue bands were for Grade One – those children who demonstrated ultimate devotion to the ideals of the Party of National Unity; white ones, Grade Two, were given to children who got good results for their admission exams, but weren't outstanding; and, finally, brown armbands were for losers, underdogs and retards. They had to wear this stigma at all times, so that everyone could see their insolvency. Boris had a gut feeling that he had all the chances to get a brown band because he hadn't done anything for the State so far to prove that he was a devoted citizen, and also his marks weren't too good to say the least.

The exam was scheduled to the end of October, the fourth anniversary of the Day of Glorious Election, and it was held in the Center's assembly hall. First came the bright students, who quickly got their bands and sat down, looking at others with contempt. Then it was the turn for the rest. Although Boris's surname came second in the alphabetic list, the commission didn't call him out at once, so he had some time to analyze the mistakes of his peers. However, the more children came on stage, the more bored he got, and in the end, he nearly fell asleep, hypnotized by the monotony of the show. When his name was eventually pronounced, he jumped from his chair and instantly felt weak in his knees. He was sure that everybody was looking at his greasy trousers, messed-up hair and artificial leather boots, which he had stained with sticky porridge at breakfast a couple of days ago and had never cared to clean.

The first part was to sing the National Anthem, and it seemed quite a piece of cake, but somehow it wasn't.

"Oh, State of good!

Oh, State of free!

Oh, State of pride and joy!"

Boris serenaded even before the music started.

"Hey-hey-hey!" interrupted him the tutor of arts. "I know singing is a hard job, and you might be born tone-deaf, so I'm not asking you to be on-key. But maybe you could at least try to hit any notes, just any of them, to make it sound less cacophonic? It is the anthem! The anthem of the country which is feeding you, for God's sake! Where's your respect? Devotion? Gratitude? Fail!"

Boris hung his head. Next came PI (political information) test.

"Name three reaches of the Commonwealth State!" ordered the history tutor – the most malicious of all the pedagogical staff in the Center because he had an artificial eye and you never knew where he was looking, which gave you an incredibly uncomfortable feeling every time you spoke to him. But the question was easy, and Boris gave a sigh of relief.

"Oil, gas and coal, sir!"

"Wrong!" cried the tutor and knocked his pencil on the desk. "The main reaches of the Commonwealth State, for your information, are its people, its government and its glorious heritage. It's a shame not to know such things at your age! Next question. Name three main threats to the State."

Boris knew the answer, but was afraid to pronounce it, so he kept silent and looked at his feet.

"Now!" the tutor banged his fist on the table.

"The… the Black Plague, the Instability and the violation of the State's territorial integrity." Boris drew his head into his shoulders waiting for another shout.

"Good." the tutor nodded. "What's the Black Plague?"

"Terrorists, foreign agents, and liberasts, sir!"

"You got this one right, strangely enough. The last question: two reasons for the defensive war with North Crestland."

Boris knew it, too. "To protect our country from the missile threat and to restore historical justice."

"Not exactly. Think harder on the first reason. It's not only missile, but…"

"Bioweapon threat!"

"Right! Who started the war?"

"Wasn't it the last question?"

"I said: who started the war!"

"North Crestland, sir, by provoking ethnic conflicts within its borders."

The sentence actually made no sense to Boris because he wasn't sure what 'ethnic' and 'provoking' meant, but, luckily, the children weren't required to understand the complicated issues of the external policy of the State. You just had to have a good memory and try to reproduce as much information received from the tutors as you could. That guaranteed that you'd get good grades and wouldn't be punished for being a stupid asshole. Boris's memory wasn't so good, and it often got him into trouble, so he was sort of angry at himself all the time for not being able to keep up with brighter children, and especially with his friend Fedor.

"Okay. Seems that it's all that your feeble brain is capable of. Pass on C," the tutor said reluctantly. "Go change for physical abilities test."

That was fun and easy. Boris quickly took off his shirt and greasy trousers and stood in front of the commission in his blue shorts and a t-shirt, which was supposed to be white, but was more of a gray.

"Twenty squats, twenty push-ups, twenty sit-ups. Seven minutes, starting now!" announced the PE tutor, who was Boris's favorite, because he sometimes gave him a ball and allowed to play with it while the other kids were running around the gym.

Boris finished even earlier than seven minutes.

"Good boy. Good shape. Pass on A," the tutor looked at the commission to see if they all agreed. No one was against, and Boris, for the first time during the test, felt proud of himself. The PE tutor gave him a hint of a smile, but suddenly looked down and frowned. "Tell me, where do these bruises and scratches come from? They look quite fresh to me."

"I don't know, sir," Boris was slightly out of breath. "Nowhere."

"Nowhere? I heard someone here likes to fight, doesn't he?"

"No, sir!"

"No?"

"If you don't have any more questions, let him go," the history tutor commanded. "We still have fourteen of them left, and I don't want to spend the rest of the day here. Arsenyev! You have eight points. Go get your white armband! And be careful with it, it's part of your land. Our land, to be exact. Say the oath!"

Boris had already managed to catch his breath and he only hoped that his memory wouldn't fail him this time. He'd spent all previous weeks learning the oath, and last time he'd recited it on PI lesson, he forgot the middle of it and messed up the ending.

"Me, Boris Arsenyev, proud and devoted citizen of the glorious Commonwealth State, true patriot and…

and…wholehearted supporter of the ideals of the Party of National Unity, receiving this symbol of the State in front of my teachers and comrades, do solemnly swear. To leave behind all my personal goals and um... urm... arm… bitions. To live… no…To direct my actions and thoughts at the prosperity of our Land. To live according to the rules and regulations of the Party of National Unity. Erm… How did it…? Ah, at all times to go hand in hand with other citizens of the Commonwealth State to the glorious future of our country. May the truth be with us!"

"May the truth be with us!" repeated the exam commission.

"May the truth be with us!" echoed the assembly hall with a chorus of dozens of children's voices.

"Sit down, Arsenyev!" ordered the director – the woman who had met him in the long and uncomfortable corridor four years ago. Boris took his armband, tied it around his right arm and put his hand on his chest – a sign to demonstrate his wholehearted devotion to the State. Then he bowed to the commission and took his seat.

As the foster kids grew older, the stories about Pravdin were becoming more and more complicated. Boris remembered some person, Pravdin's rival, whose real name seemed to be unknown, but he was called something like the Destabilizer, although, for some reason, Boris had another name in his head, which sounded even more weird – Beetlefly. Whatever he was, the Destabilizer had seized the power at some point, before Pravdin, and had begun to destroy the country and kill people who tried to oppose him. He also succeeded in making allies with several neighboring states, so that they helped him retain his power, but in the end, it turned out that they were only following their own interests and looted the Commonwealth State even more. That period was dark and gloomy, and no one could be sure of their future, and that's why it was called the Instability. This was when Boris was born and grew up, but he couldn't remember any details from that time. When Boris was about five years old, the Destabilizer was finally seized and forced to make some apologetic statements on the broadcaster, or whatever it was called back then. He repented, he cried, he swore that he'd admitted his faults, but the justice was harsh on him, and no one took his apologies seriously. Soon afterwards, there was the Glorious Election, when Pravdin became President, but Boris didn't remember it either. In fourteen months after the election, he was admitted to the Center of Patriotic Education, and there he was told about all the previous history. At first the Destabilizer was the main antihero in those stories and also some sort of a boogeyman, a scary figure to frighten kids at bedtime. However, in a couple of years, he was forgotten, and the villains became more impersonal: terrorists – those who attacked from outside, and foreign agents – the spies, who sneaked into the country and pretended to be normal citizens but were materially and ideologically supported by the enemy. Sometimes there were also 'liberasts' or 'the liberasty', defined as 'the citizens of the Commonwealth State who, under the influence of the enemy, allowed themselves to doubt the values of the government and the ideals of the Party of National Unity'. Those "liberasts" were, apparently, harmless and for the most part ridiculous, and the absurdity of their statements was a huge contrast with the sanity and the common sense of the national ideology. All the three classes of enemies were to be hated equally, and this hate was a personal responsibility of every devoted patriot of the Commonwealth State. You had to carry it with you at all times, you put it on like you put on your clothes every morning, you cherished it, you cultivated it, you fed it with appropriate broadcasts every single day of your life. And if you did everything right, if you hated correctly and according to the approved standards, you were rewarded with a feeling of all-embracing unity with those who felt the same.

In the end of the educational course in the Center, Boris had to pass an exam on the history of the Commonwealth State from

2000 to 2040, which had two parts: the first one consisted of general questions on the important dates and their background, and the second part concentrated on the biography of Victor Pravdin and the policy of the Party of National Unity, which he represented. Boris didn't learn the history because it was too boring and complicated for him, but by that time their one-eyed history tutor had been replaced by an old woman, who sometimes didn't even remember her name, so he managed to easily get minimal required points. Pravdin's biography was more of a challenge because it was to be recited before Regional Education Department Commission, and no mistakes or imprecisions were allowed. Boris spent three evenings trying to arrange everything in his head, but when he woke up next morning, he could barely remember half of what he'd learnt. When he was about to give up and started thinking of a way to use a cheat-sheet, a brilliant idea came to him, and he decided to give it a try. He pretended to himself that Pravdin wasn't just a vague figure from the numerous posters and supervisor's stories, but one of his relatives (say, grandfather), and they were sitting in some nice quiet place (a green hill, for example), and he was telling him all those episodes, calmly and amicably, in his usual lithe voice:

"Now, listen to this, chubs. Once I had to speak to a very important person. I was not a President at that time, but I was making big plans for the salvation of the country..."

"Salvation from what, Grampy?"

"From the Black Plague, of course. Listen further. The person represented a neutral state, which means that he didn't support our country, but neither did he confront us. My goal was to convince him to stand on our side because his backup would have changed things dramatically. You know what I did, chubs?"

"No, Grampy, tell me!"

"Well, I brought him a handful of earth. A piece of our land for him to hold, to feel how fragile and vulnerable it is. And you know what he said?"

"What?"

Now every story acquired a personal touch to Boris, and he even added some extra details of his own, hoping they would come unnoticed for the Commission. However, shortly after he passed the exam and got his well-deserved satisfactory grade, his mind went completely blank, and he forgot everything, including his own little fantasies. But now it was not important at all because those stories were absolutely useless in the army, where he was admitted just after he turned fifteen. And as for Pravdin, he had ever since acquired a face – a face of power, a face of truth, and a little bit a face of his grandfather.

The President's speech made everyone feel comforted and easy, and Boris even stopped feeling hungry for a while. Now he could spend some time navigating through his new environment. The broadcaster was airing current news and he called out for the National Network Assistant Katyusha. In the army there was a proprietary information field called Keen-sighted, where one could find war reports, description of the enemy and its movement, information about military equipment and, in the evenings, entertaining shows were available, which were mostly aimed at poking fun at the enemy's stubbornness and stupidity. Boris remembered how they used to enjoy these shows, laughing at smashed dead bodies of their rivals, scattered around their burning tanks.

The structure of the information space in the rear was different. It broadcast the news at regular intervals, interspersed by political talk-shows and analytical programs. In the afternoon, there were more practical shows, including music concerts, quizzes and comedy programs, and on some evenings, they showed feature-length films, mostly about war, but sometimes historical or drama. There were three broadcast channels: the National First, the Commonwealth State Today and the Heritage, but they didn't differ much, so you sometimes didn't know which one you were watching. Besides, you could always use your broadcaster to access the National Network and make educational requests, ask for advice on flat disguising and household chores or make purchases from the National Hypermarket. Part of the National Network was the National Information Portal, where every citizen could find their fines and penalties, get private account details, check the schedule of water, electricity and heating supply and inquire about current regulations in their neighborhood. Having connected to the Portal, Boris firstly decided to get detailed information on his material resources.

"There is seven million four hundred thousand three hundred and ninety-nine GKB on your account," informed Katyusha.

I was much less than he had expected.

"Katyusha, report all incoming transactions in the last fifteen years."

"Checking. Please wait. One transaction found. Display detailed information?"

"Only one? In fifteen years?" Boris was even more surprised. He was sure that every year he'd been receiving money from the Ministry of Defense, which was particularly emphasized at the combat squad reunions.

"One private incoming transaction," clarified Katyusha.

"Check money transfers from the Ministry of Defense!" insisted Boris.

"Transfers from the Ministry of Defense not found."

Boris was dumbfounded. How could it be? He was sure he'd been receiving two million GKB monthly salary, just like all soldiers. Maybe there was a mistake? He'd paid the fine at the station, and he'd bought tickets and ordered food earlier today, so there must be something on his account. Maybe the whole compensation hadn't arrived because of connection problems? But deep in his heart he knew everything. There was no compensation, at least for him. And there would never be. Startled and helpless, he leaned on the back of his chair, and the pain from the wound instantly cut through his back.

"Katyusha, tell me the details of the private transaction," he said, having regained his senses a little.

"One private transaction found. Date: 21st April 2060. Sender: Gennadiy Petrenko, internal number hidden. Amount: eight million GKB. Cover note: For Boris to learn to draw. No further information provided."

Boris couldn't believe his ears. Colonel Petrenko? Had he just received money from a person who wasn't his relative, nor even a good friend? Eight million from someone who knew that there would be no compensation from the Ministry of Defense. Eight million to fulfil his naïve childhood dream, the one that had been almost taken away from him with the toy elephant in that lonely corridor of the Center of Patriotic Education?

Boris was about to send a message of gratitude to the Colonel, but the allowed time for communication was over, and he had to wait three more hours to do it. The Regulations of the Citizens

Interaction also allowed people to use message boards, or Pools of Ideological Interchange, where everyone could post a thirty-second message on one of the topics: politics; education and childcare; culture; sport and nutrition and miscellaneous. Posts could be replied to by other users, or by section supervisors, although usually they were left unanswered. Boris wasn't sure those Pools could be of any help to him, and, anyway, he had more important business to do at the moment. He had to get some device to start working.

"Okay, Katyusha," he commanded, "show me the National Hypermarket's choice of computing facilities authorized to work with holograms."

The National Hypermarket had a wide range of goods – everything one might need at any point of their life. Clothes, hygiene products, furniture, sport equipment, toys and, of course, electronics, the section that he needed. Apart from calculating machines, Boris saw mobile transmitters, which looked like cell phones from his childhood but had more sophisticated features, wrist timers with built-in satnav and alarm clock, broadcasters, some – cheap, some – extremely costly, and something that he even couldn't name and wasn't sure what it was for. Boris could spend ages looking at all this splendor, although he wasn't sure when he'd be able to afford any bit of it. Upon his command, Katyusha read all the descriptions, and, finally, he found himself totally confused by the variety of choices offered. However, he didn't want to put off the purchase because of his own indecision and continued bombing the assistant with new requests.

It took Boris about an hour to choose a suitable machine, and he regrettably spent almost half of the money received from the Colonel, but the device was supposed to serve him for at least ten years, so he couldn't afford any compromise. Finally, he double checked the characteristics and the package of his machine and commanded Katyusha to send the order. Next day delivery cost him another twenty five thousand GKB, but he wanted to get the device as quickly as possible to start earning money, which seemed to flow like water down a drain starting from the first day of his discharge. They never had any lessons of financial literacy in the orphanage, probably because there were more important subjects in their curriculum, such as political information, contemporary history, civil defense, ideological awareness and life security. And of course, physical training, which at first was great, but eventually turned into marching, standing at attention until your legs got completely numb, and then, with your legs still numb, running around the gym for the rest of the lesson. It all came handy in the army, where Boris was among the strongest and most appreciated combatants, and even Colonel Petrenko, usually strict and unbiased, seemed to favor him slightly more than the others. And now, this generous gift of eight million GKB, once again proved his fatherly devotion.

Boris received the confirmation of the transaction and checked his account again. Considering the fine paid at the station and the purchase of the calculating machine, he had a little more than three million GKB left, and he promised himself to go through available jobs on the National Information Portal first thing next morning, so that, hopefully, he'd be able to start earning money before long. He rose his eyes from the broadcaster because he was getting tired of all these flashy images and confusing descriptions. The wallpaper on the window was the same as in the kitchen, dull and colorless and he decided to replace it with more aesthetic ones with the first received salary. "If you look at it for a long time, you can get cranky," he thought. He knew that all citizens' responsibility was to disguise their windows with opaque sheets of light-reflecting material, capable of showing pre-loaded images, as if you were really looking outside. If you wanted to change the scenery, you had to buy a new roll of wallpaper, get the permission to remove the old one, and at the designated time make all required manipulations. The presence of the disguise was checked two or three times a day by patrolling drones, and penalty for removing it was severe. Suddenly a thought hit Boris's mind. He remembered what Colonel Petrenko had told him about looking for his childhood treasures. What if there was really something, lying in a nice hiding place and waiting for him to get it back? He also had an annoying desire to look under the windowpane, and it was so strong that he could hardly resist it.

Boris came closer to the window and examined the frame. The structure looked solid and massive, without any signs of a stash or something of the kind. However, it didn't satisfy him, and he took out his army screwdriver from his backpack and scratched it on the docking seam of the pane. Of course, it didn't work. He knelt down and tried it on the plinth, but all he got was a bit of dirt, which was so icky that he decided not to continue his meaningless efforts.

Finally, Boris calmed down, sat on his wiggly sofa and commanded Katyusha to turn on the First National Channel. There was news again, and then some analytical program with a funny presenter, who started his speech quietly, almost whispering, but gradually his voice rose and became loud and shrill. The topic of the program was the Black Plague, and the presenter pronounced these words through clenched teeth with such scorn and disregard that they almost sounded like 'Bluck Plug'. There was a report from a POW camp, where captured terrorists were kept in comfortable spacious cells with all necessary commodities, and the presenter commented on it.

"Do you see, dear citizens, how merciful our President is to these degenerates? He keeps them in the lap of luxury, feeds them with wholesome products, treats them as he would treat his guests. But what do they think about it? Let us listen to what one of these retards says."

A man in black uniform stepped forward from the inside of the cell and made an obscene gesture to the camera operator.

"I am the Black Plague!" he shouted. "My only goal is to kill, to destroy as many Commonwealthers as possible! Such was the calling of my father, and my grandfather, and all my ancestors – to make your life a nightmare, to make you lose your national identity and surrender to us!"

"What can I say about it, my dear friends?" the presenter gave a sigh. "Do I have any decent words to characterize this piece of trash? Shall I forgive it? Have mercy on it? No, citizens, no, no and no. The only thing they deserve is the eternal fire of hell, which would burn their evil minds out, evaporate their wrath, leave them naked and pathetic in the face of our victorious President! Now look at what he has in his hand! Just have a look at it, my dear friends, and all your doubts, if you still have any, will vanish in no time!"

The prisoner stretched out his hand and opened it. Inside, there was a small piece of folded paper.

"What is it?" whispered the presenter. "What do we see? I'll explain, in case it's still not clear to you. It's drugs, my dears, drugs that he's been taking all this time, even in prison. How do you like it? How does it characterize our enemy? What do you feel now? How would you feel if this bantling tried to sell this piece of crank to your children? Now, I want all of you, every person who's watching me now, to stand up and say it out loud. Come on, be expressive, don't be afraid of your emotions. They are all explicable and natural, considering what you've just seen. Perfect. I think I can hear you now. Each of you is part of our struggle, and soon we will share our common victory against the Bluck Pluck! Go on, citizens! Go on and make a fight! Fight! Fight!"

Boris knew what emotions the presenter was speaking about. It was so disgusting to realize that because of such shameless inbred weirdos with a brew of hatred, stubbornness and stupidity in their heads, all citizens of the Commonwealth State were destined to endure endless hardships on their own land – the land that they had to win for themselves again and again. And the presenter – he said the right things, and he could unmistakably guess how all citizens felt, and he put it into the right words that everyone was ready to voice. Funny how the enemy didn't know such simple truths. The bad is always bound to lose, and justice will be served no matter how hard they try. That was what everyone said, right from Boris's first days in the Center of Patriotic Education, so it had to be true. It had to be, without a slightest doubt, the only truth that could ever exist in this world.

At last, time for communication was announced.

"Attention please! Message time! You may send up to ten messages to the citizens of the Commonwealth state. You will have thirty minutes starting from now."

"Katyusha, find the internal number of Colonel Petrenko," commanded Boris.

"One entry found in memory. Colonel Gennadiy Petrenko, internal number 031-BBL1984," answered Katyusha.

Boris gave a little cough and started recording the message, feeling a trifle uneasy: "Message for Gennadiy Petrenko, internal number 031-BBL1984. Start of message. Comrade Colonel Petrenko. Citizen Boris Arsenyev has arrived at the place of permanent deployment. Thanking you for the transferred money and hoping to pay it back in the nearest future. Remaining available for contact at any time. Faithful and devoted citizen Boris Arsenyev. End of message."

"Uploading message…" responded the Network Assistant. "Do you wish to send more?"

"No."

"One message uploaded. Censoring will take sixty seconds. Beginning the countdown…"

Listening to Katyusha counting from fifty-nine, Boris suddenly got an unfamiliar sense of deep inner warmth, very soothing and comforting, as if life had just patted him on his head with some invisible, yet sturdy hand. "I guess that's what they call home," he thought. The walls of his room, the old-fashioned shabby furniture, the spooky window wallpaper, the neighbors, the National Network Assistant Katyusha, even the shrill-voiced presenter – they all were becoming dear to him, and he started to make room for them in his mind and in his soul. Boris smiled unintendingly to this unexpected gift of fate, hoping that there would be more of them in the future, and he kept on smiling until he heard some voice from beyond his thoughts, which woke him up to reality:

"Sending failed. Addressee, Gennadiy Petrenko, internal number 031-BBL1984, not found. Please check data correctness."

4

A muffed humming outside the window meant that food drones had arrived. However, before getting the grocery sets, everyone was obliged to undergo an identification procedure, which implied standing still in front of the window, hands up and fingers apart, so that the drones could perform biometrical scanning of fingerprints and retina. It took about two minutes, and after this, the small door in the wall opened and revealed three brown paper bags with three blue hashes on each one, marking the number of the set. Boris noticed the printed marks, and somehow, they reminded him of his book, which he kept in his room, at the bottom of the backpack. He thought that he'd better hide it somewhere safer – under the pillow, for example. The small door shut, and the drones flew away, busily buzzing their motors. Boris thought that if they could take their biometrical data through the wallpaper, why couldn't the enemy do the same, using their spy machines, or whatever malicious equipment they had. "What are we hiding from?" he wondered but forced the thought to leave his mind because it really had nothing to do with him.

Juliana Pavlovna quickly switched on the oven not to miss the precious time and began rattling her pots and pans, which looked a bit greasy, obviously because of the lack of water. Boris opened his set, impatient to get acquainted with the butter spread and the meat product of mechanical deboning. It contained all that had been promised: bread, a packet of barley, a plastic bottle with muddy brownish drink, something wrapped in transparent film, pink and full of pieces of feathers, a small package of dried fruit, which could easily be home for little worms and larva. Breakfast was packed separately and was supposed to be eaten next morning but Boris opened it too and beheld three crunchy cookies, stuck between the omelet powder and the condensed yogurt. He stared at his riches with respect and devotion, trying to figure out how to combine all these unmatchable ingredients, when Juliana Pavlovna, laughing at his bewilderment, shoved one of her pots in his hands and pushed him towards the sink.

"Don't waste your time, dear, get some water before it's turned off!"

Dinner was ready in about an hour, and Boris noted surprisingly that it was quite decent and reminded him of his mother's cookery. Or maybe not, but still it was the first time in many years when he was eating at home. At his own home.

The smell of food made Yegor Semenovich promptly appear in the kitchen. He had changed his white shirt for a plainer one – checkered, with patches on the elbows, and looked quite relaxed and content with his life. Juliana Pavlovna quickly cut the grey bread of the third grade with rough blotches of tailings ('standard', as it was called in the description) and took out three plates, chipped on the sides, decorated with pictures of chickens and flowers on the bottom, and three aluminum spoons.

They ate in silence, each concentrated on their thoughts and trying to chew meat product without swallowing the unpluckable feathers. Juliana Pavlovna finished her soup, put aside her spoon and suddenly started speaking, addressing tenderly to her husband.

"Just look at him, honey. Such a nice boy. Reminds me of our poor Basil. It's already been almost twelve months…" she sobbed.

"Basil?" asked Boris.

"Our son. He died in early spring last year. Had just turned forty and…" she tried to gather breadcrumbs from the table with her wrinkled fingers.

"God damn these terrorists!" Yegor Semenovich said quietly, but aguishly.

"How did it happen? Was he killed?" Boris wasn't sure in the appropriacy of the question, but it looked like the neighbors were willing to share their sorrow with him.

"Worse than that. He was poisoned by them! We saw him in his room, well, your room now, he was on the sofa, almost breathless ("On the bed where I sleep," thought Boris gloomily). We tried to resuscitate him, but all in vain, we're not medics or something, after all. Life was coming out of him with every breath, so quickly, and nothing could be done about it. Old girl, she tried to call the self-aid, but they just said it was a poison capsule from terrorists and there wasn't any cure for it. Asked us to report his death not later than thirty minutes after it had occurred and promised to take the body after unblocking of doors had been approved."

"This is how we lost our sonny," Juiana Pavlovna signed and wiped a tear off her cheek. "And then, after two months or so, they told us that new people were coming to live in his room. It was so painful to collect all his things and send them to… to utilization as they call it. I kept some of his clothes, not much, actually. But those people never came, and we were sort of surprised and thought there had been a mistake. We waited and waited, and then we got a message from the army, which said we must keep the room clear for one of the former dwellers, who was coming back from the service. We wondered who it will be, we were very curious, and I thought, maybe, he… you… would just a little bit look like Basil. Our dearest Basil!" she went silent and tried to swallow her tears, some of which still fell into her chipped empty plate.

Yegor Semenovich finished eating and kept squeezing his aluminum spoon as if it was the cause of Basil's decease. The silence was unbearable, and everyone was waiting for something to happen and to take the uninvited sorrow away from them.

"Well, let us cheer up a bit, shall we?" Juliana Pavlovna gave both of them a shy yet encouraging look. "Has everyone taken their vitamin B supplement?"

No one answered.

"And what about your family, soldier?" Yegor Semenovich was still holding his spoon. "Do you remember them at all?"

"I'm not sure…" the question came unexpected for Boris. "I thought I'd forgotten them and everything from my past up to the moment I was placed in the Center of Patriotic Education. It was all blank and I sometimes had dreams which looked like memories, but I wasn't sure I could rely on any of them. And now, when I'm back, I keep getting some… how's it called? Some flashbacks, which are definitely more reliable than those dreams. I think I remember my mother – she was a good cook, just like you, ma'am. And she could also play the piano. Yes, there was a piano in your room, it looked huge to me at those times, and I always wanted to disassemble it to see where music comes from. Mother could play it a little – only a couple of simple tunes, and she wasn't too fond of it, so she hardly ever came up to the instrument. And father was always busy working. He was sort of a doctor, so he had both day and night shifts, and sometimes he spent two or three days at the hospital, so we didn't see him much. I also had a little sister; I think if I was six then, she must have been four or so when they… when they were… We were a simple family, and I can't imagine why terrorists killed… why they were after us. Grandfather sometimes said…" Boris bit his tongue.

"Grandfather?" Yegor Semenovich looked interested. "I didn't know there was a grandfather. Was he an army man, like you?"

"Grandfather… No, he wasn't. He was a traitor. A foreign agent. He betrayed our motherland, tried to sell the secrets of the State to our enemies. And also… It was him who killed my family – every one of them, even my little sister. He was going to kill me, too, but I got away. I'm a fast runner, Yegor Semenovich, I could run and hide, so he didn't get me. I know it because they told it to me in the Center of Patriotic Education. Kept telling it when they beat me in the backyard and in the toilet. That was all because of my grandfather, because of my rotten blood, that's what they said. They also said he was a killer who sent thousands of people to die in concentration camps, who stood by the enemies when they were tearing apart our country and its citizens, and now I had to pay his dues back. I heard it every day. 'Foreign agent's spawn. Criminal bastard'. And every day there were the supervisors silently watching the children doing it to me, and they had this look in their eyes – a terrifying look of silent approval, which meant that they were against me, too. You know how many scars I've got from those times? It'll take you quite a while to count them all, believe me! But there was also a woman, a nurse, called Lyudmila Ivanovna. She was also standing and watching, but I knew she was on my side. She wept a little when no one could see her, and then she bandaged my wounds and said that maybe those people, they were wrong about it. Maybe my grandfather wasn't so bad, and maybe it was all a mistake. I didn't believe in what the nurse said but I never told it to her because I was afraid of losing her. And that was when I began to hate my grandfather. I could still remember his face, but it wasn't the face of a human, a person from my family. It was cold and evil, and his eyes were… blank, as if frozen dead. I beat my pillow every night, imagining that it was him, I squeezed it, I suffocated and even bit it. I knew he'd been executed, but if he hadn't, I'd have done it myself with my own bare hands. Once, it was my birthday, I guess, Lyudmila Ivanovna asked me what I wanted most of all in my life. She said I must think it over carefully and be honest to myself because it would be my own guiding light. She looked at me smiling, and the words came out from my mouth by themselves: 'I want to kill my grandfather." She recoiled from me, but didn't say a word, and then she opened my book, you know, I'd taken one from home before getting there, and started reading. I listened to her voice and it kind of distracted me from my thoughts. No, I didn't forgive my grandfather, but I think I learnt how to cope with my emotions, to live with them like one lives with a wart on their nose. Yes, I am a criminal bastard, but I'm not a coward, nor am I traitor, and I'll do anything to prove it. Lyudmila Ivanovna taught me to read, by the way, because we didn't have any reading lessons in the Center. But one day she didn't come to work in the morning. I waited, but she didn't come the next day, and the day after next. I was afraid to ask the supervisors about her, so I thought she'd found a better job or something. I was sad because the new nurse didn't bandage my wounds, but soon I realized that I could do it myself, without any help. I could also stand up for myself and smash all my offenders, every single one of them, without letting them rise from the floor. Every evening I used to creep to the gym and train myself, work out until I was almost dead, but it was my outlet, the only thing that was keeping me afloat. All my hate, all my hurt was now in my fists. You know, Yegor Semenovich, I beat them all, even the strongest and the fiercest ones, and when they were writhing on the floor, their faces covered with their blood and snot, I spit on them with everything that had been accumulating inside me all through these years. And then I grew up and went to the army."

Boris smiled at his thoughts. Of course, he didn't say anything of the kind. He already had a ready-made answer.

"I don't remember," he said. "I don't remember anything about my grandfather."

"It's okay, dear," Juliana Pavlovna replied quietly, as if she knew what he was thinking about. "No matter what, you still have your whole life ahead of you. You'll meet the best people in this world, I promise."

5

"The electricity will be turned off and the National Network will be disabled from 22:00 until 6:00," informed the broadcaster. "Please make sure your home is safe. Have a pleasant night rest."

Boris was about to go to bed, which, after he'd been told the story of Basil, had become not so homey and even less comfortable, but suddenly he heard a knock at the door.

"Arsenyev? Are you sleeping yet?"

"No, Yegor Semenovich, come in."

Yegor Semenovich strode into the room, slightly bending, and sat down on the couch.

"I've got some business to you, soldier," he spoke. "I heard, in the army they give you… the fighters, I mean… some booze to cheer you up, don't they?"

"They do. Occasionally." Boris quickly understood what the old man was up to and relaxed.

"So…" continued Yegor Semenovich. "Maybe you have some left? Some good old spirit, I mean? I haven't seen any in… five years or so. It's not that I actually need it, but sometimes I get a feeling that it could come handy. Of course, I've got everything: food, water, a place to live, but still, I happen to sink into some sort of… yearning, which just wouldn't go away by itself," he looked at the door apprehensively, and then his eyes drifted to the window, as if he was afraid of foreign agents hiding outside the flat and listening to how miserable life for Yegor Semenovich was in the

Commonwealth State. "Maybe you'd share a drink with the old man? To our acquaintance, so to say."

"Maybe I will," Boris gave him a conspiratorial wink. "Got a glass?"

He had really received a bottle of 90% alcohol just before he was injured and got into hospital. Adding water to it, one could easily keep drinking it for more than six months, after which you could make a request for another one. When Boris returned from hospital, he found out that his squad had been relocated to another point, and there was literally no one he could consume the spirit with. He hid the bottle in his backpack where it was waiting for a chance to be opened, and it seemed that the chance had just come.

"Got two perfect glasses!" Yegor Semenovich replied willingly. "Old girl is sleeping already, so be quiet. I'll be back in a moment, ok? We'll sit together, just you and me, remember poor Basil, drink to his peace, like good old mates."

They sat together, drank to Basil's peace, to Boris's comrades who hadn't returned from war, to the Great Liberation Day and to something else. There was nothing to eat, so they just swallowed the scalding liquid, diluted by tap water, saved for morning hygiene procedures. After his fifth glass, Yegor Semenovich became merry and a bit limp, and Boris decided that he'd had enough. He closed the bottle and stuck it back in his backpack, being closely watched by his companion. Yegor Semenovich figured out that there would be no more fun and rose from the couch.

"Wait here, fighter, I'll be back," he mumbled and, staggering, went towards the door.

In five minutes, he returned, holding something behind his back.

"Here," he said proudly. "I almost forgot. Let me tell you a story. It won't take long, though, 'coz it's getting late already. So, when we got this flat, it was something like twenty-five years ago, I suppose, it was completely empty, even all the furniture had been taken away."

Boris nodded. He felt desperately drowsy.

"It was about five years from then when they obliged everyone to install disguising wallpaper on the windows. Before we had just plain glass, from which you could see the outside, remember?"

"I don't"

"Doesn't matter. Well, we did so and decided to replace the old radiators as well. They were no good, you see, leaking and making strange noises… Anyway, when we ripped off the one in Basil's room, you room, I mean, we saw something hidden behind it. Here it is, have a look. Wanted to throw it away, but old girl said we'd better keep it. You know, in case someone came back for it. So, you came back, and I thought, well, it might be yours, after all."

He handed Boris some medium-sized object wrapped in an antique plastic bag. Boris examined the gift and looked at Yegor Semenovich questioningly.

"Open it, soldier, what are you waiting for?" he smiled.

Boris opened the bag, took out the object and couldn't believe what he saw. Before him was his old toy – a stuffed elephant with big ears and a funny trunk. It was wrinkly and crinkly, grey with age, but still recognizable, and there was no doubt that it came directly from his happy childhood. Boris took the toy with great care and thought that he wanted to stick his nose in its dusty cloth and maybe it would smell the same as twenty-six years ago.

"Yours?" asked Yegor Semenovich.

"Mine, I guess," answered Boris. "I thought it was left in the Center, I clearly remember them taking it away from me on my first day. How did you say you got it?"

"Never mind, soldier, never mind. I guess we're done then," the old man looked happily drunk. "I'd best be going now, I think. You go to bed. Not a word to old girl, remember?"

"Thank you," said Boris sincerely.

As soon as the door closed behind Yegor Semenovich, he began examining the toy. Carefully, not to damage the feeble cloth, he palped the elephant and turned it in his hands to see whether there were holes, spots or other sorts of defects. There weren't any, and the toy looked quite decent for its age. The only visible fault was that in the place where the trunk was attached to the head, there were several sloppy stitches, obviously handmade, and they didn't look strong and reliable enough. "Guess, I tore the trunk off at some point, and mother stitched it back," he thought, "although she'd have done it more neatly, I suppose." One of the elephant's eyes was almost hanging loose, and he pushed it against the head so that it didn't come off at once. Suddenly, under his fingers, inside the elephant's head, he felt some hard object, either square or rectangular. Boris pushed harder, trying to figure out what it might be, but it was placed too deep between the elephant's ears and impossible to get to. Perhaps, it was some mechanism, which, being pressed on, made the elephant move its ears and sing a funny song. Such toys were very common in his childhood, as he recalled. Anyway, it didn't work, and it was time to stop torturing the poor animal and go to bed, all the more so they'd already switched off the electricity, and the room was lit only by a faint glow coming from the window wallpaper.

In the middle of the night, deceased Basil unexpectedly appeared in his former room. Surely, Boris didn't know what he looked like, but he was absolutely positive that it was him. Basil was standing next to the sofa, all blueish, with unnaturally bulging eyes and a strangely twisted left leg. He was trying to squeeze his hand under the pillow, where Boris had hidden his book and the elephant. He was wheezing and groaning, as if struggling to say something important to Boris. Suddenly, his face began to blow up, and what was supposed to be his nose started growing longer, until it turned into a large obnoxious trunk. It flopped around Boris's face like a poisonous snake, trying to find a good place for a fatal bite, and then other trunks appeared, looking just as terrifying, and Boris, frozen with horror, tried to count them. "One hungried," the ghost wheezed and with a precise movement of his hand, grabbed the elephant from under the pillow and tore off its head. The seam momentarily began to bleed, and numerous red drops fell on the floor, making an enlarging puddle on the even squares of the linoleum. "This blood is their blood. You will never wash it away from your hands," mumbled Basil through his trunks, and Boris understood that he couldn't take it anymore. Like a child, he covered his face with his hands and started whispering: "Go away, please go away!" Something moved under the pillow, and he woke up. It was dark in the room, and the darkness spoke to him.

"Poor little boy! Please, don't be so scared. It's only your past trying to take its course, or it's curse, which is actually the same. There's no need to hide from it, Boris, for it's already inside you. But there's good news, too. If you do everything right, you'll have a lot of fun, and me too, I promise. So, don't let me down, Boris. Do it! Do it now!"

Boris sat on his bed and rubbed his eyes. Of course, there was no Basil, nor blood on the floor, and both the book and the elephant were lying peacefully under the pillow. He thought that he hadn't had nightmares since leaving the Center of Patriotic Education, and what he'd seen tonight was so stupid and illogical that it hadn't been able to scare him at all. Doubtlessly, Basil was dead, as dead as mutton. His body had been taken away and buried in some common grave or somewhere else, maybe even in the hill near their house, and nothing in this world could make him leave his resting place. It was around three a.m., and he still had a chance to get a nice bit of sleep before Katyusha woke him up at 6. Boris took his stone-solid pillow in order to fluff it up a bit, and the elephant slipped out and fell on the floor, right on the spot where blood had been pouring in his dream.

"Remember, Borya, please remember one thing. It all starts inside the elephant's head."

"Who said this?" whispered Boris into the darkness.

"You know who," it answered.

He checked the elephant once again and all at once tore the self-made stitch on one side of its trunk and put his fingers inside the toy's head, pushing apart the stuffing. Soon he could feel the small flat square, grabbed it carefully and withdrew it out of the toy. The trunk couldn't stand these manipulations and tore off completely, leaving after itself sloppy pieces of artificial cotton.

Boris's fingers were squeezing a strange object – a small piece of plastic with metal contacts on one side. He thought that he'd seen one of these before and suddenly remembered that it was called a memory card. You could keep any information on it: images, documents, even programs, you just needed to insert it in a calculating machine, which Boris didn't have yet. Maybe there were his family photos, or his favorite music, or even some shows from the Fidgy Freckles Network, or anything that could remind him of his childhood. He would definitely check it as soon as he got the machine, which was scheduled to be delivered in the morning. Very carefully, trying not to damage the card's contacts Boris folded it in one of his socks and put in a special compartment in his backpack.

He could go to sleep now, only hoping that Basil had settled down and wouldn't disturb him anymore.

However, the calculating machine wasn't delivered the following morning, nor the following day, and the day after it and not even in a week. Upon every inquiry, Katyusha informed him that: "Delivery delayed due to terrorist attacks." Boris was ready to kill all terrorists himself only to get the instrument he needed to start working. Every morning he checked the Employment Section of the National Information Portal for available jobs, and the list was rather impressive.

"Content maker (educational and entertaining). Requirements: good command of grammar, knowledge of target audience. Must have necessary equipment, including speakers and microphone. No writing or reading or calculating skills required. Payment in line with current governmental regulations."

"Song composer (lyrics provided). Requirements: knowledge of music theory and basic tonal vocabulary (must provide a completed 72-hour educational broadcast course on each discipline). Portfolio or examples of work is a must. Must have necessary equipment, including speakers and hardware keyboard. No writing or reading or calculating skills required. Payment in line with current governmental regulations."

"Frontend developer (broadcasters and mobile devices upgrades). Requirements: knowledge of one of the programming languages: Niva +, 2PH, Dynamic Core. (Must provide a completed 120-hour educational broadcast course on one of the languages). Must have necessary equipment: calculating machine of not less than 5th generation. Basic reading and writing skills required (must complete an alphabet test). Payment in line with current governmental regulations."

There were also one-time jobs placed in a separate page of the Employment Section.

"Urgent: text for broadcast on environmental problems. Further details provided upon request."

"Voice acting. Two broadcasts on successful conjugal life. Due date – 36 hours each."

"Hologram design and animation. Topic – home safety. Possibility for a long-term contract upon completing the order."

In a separate section there were manual jobs, and Boris opened the page out of mere curiosity, but it was empty. "No information on manual jobs found," said Katyusha. "Please change your request."

Boris didn't want to waste his time waiting for the machine, and drew up a sort of syllabus for himself, consisting of educational broadcasts of all kinds, but mostly on graphics and design. He watched them every morning and after lunch, and the first three days were perfect, and he felt uplifted and ready to move mountains. However, on the fourth morning his wound started aching, and he allowed himself to stay in bed until almost midday and missed the scheduled lesson. "One day wouldn't change anything," he thought and missed the next day, too. The syllabus broke against his sloth, and the educational broadcasts eventually became irregular, but Boris was still proud of himself for not having given them up at all.

Sometimes he took out his book from under the pillow and read it, just because he was too lazy to do anything else. The toy elephant sat on his lap and listened to him obediently and with genuine interest. Its trunk was neatly attached back to its head with a few drops of universal glue which Boris had received from Yegor Semenovich in exchange for fifty grams of cereal from his grocery set. The old man seemed to be willing to give him the glue for free, remembering the generous portion of alcohol that he'd been given, and more of it still waiting in the backpack. But Boris decided not to overuse the neighbor's benevolence and insisted on him taking the cereal, keeping in mind that it was rather tasteless and made his stomach sick.

In a couple of weeks Boris was already feeling quite comfortable in the new world, and monotonous days, full of light-hearted agreeableness began to go by in a measured and graceful flow. Each new day looked exactly like the previous one, and nothing seemed to change, even the wallpaper on the windows sometimes froze and displayed one picture over and over again, but no one really noticed it because the remaining two were just as dull and meaningless. The broadcaster aired the same news, identical drones delivered identical grocery sets at usual time, the front door blinked with its red diode, which meant that everything was safe, and there was absolutely nothing to worry about. Juliana Pavlovna did her best to keep their little nest as cozy as possible, and Yegor

Semenovich, like a real head of the family, sat on his armchair and knowledgeably watched the broadcasts, carefully selected for him by Katyusha. All his life was in these shows, and they made his life complete, so he absorbed all information like a sponge absorbs water, and then he commented on what he'd seen with a special old man's wisdom. The world, according to Yegor Semenovich, was very plain and comprehensive. The government is good, terrorists are bad, foreign agents and left-wing liberasts are even worse, Pravdin is the savior, who will eventually kill them all and peace will settle down on the earth. There was nothing behind it and there could never be, and there wasn't even any need to analyze what he was told, or to make any conclusions of it, because all the conclusions had already been made and presented to him by trustworthy and incorruptible analysts.

Juliana Pavlovna sometimes kept her husband company, but she wasn't so straightforward and even expressed some sort of compassion towards the bad guys.

"Will you just look at what's happening!" she lamented after watching another broadcast from the frontline. "They are like children, little foolish children, they don't know what they're doing! Keep attacking us, killing our people, making us suffer, and what for? Why don't they just calm down and stay in their countries? I'm sure they have lots of things to do there. Why can't they work, learn, have children and live a decent life? Why don't they leave us in peace at last? What do they want from us? Are they just jealous that we are lucky to have our beautiful country, our wise and judicious President, that our nation has always been superior to them and to the rest of the world? Well, that's what I call childish. Yes, we have our benefits, more than they will ever have, but we are willing to share! Of course, it's not paradise here yet, but it's only because of them! Of their bombings, of their meanness, of their stubborn refusal to admit that they're nothing but losers and will always remain so. Don't they see that we can stand for ourselves, we are the nation of heroes and fighters, but we're also generous and forgiving. And we'd help them too, they only have to ask. Do you think Pravdin will refuse?"

Yegor Semenovich smiled indulgently and slightly nodded at his wife's words. Boris smiled, too. He pictured to himself that if an armed terrorist by any chance had appeared in their flat, Juliana

Pavlovna would have called him sonny, seated him at their table with a plate of soup with meat product and told him to be nice, which would have made the terrorist lay down his weapon and momentarily swear allegiance to the Commonwealth State.

Apart from the news, their life was brightened up by a game of cards, which always took place in the neighbors' room. Just after four o'clock, when the analytical program 'Time to Think' on the First National was over and there was thirty more minutes until the news report, each of them took their broadcaster and sat at Yegor Semenovich's table. There was a choice of the three leisure activities, suggested by Katyusha. Dominos was boring, checkers didn't load properly, and Boris thought it would be a good idea to play bridge for three, with one nominated dummy. Each broadcaster displayed the open cards of the owner and the back of the opponents' cards, and you had to swipe on the needed card to make a move. The game was an immediate success, especially because Yegor Semenovich often lost and it was so funny to watch him raging at Juliana Pavlona and, at times, at Boris. When he heard Katyusha announcing: "Game over. Player three wins," he struck his hand angrily at the table and mumbled: "Silly old girl! Why don't terrorists eat you whole! I tell you, I ain't no fool, no! It's you, cheaters, who have all trumps in your sleeves! Let's do it once again!" Boris laughed and told Katyusha to start a new game. They passed forty minutes playing until there was time for the news, followed by a general information broadcast, and they watched it together, like a real family. First came the summary from the Ministry of Defense with the numbers of destroyed opponents' equipment and men, then there was news about the Government's achievements in national economy, mechanical engineering and mining, followed by a report from a random factory, or a coal mine. And finally, they showed some inspiring story from the life of common people, who were happy to live in the State and saw it as their duty to demonstrate their happiness to the rest of the country.

"Today," the broadcaster declaimed cheerfully, "millions of manual workers through the country, from east to west, from north to south, stood up in front of their windows, holding national flags, in order to demonstrate their devotion and faithfulness to the President," the picture of happy smiling people, dressed in work uniform, who seemed to be suspiciously identical, appeared, and the broadcaster went on: "These simple working people know exactly who to trust. They live and work for the sake of our country, for the sake of the Party and its leader, Victor Vasilyevich Pravdin. Not a single state in the world shows such unity of people and the Government. What is more, conflicts are constantly breaking out everywhere, and only our country struggles for peace and prosperity of its citizens. Here is a coverage of another riot on the Western Continent. Warning: age restriction – twelve plus."

The news was comforting, and even Yegor Semenovich, forgot about having lost in bridge and went to the kitchen to drink his tea, which for Boris tasted like mud.

All these small pleasures made Boris reassured and convinced that everything would be just fine with him. The flat was decent, the neighbors were great people, however, the age gap between them sometimes made communication tough. Boris thought it would be a good idea to make friends with someone of his age, so he posted a message in the 'Miscellaneous' section of the Pools of Ideological Interchange asking if someone wanted to chat about art and creation of holograms. The message was approved by censorship, but its text was slightly changed, and maybe because of this it didn't attract much attention. After three days it was transferred to archive without a single response. It made Boris a bit disappointed, but just then he suddenly got a notification from the National Portal, which informed him that he was obliged to register in a database for single citizens. Usually, it was done when an individual turned eighteen, but since Boris had been in the army at that time, he had to do it now. It was supposed to be a simple procedure – a citizen just had to upload their scanned image, record a short message and after it had been approved, they could get access to profiles of thousands of single people willing to meet their match. Boris was sort of happy at the opportunity because he wasn't going to spend his life all alone in the room, which, despite his efforts, looked quite dull and untidy. Besides, he knew that if a person wasn't able to find a couple until the age of 33, a special commission could order to forcibly connect him with another citizen of the opposite sex, selected by a special algorithm, which meant that they could just bring up someone else to his room, or make him join somebody in theirs. It was called 'external matching' and although it wasn't done very often, still he didn't want to risk having an unknown woman in his premises.

Having thought it over carefully, Boris decided not to take too long and do the scanning immediately. However, there appeared to be an unexpected underlying problem, which completely stymied Boris – he didn't know what to wear. At home he dressed in a crumpled t-shirt with stains from butter product that were impossible to remove even with Juliana Pavlovna's almighty laundry soap. He had another t-shirt, which couldn't be called clean either because there was nothing he hated more in his life than doing the washing. Ever since he'd remembered himself, he'd always been dressed in uniforms, kindly provided by the State. In the Center of Patriotic Education all kids got blue clothes twice a year: t-shirts in summer and additional cardigans in winter, and all-season blue trousers. The uniform had to be worn with great care because if you spoilt it, you'd be in big trouble and would be definitely put in front of the Pedagogical Council to give explanations. From the age of four, all kids had to wash their clothes themselves, and from twelve they had to do it for the younger ones. Washing of t-shirts and underpants took place twice a week, after the shower time, and the children were split into groups of five. Each group received a basin with barely warm water and a piece of laundry soap, which stunk as hell. Boris could remember his first washing day in the Center, just three or four days after he'd arrived there, completely confused and still missing his home. He tried to copy what the other boys were doing, but the soap was so slippery that it just didn't stay in his hands and sneaked out into the basin, on the floor and even on him. After several unsuccessful attempts he gave up and started crying because the other boys were mocking him and calling him golliwog and asshole. The supervisor came to see what the fuss was about, told everyone to shut up, looked at Borya's hands and legs, all wet and soapy, and said that she'd never seen such a crooked-handed child before. Then she grabbed his clothes and threw them in his face because the washing time was over, and everyone had to go to bed. Borya hung his stuff on the rope, like all children did, hoping that when it got dry, it would look more presentable. It didn't, and when he had to put his t-short on again, all the stains and dirty smudges were there, as if it hadn't been washed at all. Of course, he got a reprimand from the supervisor and was deprived of dinner for the next couple of days, but it didn't upset him much because the food was inedible, and he had an official excuse to stay in the dormitory for the whole evening. It was then when Boris began to hate the washing, and every time he did it, he tried to finish it as quickly as possible. It became easier in the army, when dirty uniform was collected by stewards and carried away in big blue bags every four months. Underwear, however, had to be washed every evening by the soldiers themselves, and Boris sometimes skived and just dumped his socks and boxers in water and then wore them until they began to smell.

Upon hearing about the scanning, Juliana Pavlovna was eager to present Boris with clothes left from deceased Basil, but he politely refused, telling her that they were too big for him. For the sake of appearances, he tried on several shirts, which still seemed to bear the smell of another person, and they really looked clumsy and alien on him. The old lady probably got offended but didn't say a word and just put them back in the drawer, folding every garment with great care and respect, as if someone was still going to put it on.

In any case, Boris's clothes were unsuitable for scanning, and if he wanted to find a perfect match, he needed something better than that. He thought for a while and went to Yegor Semenovich to borrow his white shirt. The old man listened to his plan attentively, smiled and winked, but suddenly became serious and asked:

"So, um, where're you going to live, soldier? With your future wife, I mean."

"Yegor Semenovich, I guess it's too early to think of it. I haven't yet uploaded my profile, just getting ready for self-scanning."

"I know, I know. But young people nowadays do it so quickly. You find a match, get a route list to visit each other, usual things, I mean. A couple of months – and you're done. In our times it was different. I used to date my misses for quite a while, didn't I. No route lists, no scanning, no nothing. You just see a lady, come up to her and there you go. 'What's cookin', good lookin', wanna dance?' That's how it was. Dating we called it. Danced all night long like crazy. I tell you, they loved dancing, especially to slow music, not the one they play now. My lady was young and pretty, I was a cracker too, you see, so we got married, and we danced on our wedding: me in a black suit with a white flower in my buttonhole, she – in her frilly dress, and they all looked at us and said: 'What a beautiful couple!'. We had love, that's for sure, but I don't think you know what it means."

Boris didn't. Of course, he knew the word, but usually it was all about the love to the State and to President Pravdin and his ideology and not something that can happen between two people.

"Basil wanted to meet one, too. A lady, I mean," continued Yegor Semenovich. "I told him, you can't live without a wife, son, like a lonely tree. Lightning strikes at lonely trees first, right? He even went to see some of them, but in the end of the day, old girl decided that he'd be safer with us. You never know what's going to happen to you out there with all these terrorists and viruses. But it still happened to him, no matter how hard we tried to protect our only child. We just couldn't save him… I sometimes think that if… Ok, enough of this chitchat, news is on!"

Yegor Semenovich gave Boris the shirt, winking and reminding him that "women are all like this, soldier." What women were like, Boris didn't understand because he hadn't met any, apart from the supervisors and the nurses in the Center. He put on the old man's shirt on top of his own t-shirt, ran another scanning and was finally happy with what he saw. Then he recorded a cover note about himself ("Born 7th January 2029, grew up in the Center of Patriotic Education, after which went to army and had served there fifteen years before being transferred to reserve because of health conditions. Currently living in the capital in own room (GPS coordinates attached). Would like to meet a woman of corresponding age from nearby districts. Ready for friendship and more."). In the next time for communication, he found out that his profile had been approved and he could browse the information of other citizens. He filtered it according to sex, age and location and spent another couple of hours looking at women's images and listening to their stories. They all seemed nice and attractive, but he somehow couldn't find the courage to message any of them and decided to wait until 'a lady', as Yegor Semenovich would put it, contacts him first.

Finally, about three weeks after Boris had placed his order, Katyusha gladly informed that the calculating machine was ready for shipping and would be delivered in the evening, together with the grocery sets. Boris spent the afternoon waiting impatiently for the drones and even didn't feel like playing cards with the neighbors. From five o'clock he began listening to noises outside the window and, at last, heard the familiar humming of motors. This time the identification procedure seemed to take unusually long and when it was over, four parcels stuck in the window, one of which was obviously bigger and heavier than the others. Boris grabbed it, threw his grocery set on the table and rushed into his room, leaving behind bewildered Juliana Pavlovna holding a rusty pan, which she was about to put on the burner.

Boris opened the package and made sure it contained everything he needed: the device itself, a drawing controller with several pens, a graphics tablet, wires and, of course, a screen, which was only about ten inches wide, but otherwise it just wouldn't have fit into the delivery window. Boris stretched his fingers and began connecting the machine. Firstly, he had to plug it in, but, to his surprise, there were no free sockets in his room. One was placed under the window and designed for the window wallpaper and the air conditioner, and the other one was for the broadcaster, so neither of them could be used for his calculating machine. Boris stood in the middle of the room and wondered how he have been so short-sighted as to not have checked the room in advance.

He kept cursing himself and trying to come up with some idea of how to get the machine running, when his memory flashed with a picture of his grandfather sitting at his desk in front of his (what did they call it? Top… lap… laptop!). It was definitely plugged in somewhere, probably right under the desk, which meant that Boris just had to palpate the wallpaper and find the socket hidden under it. He took his army knife, knelt down with a slight grunt and started fingering the wall, checking carefully every inch of it. After a while, he felt a bulge just between the legs of the table and, having cut through the wallpaper, beheld a nice socket with two outputs. He quickly plugged the calculating machine in, and, surprisingly, it responded with a short beep and started loading. In about thirty minutes, all equipment was connected, and the monitor showed a starting screen, which was instantly revealed by Katyusha.

"New complimentary device of data input, storing and processing found. Model: B-3007. Revision: U-001. Contents: empty," it informed.

The diode on the calculating machine started flashing, which meant that it had also been connected to the National Network.

"Reporting the device to the Ministry of Communication," continued Katyusha. "Approval may take up to seventy-two hours. Please note that the device cannot be used until approval is received."

Boris had suspected something of the kind. Of course, there had to be a firewall against all these foreign agents and dirty liberasts, and the Ministry should check all equipment carefully, not to let any information leak out to the enemy. However, he was a trifle disappointed at the fact that his work was delayed again, and, reluctantly, commanded Katyusha to turn on another educational broadcast.

Approval, indeed, took exactly seventy-two hours, and the message that the device was authorized to be used in the National Network came in the evening, two hours after the food drones had arrived. Boris was overjoyed and immediately started configuring his machine, which responded willingly to all his manipulations. The rest of the evening, right until the electricity was switched off, he spent tinkering with his purchase. It was at times slow and out of memory, so he didn't manage to finish it before bedtime. He loved everything connected with technology and it was one of the few things in which he found real enjoyment. In the army he was responsible for connecting wires, hacking enemies' databases, overtaking signals and sending important information to the frontline. During one of such operations, he accidentally connected to an unknown transmitting station, which he identified as hostile. Boris quickly decided to record the transmission and report it to the superiors, after which he could start working on the decoding. The cypher was unfamiliar to him and didn't match with any coding systems he'd met before, so he became extremely rattled and looked forward to several sleepless nights spent on searching the key. After the transmission ended, he rapidly collected the equipment, put it in his backpack and ran to the staff, where he primarily informed the platoon commander about the incident. The commander listened to Boris quite indifferently, but in the end promised to report it to Colonel Petrenko at the morning meeting of the battalion. Boris was sure that the recording would intrigue Petrenko just like himself, at least because the new cypher meant some significant changes in enemies' tactics. Next morning, soon after the meeting, the Colonel walked into the barracks, where Boris was getting ready for another field mission. Petrenko looked unusually anxious and alarmed. He quickly came up to Boris and asked about the location of the recording.

"Comrade Colonel, the memory device with the recording of enemies' negotiations is currently located in my private backpack, protected by third-level password!"

"Was it decoded?"

"No way, sir! Do you order to start?" Boris stretched his hand towards the backpack.

The Colonel seemed to settle down a little.

"As you were!" He commanded rudely.

Boris obeyed, although he couldn't understand why. He was confident that sooner or later he would be able to decipher the transmission and obtain information, which, doubtlessly, was vital for the State, so the Colonel's decision seemed illogical and unexplainable. "Unless," thought Boris, "he wants someone else to do it." He opened his mouth to give some more reasons why it was his, and not someone else's job, but Petrenko was inexorable. He immediately confiscated the backpack with all equipment and ordered to give him the main and the reserve password.

"The information received during the operation is the official state secret and should not by any means be disclosed," he clarified before leaving. "Proceed with duties! At the double!"

Boris went outside, still puzzled and suddenly saw two combatants standing near the barracks, who, upon seeing him, quietened down, but still looked unnaturally tense. He pretended not to notice them and quickly marched towards the staff, as if he had some urgent business there, when some sudden crashing wave hit him and covered him with millions of shards, which smashed into every nerve of his body. Boris didn't remember how he fell on the nacreous snow and momentarily stained it with red. He woke up only in hospital, bedridden by the wound, which since that very day, had forever settled down deep in his spine. He hadn't heard of the recording anymore, and every time he wanted to ask about it, something made him numb, and he decided to listen to this sensible part of his brain, which had always been saving him from getting into trouble. But the recording didn't make too much difference, anyway, because in two months he was found unfit for military service and transferred to reserve, away from his wires, machines and transmitters, which he used to love so much.

When Katyusha wished Boris good night, precisely at 22:00, he knew that now it wouldn't take him long to set up his device, as there were merely a few things left to do, so he went to bed, imagining that right in the morning he would already be drawing his own holograms. He habitually felt the book and the elephant under his pillow and suddenly remembered about the memory card, withdrawn from the toy's head, which was still in his backpack. He thought that, probably, he'd be able to connect it tomorrow and finally reveal what it had been storing all this time. The thought made him wait for tomorrow even more impatiently, and he closed his eyes, hoping that the night would pass on quickly. He didn't dream of anything, and right at six o'clock he was woken up by the broadcaster's greetings:

"We welcome all citizens of the Commonwealth State! Current time is six o'clock of the 6th of May 2060. Starting with the latest news."

Listening to another patriotic broadcast, Boris got up, finished his yesterday's tea drink with dried fruit and condensed yogurt and turned on the calculating machine. After a couple of hours, he could finally connect and set up all peripheral equipment, checked all the wires once again and, finally, with some unexplainable devotion, took a pen and drew an oval on the graphics tablet. The machine scanned his movement and obediently displayed it on the screen. "It's working!" rejoiced Boris and held his breath. He had to create something straight away, something, anything, everything he'd been keeping inside his head all these years. The images that had been waiting to be released, and being released, would exempt his mind of the shadows of the past and the present, which he could not express verbally. He took the controller and closed his eyes. But he had no ideas. The oval was looking at him from the screen like a silent reproach to his creativity.

Boris decided to take a break and connect the memory card from the elephant's head. He took it out of the backpack, cleaned the contacts from rust and was about to insert it into the universal slot, but then he paused. He remembered the evil eyes of his grandfather, a traitor, who could have easily infected the card with viruses, capable of smashing his brand-new machine into pieces. Yes, the old rat could have done it, but of course he couldn't have known that Boris wasn't that stupid.

"Katyusha, check antiviral software," he commanded.

"Checking…" responded the machine. "Antiviral software Steel Fortress 2058 found. Software Last update: May 1st, 2060. No further updates needed. Software functions properly."

"You heard it, asshole?" Boris gave a malevolent chuckle. "It functions properly! You lost again, you, old fart, you always lose to me, no matter how hard you try!"

Suddenly he heard a knock on the door and thought that his cry of victory might have been just too loud for the neighbors.

"Sorry!" he cried in the direction of the door.

"Are you ok, sonny?" Juliana Pavlovna's voice was as soft and delicate as always. "Can I come in?"

Boris quickly put aside his memory card, took the controller, which was lying on the table, and started moving it on the graphics tablet.

"Come in!" he said, and the door opened.

Juliana Pavlovna slowly entered the room, holding a small cup in her hand. The cup suddenly seemed familiar to Boris, and he was almost sure that there was a picture of an elephant, making a fountain out of his trunk, but of course, it was nothing but a piece of an ugly childhood memory.

"Here, sonny, I've made some stewed fruit from yesterday's delivery. It's a bit sour, you know, we're short of sweetener at the moment. But I thought maybe you would like to try it? Yegor Semenovich is quite fond of it, and he…"

Suddenly her eye caught the machine which was placed right in the middle of the former Basil's table.

"My goodness, what's that for, I wonder!" she walked closer and started examining the device but didn't dare to touch it. "Is it to fight terrorists?"

"No, ma'am, it's to draw pictures," answered Boris proudly.

"Pictures? You mean, holograms? Like they show in the broadcaster?"

"Exactly, ma'am. I've always wanted to draw, right from my childhood. I can finally do it! Do you want me to make something for you?"

"Well, it must have cost an arm and a leg, I assume," she said thoughtfully.

"It did, ma'am, but it doesn't matter. It will soon pay off, I promise. So, what can I make for you?"

"Oh, sonny, you've befuddled me, really. What sort of things can you draw with it?"

"Anything, you just name it."

"Oh, let me think, sweetie… Maybe…" she looked around and then her eyes stopped at the cup she was holding. "Can you picture Basil? I know it sounds stupid, but before you do, can I tell you something?"

"Of course, ma'am."

"Please don't be too hard on the old maudlin woman, will you? I promise not to take too much of your precious time. So, well, do you know where I got this cup from? You surely don't, so listen. It was the year 2036 or 37, I'm not sure, but what I do know is that it was the last happy year of our life. Mine and my family's, I mean. We still celebrated the New Year at those times, you must have done it too as a child," she looked at Boris hesitatingly as if not sure whether she should continue or not, and he gave her an approving nod.

"So, it was the 30th of December, and we were getting ready for the celebration. There were shops open, not the provision points that we have now, but the real ones, where you could go and choose whatever you wanted. Everything looked so beautiful there: the decorations, and the music, and the people, real people walking past each other; everyone was sort of united by the joy of the coming holiday. I went there with Basil. He was... let me see... seventeen or so, and he was going to celebrate with his friends, but it all got canceled at the last moment, so he decided to stay at home, with us. I was happy, I was always happy when we got together – our little family, and our dog... So, we went to buy the best treats for this special night. We could afford meat, and cheese, not the cheese spread we get in grocery sets now – real cheese, which you could cut

with a knife and put on a piece of bread with a tomato on top, or... I
do remember what it's called, it just slipped out of my head... Olive!
Yes, olives, they were perfect with fish and in salads, you see. So,
we got it all, and it was a bit too expensive, even for those times, but
it was ok, we could manage it once a year. And then Basil said:
'Mum, we need some nice tableware for such a feast,' and I agreed,
and we bought six beautiful plates – three big and three small ones –
and three cups, like this," she turned the cup in her hand, inviting
Boris to see it from all sides. He nodded again.

"We had a quiet family celebration, and when the clock
struck twelve, we all made a wish. I wished that this time next year
we'd be sitting like this, at the same table, eating from the same
plates and drinking from the same cups, together, with our dog, in
our flat, feeling as happy as we did then."

"Nice story." Boris remarked when the old lady paused.

"However," Juliana Pavlovna seemed to be lost in her
memories and ignored his words. "my wish never came true. Next
year we were hiding in a temporary accommodation center, because
of the virus outbreak. We never celebrated the New Year again, well,
we tried to, but there was no food, and all big shops were closed, and
we had more important things to do. And then it all became even
worse. The war, the lockdown, the terrorists with their bombs – they
ruined our small home, and we had to move here, to your flat.
Finally, Pravdin managed to take it under control, but it has never
been the same to me. Ever! All our plates and cups were broken or
left in the homes where we had to hide until we finally came here.
All, except this one. And it is so dear to me... So, I thought, sonny...
I thought you could try to capture that moment. Me and Basil,
together, in winter, before war, before virus, walking home after
shopping, or just walking somewhere... Could you?"

Boris hesitated for a while, trying to gather his thoughts, and
then took the controller again. He was sure he'd finally caught the
inspiration that had been escaping from him all this time. First of all,
he drew a hill covered with shining snow. It was so easy to make all
these sparkles, just with a wave of a pen, and they looked so real in
the monitor that he could almost feel their refreshing cold. Then he
placed a figure of a young man in the distance, wearing a black coat
and rubber boots and looking upwards, right into the sky, which he
made light blue, with a hint of frosty fume. Beside the man he drew

a woman, she was holding his hand and looking at him, her colorful kerchief tied above her grey hair, some of which got from under the cloth and was gently blowing on the wind. A couple of strokes – and the drawing started to glow, like it was a real winter landscape, peaceful and serene, the one that came straight from his childhood, when there were no terrorist attacks, no war, no fear, and no one was going to die, and life promised to be as bright and sparkling, as the snow, falling on the hill. He finished and put away his pen. Juliana Pavlovna was looking at the screen intently, one hand resting on the table, where she had put the cup with stewed fruit. She secretly wiped a tear from her cheek with her other hand and gave a smile with her wrinkled lips. The image now could be transferred into hologram and shown on the broadcaster, but for some unknown reason, she refused, although Boris tried to convince her that it would look much better in 3D. Then he took the cup and drank the fruit stew, which was really a bit sour, but not bad at all. Juliana Pavlovna looked at the picture for the last time and asked him to delete it. “I don’t want Yegor Semenovich to come across it,” she said bashfully. “He doesn’t like me being sentimental, you see.”

When she left, Boris returned to the card. It was old-fashioned and looked weird, as if it was handmade, not like the ones he was familiar with. However, it seemed to be able to fit into the universal slot, and, after a couple of minutes of hesitation, he pushed it inside, and it slid in willingly, with a frightening click. Boris felt that his hands and his armpits went sweaty while he was waiting for the machine’s reaction. A few minutes later the screen showed a blue bar and the broadcaster announced: “New complimentary device of data input, storing and processing found. Model: not found. Revision: not found. Contents: unknown. Reporting…”

Right at this moment, on the other side of the city, a middle-aged man quickly put on his massive glasses and, astonished, stared at his monitor through their thick lenses. “That can’t be true!” he whispered. “There must be a mistake. I must check... I must…”

“Reporting…” Katyusha repeated and paused. “Device disconnected. Please check your settings.”

Boris waited a couple of minutes more, but nothing happened. “Duped again,” he said to himself. “Just like a barmy pigeon. Typical! That’s just what I’d expect from you, doddery zealot! Okay, okay, you fooled me this time, but I swear I won’t be that dewy-eyed in the future. I'll take this one out just in case, so that…" he pressed on the card to withdraw it from the slot, but it was stuck. He pressed harder. The card stubbornly remained inside his machine. Outraged, he took his army screwdriver, the only tool he had in his backpack, and started picking the slot with its sharp tip. The card was unswerving. Boris was afraid to break the slot completely, so he promised himself to try to fix it later and went to the kitchen to eat yesterday's barley. On his way he thought that he'd better find a partner because Juliana Pavlovna's stewed fruit tasted ok, but obviously was not enough to live on.

Chapter 2. 2061

1

The winter of 2061 was extremely cold and changeable. The temperature went down as low as minus twenty-five degrees, then suddenly rose to minus five, and fell to minus thirty again. Boris could feel these fluctuations very sharply because to every one of them, his back responded willingly with a stroke of blunt and irksome pain. The heating in the flat was turned on twice a day, from six to ten a.m. and from six to ten p.m. Boris was ok with it because for him it had always been like that. Back in the Center of Patriotic Education it used to be even worse. At times, there hadn't been any heating at all for the whole day because the boiler broke down or a heating pipe burst, and the winters had never been warm in this part of the country. On such days, all children had to sleep in their clothes, and in the morning, warmed themselves up in the kitchen, where the supervisors turned on the ovens and put chairs in front of them. The quickest kids occupied the best places, but even if you were sitting far from the source of heat, you could still feel its warmth and comfort. Borya liked such mornings, when there was no school because the classrooms were frozen out, and you could just sit in the kitchen, which smelled of food, and listen to the morning silence. It was still dark outside, and there was no wallpaper on the windows at that time, so Boris watched the snow falling slowly on the ground, forming snowdrifts, which nobody was going to clear, and the view was so peaceful and meditative that it made his eyelids feel as heavy as lead. He sometimes fell asleep on his uncomfortable chair, but no one cared to wake him up, before, at some point, his muscles completely relaxed and he nearly fell on the floor, waking up at the very last moment.

Unfortunately, in a couple of years, these gatherings finished due to some fire accident, and no unauthorized people were allowed in the kitchen anymore. Boris regretted it a little but didn't say a word because arguing with superiors never worked and only made things worse for you. However, his companion, Fedor, a plump funny-looking fellow with small sneaky eyes, was completely put out. Fedor was sort of Boris's friend, not a real friend, but at least they stuck together most of the time. They were both outcasts, but this was the only thing that they had in common. Boris was quiet and preferred to listen and obey what he was told, never asking questions or thinking it over too much. Fedor was just the other way around. He seemed to be able to produce a contrary opinion on everything, and it wasn't in his nature to take things for granted. He got to the Center of Patriotic Education when he was about seven, just a couple of months after Boris, but unlike Boris, he didn't cry his eyes out, nor did he call his parents, he didn't even try to run away, like Boris did on his second week. Fedor's power was in his ability to ask questions and make his own conclusions, so he spent all his first days interrogating the supervisors about the procedures in the Center, not paying a slightest attention to their annoyance and frustration. Both Fedor and Boris were beaten unmercifully by their peers, but while for Boris the execution was always fierce and very painful, his friend just got some routine, as-a-matter-of-fact thrashing, more for entertainment, than for any practical purposes.

When the accident with fire in the kitchen happened and it was announced that there would be no more sitting at the stove, Fedor was the only one who raised his hand.

"Where's the justice?" he asked the supervisor.

"What do you mean, justice? How can an eleven-year-old boy know anything about justice?" she said looking down at him with barely contained contempt.

"I mean, instead of arranging additional fire protection systems, replacing hazardous ovens, buying fire-extinguishers after all, you just close the kitchen for everyone. Do you know that the optimal temperature for growing organisms is from 21 to 24 degrees Centigrade? My feelings tell me that we hardly have fifteen here, and in the mornings it's even colder," answered Fedor tediously.

"Where did you come up with that? This rubbish about optimal temperature, I mean," the supervisor's voice was trembling with anger.

"I read it in the brochure."

"In the brochure? Did you read it? Do you know that reading has been excluded from the timetable since last year? Where did you get it?"

"In Classroom Five. Our history teacher kept me after lessons yesterday for asking too many questions and went for a lunch, so I was all by myself there. I had nothing to do, so I went through the books that were on the shelf. One of them was a brochure called 'Hygiene requirements for children in educational institutions', and it seemed very interesting to me. I found the information about the optimal temperature there, and it also said that we're supposed to go for a walk twice a day and get seasonal fruit and vegetables for lunch. I haven't seen any fruit on our menu for fifteen months, I guess. Or even seventeen, but I'm not sure, so let it be fifteen."

The supervisor said something under her breath, and the other children sat still, waiting for the discussion to be continued.

"It's always twenty-one degrees here," she finally pronounced.

"How do you know?" Fedor wasn't obviously satisfied with her answer. "You don't even have a thermometer to measure it."

"Because if it's said in the brochure, it is true."

"No, ma'am, it doesn't work like this," it sounded a bit rude, but everyone knew that it was just Fedor's manner of speaking, his way of communicating with the world. "We mustn't trust anything except for our own conclusions. That's what we've been given our head for, not just for putting food into it."

Boris felt that it was too much. He saw the look in the supervisor's eyes, which didn't bode well, pinched his friend in the ribs and whispered "You nuts?" in his ear. Fedor ignored both the poke and the words and continued in his provocative manner.

"And what about the fruit?" he asked.

"You got your orange juice drink yesterday, didn't you?" the supervisor narrowed her eyes at him.

"I remember it said 'fresh'…"

"It was fresh!"

"And 'seasonal'? It was orange juice, and I don't think winter is a good season for oranges."

"It is! On the opposite hemisphere!"

"Overseas import is prohibited in the Commonwealth State. Our history teacher told it to us several times. Or, maybe, he was mistaken?"

That was it. The supervisor took Fedor by the hand and pulled him out of the room. The Pedagogical Council was called, and he was unanimously punished and put to isolation room for the rest of the day, and the next two days, too. The isolation room was located in the basement, and all kids were terrified of it. Some spoke of ghosts and evil spirits there, more pragmatic children mentioned rats and cockroaches, but in any case, it was an awful place, which was intended to beat sense into the most stubborn rule-breakers. However, Fedor went there quite calmly and only asked if he could take some books from Classroom Five with him, but, of course, he was refused. In three days, Fedor came back into the dormitory, like nothing had happened, sat on his bed and looked at the others, who quickly had started gathering around him.

"Is it really so scary?" someone asked.

"It depends on what you're scared of. I can't say I had a time of my life there, but it wasn't too bad either. Bearable enough, to cut it short."

"Are there ghosts? Spirits? Rats?"

"I haven't seen anything paranormal, although there were some traces of rodents. And spiders were quite numerous, but it was something I had expected, because these arthropods just love dark and humid places. Fortunately for us, no poisonous spiders are found in this region, so I was certainly out of danger."

No one expressed it verbally, but, instead of teaching him a lesson, that isolation room made Fedor a hero for some time. He wasn't even beaten as often as he had been before, and Boris envied his friend, because now all the force was directed mostly at himself. But the triumph didn't last long. In the end of that winter, during the walking time, Fedor took a spill off the slide in the backyard and nicked the side of his head badly. It was strange because he never fancied outdoor activities and preferred a quiet stroll around the building all alone, or with Boris as a silent company. He was immediately taken to hospital, and that was the last time Boris saw him. In ten days, the supervisor collected Fedor's things into a burlap bundle and carried them away. Boris thought that they'd probably found another Center of Patriotic Education for his friend, or maybe even a foster family, but later that day he saw through the window the janitor emptying the bundle into a garbage container, which did not fit into his theory. After getting rid of Fedor's possessions, the janitor brought another bag, which looked heavier and was torn on one of the sides. Boris noticed a book cover poking out of the gap and understood at once that it came from Classroom

Five. He was right. Next morning, the shelf in the classroom was occupied by black-and-white portraits of Pravdin and handmade symbols of the Commonwealth State. No one seemed to notice it, which didn't surprise Boris because he was used to the fact that things and people could disappear at any moment and if you pretend that they had never existed, you didn't even get too much upset about it. He decided not to mention Fedor to anyone, and soon another boy took his bed and desk, the boy who never asked questions and believed everything he was told. Just like all the other kids in the Center of Patriotic Education.

Boris had never had a close friend again, and friendship was not in the list of virtues of the Commonwealthers. So, he was very surprised when one winter afternoon, in 2061, during the message time, he received a notice from the National Information Portal: "You have one incoming message from private citizen. Play now?" Boris was intrigued and commanded to reproduce it.

"Dear Boris Arsenyev. I have found your profile in the single citizens' section, and it seemed interesting to me, so I decided to contact you. My name is Olga Klein and I happen to live just a few blocks away from you. I am 27, and I am a home safety and healthy lifestyle consultant. My father is a Chief Warrant Officer in the National army, so I thought that he would approve of our communication, since you were a soldier, too. Attached to my profile, please find my image and GPS coordinates. If you are interested, please message me back. Best regards, Olga Klein."

Boris loaded the image. It was a round-faced girl with rather strong chin and plump lips. Her eyes, deep-set and widely spaced, gazed at him with a hint of disdain, although they weren't repellent or disagreeable. She could be described as a girl who is aware of her worth and who knows exactly what she wants from life and from the others. Boris realized that it was just the way a CWO's daughter was supposed to look like, not more and not less, and he was attracted by her self-sufficiency and grace. Of course, he messaged her back, feeling slightly nervous and flattered that she had picked his profile among hundreds of others, who, undoubtedly, would gladly go out with her.

They kept messaging for a couple of weeks, and Boris learnt that Olga lived with her mother and younger brother Max, and her father, Solomon Klein, was currently on a mission at the frontier with North Crestland, the neighboring country, with which the Commonwealth State was permanently in conflict. Such trips were not uncommon for him, because the conflict subsided and then broke out again, and the troops were always ready to relocate to the hotspots. Olga didn't reveal much about her dad's missions, but Boris could imagine what they were about. He knew such soldiers – focused and terse, unreservedly committed to the State, ready to give their lives for the sake of their country. Boris himself used to be desperate to get to one of such places, where he could feel real war and demonstrate his martial skills, but Colonel Petrenko, who at times acted like his supervisor, kept saying no to all of his pleas. "I know what I'm doing, Arsenyev! Your mission is here and not anywhere else, understand? And I'll send you to rub the toilets with your toothbrush if you go on arguing with superiors. Attention! About turn! Dismiss!" "Yes, sir!" Boris obeyed and went back to his wires and installations.

In order to get a route list and unblock the doors to see each other, it was necessary for Boris and Olga to provide evidence of their close connection. Normally, people had to know each other for at least six weeks to be able to get a permission for 3-hour dates two times a month. However, for Olga it was easier. Being an army man's daughter, she had some privileges, unknown to common people. She could arrange a pass after just three weeks and invited Boris to a dinner with all her family (excluding Officer Klein, of course). Boris wasn't quite prepared for the outing, but it would have been rude to decline the invitation, and he started thinking it over and figuring out how not to hit the dirt at the first acquaintance. The neighbors were, as usual, there to help, and although their views were rather old-fashioned and a bit primitive, some of their tips seemed reasonable enough.

"First of all, soldier," began Yegor Semenovich instructively, "be natural. Don't take too many bows, I mean, but don't act too rough either. Find a golden mean and stick to it no matter what, okay? If you're too nice, they'll probably think you're too interested, and will kinda take advantage of it. Let them be the first to make a move, so to say, got it?"

Juliana Pavlovna disagreed with him. "What are you saying, you old Casanova? It's the boy's first date and you're teaching him to be contemptuous! Listen, sonny, being nice to people always pays off. It's true that we've become sort of crusty these days but look at our life! It's no fun at all!"

"What?!" Yegor Semenovich's voice soared with indignation. "You mean you don't like our life, if I understand it correctly? The State has given you everything! Everything! Freedom, security, protection from all those enemies, lurking everywhere. Or might you want to return to the thirties? The instability times, when our State was nearly ruined by that one… what was his name…?"

Juliana Pavlovna pursed her lips and covered them with her hand, having realized that she'd said something reprehensible.

Boris suddenly felt interested.

"Are you speaking about the Destabilizer?" he asked.

Yegor Semenovich pondered. "I guess they called him something like this later. He had a real name, though. What was it, old girl, Ma... Manilov? Marinin?"

"Don't you pronounce it in our home!" said Juliana Pavlovna quietly, yet ragefully. "The boy's too young to know, anyway."

Boris looked at both of them for a moment and then spoke again.

"Was it really so bad in the times of the Destabilizer?"

"Awful!" keened Juliana Pavlovna. "We were starving, we were freezing, and the country was going to hell in a handbasket!"

"And there were strikes everywhere. All you could hear on TV was 'strikes, strikes, strikes…' At some point it just felt like the whole country was on strike," added Yegor Semenovich.

"And the Destabilizer? What did he do about it?" asked Boris.

"He was…" Yegor Semenovich pondered again. "Funny… Yes, I guess that's what I can call him. A weirdo. Today he said one thing, tomorrow – the other, as if he had a dozen of personalities inside him and none of them was aware of what the others were doing. Seemed to have lost control of the whole thing finally and was about to sell our State to the one who pays most. That was when all those terrorists and foreign agents began to flock up here, like flies to manure, I tell you. They bribed him, I guess, or something of the kind, they've always looked for weak spots in our country, and he wasn't strong enough to resist them. If not for Pravdin we'd all been under their control now, that's as certain as gold."

"And what happened to the Destabilizer after Pravdin?"

"Fled to North Crestland, that's what he did. Well, at least no one's ever seen him after the Glorious Election in 2036. The last time he appeared in public he was completely off the rails. Cried and repented, but then started yelling and promised to return and destroy us all. I said he was funny, and no one really took him seriously. I think he might be still there, in North Crestland, arranging all those attacks and bombings, or just living peacefully on the money from our enemies and hating us and Pravdin for stopping him. He just couldn't let it go, could he, old girl?"

"No, no and no!" Juliana Pavlovna shook her head. "I don't want to listen to this anymore. The boy needs some help with the date and not all this heresy from the past."

Four days before the visit, Boris got a route list for the purpose of performing hygienic procedures. He had to take the tram to the only barber salon open in their borough, and there he got a pretty haircut which was a lot better than the one he'd mage himself three months earlier, using Yegor Semenovich's trimmer. Next day, he ordered grocery set number one, which was a bit out of his budget, but he wasn't going to eat it all by himself. The first set contained a dessert, and that day it was a box of jelly beans of orange, strawberry and minty flavor. He couldn't help opening it and smelling the contents, and the smell was so alluring that he almost took one bean and stuck it into his mouth. But the treat wasn't for him no matter how much he wanted it. He would take this box and present it to Olga's family and, probably, they might open it at dinner and offer him to take one, too. Boris licked his fingers and closed the box, thinking about tomorrow and feeling a trifle uneasy at these thoughts.

He was expected at Olga's place at 17 o'clock and could stay there until eight. Usually, the first date lasted not more than two hours, but with Olga's family's privileges, it could be extended one hour longer. Boris woke up early, even before Katyusha announced the beginning of the new day and took out the clothes that he'd selected the day before in order to make sure that they were still good. Of course, it wasn't something outstanding, just a white t-shirt he'd bought on sales especially for the visit, and some clean black pants, which, quite surprisingly, turned out a bit too tight at the waist. He remembered that back in the army they fitted perfectly, and even loosely, but now his lifestyle was completely different and it must have awarded him with a couple of extra kilos. He still looked quite fit, at least he didn't notice any significant changes in the foggy mirror, attached on the only door of his wardrobe, and his athletic build was still there, so for the time being there was nothing to worry about. He'd have to make an exercise schedule later and stick to it, or even order some training device from the National

Hypermarket, but he'd think about it after it all was settled down with Olga, who was his priority at the moment.

Boris put on his self-disguising set, left from thc time of his first arrival in the city, and swiped his micropass against the door controller at exactly 16:45. The mechanism was silent for a couple of seconds and then the diode went green, which meant that the path was clear. "This micropass is allowed to unblock the door. Warning: according to the Order of the Government Committee of Migration Control, all unauthorized attempts to leave the premises during the unblocking will be suppressed," the lock informed routinely. His neighbors hid in their room, obviously afraid that there would be a terrorist hiding outside the flat, waiting to break in and kill them all. But of course, there were no terrorists there, and the corridor was dark and completely lifeless. Boris had his biometry checked and when the procedure was finished, he stepped out and walked slowly to the staircase. Suddenly, his legs began trembling and his palms went wet, and he could barely breathe, while a wave of panic struck him and nailed him to the ground. "Stop!" Boris suddenly heard behind his back and turned around, but there was no one, and it made him even more terrified. "I command you to stop!" shouted the invisible pursuer. And Boris started to run. "Run-and-hide! Run-and-hide! Run-and-hide!" ticked in his ears, and it didn't make any sense at all, but this absurdity made the order impossible to disobey. He rolled down the stairs, pushed the door open, clearly feeling persistent footsteps behind his back, and continued running until he suddenly found himself standing on the hill, where he'd met the guy with the cat six months before. He finally caught his breath and looked around. The landscape was quiet and serene, so contrasting to his galloping heartbeat and drawn face. Everything was covered with beautiful nacreous snow, perfect for skiing or sledging, or playing snowballs with someone, who could just as well be his grandfather.

Olga's block of flats could be seen from a distance, and Boris didn't even have to use his satnav to find it. He didn't have a proper winter coat or shoes, and he soon started to get quite chilly, but still walking was fun and made him feel warm inside, so he even tried to whistle a simple tune with his frozen lips. He met a couple of self-registrators on his way, which were lazily cruising on the snow, leaving orderly tracks everywhere they went. It was getting dark already, the special darkness that could be felt only in winter – viscous, retractable and soothing, the one that makes your insides shrink in anticipation of unfathomable miracle. The city seemed to be sleeping and breathing peacefully, its windows blinded by wallpaper, like eyelids, and the snow blanket covering its lumping body with grandmotherly care. The scenery was so unnatural, as though coming from a page, torn out of a fairy-tale book – the image, which imprinted in your mind, although you didn't remember what the story was about. Boris bended and grabbed a handful of snow. It immediately started melting slowly between his fingers, making them cold and wet, yielding its charm to the warmth of his body, giving in to his human supremacy and losing its fragile magnetism, leaving him all alone in the cold embrace of the winter twilight. Boris shivered and continued his way.

Olga's house had a double identification system, both at the front entrance and at the apartment door. There was an elevator, which even seemed to be functioning, but Boris decided not to use it, even though the flat was on the eleventh floor. His pass worked okay, and soon he found himself in front of the whole family of his new acquaintance. The mother was wearing an elegant brown dress, quite smart, but not too chic – just enough to show her respect to the visitor. She looked calm, but the constant movement of her hands gave out her inner tension and uneasiness, so Boris felt uncomfortable too and bowed at her, which made the situation even worse. Beside her stood a young guy of approximately fifteen years, who, upon seeing Boris, scowled and mumbled something inarticulate, which could mean both "hello" and "piss off". Olga herself turned out a bit taller and more broad-shouldered than in the image, but her dignity was all there, behind her deeply set eyes and firm chin. After accomplishing the formalities, they all proceeded to the living room.

Dinner had already been served, and Boris remembered about the jellybeans, which he'd left in the pocket of his coat, hanging in the hall. However, soon he understood that there had been no need to bring them at all. On the table he saw various dishes, and only a half of them was familiar to him. There were real vegetables, not vegetable chips, cut in small pieces and dressed with thick white sauce. There was salted fish – Boris was sure his mother had made something of the kind for special occasions, but he'd never tried it because it hadn't looked as something a little boy might like. The fish was garnished with eggs, grated carrots and beetroots, and on top of it there were onion rings and a few sprigs of parsley. The middle of the table was occupied by a large dish with meatballs in tomato gravy, some long white stripes of dough with red sauce, presumably called pasta, and, finally, came a plate of bread, which, again, was very different from what you got with the third, or even the first grocery set. Boris remembered the words of Juliana Pavlovna: "Eat a bit of everything, but not too much," and decided to start with the bread, which turned out to be the most familiar object among all those delicacies. Olga's mother looked at him with insolent surprise but didn't say a word and just kept poking her fork in the plate with spaghetti and meatballs.

"So, erm… Boris," she wasn't obviously keen on small talk, but her manners didn't allow her to keep silent in this awkward communicative situation. "You are a soldier, aren't you?"

"I am, Madam. Retired to reserve."

"Well, what's the matter with you? What was the reason for retirement?" Mrs. Klein's look was still blank, and her voice didn't show any concern, although the question was rather personal and, perhaps, shouldn't have been asked so straightforwardly.

"I was injured, Madam," answered Boris politely. "I didn't want to leave, but my commander said I was no good for service anymore. I had to accept it, and it was a tough decision to make, believe me. But now I am here, and I think I can be of some use in the rear as well."

"Boris is an artist," clarified Olga and smiled gently at him. "He makes holograms, and I saw some of them. They're really nice and original, mum, believe me."

"Good," the mother seemed to relax a little, but her fingers were still squeezing the fork too tight. "I do trust my daughter; she knows all about art."

The dinner went on for half an hour more, and the jellybeans were still lying in Boris's pocket in the hall. Finally, tea was served – real hot tea with muffins, so soft and gentle that Boris for a short moment thought they might have been freshly baked and not delivered by drones. His own mother used to bake pies and buns quite often because she sort of liked cooking, and there was a decent oven in their kitchen, which could be turned on at any moment, not according to the schedule. Little Borya always managed to sneak into the kitchen and steal some goodies, like a handful of raisins, or a few chocolate chips, which his mum used as decorations. He dreamt that when he grew up, he would be able to eat any sweet at any moment, without being punished for it. Funnily, up to this moment, his life was just the other way around: he got enough punishments, but hardly any sweets.

After he finished the muffin, Olga suggested that they go to her room, and her mother made an uncertain movement of the head and started clearing the table. Boris wasn't sure whether he should offer his help to her, but finally decided that he'd better not and stood up clumsily, almost dropping his glass with ruby cranberry drink.

When they were finally alone, they sat on a nice little sofa, too small to provide enough distance between them, and this sudden intimacy seemed to embarrass both of them, but it was a pleasurable embarrassment, too pleasurable to be interrupted.

"So, what can you say, Boris?" Olga was the first to break the spell of the moment.

"About what?"

"Everything. Your life, my life, the whole thing."

"Well, I'm a bit surprised at all this… variety. I've never seen so many viands in my life. That's not the sort of fodder they put in our grocery sets."

"Not in the common sets, that's true. But yours should be different. Do you mean you get regular food, like all unprivileged citizens?"

"Well, yes, why shouldn't I?"

"Because you are a soldier, Boris. It should be different for you. My dad enjoys all the benefits of the army service."

"Well, that's sort of fair. He risks his life for the sake of our State."

"It was his choice, after all. Killing people and getting his piece of loot in return. Is it fair? I don't know. Fairness and truth are the first victims of any war."

"You can't say that! This war is hard for all of us, but it's essential. We have to fight until the last enemy is destroyed, otherwise they will destroy us, and the rest of the world, too!"

"The enemy?" Olga smiled bitterly. "Whose enemy?"

"Ours, of course!"

"It might be true, but there's one little thing that changes everything. They're not our enemies, Boris, that's what I think. And it's not our war – not yours, not mine, not even my father's. It's nothing to do with us, believe me," she whispered, lowering her eyes.

"Whose is it, then?"

"I have no idea. But you know what they say? The best and the most important agreements are made on the battlefield. Those who get benefit from these agreements and from this war are those who are responsible for every single death, every single drop of blood that it entails. And we'd better not mess up with it, otherwise we might get ourselves stained in this blood, too."

A wave of uncontrollable fury rose from Boris's stomach and echoed in his wounded back.

"But this war is real!" he insisted. "I was there! I saw it with my own eyes! I was even injured in it!"

"Where? At the frontline?"

"No. Well, not exactly. I was in the provision unit, about 50 kilometers away from the frontline."

"That's good. The further – the better. But how did you manage to get injured in a place that was supposed to be safe?"

"Well, I caught some hostile signals and recorded them. I'm sure they belonged to the enemy, because the cypher was unknown to me. And then they, the enemy, I mean, tried to kill me, right in front of my barrack. I was lucky to survive, my colonel said."

"Really?" Olga sounded skeptical. "What was there? What kind of signal did you catch?"

"I don't know. I didn't have a chance to decipher it. I was taken to hospital, so, probably the recording went to someone else."

"Oh, now I see. You remember what I told you about agreements in the battlefield? Maybe your signal, your recording, was one of those? I heard about some negotiations through protected channels from my dad. In this case, your Colonel was right. You're lucky you didn't get killed. And you must have a very strong patron if you managed to get away with it. Who protects you, Boris?"

"No one. I'm all alone in this world. Grew up in the Center of…"

"Yeah, I know. An orphanage. And that's even stranger."

"Why?"

"Because orphans never go to elite provision units in the army. They either patrol the city streets and die from toxic waste when they are forty, or do manual jobs on factories or mines, which kills them even earlier. Believe me, Boris, you aren't just some orphan. There must be a story behind you. Who's your family?"

"I don't remember… I think, dad was a doctor, mum was sort of a home person, sister was just four when they…"

"And this is it?"

"Well, yes, mainly. What are you asking me about? I was just six when it all happened!"

"They're all dead, I suppose?"

"I don't remember, really. At least that's what they told me in the Center. They said I must stop crying because no one in this world would hear me now. They said I'd better be nice and well-behaved because the State is my only family now, and it doesn't like bad and naughty children. They said I'm blessed to have been born here because our State is strong and forgiving, and it would take good care of me. And so it did and is still doing, that's for sure."

"Sorry, Boris, it may sound insensitive, but did you really see your family dead?" Olga's sharp voice rung in his ears, and he wanted to go deaf and stop hearing it because some memory, some very small piece of the past suddenly emerged in his head and disappeared almost at once, leaving behind an aftertaste of ultimate despair. He stood up and turned his back on Olga.

"Yes. No. I don't remember. Terrorists broke into our flat, I think. I can recall the shots. There were exactly three shots – one for each of them, and then... I started running. I think I managed to dodge their bullets and hold out until the National Army arrived. They took me to the orphanage. I was in this corridor – it was long, very long, and I had to walk through it, and when I finally reached the end, I was another person. A foundling. An orphan. A proud son of the Commonwealth State."

"I'm so sorry for you, Boris," she gently touched his clean-shaven cheek. "You must have been through hard times. But I still don't believe you. If a child has actually seen his parents dead, he'll by no means forget it. Ever. And the terrorists don't just break into anyone's flat and kill people for nothing. There's something more to you, I'm sure. Anyway, you can't hide from the past, Boris. It will overtake you sooner or later, and, you know, I'd like to be there when it does. And now take my advice if you will. Don't go telling strangers like me about your life, especially your past. Hold your tongue, or you'll have problems before you know it, okay?"

"I know. I always say I don't remember, it's like a spell that keeps me safe," answered Boris. He felt like changing the subject and suddenly smiled. "Who was your favorite character from Fidgy Freckles?"

"Oh, that one!" Olga laughed, too. "Funny how I almost forgot about this network! Mine was definitely Budgie from 'Avian Force'. She was so swift and fearless, remember?"

"No, that was for girls!" Boris shook his head, still smiling. "I liked Fabio from 'Ninja Cats', Doctor Easemypain from 'The animal doctor' and Cloudy from 'Cars and Monsters'."

"Cars and Monsters, I liked it too. But Cloudy seemed too brazen to me, so I preferred Buzzy."

"Yeah, it was fun. It's incredible how much stuff for kids was at those times! Where is it now, I wonder. I think they closed the channel soon after the Glorious Election, didn't they?"

"Not really." Olga went thoughtful. "They replaced it with another one, called United Stars. It was nice and instructive, but somehow not as popular as Fidgy Freckles. I think it's because it lacked this meaningless fun that all children like, you know, when you just enjoy yourself without thinking too much about it, without having to split the world into good and bad and being obliged to follow the good. I missed my favorite characters, especially Budgie. Oh, Boris, I have an idea! Can you draw her? Please-please-please!"

"I might give it a try, I suppose."

Three hours of permitted visit were coming to an end, and Boris proceeded to the hall, back to his lonely jacket. Olga's mother was in her room and her broadcaster was already airing evening news.

"Muuum! Boris is leaving!" Olga informed her, but there was no answer.

"Don't mind my mother," she whispered to Boris. "She's unwell at the moment. I'm sometimes scared for her, especially when she stays in bed for days and refuses to go out of the room. You're actually lucky that she agreed to make dinner and stay at the table with us. Perhaps, that's because my dad's away... I don't know. So, now it's time for me to see your home, I guess."

"Sure," Boris replied, tightening his shoelaces. "In a couple of weeks, right?" he tried to figure out how much time he had left to produce something decent out of his den. Olga read his thoughts and laughed.

"Don't worry, I'll not inspect your room, or anything! I just want to see you again before my dad comes back."

"Why? Do you think he'll have something against me?"

"I hope not. But you never know my father. He might end up shooting at clouds in the sky if they appear when he doesn't want them."

3

They went on messaging each other two or three times a day, and Boris thought that his fortune had, for the first time, been kind to him because Olga was just the girl he needed. She was a perfect combination of a friend and a supervisor, and she had a deep and profound understanding of how this world worked, and it looked like the world, in its turn, took marching orders from her and obeyed her in every way. Nothing could hide from her piercing eye, and Boris wondered what it would be like if they, by any chance, had started living together. He tidied up his room several times during these two weeks, but it still looked desperately shabby and unsuitable for living. He remembered his promise to draw the bird from 'Avian Forces' and he even made some sketches, but what he got was nothing comparable to real Budgie. He finally gave up and made a stupid little hologram of Olga surrounded by roses. It looked rather romantic and would perhaps distract her from the mess in his room.

Finally, the day of return visit came, and Olga was standing in his doorway, dressed in gorgeous fur coat, sprinkled with snow. Yegor Semenovich and Juliana Pavlovna were quiet in their room and even their broadcaster was off – a thing, which had never happened before. Olga hugged Boris, and he responded, clumsily, yet ingeniously, and it was so nice to smell winter in the villi of her coat. She took it off and looked around, nodding understandingly, which meant that she had expected something of the kind.

"Care for a dinner? The food drones are just about to arrive," asked Boris, more out of politeness because he knew she would refuse.

"Well, not now, thanks. First thing I need to get warm, it's freezing outside. Is the heating on?"

"No, it'll be given at 18:00, so it's about an hour…" Boris felt guilty.

"No problem. I guess *you* will have to be my heating for this hour," And she shot a conspiratorial smile at him. "Which one might be your chamber, sir?"

"On the left, my lady, and be careful not to bang your head on the doorway, The ceilings are pretty low here."

Olga brought a small bag for him, which looked like a birthday gift, and Boris felt absolutely delighted because he didn't remember receiving any of those since he was six. She insisted on him opening it straight away, and so he did, wondering what treasure it might contain. First thing he found was a set of felt pens, which looked exactly like those he'd seen on the stalls when he was a kid. He wasn't sure he'd told Olga about it, so he was amazed at the fact that she actually managed to guess his dream.

"It's my brother's. Dad bought them five years ago or so, but Max isn't keen on such things. They were all dry when I found them, so I had to use my perfume to get them back to life. Just smell one, will you? I thought you might want to try real drawing, but I couldn't find any decent paper. You may use grocery wrapping for now and I'll try to think of something more suitable. Go on."

There was also a box of sweets, called Zephir, something like rose-shaped apple marshmallows, very light and fluffy.

"You look like a person who may have a sweet tooth. You have this bread-and-butter look in your eyes, like a child, and all children are crazy about sweets. These ones are really good, better than anything you get in your grocery sets. No, don't share with me, I had tea with mum's muffins before I left home. These are entirely for you. There's one more thing."

It was a military mug of khaki color, like he sometimes saw on Colonel Petrenko's table. It was solid and heavy, just the one to be held in a commander's firm hand, shining with the glory of his battles won.

"There's something written on it. Can you read, Boris?" Olga asked.

"No, reading wasn't in our curriculum in the Center," he thought he'd lie this time, just once. He'd maybe tell her later, and even show her his book, but now it just wasn't the right moment to give explanations. "Did you go to school, by the way?"

"Oh, yeah, I did. It was a special one, for army men's children only. You know, we had lessons every day, except weekends, of course, and it was something outstanding because after the National Lockdown all children had only two school days a week. Oh, and I had a white armband in the National Youth Organization! And you?"

"Me too," it was the second lie in the past fifteen minutes, and Boris didn't understand why he did it at all, but the words just slipped out of his mouth and couldn't be taken back.

"I knew it," Olga smiled. "I didn't like learning, but my dad said I must be the best in my class. And, naturally, I was. But then again, we didn't have any reading, or writing, or anything of the kind. Mum tried to teach me because she thought it was sort of important, but when father learnt about it, he forbade her. I can still remember some letters, the ones which come first in the alphabet. And also, of course, the letters of my internal number. When I was fourteen and received my ID, I hoped I'd have some nice letters in it, but they were all ugly. Look at the slogan here, on the mug. This is 'f', the next one I don't know, then comes double 'e', then 'd'… Dad could read the whole lettering and said it's bullshit. He put the mug in a drawer and never went back to it, so I thought of bringing it to you. Do you like it?"

"It's wonderful. I promise I'll remember you every time I use it. And your father, of course," he smiled.

They sat on his sofa and kissed for the first time. The feeling of holding a woman was so unusual for Boris, and so inconceivable that he decided to disable his rational thinking and just go with the floor, wherever it takes him. They hardly spoke at all, and when they heard the floor creek behind the door, Olga suddenly got up from the sofa and declared that she would like to meet the neighbors. Boris didn't think it was a good idea and wanted to stay in the room a bit longer, but he obeyed her, as he'd always done, and walked to the door. Of course, Yegor Semenovich was behind it, pretending to be looking for something in the corridor, and when caught red-handed, started to look like a child stealing up to a box of forbidden sweets. Olga went out of the room, putting on a wide smile, and approached the confused old man.

"You must be the brave and wise citizen Boris told me about? Yegor Semenovich, if I'm not mistaken?"

"Quite so," he straightened up and Boris noticed that he was wearing the familiar ceremonial outfit – the white shirt and the black sweatpants.

"Well, I'm delighted to meet you," Olga said warmly. "Boris spoke highly of you. And your wife? Would she like to come out, too?"

Yegor Semenovich looked even more pleased. "Old… Juliana Pavlovna! Come here a second. There's someone who wants to meet you here."

The door opened, and first thing that Boris saw was a colorful kerchief sticking out of the room. Olga gave another smile and offered her hand for a shake, the other one supporting the old woman's elbow.

"I must say you look so active for your age," she said to both of them. "You know, these days people lose their vitality when they don't go out for a long time. Do you use a UV lamp?"

"What lamp? Never heard of it," Yegor Semenovich answered skeptically. "What's it for?"

"Vitamin D and melatonin synthesis. It's an indispensable device for home people nowadays, don't you know?"

Juliana Pavlovna looked extremely interested. "What? Where can we get one?"

"From the National Hypermarket, of course. If you let me into your room, I can help you select the best one for a reasonable price. And next time I'll bring you some vitamins. They're for soldiers only, and I'm sure Boris received some in the army (he didn't). But they're good for everyone, especially with poor diet. These common grocery sets are… you know… to feed livestock only."

They went to the neighbors' room and logged in to the National Hypermarket. While Olga was choosing a suitable UV lamp, Juliana Pavlovna sat at the table, with her hand propping up her chin and looking at the guest with genuine obeisance and delight.

"Ok, that one seems rather decent," Olga said at last. "I think I can use my promocode here, so that it'll be cheaper for you. Let's see if it works. Yeah, perfect. It'll be only fifty thousand GKB and, considering that you're going to use it for at least ten years, it sounds like a good investment. Ten minutes every day will be enough to get all the light you need. What do you say?"

"I like it!" answered Juliana Pavlovna mesmerically.

"I might try it, too," echoed Yegor Semenovich.

They ordered the lamp and sat in the neighbors' room for a while because Yegor Semenovich by all means wanted to hear some stories from the army, and Olga gave him some short indefinite answers, which didn't satisfy the old man. Eventually, they managed to escape and went back to Boris's room, where they spent the rest of the allowed time. They didn't talk much because talking could wait until message time, but Boris felt that all uneasiness between them had been gone, and now they were okay. Yes, they were just perfect.

"Were you in a relationship before, Olga?" Boris was afraid of the question, but it had to be asked.

She smiled as if she had been waiting for it. "I'd lie if I said no, so, yes, I have."

"What happened? How come you're not together?"

"It's a long story, Boris. All I can say is I'm happy I'm over it now."

"Does your father have anything to do with it?"

"It was complicated. The best answer is yes, it was he who got me out of it. Don't think too much about it, please, I don't want the past to come between us. I'm sure we'll be fine; I have this feeling that it'll all be different now. And, you know, my feelings never fail me."

When Olga left, he stood in front of the closed door and thought of her. He thought and thought, and he liked what he was thinking about, and then Yegor Semenovich went out of his room and tapped him on his shoulder.

"Good job, soldier," he said as though it was all Boris's merit. "Do your best not to lose her, got that?"

Of course, he would never let her go. He'd fight for her, for himself, for their future, and no one would ever take her away, not even Officer Klein, whom he didn't fear at all. He now couldn't imagine his life without this woman and if anything happened to them, if anything in this world tried to break them up, it would be the worst slap in the face that life could ever give him. In the evening, he messaged Olga to wish her good night, and in the morning, she messaged back, telling him that her father was coming home for a short stay, and it would be better if he met Boris now, and everything would be settled down. Her mother was unwell again, and there wasn't going to be any dinner, just a conversation between the three of them, after which, hopefully, they'd sit in her room and think of their further actions, depending on what the father had decided. The next route list could be arranged only in two weeks, even with Olga's privileges, so they started waiting, with their hearts in their mouths and their fingers crossed.

That was again the occasion for Yegor Semenovich's white shirt. Juliana Pavlovna washed it with laundry soap and hung it out to dry in her room. She said she had an iron somewhere, and she even found it, but when they plugged it in, it wasn't heating up, so Boris decided that there was something wrong with its power controller. He disassembled it and looked into the inwards, trying to figure out what can be done about it. But everything was all so rusted and friable that the more he tried, the worse it became. He assembled it back and gave it to the owner. However, Juliana Pavlovna didn't want to give up so easily. She carefully examined the iron and said she had an idea. Next time the oven was turned on, she put the iron on the burner and waited for its sole to heat up, after which she pressed it on the shirt, which was still slightly wet, and went on doing it until the cloth became smooth, and the wrinkles were almost gone. She then checked that all the buttons were tight and were not going to come off at the most inappropriate moment and, finally, handed it to Boris, who had been watching her open-mouthed, as if she was a magician performing tricks on stage. He also noted that the UV lamp, which had arrived about a week ago, was placed carefully in the corner of the room, still wrapped in transportation film, and no one was obviously going to unpack it. He wanted to offer his help with unboxing and tuning it, but for some reason decided that the neighbors would feel uncomfortable about it, and just pretended not to notice.

The evening before the D-day, Boris got a notification from the Portal that his visit was approved and scheduled for the afternoon, from twelve to two p.m. "Two hours is just the right time to get to know each other," he thought and felt the chills run up his back. What impression would he make on the Officer? Was he really a good match for his daughter, or does she deserve better than a second-rate artist afraid of his own shadow? He would find it out soon.

Boris stood at the front door and looked at his wrist timer. He felt uneasy about going out in the corridor, remembering the panic attack he'd gotten there last time, but there was no other way to leave the flat, so he made a deep breath and stepped out. The darkness was familiar to him, but this time it looked friendlier, and the red flashes of diodes above each flat door were nonthreatening and even mollifying. He already knew the way and headed straight to Olga's house without stopping at the hill, although he had a weird feeling, some irresistible itch to go there once again. The desire was strong, but he didn't have time for it now, because he knew that Officer Klein was waiting and surely, he wasn't going to put up with him being late.

Boris met only one self-registrator on his way and one human patrol, consisting of two unfriendly-looking police Officers with faces hidden behind bulletproof visors. He prepared to submit his micropass for verification, but they just pointed their biometrical analyzers at him, checked the data and ordered him to speed up.

"There's information about a terrorist attack planned for this spot. Get out immediately, or you'll be taken to a bomb shelter until the threat is gone."

"Yes, sir!" Boris stood to attention and the police Officers waved him away. "Permission to go?"

"Go!"

Boris doubled his pace.

He came to Olga's place at exactly five minutes to twelve, a bit breathless after the race from the police Officers. He rang the doorbell and swiped his pass on the door lock. The diode went green, and the mechanical voice announced that the pass was verified. Just after that he heard strong footsteps behind the door, which scared him so much that he thought he might have a panic attack again.

"Come in!" commanded the voice from behind the door. He drew his head into his shoulders and went inside.

When Boris entered the flat, Officer Klein and his daughter were there, and he noted that Olga had taken after her mother more than after her dad. The Officer was a rather short man with disproportionately big hands and large feet, which made him look like a monument to his own self. Olga stood by his side, but as soon as she saw Boris, she made two confident steps towards him and remained there, between the two of them, ready to intervene at any moment.

Boris wasn't wearing a uniform and could not salute the superior properly, so he just stood straight and made a small bow at the Officer.

"Reserve Sergeant Boris Arsenyev at your service, sir!" he reported.

"Officer Solomon Klein," the father extended his hand for a shake, and Boris took it with reverence. Stepping closer, he could clearly smell alcohol vapor coming from the Officer's mouth.

"Take off your stuff and go in," Klein spoke casually as though he was talking to someone he'd known for ages. "I can't offer you any grub, but there's plenty of booze to load on. And don't be long, or I'll finish it all myself."

The Officer was certainly drunk, but still, the way he held himself revealed his special status in society. He walked away, slowly and with dignity, and Olga shot at Boris a look that said: "Don't worry, it's all been going not bad so far." That look meant a lot to him, and he responded with a slight nod and a grateful smile. She hung his coat and flipped her hand on Yegor Semenovich's white shirt to smooth out the wrinkles. Then they followed into the room.

Officer Solomon Klein was already sitting at the table with two bottles in front of him, one almost finished.

"You can go, Olya," he said to his daughter in an unanswerable voice. "It's all men's business that we'll be discussing."

She seemed to be unprepared for such a turn and froze in the middle of the room.

"I said, go!" The Officer repeated, and his face went pink.

"Promise to be nice, dad, ok?" Olga's confidence was all lost, and she resembled a little girl, so helpless and infirm that Boris felt sorry for her and angry at the person who made her look like that.

"What are you speaking about?" Klein's face went even pinker. "I'm always nice to people. If they are not a threat to me, of course. And does this boy look like a threat? No, he doesn't. I'll be all niceness to him, I promise."

When Olga left the room, Boris was still standing in the middle of it, wondering if he should wait for the Officer's permission to sit down, or do it voluntarily, or maybe just walk away, because he suddenly felt sick for no reason at all.

"You gonna stand there until you rot or what?" the Officer put into his mouth a piece of pickled cucumber, which looked like a frog, and waved Boris to the chair. "Sit down, kiddy, you won't seem any taller like that, anyway. Pour yourself as much as you want. I've already had enough, but I'll make you company on such occasion."

The first glass of whisky burned down Boris's throat and stuck somewhere between his heart and his stomach. Before he could take a breath, Officer Klein spoke again.

"So, Sergeant, are you any good? Any medals, or military awards you can boast?"

"No, no, I didn't have a chance. I was in a provision unit, and it might seem too easy, but, believe me, it wasn't."

"I know. The selection there is high, I heard. How did you manage?"

"Well, I was in the Center of Patriotic Education and then I passed my exams and physical training standards. I was awarded A's in almost all disciplines: jumping, cross country running, wrestling, track-and-field. So, they said I could try to join Colonel Peternko's unit. It was in the south, three hundred kilometers from here."

"Colonel Petrenko? Yevgeniy or Mikhail?"

"Gennadiy."

"Really? I knew one Petrenko, but I'm not sure about his first name. A murky business it was. I think I heard about him some twenty years ago, and I was a simple sergeant back then, just like you." the Officer swallowed another glass of fiery drink. "Help yourself, there's some more pickles left. I think we should have crackers somewhere; can you check the upper drawer? And bring me my broadcaster from the shelf, that one, with a number plate on it."

Boris had to drink again and again until he felt queasy. The crackers were nice, but too dry to be a proper drink nibble. Officer Klein looked at him with his watery eyes and shook his head sympathetically.

"Not used to drinking, are you, Sergeant… what's your name?"

"Arsenyev."

"Arsenyev, right. You should receive a bottle in your army sets every second month. Don't say you're storing them for a rainy day!"

"I don't get army sets, Officer," Boris tried to focus on what he was saying and not to reveal any unnecessary information.

"That can't be true!" Klein was genuinely surprised. "You mean, you live on common people's ration?"

"Well… Yes…"

"And other stuff? Passes, broadcasts, access to 'Keen-sighted' network?"

"None of these, sir."

"Well. Let me check then. You came here last spring, right?" Officer Klein turned on his broadcaster, the one with the number plate on it, and made a request. "Keen-sighted, load database of sergeants transferred to reserve in the past year!"

The broadcaster thought for a second and for the first time in more than six months Boris heard the voice of Keen-sighted assistant, so different from familiar Katyusha: "Information loaded."

"Search for Sergeant Boris Arsenyev, internal number… What's your number?"

"Sergeant Boris Arsenyev, internal number 152-AH1021."

The broadcaster paused. "Information not found."

"Search again, you bloody machine! Search the previous year!"

"Information not found," insisted the bloody machine.

"What?!" Klein's face was now more than pink – it was almost purple. "Looks like you're not on the list, Sergeant. What's the matter with you, I wonder?" Klein looked at Boris suspiciously. "What are you keeping back?"

"Nothing, why would I? It's just a mistake, I swear!"

"In this case you wouldn't mind if I ask Keen-sighted one more thing."

"Please, ask whatever you want!"

"Ok, when were you accepted to the forces?"

"In 2045…"

"Keen-sighted, load the list of all accepted to provision units in 2045!"

"Information loaded."

"Search for internal number… What's your number once again?"

"152-AH1021"

"Search for internal number 152-AH1021!"

Boris's palms went wet, and during these two seconds while Keen-sighted was searching for the information, his whole life flew before his eyes.

"One record found. Display?"

"Yes!"

"Sergeant Boris Arsenyev, internal number 152-AH1021 currently serving in unit U-486 since May 9, 2045."

Boris gave a sigh of relief. Officer Klein chuckled.

"That proves that you are not some liar," he said, "and explains why you weren't receiving all the army privileges. They just forgot to add you to the list of retired to reserve, as simple as that!"

"And that why I didn't get my allowance!"

It all became so clear and explainable that Boris laughed like a child and, without permission, poured himself another shot of whisky.

"You didn't? You mean, you came here from the frontline without any money at all?"

"Not exactly. Colonel Petrenko, Gennadiy Petrenko, made a transaction for me. It was enough to buy a calculating machine and start drawing. I sold my first hologram rather quickly, and the others were good, too. Now I make about three of them each week, and that's enough for me. I can do more, believe me! If I have a family… When I have a family, I'll work harder!"

"Petrenko gave you the money? Did you pay it back?"

"I tried to, but, somehow, I couldn't reach him. My message just didn't go through," Boris suddenly had an idea. "Officer Klein, maybe you could look in your database? Maybe there's another way to contact the Colonel?"

"Of course, I can. Do you know his internal number?"

"Yes, I remember it. Colonel Gennadiy Petrenko, internal number 031-BBL1984."

"Keen-sighted, search for Colonel Gennadiy Petrenko, internal number 031-BBL1984!"

"One record found. Record classified. Please confirm your access."

The Officer put his greasy thumb on the broadcaster's sensor for it to read his fingerprint.

"Access confirmed," responded the broadcaster. "Retrieving information…. Colonel Gennadiy Petrenko, internal number 031-BBL1984, 3rd July 2003, deceased 23rd April 2060. Last position – Provision unit U-486. Display further information?"

"Deceased? What does it mean?" Boris felt that something was extremely wrong, something bad had happened to the Colonel and he wasn't there to prevent it. 23rd of April 2060 was the day he had arrived at the capital to start a new life, and that couldn't be a mere coincidence.

"It means, he's dead, Sergeant," Officer Klein stood up and bowed his head so that his fat chin touched the collar of his shirt. "Colonel Gennady Petrenko is dead." he repeated solemnly and bowed even lower.

"But that can't be true!" cried Boris. "Who could do this to him?"

"There-there, son. I'm sure he fell in the battle. He died a hero, and we'll always remember him as a fearless fighter and a distinguished leader. I know how you feel now, son. I lost my first commander too. It's like losing your father, your family, your own life."

Boris nodded. He knew what it was like to lose a family and he thought that now he felt even worse, because he was mature enough to understand the meaning of death and the meaning of loss. He remembered the Colonel's shrewd eyes and his instructive tone, his discreet concern and weird sense of humor, which he had been extremely proud of. All of it was gone now.

"Look here, son," Officer Klein leaned towards him and exhaled a cloud of alcohol vapor into his face. "Since there's no one to take care of you now, I'll see to it that you have everything. Tomorrow I'll make some inquiries and make sure you're included in the retired army men list. You'll get your allowance, and the food sets will be different for you now. You'll be able to go out without a reason two times a month and once a day your windows will be unblocked so that you get some fresh air. There are plenty of other things you can enjoy, I'll tell you later, okay?"

"Thank you, Officer!" Boris felt light in the heart, but then remembered about the Colonel, and the smile faded from his face. He stood up and knocked down another shot, which went down so smoothly that he hardly even noticed it.

5

All the next day Boris had a terrible headache and didn't go out of his room. Olga messaged him to find out about his condition and he assured her that he was okay. In the next message she said that the acquaintance had gone perfect, and her dad was extremely excited about the whole thing, which meant that his approval had been received, and they could start planning their future. Boris knew it and thought that Officer Klein was a great guy and would make a perfect father-in-law if it goes as far as this. He wanted to hug him, and Olga, of course, and everyone, including his neighbors and even their Basil. Soon he would finally have the life that he deserved. Officer Klein might already be making all necessary arrangements, and he just had to wait, maybe, for a couple of days, when he starts getting all the promised privileges.

When the food drones arrived, Boris came out of his room for an identification procedure. The neighbors were already in the kitchen, and Juliana Pavlovna was preparing the kitchenware for dinner. Boris didn't feel like eating, especially when he thought about all the delicacies that he'd tried at Olga's place, but the grocery set still had to be received and the identification procedure – undergone. He opened his bag and stared at the barley and the meat product, and then he turned to Juliana Pavlovna.

"Do you want to have my food, ma'am?" he asked her. "I had too much yesterday, so I'd better skip this dinner."

"Are you sure, sonny?" she looked at him incredulously. "Let me just keep it for you, and you'll have it when you feel better, okay?"

"No need to do it, ma'am. Soon I will have something… something else… different from what 's inside this bag."

Yegor Semenovich stepped closer.

"What do you mean, different?"

"I can't tell you for now, but, believe me, in three days maximum I'll surprise you with what you've never eaten before."

"Us?" Yegor Semenovich curled his lips, which looked like a smile, but Boris wasn't sure whether it was content or bitter. "We've eaten lots of things, soldier, I tell you. We went through happy times and bad times, we ate enough, and then we starved, and we've kind of got used to be thankful for what we have, even if it might seem meager. You remember, old girl?"

Juliana Pavlovna nodded. "I do."

"Really?" Boris was touched by the way these old people spoke of the years which they went through together, all these joys and sorrows, all these little moments that took them where they were now. "What was the most delicious thing you've tried?" he asked, preparing to listen to another story from those times.

"Let me think…" Juliana Pavlovna took the question rather seriously.

"I know!" Yegor Semenovich looked quizzically up at his wife. "It might sound a bit... gooey, but that's the way it is, soldier. Listen. It was before the war, before the current war with North Crestland, I mean. In the 2030's I saved enough money and bought a piece of land about six acres, just plain land with no buildings or anything. It was in the suburbs, and it hadn't been cultivated before, so it was quite affordable for us. I built a shed on this land; it wasn't a proper house, but you could live there throughout summer months and even autumn if you arrange the heating, and kind of enjoy the wild nature. There was a forest and a lake close to the place, so people came there with families and kids, and it was very busy. We took Basil there, too, he was about twelve or thirteen, something like that, and he made tons of friends. They were always running around, inventing games and chasing each other, swimming in the lake on hot days, or just hanging out at someone's place. There were no fences or hedges, so you could talk to the neighbors at any time, and it was like a commune. Called it 'dacha', right, old girl?"

"Oh, yes!" confirmed Juliana Pavlovna. "You were very fond of it, honey, weren't you?"

"Old girl made some beds and ridges there," continued Yegor Semenovich. "And we had roses, and peonies, and golden daisies, but also, she planted strawberries, and carrots, and parsley – all the simple stuff that you could grow yourself. Our neighbors gave us three saplings of apple trees, and I planted them too, but I wasn't sure they'd grow properly on this soil. Nor did I hope they'd bear any fruit there. Basil kept asking when he'd try his own apple; he'd seen wild apple trees, but he'd never thought he could have one of his own. I told him that if he took good care of those little trees, he'd be able to get his first crop in five years or so. We watered, fertilized and pruned them together, my son and me, and you know what? In five years, we got our first apples! They were small and sour, but it was the most delicious thing I've ever tasted. There were not more than six of them, from the three trees, and they were so tiny, and hard, and tasteless, but we ate all of them. I promised that they'll become bigger and sweeter with every new crop. But next year the trees were empty, you know, apple trees bear fruit every other year, and then it was 2036, the year of the Glorious Election, after which all those terrorist attacks began, and foreign agents invaded our country. Our land was taken for some military purposes, and the apple trees were probably cut down, or not, I don't know. Anyway, we never went there again, so it really doesn't matter. In 2038 the National Lockdown was announced, and at first, we thought it wouldn't last long and it would get back to normal pretty soon. But, as you can see, it hadn't, and we are where we are now, and this is it. You know what I sometimes think about? What if our trees are still there? We took good care of them, so they might have grown tall and strong and likely to survive the attacks. What if the dried fruit we get in the grocery sets now have our apples inside them? It's all nonsense of course, these thoughts, I mean, but they make me kind of… happy, don't they…"

Boris looked at the old man, who spoke about happiness, but had a fey and weary look in his eyes, as if he was talking to someone really close and maybe saying goodbye to them. He had a feeling that all his neighbors' life now was based on losses and sorrows, which they mistakenly called 'memories'. It was just not right. It didn't have to be like that – life, which is granted to everyone only once, was supposed to be lived decently, with ups and downs equally disturbed throughout its course, and people didn't have to hold on to their scarce memories of happiness to convince themselves that they'd lived well. Whoever did it to them, whoever deprived them of what they naturally deserved, was not just cruel – he was inhuman. Boris looked at Juliana Pavlovna to confirm his hunch, but the aloof expression on her face didn't mean anything definite. She stood in front of the disguised window and looked at the loop of images which it displayed, thinking, probably, that it had to have all the answers. The rusty pan was already heating up on the burner, so there was no time to waste.

Boris went back to his room. He hoped that his headache would have ceased by then, but it was nowhere close to it. The heating was turned on, but the flat still felt cold and lonely, just like in the evenings back in the Center of Patriotic Education, when the children had a couple of free hours before bedtime, and there was absolutely nothing to do. Boris waited for the last message time for the day, but there was nothing for him, so he recorded a short 'goodnight' to Olga and stretched on the sofa. He suddenly wanted someone to read to him about Cock-the-Roach, so he took out his book from under the pillow and opened it at a random page. He remembered the story by heart, and now it didn't seem as amusing as it did when he was a kid. It was about some fairy-tale land inhabited by various animals, whose comfortable existence was all at once broken by an annoying cockroach, who proclaimed himself their ruler and demanded blood sacrifice. He started reading, partly by heart, partly from the page.

Cock-the-Roach was named the Victor Great and
Grand,
King of Field and Forest, Lord of All the Land.
Ginger-Whiskers ruled – life was at its worst,
Birds and beasts were fooled. (May his name be
cursed!)
He struts and rubs his yellow tummy
As he orders every Mummie:
"Bring your little ones to me.
I shall take them with my tea,

Or eat them up at supper!"
Oh, those wretched Beasts!
How they howl and growl!
They declare in every lair
That the glutton and his feasts
Are unfair and foul.
"Why! It breaks a mother's heart
With her little one to part,
Chubby Jumbo, Baby Hare,
Or a cuddly Teddy Bear.
The rogue, the scoundrel! Oh, how cruel
To use our babes to make his gruel!!"
How they weep no words can tell.
Mummies bid their babes farewell…"

"Time to sleep, Borya."

"Lyudmila Ivanovna, and why couldn't the animals defeat Cock-the Roach? Was he really so strong?"

"No, that's not the point, Borya. It usually doesn't matter how strong you are. It's all about what the others think of you. But those who can see the real thing, who are wise enough to find the truth behind thousands of imposed lies and delusions called 'public opinion', those people can face any enemy and eventually defeat it. Because they are free."

Boris was sleeping soundly, the book lying on his chest, open at the page with a picture of a big and fearful insect holding a tiny baby elephant in its paws and trying to nip off his head. He hated this picture when he was a kid because it made him feel insecure and completely helpless, so he even tried to remove it from the book, and it was sill torn on one of the sides.

Next morning, he felt better. There was no message from Olga in the first communication interval, which was quite strange. She hadn't even replied to his 'goodnight', although she always had, and Boris wondered whether he should send her something, or wait for the next message time. He decided to wait and went to the kitchen. His yesterday's grocery set was lying unpacked on the table where he'd left it the previous evening, and he was happy the neighbors hadn't appropriated it. He took out the breakfast box and started eating, thinking about Olga and becoming more and more worried with every minute. Then he ordered a set for tonight and found out that all the food in the provision point was the same as before. Officer Klein had promised that he'd start receiving new sets in a couple of days, so he hoped that today it would be different. But it wasn't. The neighbors were listening to the broadcaster as usual, and Boris went to his room to wait for the next message time. But there was nothing for him again, and he felt sure that it just wasn't right. He thought his heavy thoughts, imagining the worst things that might have happened to the Klein family, and got more and more anxious, walking round his room in circles, looking at the window wallpaper and listening to the mumbling of his broadcaster. He had to get to work because he had taken an order for a hologram a few days ago, and the deadline was tomorrow, but he couldn't concentrate on what he was doing. When the food drones arrived, he was already going mad from the suspense and the obscurity of the situation. He got his set, hardly speaking to the neighbors, and quickly left the kitchen, trying not to seem too rude and at the same time not to reveal his anxiety.

The last communication time was at 21:00, but Boris was sure that the mailbox would be empty again. However, he jumped on his chair when he heard Katyusha's "One incoming message. Sender details withheld. Reserved encrypted channel used. Play message?" Finally! Of course, Officer Klein had used the reserved military channel, he would by no means send it through the common citizens' network! It had taken him some time to arrange everything, but he managed – he was as good as his word, like all army people were! It was a huge load off Boris's shoulders, and he commanded Katyusha to play the message.

"Starting playback. Sergeant Boris Arsenyev! As promised, I made all necessary inquiries about your case in order to reimburse certain inequities that you had undergone. However, checking your family background, I came across some facts that point out to your connection to one of the state criminals, who, supposedly, was your grandfather. I have double-checked the information and made sure that it was not a mistake. I admit that this fact might not have been known to you, so I will not accuse you of lying or concealing it. What is more, I will not take any further actions against you, and sending this message through reserved communication channel, which is not censored, proves my intentions. In return, I demand that you immediately terminate any contact with my daughter, myself and all our family. By no means should you mention our names and details or keep any messages that you have exchanged with my daughter so far. Otherwise, I will be forced to resort to the help of higher authorities. Finally, I suppose, that my duty is to inform you about the cause of death of your Colonel. On 23rd of April 2060, he committed suicide using his service weapon. He left no note, and the investigation team couldn't come up with the cause of his action, but some details from his past make me think that your grandfather might be involved in it, too. This fact implicitly explains why you weren't added to the list of retired to reserve. And this means you will not get the privileges we were discussing. My last advice to you is to break with your family history completely and live as if they never existed at all. Keep serving our country, and you will be able to purify yourself of your inglorious past. This is a one-way message and cannot be replied to. End of message."

Boris understood everything. He felt an overwhelming wave of abhorrence covering him from head to toe, and the old familiar feeling which he thought he'd left in the dormitory of the Center of Patriotic Education, rose again, leaving him no chance to breathe. He hated his grandfather, more than he had ever done, more than any words in this world could express, he hated him so much that he was afraid of himself, but there was nothing he could do about it. "You, old mean creature! A traitor! A foreign agent, a destroyer, a murderer! I will kill you! I swear, I will find a way to kill you once again and send you to your foreign-agent hell so that you suffer and agonize, so that your rotten bones burn in its flames, and your little ghoulish soul is torn apart by my hate and scorn! I will stand there watching you, and I will laugh at your torments. Yes, I will laugh and watch you die over and over again, slowly and painfully, and I will keep on laughing until you stop wriggling and begging for mercy and die down forever. I will do it because I have nothing left now, because everything I've ever had, has been touched upon by your filthy hand, and my whole life smells of your lousy self. I hope you hear me, duffer, and if you don't, I will go on saying this every time you try to creep into my mind: I hate you! I hate you! I hate you! Burn in hell!"

Boris grabbed his pillow and started beating it, like in his childhood, hoping that it would make his pain go away. A small toy elephant slipped out and was lying on the linoleum, looking at him amazedly with his half-torn eye. He wanted to stomp on it and trample it into the floor, but suddenly he stopped and bent to pick it up.

"Grampy! Did you buy me an elephant?! A real elephant?!... Nastya, look at what Grampy's got for us! You can press on its head, like this, let me show you! I know, Grampy loves us, even when we're naughty and misbehave..."

Boris picked up the toy and cradled it, and suddenly, for the first time in twenty years, he felt a tear rolling down his cheek. The window wallpaper changed the image and showed a path, running into a quiet summer forest, tempting him to follow it to its artificial enticing calamity. He carefully put the elephant on the sofa and went into his backpack to find a tube of universal glue for its damaged eye.

"It's too early, Sergeant Arsenyev," echoed the darkness hollowly. "It's too early to kill your grandfather. You'll do it a bit later; you just wait for it. And after it, I'll kill you, of course."

Chapter 3. 2035

1

It was the middle of the summer of 2035, and the State was on the edge of a new epoch. Not a single person could imagine how life would change and what their existence would be like in the next several years. People lazily walked along the streets, minding their own business and suffering from a deadly heat wave that had swept throughout the country in the past weeks. The distraught summer sun was obstinately burning the red-hot streets of the capital, which were generously covered with stinking waste, dried leaves and bird's dung. The boiling air was now and then pierced with high-pitched squeaks of starlings, flying through the faded sky and not daring to get close to the silhouettes of the melting roofs. The city was taken up by the wind, but it was not the kind of wind which brings comfort and relief from the heat, but the one that only throws itself in your face, making it even harder to breathe. It casually played with the rubbish that hadn't yet been eaten by the sun: candy wraps, empty packs of cigarettes, torn plastic bags from the supermarkets and crumpled fragments of newspapers, which nobody had ever read.

One of such newspapers was picked up by a professor at the State University of Economic Management, Vladimir Ivanovich Rogov. He did it in order to protect his almost bald head from the sun, which was already making him dizzy, but then he unfolded it and started studying an article on the front page. It was headed 'President of the Commonwealth State S. A. Malinin to negotiate with the miner's union.'

"During the long meeting with the miners from the Southern Region, the President discussed the most vital issues with the workers of the regional coalpits. Due to strikes, overwhelming the whole country, Sergey Malinin was forced to discontinue his summer vacation and start an unplanned trip throughout the State. Later, he had a series of consultations with ministers of several offices, resulting in issuing a new anti-crisis plan, which is supposed to be released shortly. Despite this, the strikers have informed that their protests will continue until each of their claims is fulfilled."

The article was accompanied by a photo, on which President Malinin was standing in a circle of workers, who, like beasts of prey, seemed to be ready to tear him apart as soon as he loses his vigilance, ignoring the object-glasses of the journalists. Vladimir Ivanovich sighed.

"Tell them about the dream, Sergey. Tell them about the dream," he whispered, but the photo was frozen.

The news and the whole look of the President made the professor extremely frustrated, and he had a good reason to feel like this. There was a story, a life-changing story, which had happened to him quite a while ago, and he couldn't stop thinking it over, especially now, when the situation seemed to have gone out of control.

2

Six years ago, a young student of the Law department entered the professor's office and asked Vladimir Ivanovich to supervise his diploma work. The man was well-mannered and polite, which made a very favorable impression on the professor. However, he was about to refuse him, motivating it by the fact that he was too busy rearranging the students' assessments on his desk, delivering lectures to empty lecture halls and taking part in lively disputes with his colleagues in the smoking room. But the student was so appealingly insistent that Vladimir Ivanovich stopped short in mid-sentence. He'd been teaching young people for almost twenty-five years now, and he'd met hundreds of them, but some professional flare prompted him that this one was different, and it would be stupid to miss the chance of having an interesting conversation at the dawn of his career. The student's name was Sergey Anatolyevich Malinin, and apart from learning, he had a full-time job as an Assistant Senior State Advocate in the Public Court.

The professor offered Malinin a seat, poured him a cup of instant coffee and began interrogating him about the topic of his diploma.

"It's called 'Objective preconditions for reforms in the modern economical system of the State'," he answered. "I looked in our university library and couldn't find anything on this topic. Why is that I wonder…"

The professor was vigorously stirring sugar in his coffee as if it was the most important business in the world.

"You know what?" he finally said. "What's your name again?"

"Sergey."

"Sergey… I think I know the answer to your question, but I'd better keep it to myself. And you'd better change the subject of your work, okay?"

"Why?"

107

"Because reforms are not welcomed in the Commonwealth State," said Rogov and momentarily regretted it.

"I know," Malinin's eyes shone with excitement. "I know more about the State than is necessary for a simple citizen. And that's the reason why I chose this topic for my diploma."

"You chose the topic that will never get through the censorship? What for?"

"To antagonize them, of course. Just to rock the boat a bit."

"And why are you telling it to me?"

"Because I was in your lectures, professor, and I noticed that you're different. I dare say, you look like a boat rocker, too. And I'll change the subject of my work if you agree to supervise it. Which one do you prefer?" he laughed like a naughty child, who said 'I'm sorry' but wasn't really sorry at all.

The student and the professor went on talking for another two or three hours, every time finding a new topic and arguing vigorously about it. They discussed the current situation in the country, its possible outcomes and consequences, the past and the future, the background events behind it all – everything that worried both of them, and what they had been afraid to discuss with anyone else before. When the scrubwoman Nadezhda Mefodievna came to the office with her crook-handled mop and a deformed aluminum bucket, Vladimir Ivanovich understood that it was about time for him to go home.

"So, student, tell me, what're you up to?" he asked Malinin just before leaving. "Don't tell me you're considering a revolution!"

Nadezhda Mefodievna groaned, dropped her mop and started crossing herself hastily.

"Who knows, Vladimir Ivanovich, who knows," The student winked at the professor and offered his hand for a goodbye shake.

And no one really knew because there was still a long way ahead of them – the way that took four years of their lives.

Vladimir Ivanovich could clearly remember that day when Malinin first openly spoke about change of power in the country. It was the day when his, or their, diploma was successfully defended, and they celebrated this victory in the park near the university, with a bottle of champagne, as if they had just won a war.

"I'm going to move on," Malinin suddenly said and looked intently at Rogov.

"Where to?" What for, Sergey?" asked the professor, who was already a bit drunk.

"Upward. To the source of it all. I'm going to make this country into a different place."

Vladimir Ivanovich put aside his plastic glass of champagne and looked around.

"Are you talking about revolution again?" he whispered.

"Not exactly but let us call it that for the time being."

"You can't be serious, Sergey! It's not a child's game, do you understand it? Revo... these things are not done overnight, moreover, they hardly ever turn out good. In the long run, I mean. Why on earth do you want to get involved in this?"

"Because I had a dream, professor," answered the future President with a mysterious smile.

"A dream?!" Rogov laughed, intending to make the laughter sarcastic in order to beat the crap off his student and put his feet back on the ground, but it sounded too posed and artificial, so he ended it abruptly, even with a more artificial cough. "What kind of a dream?"

"I had a dream that all people of the country left their shelters and went out in the streets. They all, like one person, raised their eyes to the sky because they didn't have to look for crumbs under their feet to feed on. And each of them saw something out there, and they wanted to share it with the others, and everyone listened, and no one said that it was a lie. And people, for the first time, could hear and understand each other, and that was called – freedom.

I had a dream that we could choose our own leaders, basing out choices on their actions, and not promises; to choose them not in fear of the past, but with a hope for the future. And these new, freely elected leaders were not afraid to come out to their people and they were not afraid of people coming out to them because it was their common choice. In my dream the government didn't deprive people of what really belonged to them but tried to give them more of it because real wealth lies in the trust and support of those, whose interests they represent.

I had a dream that every single man has a right to make a choice, which is called 'voice', and this voice cannot be stolen or forged because this is the biggest and the most terrible fraud that can be committed by the power. Moreover, it's a self-delusion, stealing from one's own pocket, forgery of one's own soul, sinking into lies and insolvency. And never, at any moment of the history known to me, could a state be based on lies and forgery. It's just against the order of things, so it has to be changed. And now, right in this moment, there is an opportunity for this change, for the curtail of power so that it cannot lie to people anymore. I hope that this will make my dream come true, and soon we will hear our own voices, and will be proud of them, no matter who we give them to."

The professor stared at Malinin for a moment and then laughed again, but this time the laugh was heartfelt and snide because the speech was so pathetically stupid and utopic that it was the only reaction it could provoke.

"Please continue," he said finally, wiping tears off his face.

"What is revolution, professor? How can you define it?"

"It depends on the nature of revolution, doesn't it? In politics it usually means violent overthrow of the current government or social order involving radical changes in the state organization. Is this the correct answer, student?"

"I guess so. Well, I don't want violence, professor. It means I don't want revolution. Although I am fully aware of the fact that the situation in the State now might require some hardline actions."

"So, what do you want then?" Vladimir Ivanovich seemed to have lost it again.

"I want to give people the possibility of choice. I know how to tell them the truth about what's happening in our country now. I will present them with only the bare facts. With the evidence of lies and falsifications in all spheres of their life. They will learn that this State, which is supposed to constantly develop and improve, is stuck somewhere between 'timocracy' and 'tyranny' and doesn't even try to carry out its functions, which is to control, to defend and to produce material goods. People will be able to realize that, actually, they've been living without any State for hundreds of years, and if they have any dignity and self-respect left, they'll probably ask if they really deserve it at all. And then I will tell them about my dream. And if they decide to follow me, we'll work together, and if we work together, we'll win. So, how does it sound to you, professor?"

"Woah-woah-woah, it doesn't have to be so bombastic! You know, Sergey, your pathetic attempts to sound lofty are complete and utter nonsense, which has nothing to do with reality, and the worst thing about this crap is that it is pronounced by one of my best students. Aren't you afraid, after all?"

"Afraid? Of what?"

"Don't fool with me, Sergey, you know what. Them… Those who you're going to fight. Do you really think they're just sitting there waiting to give in to you?"

"No, Vladimir Ivanovich, I don't think so, and I'm not afraid of them, as you can see. We are living in a rough time in a rough country, but even in this situation we must still remain ourselves – human beings, with our own feelings and our own rights that are granted to every one of us automatically, from birth. But those whom we call 'the State' act as if they've never heard of anything of the kind and try to take these simple things away from us, turn us into rubbish, into nothing but the source of their power, their ambitions, their enrichment. They keep us under control using our most primitive emotions: guilt, resent, aggression and fear. Our fear is their weapon against us, but it could be used against them just as well. I don't want to be their source of enrichment, so I chose not to be afraid. What should I fear? Death? We'll all die, sooner or later, so maybe, Vladimir Ivanovich, it is better to die a human being, rather than to live a long life being a faceless puppet? For me the answer is obvious. And for you? Have you ever had a dream, professor, but waited for a moment to make it come true? Don't you think the moment is now?"

"I really don't know, Sergey. Suppose you do it. Suppose you, by any incredible stroke of luck are able to get the power under your control. Can you imagine what huge load of responsibility it will be? Millions of lives will now depend on you, and there will be no margin for error. And don't forget about the external policy, too. I've been studying it for my entire adult life, but I still have no idea who is who outside our borders. Isn't it too much for one man, even as articulate as you?"

"It is, and that's why I'm asking you to help me. And not only you. I need a team, Vladimir Ivanovich, and I already have some concepts and some very important connections, which makes me think that I might try to unlock the current stalemate. And, what's more, I have money. Don't ask me where I got it from, and, technically, it's not all mine, but during the last three or four years I've been able to raise a start-up sum that'll be enough to cover our first essential needs. More of it will come in if everything goes well."

"And if it doesn't?"

"If it doesn't, money will be the last thing that matters. So, professor, what do you think about it? Does it still sound like a complete bullshit to you?"

It was dark in the park and the darkness smiled at them with its blood-thirsty mouth. "What a clever guy," it spoke. "Pity, but I can hear the tocsins ringing and I can smell the fire burning on my altar for him. It won't be long till he dies, of course, but his death won't be such as he imagines it. Just another death of another sacrifice, which will very soon be forgotten by everyone, even by myself."

Rogov was listening to Malinin and thinking that such were the people who had always made this heavy world go round. It was a hard decision, and there was absolutely no one to ask for advice, so he went home and started thinking. But the only thought he had inside his almost bald head was something he'd heard in his childhood, something he'd never dared to question. 'Go on risking your life for the sake of your ideals. Life without risk is nothing but a senseless existence.' The professor knew that he'd already made up his mind the moment he first saw his student walk into the room. He now was ready to work with him, to follow his dream, this unreachable, yet beckoning Utopia, which he seemed to have adopted in his heart, too. What did he have to lose? Nothing or everything? It all depended on his choice. After that talk in the university park the professor's life had acquired a meaning, it had become what he'd always wanted it to be, and, finally, after so many years of wandering in darkness, he had found his passion and all he had to do now was to follow it because, as he'd been told, 'compromise never works out in the end.'

Their next meeting with Malinin was in a semi-basement premise of an abandoned boiler house in the outskirts of the city. There were four of them, including the professor, and they started making sketches of their plan for the next years.

"I happened to come across a person a short while ago," Malinin said and made a pause. Rogov noticed the way his former student looked at them and thought that it was the look of a real leader, and his words about not being afraid hadn't been said just for effect. Malinin continued. "This person is pretty close to the current government, and he revealed some facts that might prove useful to us. He confirmed my ideas that now all power is merely based on money. Those who have it in abundance, are able to control, aka to buy the whole country. But the time is getting rather difficult for them because the population is growing, despite the conditions they are subjected to, and some of them are starting to think inappropriate thoughts and ask uncomfortable questions. But the authorities aren't just sitting around waiting for the situation to escalate. According to my information, soon things might change, and all controlling functions will be done automatically, by machines, which cannot be bribed or nobbled, only reprogrammed. It seems that something should be done straight away, before they manage to realize their plan. I know how to talk to people, but I don't know how to talk to machines."

"Sounds reasonable," agreed Vladimir Ivanovich and everyone in the room nodded too.

"First, we must provide people with fuel for thought. All evidence of cheat, fraud, swindle, false pretenses – everything will do. Even the smallest larceny can make a difference. I'll explain. At the moment, the state power is sewn into every citizen. Everyone has a small transmitter in their head that is constantly replacing their own thoughts with the ones that are advantageous to the State. All we need to do is to switch it off, to extract it, so that people could think for themselves."

"Extract?" wondered one of those present. "That might be painful."

"Not literally, of course. And there will be no pain, my friend," smiled Sergey. "There is always such thing as anesthetic. Doctors have been using it for quite a long time. And we'll use it for our purposes too."

Their primary task was to form a team, the core of their forces, which consisted of carefully selected people, ready to follow the dream of their leader. Professor Rogov found out that he had some inner feeling that helped him identify the right candidates, for he could listen to people and see the meaning behind their words. Malinin, on the contrary, had the ability to speak in such a way that you couldn't help but believe him, trust him completely and, what's more, relate to his ideas as if they were your own ones. It kept them busy for a year or so, and after this year, they had their offices in the most important regions of the country. The team consisted of lawyers and scientists, students and teachers, workers and managers – and each of them contributed their equal share to their goal. Of course, there were those who just came to see what the fuss was all about and even those who openly hated the new movement and even gave a nickname to it – 'the dirty liberasty'. "I don't mind being dirty," smiled Sergey. "as long as it is the dirt that I've dug out of your heads."

By the time their first year of struggle was over, the name of Sergey Malinin had become known throughout the Commonwealth State and it had become a symbol. For someone it was a symbol of madness and rage, and for someone – the symbol of courage. Malinin celebrated this one-year anniversary in prison where he'd been put for no reason at all. In six months, he was released on probation, and everyone thought that it would settle him down a bit, but the moment he stepped out of the prison gate, he started to prepare for another pitch. They set up their own information resource called 'The Voice of Liberty', and the first article that was published there came under the heading 'Objective preconditions for reforms in the modern economical system of the State'.

It was amazing how quickly and effortless it was to shift the vector of some people's thoughts or 'to extract their transmitter', as Sergey would put it. It seemed that something of the kind had been burning inside the society for a long time, and their group only had to turn it into the right direction. However, there was quite a big layer of those who were tangled up in the state propaganda net and were drowned in the cloudy water of the national broadcasting channels. These people were numerous, and they all said similar words and shouted out identical slogans against all Malinin's evidence.

"There's no alternative to our President," they said.

"Why? There are 80 million people living in the Commonwealth State, and it's impossible to find a right candidate? Is it acceptable for a state to depend on one person only?"

"It's you, filthy liberasts, who don't let our government work properly. If you shut your stinking mouths, things will improve faster, you'll see!"

"Pluralism and freedom of thought have always been an engine that pushes a state forward. Only someone who knows he's wrong is afraid to listen to the others."

"How dare you criticize the State that has given you everything? People now have far more than they had thirty years ago! Where do you think all this well-being comes from? Doesn't it mean that the government is doing the right thing?"

"It only means that people have learnt to survive without any outside help. All the benefits I've received were not because of the government, but in spite of them. Security? Medicine? Education? Are you sure it all comes free for everyone?"

Such discussions continued, some of them were successful, some – not, but the mere existence of them was a benefit for Malinin because it meant that his plan was working. As time went by, he learned to speak even to such wayward souls and find triggers they responded to. The only problem was that there were very few ways of communicating with the masses, but then, as the team grew stronger, they found options to use the same channels as the government, but for their own purposes, for the purposes of liberation. The state media was too straightforward, resorting to the old habitual methods over dozens of years to transfer its ideas to the population, thus killing itself with its own weapon. It kept on pulling the same strings without realizing that there were very few puppets left on their other ends, and pushing itself deeper and deeper into the dead-end, full of pathetic lies and glaring inconsistencies. People were just getting tired of what they'd been told over and over again and started to suspect that repeated lies might not always turn into truth. That feelings produced a favorable ground for Malinin's team, which little by little, started giving them new information, some fresh food to digest, something to make them think instead of barely sticking into their brain. The propagandistic lies were so easy to refute that it didn't acquire much effort to prove their insolvency. Finally, the group stepped out of the shade and openly spoke of their plans to change the situation in the country. They wondered how many people would follow them, and, surprisingly, a rather number of them did, so the government could not keep ignoring the newly emerged opposition anymore.

This was time to involve as many associates as possible, mainly, from the military forces, the only stronghold of the existing power. The forces hesitated, but, Malinin made some very bold promises and they, having not much to lose, believed him, and about thirty percent took his side. It was more than enough to start the real action – to get people out in the streets. At first, there were some small gatherings, rather peaceful and harmless, but the keenest participants were indicatively arrested, and some of them even killed. It took the edge off Malinin's team a bit, although they were prepared for such an outcome, but, at the same time, it outraged those with more radical views, and they were ready for revenge. Having studied the government forces' technique, Malinin gave his people weapon, self-made at first, because he had to save the real arms for the final shot. Again, the conflict resulted in victims, but now they were on both sides. As an extreme measure, the State introduced tanks, one of which was burned by the rebels with the full crew inside. Shortly after it, another 10 per cent of the military forces joined Malinin, who guaranteed them safety and multiple benefits after the victory. The revolts continued, and at some point, it was clear that the state started losing control of them, and Malinin again was arrested and taken into custody, together with a dozen of his most zealous associates. They took it with disregard, and even humor, and in the evening news millions of Commonwealthers saw them smiling conspiratorially into the cameras, while being escorted into jail. That very evening, the country, with a fainting heart, watched some of the important official buildings engulf in flames of revolution, and thousands of Molotov cocktails flew across the streets of the biggest cities. In a fortnight, Malinin was released, only to face an assassination attempt shortly afterwards. He got away only with an injury in his left arm, mainly because he was prepared for it, maybe even warned by someone, and he replied by sending out even more people into the streets.

The State, already agonizing, turned for help to its remaining allies – the countries which lived on its resources, and, in return, provided it with a simulacrum of faithfulness and respect. Surprisingly enough, the government didn't get any serious support, apart from vague promises and big pronouncements. Instead, some of the radicals outside the borders of the Commonwealth State joined Malinin's revolution, hoping to crank something of the kind later in their homeland. With their help, in about three months Malinin gained control of almost a third of the country, and some point operations enabled him to get to several strategical locations and bases. All his efforts resulted in an unprecedented event – the dialog between the officials and the opposition, which nobody had taken seriously before. The negotiations took several days, during which the mob violence continued, and the only demand of Malinin's Team was for the Parliament to impeach the President and appoint early election. The government finally agreed, hoping to win the election using its old mechanisms of falsification and fraud. However, quite unexpectedly, even with all their efforts, the number of carousel voters was smaller than it was expected and proved not sufficient to overweigh the rest. The new leader got the majority of votes – 53 per cent to be exact.

It was the long-awaited victory, and that night Professor Rogov, his hands trembling with excitement, dialed the number of the new President to congratulate him and heard his usual "At your service, Vladimir Ivanovich." Malinin spoke in a calm and confident voice as if he had always known that it was going to be like this. He offered Rogov a consulting position in the new office, but he refused. He was too old and sort of devastated by the struggle of the last years and just wanted to enjoy life as a simple citizen of the newly reclaimed state. That was when they made a deal: whatever happens, in any circumstances, they would never lose contact, even if it proved difficult for both of them. They kept this promise until something happened two years after the election, and that something was Victor Vasilyevich Pravdin, an unknown official with plain biography and excellent reputation, who suddenly took place of an economic adviser in the President's office. That was when everything started to go wrong. The Hydra, which seemed to have been defeated and unable to raise any of its heads, had been in fact just lying low and waiting for the right time to take revenge. Now it was stronger, fatter and smarter and by no means would it release its loot.

"We need another revolution. A proper one this time," said Vladimir Ivanovich to himself, folded the newspaper and tucked it in his pocket, where he already had a pack of cigarettes, an old mobile phone with a cracked screen and some breadcrumbs.

The way to the university was long, and Vladimir Ivanovich was walking slowly, trying to stay in the shade whenever possible. However, on top of the roofs, through the mist of the boiling air, he noticed a cloud with gray edges, threatening him with pouring rain, or even thunderstorm, typical for such hot summers. It seemed that the nature was against the professor this time, and it was trying to stop him by all means available to it, before he did something extremely stupid. But it was too late.

At last, when Rogov reached his office, the storm broke out, both in the sky and on earth. All magistral staff was gathered in a stuffy meeting room, and an old television, which had been pretending dead for many years on a dusty cabinet, was turned on.

"All citizens, your attention, please! At 13:00 President Malinin will make an urgent address to the people of the Commonwealth state!" croaked the TV box.

Everyone knew or at least suspected what the address would be about. It had to happen, sooner or later, but deep in his heart, Rogov entertained a delusive hope that it would all settle down one way or another. There were seven more minutes until 13:00, and the rain was hitting mercilessly against the window glass. Vladimir Ivanovich was sitting in the meeting room, surrounded by his colleagues, and secretly looked at their faces in order to make out what they were thinking about. He imagined that at least some of them were hiding their emotions under their poker faces, and what was about to happen concerned them as much as it concerned him. What if there still were people in this hopeless country who, right at this moment, were standing at the doors of their flats, ready to break them open and jump out in the streets to protect what they had once gained. He thought that if he could collect them all, poor, hopeless and deceived, thousands of times betrayed and left all by themselves, they would be able to turn the tide and finish what they had started six years ago. This thought was piercing his brain, killing him from the inside, and he kept on waiting for the speech and crumpling the newspaper with Malinin's photo, which had already become limp and faded and turned into a selfless wisp.

On the dusty screen of the old TV set, the president's face looked especially pale and unnatural, as if carelessly painted by some unknown beginner artist on a cheap lumpy canvas. Malinin started his speech on time, as always, and, as always, he was laconic and persuasive.

"Dear people of the Commonwealth State! I have always been honest with you, and I have always asked honesty from all of you in return. This time is no exception. We all feel that the current situation demands urgent and strong actions, both from me and from you. Therefore, I am here to announce one of the hardest decisions I have ever had to make, which, in my view, is the only way out of the growing crisis. I've been thinking it over and over again, I discussed it with my colleagues, advisers and close people, whose opinion I have always valued so much. As a result, we came to the conclusion that the state needs profound and fundamental changes. I have always done my best to fulfill the will of each of you, of every citizen, who had voted for me, who had entrusted me their present and their future. And now, as the legally elected president, I announce I am leaving this post. I am entrusting your present and future back to yourselves this time, and I am sure you will make the right choice. I do hope that you will elect a capable leader, the one who will take you where we have all been heading to – to the goal that you set for yourselves and for the next generations – the freedom. I call the election of the new President of the Commonwealth State to the twenty-fifth of September 2035. (Pause) I realized that I have to resign, perhaps, for a while, perhaps, forever, leaving you what you have deserved – your freedom of choice, your freedom of will. This is our most important achievement – the liberation of our country, so that it could not go back into the past. I also managed to form a team of energetic, knowledgeable and vigorous politicians, who will continue my work and guide you throughout this borrowed time to our common aspiration. However, I haven't managed to do a lot of things. Not all of our plans have been realized, not all of our dreams have come true. But, believe me, I have done what I could. And now I am making way to a new person, the one who will do more, who will do better than me.

Finally, there's one last thing I wanted to tell you, which I have always told to myself in times of doubt. Anywhere you go, in every situation, however complicated or desperate it might seem, always root out for the truth. It will make you free.

In the upcoming fair election, you are going to make up your mind, just like you did almost three years ago, and you will vote for the one who, in your opinion, deserves your valuable voices. The names of the candidates will be announced shortly. Currently, I appoint acting President the State Secretary of Defense Victor Vasilyevich Pravdin. I would like to thank all of you, and I hope that you will take an active part in the vote.”

The doors closed. No one came out.

In a couple of hours, Vladimir Ivanovich Rogov was at last left all alone in his office. Everyone had gone home to discuss the latest news or hurried to the shops to get some essential stuff, like pearl barley, or toilet paper because they knew from their own experience that every change of power meant shortage of their habitual amenities. The professor took out his mobile phone and, after a moment of hesitation, dialed the number, which he had been carefully keeping in his contacts for so many years. There were two or three long beeps, and then an unknown voice answered unemotionally: “You’ve got the wrong number,” and the line went dead. Rogov knew that he hadn’t got the wrong number, nor the wrong person, and tried again. This time there was no connection at all. “Got blacklisted,” he thought. He hoped that maybe he might try calling from a different number, but, as his ill luck would have it, there was no landline phone in the university. He stood in front of the window and thought. A pink wave of summer twilight was descending on the university park, and he could hear some parting strikes of thunder in the distance. The storm was coming to an end, leaving behind numerous sparkling puddles on the soaked ground. Suddenly, the professor noticed something, which he had already known, but felt like seeing it for the first time. In the middle of the park, on a small concrete pedestal, there was a bright blue telephone booth, combined with an SOS-pole. Those poles had been ubiquitously installed throughout the capital in the last couple of years, especially in crowded places and social institutions. Rogov hoped that it had already been connected to the telephone line, and he’d be able to use it right now.

The professor went down to the park and walked straight through the puddles, ignoring his wet shoes, and the cheerful drops of rain were sliding down his neck from under the collar of his shirt. He picked up the receiver and, to his relief, heard the signal. He dialed the number from his contacts, not sure where it would get him. The handset answered with long beeps: one, two, three…, and with every beep a little drop of hope was leaving him, like a drop of rain rolling down his spine. Finally, after the seventh signal, he heard some annoyed rustling, and desperately cried to it: "Tell President Malinin that Professor Rogov called! You hear me? Tell him…" The line went dead again. Vladimir Ivanovich wiped the sweat off his forehead with the newspaper he'd been keeping in his pocket all this time and threw it in a puddle. He stood there for a while, wondering whether he should try to dial once again, or write a text message, or just give up and go home. After a few minutes he lowered his head and went back to the university. The sky was turning from pink into deep blue, which meant that it was time to go home.

The professor looked at his desk and thought that he'd better collect his things and take them home now, before someone else comes for them – someone who was aware of his role in the so-called 'Malinin's Revolution'. He looked around just in case, and then he switched off his laptop, closed it and put it in his bag. The storm was almost over, and somewhere, on the edge of the world, behind the endless roofs, he could see rays of the dawning sun coming through the clouds. Some odd drops of rain were hitting the window cornice peaceably, which meant that now he could get home without an umbrella, which he in fact didn't have. Rogov turned off the lights, jingled a bunch of keys in his pocket and headed to the exit, lifting the collar of his shirt, still wet and smelling of sweaty summer ardor. He was about to lock the door when suddenly he felt a slight vibration in his pocket. His cell phone, which he thought had run out of battery, came back to life.

"I'm at your service, Vladimir Ivanovich." Malinin's voice was calm and barely trembling.

The professor and the President met in the middle of the night in the university park, where they had celebrated the defense of the diploma work five years ago.

"Well, I sort of came to say goodbye," Malinin said gloomily, sitting down on a wet bench.

"What do you mean, Sergey?" Rogov was shocked. "What the bloody hell are you talking about? Are you going to give up now, when you still have your team, your people? When there's still hope?"

"There's no hope, Vladimir Ivanovich. You are a wise man and should understand what's going on."

"But I don't! And neither do the others. Sergey, would you care to explain it to me and to all of those who voted for you almost three years ago?"

"No. I have nothing to explain," Malinin said coarsely.

"But the coming election! You could run this time too, couldn't you? I'd vote for you again and again and millions of times if it makes a difference."

"There will be no election. They've already used your vote. Yours and everyone else's."

"What? How did they do it? Why can't you just give it another try?"

"Professor," Malinin made a pause and for the first time rose his eyes from the wet ground. They were desperately tired and colorless, just like the ones in the newspaper Rogov had found that morning. "I will not take part in this election. Nor in the next one. I'll be dead. As soon as my physical presence and my signature aren't needed any more, they'll kill me," he said it as regularly as if he was speaking of what he was going to have for breakfast tomorrow.

"No, no, no, I don't believe you!" Rogov waved his hands, trying to kick away the words, too cruel for him to handle. "They can't just get rid of someone who's known to the whole world!"

"The whole world doesn't give a damn, professor. It knows me and it knows them equally."

"That's bullshit!"

"Maybe, but it doesn't change anything. I'm already dead, if I may put it like this."

"How can you say so? You are here, I can touch you, hear you, how can you be dead?"

"Right. And at the same time, while we are here, I am giving an interview where I'm going to repent and agitate people to support Pravdin on the election. Does it give you any hint? Does it, professor? Ok, I won't hold you in suspense any longer. 3-D modelling, Vladimir Ivanovich, that's what it is. You thought they'd been developing it for movies? Computer games? No, professor, there's much more to this technology. Could you ever imagine that half of what you're seeing on TV now is an illusion? Artificially created images and people? And I am the biggest illusion. I hardly exist at all. Vladimir Ivanovich, they are developing something else now – the new generation of more sophisticated devices. They call them 'broadcasters'. They are also getting more and more people hooked on what they show on the national channels by using prohibited, yet the most effective methods. NLP, false feeling of unity and affiliation, fear to lose control of the situation – the best psychologists have been working on these ways of distraction people from the reality and getting them deeper into illusion. And it will become worse, much worse, believe me, professor. I was there all this time, and I did my best to stop them. But the more I tried – the worse it became. It's time to stop now before they kill the remnants of the people whom I value so much."

"So, does it mean that you are also artificial on TV now?"

"Mostly"

"And Pravdin?"

"Does it matter? It's nothing but *commedia dell'arte* you're watching now, Vladimir Ivanovich, a kind of art as old as this world. The roles are pre-determined, and the masks are molded and painted according to the long-established patterns. The masters, the servants and the clowns – the actors may be replaced, but the point stands. Pravdin plays the central role, but he is also a mask. Who is the director? I don't know. Sometimes there is no director at all, and the troupe has to improvise in order to keep the audience focused. But whatever he is, Pravdin is the State. He is what was before us and what will remain after. I tried, Vladimir Ivanovich, I put everything on the line, but it wasn't enough. I was prepared to fight with enemies, but I can't fight with my people. The State, it has penetrated everyone, it's what we are breathing with, what has caught us up and has become ourselves. I wasn't aware of this, and it was my most crucial mistake. And now that you know it, I only beg you to forgive me. I haven't done anything of what we'd planned, and I will do nothing more. People who'd trusted me have become pathetic almsmen and criminals again. No one reads books, no one paints pictures, creates new machines, conquers space. I failed all of you. And I lied when I said that I'd done what I could."

"No, Sergey, you didn't lie. You did a lot, and our country will never be the same. People, for the first time, maybe, got such a chance! You should fight, we should fight, even if there is no hope left."

"Vladimir Ivanovich. Just trust me, like you did all these years. And listen to me very carefully. If you don't want to lose your life, the lives of your close people, you must run. Forget about me and pretend that you've never met me. They will reach you sooner or later, but they have more important business to attend to now, so you have some time. Not much, so please don't waste it. Of course, I've taken some precautions, concerning you as well, but when I'm gone, you'll have to defend yourself. Please take it seriously this time."

"I don't know. It seems to be such a miserable endgame…"

"It is. But it's the only one we've got. However, it could be worse, I suppose."

"And what about you, Sergey?"

"What about me? Nothing. I'm still not afraid of them, but it doesn't mean anything. I'll die, and everyone will forget me. They'll make you forget. In a couple of years, everything I've made will vanish in history, and there will be a new story, a story of the glorious Commonwealth State, which has always been like that. But there's one more thing, professor. I'm going to tell you something, which might prove useful later. Remember it and don't let them fool you, at least for some time. There is a detail which can help you to tell illusion from reality. I'll show you and that's all I can do for you now."

Soon Malinin was gone, and the professor kept this conversation in his mind till the end of his days, which was exactly in fifteen months and a half.

When he went out of the park, it was already half past five in the morning. The new day brought the new heat and the new asperities, but he didn't care. He wanted to call home, but the phone was out of power, so he wandered the streets a little, waiting for his head to clear and for shops to open. He needed a drink. Not less than two bottles of vodka because he had a lot of thoughts to think. Being sober, his only desire was to hide in some rural area and stay there until the country cools down from the summer heat and the election. Fortunately, he soon found a scruffy booth with third-rate alcohol and got himself two half-liter bottles of 'The Drink of Bravery'.

Professor Rogov was finally approaching home, completely exhausted and out of breath, when his eye caught a glimpse of something on the nearby stalls. He slowly came closer and took out his wallet with a strong intention to buy it. All at once, a cheerful open-armed saleswoman stepped forward and welcomed her first customer.

"Vladimir Ivanovich! It's been years since I saw you last! Looking for something to read? A paper, maybe? All the news is already there! You've heard it, haven't you? I'm talking about the election, of course! So unexpected! What do you think will come of it? This Malinin, I've never really taken him seriously. We'll see what kind of fellow Pravdin is, and I only hope he won't make it worse. So, 'The Morning Herald' or 'The Star'?"

"No," the professor cut her short. "I want this one."

"A toy? The elephant? Of course! They've just arrived and I'm sure they'll be sold out in no time. You just look at it, so cute and funny! Oh, and there's a button inside its head, and when you press it... Let's see what happens... My God, it's singing! What a nice song it sings! Amazing, isn't it?"

"I'll have it. How much?"

"For your grandson, right?" the woman didn't seem to notice the professor's annoyance.

"What?... Ah, yes..."

"A perfect present. And I'll make a nice reduction, just for you. Only 800 libs, how does that sound? Listen, why don't you take another one for Nastenka?" she worked on commission from sales and was more than happy to sell something more expensive than penny-worth newspapers. "The younger always follow the elder, and Borya is a perfect role model, that's what I tell you. I often see him, his sister and their mother, your daughter, I mean, and I think to myself, what a beautiful family. Always walking with dignity, and dignity means a lot these days, doesn't it? And I also say 'this boy's gonna be no less than a captain.' So calm and sensible and talks like a real scholar. An adorable young man, indeed! And his sister, of course, a little princess! You are so lucky to have them all, Vladimir Ivanovich. In times of test, family is best – that's the real words of wisdom. And we must by all means keep them happy, that's our most important goal."

"Our most important goal..." mumbles Vladimir Ivanovich mockingly, takes the two identical toys and slowly walks away, towards his home, passing by a small hill, where they sat with Borya the other day and laughed at a pigeon, which tried to shove an enormous piece of stale bread down its throat. The hill smells of morning dew, which catches the reflection of the sun and keeps it for a while, so that everyone could enjoy its generous grace.

Meanwhile, the State started to prepare for the National Election Day.

Chapter 4. 2070

1

It was the autumn of 2070, and the State was also preparing for the National Election Day, or the Day of Glorious Election. For Boris it was a normal day, and he was quietly doing his job, which, for some reason, seemed unexpectedly hard. Not too hard, but it somehow just went wrong, and nothing could be done about it. Boris had already spent half of the morning trying to select the right color for the enemy tank, which he'd been drawing for a junior educational broadcast. But even such commonplace task appeared to be an impossible quest. Black was too deep, dark blue seemed too artificial, and khaki made the tank look like a shapeless spot of mud. Boris was angry at himself, and at the tank, and at the whole world, but stubbornly carried on sifting through the virtual palette of available colors. His neighbors were arguing again, and it distracted and annoyed him too, making it even harder to concentrate on what he was doing. Suddenly, Boris heard the door slam in the corridor and right after that Slava tumbled into his room.

"Wakey-wakey, Bobby-boy!" he thundered. "Just thought of calling in to check if you are safe and sound and enjoying the day, whatever it might mean to you."

Boris pursed his lips not to let any swear words come out of them. His neighbor was apparently not going to confine himself to a bare greeting and advanced further in the room, finally stopping beside the desk.

"Busy with anything exciting?" he continued. "Drawing, aren't you? So, what have we got here? I'll have a look if you don't mind. So, what is it? It's a tank if I'm not mistaken! Yes, this is it. Strong and fierce, just the way a real killing machine should be.

These firm lines, this brawny body and the muzzle, of course – it's got all it needs to destroy anything on its way. Wait, isn't the muzzle a bit too long? Doesn't matter. I like it like this. I really do. I'd call it a masterpiece if not for one thing. You wanna know what?"

"Well, I've not colored it yet, I suppose…"

"Wrong answer. Anyone can color, even a stupid baby. And you bear the glorious name of an artist, remember?"

"So what?"

"So… You must do something more than sketching and coloring. You must serve art, and what I can see now is a bare doodling. It won't get you anywhere, believe me. Do you know what your problem is, Bobby-boy?"

"I don't have a problem, and, on top of that, I'm not Bobby-boy."

"Your problem, Bobby-boy," Slavik was deliberately ignoring his indignation. "your problem is that your picture hasn't got an idea. It doesn't make any sense. What does it want to say to the rest of the world? What message does it convey?"

"Well, it's big and evil and kills everyone. Especially those who disturb the others when they're working".

Boris imagined his uncolored tank crushing Slavik's skinny body and smiled to himself.

"Let me put it like this," the neighbor's repugnant voice was ringing in Boris's ears. "It's nonconceptual. It hasn't got an inner conflict. There should be one, in every thing, in every person, and this conflict keeps us going, struggling, vanquishing ourselves. It brings sense into our life, and our goal, as artists, is to discover it, to expose the essence of things to the world, make it suffer from its own imperfection, and, through this catharsis, to purify itself. I know what I'm saying, I've seen it on one of the educational broadcasts. Spent quite a lot of money on it, by the way. You know what? Maybe you should at least put a sticker with a heart on one of the tank's sides. As if some vulnerable and delicate soul is trapped inside its impregnable armor. Agreed?"

"It's a junior broadcast. I guess it's too early for them to think about hearts."

"Junior? For kids?" Slava looked at the drawing once again. "That changes everything, my friend. In this case there should be a rabbit. Wait a moment… Yes, I'm sure a rabbit will be perfect here".

"An elephant, maybe?" Boris gave a chuckle.

Slavik stared at him as if he was completely out of his mind.

"What do you mean an elephant? Have you seen elephants? I haven't, but I tell you, they are disgusting and totally nonconceptual."

"They're wise at least. Unlike some of the people I know…" he hoped that he hadn't said it aloud.

"Wise? Since when has wisdom become a virtue? Who needs your wisdom? Who needs *my* wisdom, after all? No one, Bobby-boy, let's face it. We're so detached from the world now; our existence is so solitary and withdrawn that no one really cares about what's happening in our heads. Who are you going to expose your thoughts to? What subjects are you going to discuss? The current situation on the western front, perhaps? Or your ideas of redecorating the kitchen?"

Boris would gladly talk to anyone right now, an elephant or even a fly, but not to this annoying little freak, who kept bombarding him with his pseudo-philosophical quirks. But the conversation was amusing Slava, so he was obviously going to continue until he runs out of his platitudes.

"Remember, Bobby-boy, what people need these days is conceptuality. Something that can get them out of their comfort zone. This is my advice to you, sincere and, more importantly, completely free. Look for an internal conflict everywhere, and you will be rewarded. Even in yourself, although you might not find it because you probably don't have it whatsoever."

Boris felt an overwhelming desire to throw something at his neighbor, so he took his pen and squeezed it in his fingers.

"Anyway, why are you drawing war all the time?" he looked back at the monitor. "Tanks, submarines, choppers and other masterpieces for the Ministry of Defense? You got a lifelong contract with them, or what?"

"Sort of," said Boris insinuatingly.

Slava shrugged his shoulders and it seemed that he was finally about to leave. Suddenly, he stopped where he was standing as if he'd seen a ghost.

"What's that, Bobby?" he asked, pointing his finger at Boris's sofa. Boris turned around to see what had been able to surprise his neighbor so much, and to his dismay saw the old book, which he had been using to select the right color for his picture. Before he could do anything to prevent it, the intruder leaped to the sofa, crooked the book and opened it with a barbaric crunch.

"Slava," Boris tried to make his voice sound firm and convincing, "please put my thing back where it was. Do it now, Slava!"

"Just a moment, Bobbin-the-Robin. I'll only read a few pages and give it back to you, safe and sound, no worries, my friend."

"You mean you can read? Artists are not supposed to have reading skills, as far as I know. Who taught you, if I may ask?"

"No one. Did it all myself, dude. You see, I keep learning, developing my mind all the time, even if it's only for my own sake. Have you heard of third-level broadcasts? What access did they give you, by the way? Fifth?"

"Fourth," lied Boris.

"Not a big difference. There are tons of sapid information starting from the third level, for the privileged ones. But you won't get it, anyway, at least not through your Ministry of Defense, that's for sure".

And Slavik began reading the words that Boris knew by heart, that had been mouthed first by his grandfather, and then by the nurse in the Center, and it was so strange to hear them now, from a person who had no connection to both of them.

"Be-ars went to… the… hike…A-riding on a bike. What's 'a bike', Bob? And how can bears be a-riding anything? Unless it's not a metaphor… Or a hyperbole? Or whatever the hell it is…"

"A bike?" Boris knew the answer and he was pleased he could outdo his neighbor this time. "It's in the book. Here, in the picture, look," the word 'bike' suddenly stirred something in his memory, but that something was lying deep in the forbidden realms of his mind and refused to come out no matter how hard he tried. "It's a sort of transport. Like a… a tank, for example."

"A tank?" Slava looked at him incredulously. "You must be mad. Who's gonna put bears inside a tank? They are animals, for God's sake, they'll flatten everything around them! Unless it's meant to be their catharsis… No, catharsis usually comes in the end, and now it's only the beginning. Ah, yes, I think I found it! Is it this thing with two wheels and a funny broken steering wheel? Man, it looks embarrassing! How can anyone ride it? Yes, I remember, I think I saw it in one of the broadcasts about the past. It actually moved, and you were supposed to balance on it somehow. I wonder if there are any of them left now, or they've been all melted down into weapons. Okay, what's next? 'Then came…' what? You'll never believe it, Boris, you know what came next? Tom-the-Cat! And… 'back-to-front he sat'! Good. It still doesn't make any sense, but it's becoming rather intriguing. Where did he sit? On the bike with the bears? Or on the ground, watching them go by? No, wait, how could he be watching if he was sitting back-to front? I guess it's its personal tragedy. He'd been dreaming of seeing bears riding a bike all his life, but exactly at the moment they actually did it, he happened to look in the opposite direction. So… let's skip this page, it's senseless… Where does the action begin, I wonder? Who's gonna be the main hero in this circus?... 'Suddenly a Titan crawls beneath the gate. Whiskers meant to frighten. Very stiff and straight…' I don't know what a Titan is, but I'm already frightened to death. Is it supposed to be a children's book? Like: 'Kids, finish your soup, or a Titan with whiskers will come and eat you whole. And the soup as well, of course'… Cock-the-Roach, Cock-the-Roach, Cock-the-Roach the Great!!... What-the-Roach? It's a poem for kids, author, come on! Man, it's disgusting! Or am I just too spoilt for a kid's book?

'Sharp and loud his shout rings out,
While his whiskers wave about:
"Don't you worry, I shan't hurry,
But I'll gulp and gobble you!
That is true! Oh, too true!
There's no hope for you!"

Slava closed the book and put it back on the sofa.

"Tell me just one thing, neighbor," he uttered at last. "You probably know the story by heart already. Is it really something worthy, or just a piece of crap? I think it's crap because this parade of contused animals riding on prehistoric transport was just written for nothing. Books of this sort are completely useless, and children won't learn anything from them. I'm so happy they are illegal now. Books, of course, not children, although if you ask me, I'd ban children as well. By the way, you'd better hide your bears damn well, or you might have problems. Did you know that drones can scan not only your biometry through windows, but see the inside of your room? I'm not sure if these things are illegal now, but to be on the safe side, don't demonstrate it so unequivocally to them, okay? Well, I'd better go now. Got some pressing business in the toilet, while the water is still on."

Boris smiled and thought that his neighbor was at times okay. Not the best one in the world, and surely, not better than the previous ones, but still, it could be worse. He took the pen again. It was finally quiet in the flat, and he could get back to work, but his mind was still blank and all it could produce was images of was reversed cats, mosquitoes stuck around white balloons, bears in tanks and, surprisingly, an elephant with one hungried (or one hundred) trunks. He started to transfer these images from his head onto the screen, and in about half an hour, his drawing was finished and, although it looked quite silly for a forty-year-old man, he liked it. He even had an impulse to show it to Slava, in case he might want to look for his much-valued catharsis there. But in the end, giving it a second thought, he commanded the machine to delete it. "What if he really finds it?" he thought to himself.

As usual, the provision drones came in the evening, and the tank was still not ready. Its transparent body was hanging in the middle of the monitor, an irrefutable proof of Boris's talent slowly leaking away with every hologram drawn.

"Your attention please! Everyone present in the premises must undergo the identification procedure and receive their grocery sets," announced the broadcaster after getting signal from the food drones. On the one hand, Boris was happy to leave his room and distract from work for a while, even if it only meant walking five meters to the kitchen and spending about half an hour cooking his routine dinner. But on the other hand, he was absolutely reluctant to meet his neighbors again, even though they hadn't really done him wrong. It was just that at times, he desperately needed privacy – just a few hours of peace and quiet in his own flat. To engage in conversations when *he* wanted to, to draw what *he* found appropriate, to stop being in this foolish competition with his neighbor, who always won, who always surpassed him – in work, in education, in love life. It wouldn't be so bad had Slava had at least a slightest fraction of tact and empathy, but he preferred to be a pain in

Boris's arse and just wouldn't stop torturing him with his constant molestation. His wife Angie was, in her turn, so utterly stupid and pretty-faced that Boris didn't know how to behave with her, so he usually limited himself to a pleasant expression and a meaningless smile. For several years he'd been missing the good old times when no one broke into his room while he was trying to work, interrupting him with unwelcomed criticism and useless comments, and grabbing his things without asking for permission. Yes, those were happy days, and Boris felt sad they couldn't last forever.

The drones delivered three grocery sets: two of them, for his neighbors, were number one, and number three was of course for Boris. Slavik opened his bag with posed disgust and called to his wife:

"Angie, come here, darling, will you? I just wanted you to have a look at what's inside our surprise bag today!"

"What?" big-breasted Angie seemed unfamiliar with the concept of sarcasm and started rummaging through the bag's contents.

"No-thing!" declared Slavik. "Completely and absolutely nothing. Or let's call it 'shit', maybe? The same shit as yesterday, and the day before, and all the previous goddamned days. Bagged shit. Cubed shit. Shit elevated to absolute".

"Aren't you cubed shit yourself?" wondered Boris to himself. "You keep getting number one sets almost every day, which is far more than common people can afford, and you still turn your nose up on them, you overindulged brat?"

He opened his own parcel, knowing already what it contained, and Slavik instantly poked his head above his shoulder to see if he could make any more felicitous remarks.

"M-m-m-m-m…" he hummed emphatically. "Dried peas. Food for gods and unclaimed geniuses. Looks yummy to me. You know, Boris, I gave it a thought and decided to go without dinner today. Like some great person said, I don't remember who, 'It's better for an artist to be hungry'. But then again, it doesn't concern you, of course."

And he provocatively slapped his hand on Boris's belly, which was hanging loose from his pants.

"So here, neighbor, help yourself. It will cheer you up a bit. Sorry if I was rude or something."

Slava fished out of his bag a small carton and handed it to Boris with a generous smile.

"He might be right." Boris thought grabbing the carton. "I must get fit, I guess. It's not that I'm overweight or something, but a little exercise wouldn't be superfluous. Used to be an army man a while ago, and look like a real hobgoblin now."

But he still was happy to get a package of caramel sticks from Slavik's set number one, and he was going to indulge himself on them for at least a couple of days.

2

Boris's room was quite different from what it had looked like when he'd just arrived here, ten years ago. When he got his first salary, he immediately, just like he was intending to, replaced the window wallpaper with a new one, showing six, instead of tree, landscapes. Having done that, he noted to himself that the room had livened up, but there was still more to be done. Another thing was to clear it of all the dirt and rubbish, which had been lying there since the times of Basil. He wiped all the dust from the furniture, washed the floor with water that he'd been saving for this purpose for several days, and even moved the furniture to get to unreachable places, hoping to find some more of his childhood stuff there. Expectedly, there was nothing of the kind, except for empty packages of food, spider web and fluffy lumps of dust.

The second major cleaning took place in the spring of 2061, just after Boris was forced to break up with Olga. He felt extremely depressed and disenchanted and decided to delete everything connected with her from his memory and throw all her things away, further from his flat. There were not many of them – just a nice little present she'd brought him on her first and last visit here – a set of felt pens, a box of marshmallows, which he hadn't opened, and a mug with a motto that he never understood: 'Freedom has a nice ring to it and a bit of recoil'. He looked at the gifts again to make sure he didn't want to keep them, and then, quite abruptly, flicked them all in a rubbish bag and tied it up before he changed his mind. Then he put the bag in the corner of his room, where it had to remain for about a month until he could take it out to the landfill. He wanted to do it himself, not trusting it to the utilization drones, which came weekly to collect the waste. Boris could try to get a route list to go out in a week or so, but he couldn't find the reason for the request, and what's more, he was afraid that Officer Klein was still watching him and controlling his movements, and he might consider his attempt to leave the flat as a breach of their contract. The sanest option in his situation was to wait for official unblocking, which happened twice a year – on the Great Liberation Day in May, and on the Day of Glorious Election in October. The closest of them was the Liberation Day, so Boris had to merely wait for four weeks and a half to get an official permission for the exit. Two days before the event, the government, as usual, published the exit and return schedule on the National Information Portal. Boris found out that he could stay outside from five till seven p.m., and he was more than happy with the timing. He thought it would be a perfect opportunity to catch his share of the spring sun and enjoy the warmth of the city vibes.

Yegor Semenovich and Juliana Pavlovna, however, decided not to take advantage of their allowed time outside and stayed at home, although they were still granted two hours to have a walk – from nine to eleven a.m. "I've seen it all, soldier," explained Yegor Semenovich. "We used to walk every day before it all began, and where has it taken us? Nowhere exciting. Had enough of it, so to say." And then he lowered his voice and continued in Boris's ear: "Maybe, we could have a drink later on? In the evening, I mean. For the Liberation and everything?" Boris suddenly felt that he didn't want to spare his alcohol this time, but somehow, he couldn't refuse the old man either. He decided that he'd pour him a glass of respect and then send him out to celebrate with the old girl.

Boris's pass worked exactly at three o'clock and this time he didn't have to wear his self-disguising set. He quickly ran down the familiar staircase speared by the empty elevator shaft, and pushed the loose front door, which gave him a weary and displeased creak. Finally, after a more than a month of voluntary retreat, he was outside, and he eagerly breathed in his first portion of the soft spring air. The nature was kind to him, and the weather was really warm and tender. All the dirt, which had remained after the winter, was already gone, and everything was so bright and green, that for a short while he stood still, blinded by this splendor. He looked around for some nice dump to throw away the things left from Olga, and it was there, just around the corner of his house – a big hole with a mixture of sewage water and organic waste inside. The plastic bag flew into the stinking goop, floated there for a few moments, and then sunk slowly into its depths. Boris walked away. He wanted to take part in the celebration, which he hoped would shake his blues right away.

Having walked a few miles further from his house, Boris started noticing other people in the street. They were also heading to the square, hidden between the identical blocks of flats. A few of them were wearing their disguising masks, hats and gloves, although it was not obligatory on the days of national celebrations. Boris walked together with the crowd and soon heard the sounds of music and laughter from the square. When he was small, this place was the unofficial center of the neighborhood's life. Children went there to play and eat ice cream, which was taken out of wheelie refrigerators with a bit faded, yet delicious-looking pictures on their sides. Grownups followed them, talking to each other, or just looking into their mobile phones, some of them with dogs which ran free and enjoyed the walk even more than their owners. The square was still there, of course, and now it looked alive again, as if he had suddenly returned to his childhood and was a six-year-old boy, asking his mother for a chocolate-coated ice cream cone.

The sensation made Boris absolutely delighted, and all those people around him contributed to his joy because they were real – not holograms from the broadcaster, nor his neighbors, just human beings with completely unfamiliar faces he saw for the first and for the last time in his life. They were all different, but there was something that united them all – the Great Liberation, which was doubtlessly their common achievement, their holiday, their well-deserved reward for being part of the glorious nation of fighters and emancipators from the Black Plague. "Just look at these faces," thought Boris. "No one will ever defeat us. No one in the whole world!" and he felt even happier at these thoughts. Several defending drones flew above his head, watching for foreign agents, and he waved his hand at them thanking them for their job.

"In case of any sight of danger," informed the loudspeaker on one of the drones, "please keep calm and immediately proceed in an air-raid shelter following the street signs."

Some people stopped to look for the signs and, having found them, nodded in recognition and in relief that they were out of danger, and continued their way. Civil defense was one of the most important aspects of their current life, and by no means was it to be neglected.

Among the other passers-by, Boris spotted a young eye-catching couple: the guy was wearing thoroughly ironed shirt and stylish brown trousers, and the girl was in a short navy-blue dress, which looked too light for this time of year. They were holding each other's hands and it looked like they'd been waiting for this moment for ages. Their cheeks were red with fresh air, so unusual for home people, who mainly breathed with what was provided by their conditioning system in locked apartments. The couple's eyes reflected the spring sun, and its sparkles made them glow with something that Yegor Semenovich would call 'love'. Boris tried not to think about Olga, but he still did, however, to his relief, it didn't ruin his blissful mood, so he followed the young people for some time to see what they would do next. They were chatting happily when suddenly the guy stopped, looked at his wrist timer and then at his satnav, and his face darkened. He hugged his girlfriend and held her for a few seconds, and then rapidly walked in the opposite direction, turning behind now and then to see if she was still there. Boris understood that it was because their schedules didn't match, and his allowed time outside was just about to finish. The girl waited for her partner to disappear in the crowd and then slowly strode away, shivering because of the wind, which blew her light navy-blue dress.

Right at the moment Boris entered the square, he was approached by a volunteer in white uniform and an orange tie, wrapped around his neck. He was holding a bunch of white balloons, four or five, which were swinging in the wind, rubbing against each other, eager to be released and reunite with the clouds in the sky.

"Are you enjoying yourself, citizen?" inquired the volunteer cheerfully.

"Yes, sir!" Boris stood to attention out of habit, although the guy was no authority, nor even a human patrol.

"Do you need any help?"

"No, no, I'm fine. I was just about to watch the performance."

"You are right on time, citizen. The show is to start in seven minutes, so you'd better hurry. Today we have prepared something special, something to surprise you on this solemn occasion. Have you watched the President's speech on your broadcaster?"

"Certainly, sir. I watched it yesterday and the day before yesterday, three or four times in total, I think."

"Now this is laudable. Keep it up."

"I will, thank you, sir," said Boris with a slight bow.

"Here. Take these symbols of Liberation." the volunteer detached one of the balloons from the bunch and handed it to Boris, together with an orange ribbon, which had to be tied around his arm.

"Thank you, sir!"

"Release the balloon before you go home. Watch it fly freely into the sky and embrace its freedom in your mind. This will be the real spirit of Liberation, citizen. May the truth be with you!"

"May the truth be with you!" answered Boris and put his right hand on his chest.

In five minutes, he was already close to the stage – a massive construction with a screen and several speakers, which were playing a slurred tune, consisting mainly of brass shouts and snares of drums. When it was over, several projectors lit up, and a group of four elderly ladies stepped on the stage.

"The Song of Liberation!" announced the speakers. "Performed by the Quartet of Unity!"

The ladies stood waiting for the music to start, and the crowd cheered them with applause. The first chords were so loud that Boris thought of covering his ears, but then he looked at the others and decided not to. He knew this song from his early days in the Center because it was a tradition to play it on every Day of Great Liberation. The music was probably composed manually because it was different from most of the contemporary stuff – it was solemn, moving, artfully arranged and extremely absorbing, making your eyes wet from the noble sorrow for everyone who hadn't lived to these happy times. The lyrics were heartbreaking too.

Day of Liberation! Coming from the past!
Fire, death and sorrow – finally they passed.
Tanks and planes were burning. Millions were killed.
No one is forgotten! New world shall we build!

Day of Liberation! Smells of dirt and pain!

Guns are in our blood now, freedom – in our veins.
Grief and joy, together – that is how we feel.
Young and old, no matter what, we're standing for our will!

Boris stood there, letting the spirit of Liberation penetrate himself through the glorious song, and when it was over, the audience exploded in ovation. The choir bowed and split into two groups, and each group made a few steps to the sides of the stage. Suddenly, from behind the stage, came a procession of three volunteers: one of them carrying a national flag, and two others – some wooden object, which resembled a scarecrow. Another – fourth – volunteer jumped out and quickly covered the scarecrow with a large piece of black cloth. The national anthem started playing, and the performers stood still, each exactly on their place. The choir sang along to the music, and when the chorus began, one of the volunteers came up to the scarecrow and hung a wooden sign on its neck. "THE BLACK PLAGUE", said the sign, and when people in front of the stage read it, they started booing and shouting. Some of them threw at the scarecrow whatever they could find: dirt, twigs, rubbish, and some just closed their eyes, put their right hands on their chests and sang the anthem together with the choir. Then suddenly someone, maybe a volunteer, said: "Burn it!" and the crowd momentarily picked up the call, spreading it over itself, making it more intensive every time it was repeated. "Burn it! Burn it! Burn it!" Boris cried with the others, but he couldn't hear his own voice, so he cried louder until his throat began to hurt. It was the last verse of the national anthem, and the volunteer came out with a flare and pinched the scarecrow with the flame, which instantly caught the black cloth. The crowd cheered and screamed as the dry wood was burning, flashing on the faces of those who were on the stage, and even the wrinkles of the old ladies from the choir looked sharp and sinister.

When the scarecrow had been eaten by the fire, the volunteers emptied three buckets of water on what was left from it and carried it away, and the projectors went dim. The crowd calmed down and adopted its usual expression of submissive aloofness.

"Your attention please!" Announced the loudspeakers. "You will now hear the speech of the President of the Commonwealth State Victor Vasilyevich Pravdin!"

The last word echoed against the walls of the nearby houses and flew throughout the square: "Pravdin... Pravdin... Pravdin..." and the built-in projector in the middle of the stage shone a ray of light in the air, which in a couple of seconds revealed the image of the President.

"Dear people of the Commonwealth State!" the words came out of his sharp mouth and rolled across the square, reinforced by numerous loudspeakers. "There is no need to remind you what great day we are celebrating today. You all know that it is the 90th anniversary of the Victory that we all remember, as if it happened yesterday. We are here to honor our past, and our present, and our future. Today we are bowing our heads in commemoration of that dreadful time, when our free country was attacked by a savage and merciless enemy, which tried to capture our land, demolish our people and devour everything it could reach. We remember our forefathers, who stood tall against the foe, who were wounded and crippled, who died in violent battles, but didn't give up and defended our freedom. They alone, with the whole world turning its back on them, could achieve what we now call the Great Liberation. Their blood is now in our veins, dear citizens, and we are their only successors and the heirs of the victory. Not a single person in this world can take it away from us. And we are going to keep on fighting for as long as it takes us, we will never give a single inch of our land to those who do not deserve it. This is a hard battle, my dear friends, but we will win it. The victory is close, so close that the enemies can feel it too and are gathering their last strength to give us their final blow. But they don't know that we are ready for it. Every minute, every second, we are watching them, controlling every move of their forces and now, as always, I promise you, I will never let a single hair fall from your heads! We will fight together, even if the whole world rises against us. And now I would like all of you to stand up and remember those who gave their lives for you. I announce a moment of silence, after which you can continue your celebrations."

A mechanical watch was displayed, watch solemnly and abruptly ticked away sixty seconds, and everyone stood up with their arms on their side and stayed still in complete silence, interrupted only by the buzzing of defending drones. Boris stood too, sincerely thankful for the opportunity to be with all these people now, who didn't notice him, but it didn't matter at all. They were *his* people, and Pravdin was *their* President, whose invisible presence brought meaning into everything they did. Sixty seconds were over, and it was time to take a little walk.

"Attention everyone!" announced the mechanical voice from the loudspeakers. "You are required to leave the place in five minutes. The next session of celebrations will begin in thirty minutes. The location must be cleared to make it accessible for other citizens."

The crowd started to move in the direction of the two exits, which were located on the opposite sides of the square. Several defending drones were hanging above the place, guaranteeing that no terrorist would infringe on their security, while volunteers with wide cheerful smiles on their faces solicitously directed the flow of people so that no one lost their way or got hurt. The loudspeakers were playing some upbeat march, which made everyone walk in lockstep, keeping pace with the rest of the crowd. Boris strode slowly behind a group of young people, who were loudly discussing the performance.

"Now that was a darn spectacular burning, I tell ya!" said one of them.

"Absolutely hilarious," confirmed another one. "Next year they'll destroy it with lasers, or power blasters, I promise!"

They all giggled in chorus and fist-bumped each other.

"You know what?" continued the first fellow. "They showed dead bodies of North Crestlanders this mornin', you saw?"

"They were fakes, man!" answered the third one, who had been keeping silent all this time. "I saw real dead bodies, and they're different!"

"You haven't! And they never show fakes in broadcasts! Never, man!"

"I swear it on my mother's grave!"

"So how do they look then? Ah? Tell us!"

"They're... kinda frozen, I'd say. Their eyes are blank, and their limbs are unnatural, like they're made of something soft and malleable."

"Anyways, it was fun to look at those bodies in the broadcaster. Man, they're so stupid, those North Crestlanders! Presenter said they'd killed themselves, literally, they were shooting at each other like crazy, and finally everyone was shot, can you imagine?"

"Yeah, man!" laughed the third guy. "They're freaks! They'll die like cattle, every one of them! Pravdin's just too merciful to these imps."

Boris walked out of the square and looked around. The facades of the houses were decorated with flags and holographic images of weapons and military machines, and everywhere he saw pictures of Pravdin smiling at passers-by. He walked a couple of blocks, watching the posters and breathing the spring air, which was becoming chillier with every minute. He had absolutely no idea where to go, and he hadn't taken his satnav, which was a bit short-sighted of him. There were about two hours of permitted outside time left, but Boris was afraid of getting lost in these unfamiliar surroundings, so he decided to walk in the direction of his home. The balloon given to him by the volunteer was still tied on his wrist, dancing in the air and pulling the string impatiently in accordance with gusts of wind, calling it to join them in the velvet softness of the sky. Boris stopped, looked up and suddenly had an idea, which brought a satisfying smile on his face. His legs knew where to go. They carried him directly to the hill near his block of flats – the spot of happiness from the past. He was sure that it would be a perfect viewing platform, from where he'd be able to trace the way of his symbol of liberation and get inspired by it before he went home to spend another six months in lockdown. He wasn't mistaken. The sight of the hill was absolutely amazing, with young shoots of fresh grass, covering all the ugly piles of rubbish and scrap, which seemed to have been lying there since the first dawn. Some nimble little birdies fluttered from the ground with high-pitched chirping, made several circles above his head and then went down again to continue digging for worms in the warm generous soil. The scenery matched perfectly with snow-white patches of clouds, embroidered in the deep-blue canvas of the sky, and the golden rays of the sun were persistently making their way through the gaps between them.

Boris closed his eyes and was about to breathe another portion of the air and let himself be carried away by this feeling of freedom and joy, but instead of it he was momentarily seized by the strongest panic attack he'd ever had in his life. A bullet from his memory shot right at his temple, completely stunned him and made him a helpless six-year-old boy, screaming for help. He was thrown back into the November of 2036, when he was also standing here, right on this hill, with his eyes screwed up, and, presumably, he was crying. However, he wasn't sure it was a real cry, or it might have only rung in his head. The only thing he was sure of was that it sounded like a desperate cry of a child, strangled by a long run and overwhelming terror. Borya tried to open his eyes, but the picture didn't change. It was there, and it would always remain somewhere in the back of his mind, no matter how hard he tried to delete it. His Grampy, his beloved Grampy, the one who walked with him, who read to him, who watched silly TV shows on Fidgy Freckles with him and laughed like crazy; the Grampy, who had always been there, and when Borya fell off his bike, injuring his knee badly, he cuddled his head against his chest, as if trying to absorb his pain and hurt; his only Grampy, his friend and his tutor, was now lying on the worn-out linoleum of his own room in the middle of the pool of his own blood, with unnaturally twisted left leg, and the frozen look in his eyes, stopped by a deadly shot, was directed at something past Borya, past the soldiers, stomping loudly through the rooms of their flat, past the sky, past the life – to nowhere. And little Borya started to run – away from this flat, which had momentarily become cold and alien, away from the blood and the look in his Grampy's eyes, away from the soldiers and their commanding shouts. He squeezed the two things, most dear to him, and kept holding them all the way, although they obviously slowed him down, and he kept on running, urged by the soldiers' voices behind his back: "Stop, kid, you hear me! Stop immediately! I command you to stop!" The elevator was there, on the fifth floor, and although his parents prohibited him to use it on his own, he jumped into it and frantically pressed the ground floor button. It surely gave him a good leg-up. He heard the soldiers running down the stairs, and when he reached the ground floor, he pushed the door open and darted into the street. He ran and ran until he was totally out of breath, and the air couldn't go in his lungs anymore, and his heart was about to jump out of his mouth. Then he stopped on that very hill and silently yelled with the last bits of his escaping consciousness, listening to the soldiers' heavy footsteps behind him. This is it, and now several cold muzzles are looking at him, blindly and indifferently, ready to fire right in his head. This is it, and he can almost hear them pulling the triggers.

This is it, but suddenly there is another voice coming from behind them: "As you were! I need the kid alive!" Boris raises his eyes to the sky. The white balloon is going up, slowly and fatedly, until it disappears in its gentle bottomless azure.

He returned home an hour earlier than it was scheduled and, in the evening, got completely wasted with Yegor Semenovich.

3

"Stupid," thought Boris. "Soldiers, grandfather, the hill. Where did it come from, I wonder? That balloon flew away almost nine years ago, but why does it still feel like it's here, and if I had a chance to look outside through the window wallpaper, I'd see it right above my house? Isn't it stupid? Time to get back to work, anyway."

He had to finish the tank no matter what. It seemed weird, but Boris, having drawn hundreds of war machines, still found it difficult at times to make it right. It was not that he was a bad artist, of course, but he still sometimes felt like he could do better. Maybe that was the reason why there hadn't been too many orders for him recently, which, in its turn, didn't give Boris any sense of security at all. He knew that there was a complicated system of jobs distribution, so that every citizen could receive minimal wages to live on, so he wouldn't starve to death, of course, but settling for grocery sets number three and wringing the last wits out of his old calculating machine was not what he wanted from life. He thought of finding a different source of income, but for the time being, creating holograms was the only thing he could do for the living. He sometimes remembered the guy with a funny name, whom he'd met when he first came to the city. He said something about going to the factory, and Boris wished he'd taken his internal number so that he could message him now and see if the job is still available. He wasn't sure he'd like it, however, but he'd definitely give it a try. The State had been so kind and generous to him so far, providing him with accommodation, and food, and protection, and everything he might ever need, so maybe it was time to pay it back with something more significant than silly drawings, which seemed to go to waste right after he'd sent them to the client. These thoughts were rather depressing, but, fortunately, they visited Boris's head not often enough to darken his life.

Boris took his pen and loaded the palette. He was sure he'd be able to find the right color now. Black, dark blue, emerald green and a hint of white. He was finally satisfied with the shade and spread it over the whole machine. The tank looked pretty ominous, but not too scary for the children who were going to see it. In some sudden fit of creativity, Boris changed the pen color into white and drew a rabbit on one of the tank's sides, with a tiny pink heart in its paws. Of course, he'd delete it later, because the Ministry of Defense would never accept such liberty, but he thought that kids might find it amusing. When he was little, he enjoyed silly shows about animals and fictional superheroes more than all the patriotic stuff they started showing after the Glorious Election of 2036. He sometimes imagined saving the world all on his own, just like Mister Jaws or Steel Rider from the Fidgy Freckles Network. One of them might want to use his tank, he thought, and started programming its movements. The tracks were gnashing, and the muzzle rotated heavily and majestically, revealing all the destructive power of the machine. The text of the translation had already been stored in the calculating machine's memory, and Boris only had to select the right voice for it. "Look, children. Look and listen. This is the most advanced model of military vehicles available to our glorious army. It can kill up to fifty enemies in one shot, more than any other machine of the kind. And it doesn't just destroy enemies, it smashes them, turns them into dust, blasts them out, leaves nothing but a wet stain instead of them. Just imagine how helpful it will be for our army forces which…"

"Blah bah blah…" thought Boris wearily.

He listened to the words again and decided not to make the timbre too low. He put the sound slider to the middle of the scale, and the recording began to sound insinuate and confident, which made a dramatic contrast to the drawing. It was more of a female voice now, and that was just what he wanted. "Kids kinda trust women's voices," he thought. "They remind them of their mother." Boris could hardly remember his own mother, but for some reason he was sure that it was exactly the way she'd have told him about the might of the army forces of the Commonwealth State.

As usual, the electricity was turned off at 22:00. The room sunk in darkness, diluted by the glow coming from the window wallpaper, which was enough to get undressed and prepare the bed.

Boris squeezed his hand under the pillow and felt a box of caramel sticks – a generous gift of Slavik, which he'd received at dinnertime. He took out one stick and munched it with appetite. The taste of burned sugar was gorgeous, and by 22:30 he'd eaten the whole box, hoping to get some more from the neighbor in the nearest future. He thought that it hadn't probably been the wisest thing to do and promised himself that he'd start getting fit right from tomorrow, and at these thoughts he fell asleep, with pieces of caramel stuck between his teeth.

The broadcast was to be sent in the first communication interval, and in the morning, Boris only had to add some slight improvements and final essences. Very fortunate for him, the neighbors were still sleeping, and not a single noise came from behind their door. The broadcaster was airing the news about the situation on the border with North Crestland, and then started playing a health show with a funny little woman as a presenter. She was speaking about life expectancy, which in the previous ten years had increased by seven per cent, and then she gave some useful tips on using salted water as a digestive. Listening to her monotonous voice, Boris tested the tank's mechanics. He loaded the scenarios and made sure all of them worked properly, after which he started forming the message to the Ministry of Defense.

He sent the broadcast, accompanying it with some comments, and asked Katyusha to check for new orders. The mailbox was empty, which meant that today he would be completely free, and it was quite a relief, because he didn't feel like doing anything at the moment. He thought that it was a perfect time to have a mid-day snack and regretfully remembered yesterday's caramel sticks, which he'd so wastefully finished in one single sitting. Together with tea drink and condensed yogurt, they would have made a perfect feast for a perfect guy. He thought that he might find some leftovers, which he hadn't noticed in the darkness, and shook the box. Indeed, it made a noise as if there was something inside, and he squeezed his finger through a hole, which he'd made at night. Inside the box, Boris could feel something of suspiciously familiar shape, and when he pulled it out, he was surprised to discover a square object, which looked exactly like a micropass everybody used to unlock the doors to different premises. He turned it in his fingers, wondering how it might have got into the candy box, and, remembering that it had been initially sent to Slava, decided to ask him for the explanations.

There was some rustling coming from the neighboring room, and Boris firmly knocked at the door, prepared for a serious talk. It was silent for a while, and he thought that no one was ever going to come out. He was about to give up and try later, but the door finally opened, and Slavik's disheveled head poked out.

"You either have something absolutely urgent to tell me, or I'll kill you, and, believe me, it's not the worst thing I can do to you now!" he hissed furiously. 'Good morning' was obviously missing from the neighbor's vocabulary.

"What's that?" Boris handed him the box.

"Oh, my goodness!" cried Slava. "Did you just make this exhausting two-meter journey in order to give me this thing of enormous value? That's very, very generous of you, little Bobby, but I bestow this empty box to you, as a symbol of your outstanding intellect!"

Boris shook out the micropass.

"This is yours, I assume?" he squinted at the neighbor, anticipating his embarrassment. Angie came out too and looked through his shoulder.

"Slava, what's that?" she asked.

"It's a micropass, isn't it?" Boris smiled viciously.

"It surely is," confirmed Slava. "Third-level, by the way. I was… making something for one big person from the Government Committee of Migration Control, you remember?" he pointedly glared at his wife. "And, as a gratitude for my small service, this big man awarded me with something more significant than money – freedom. Relative freedom, of course, but in our times it's a huge thing, believe me."

"Does it mean that you can have access to locked places?" wondered Boris.

"It does, partly. Like everyone, I need a route list to authorize my access, but, it's much easier than to receive than the pass. What if I tell you that I've just got a month's route list to the neighboring locations, so now I can wander the deserted realms of this godforsaken city and look for… what's it called? Ah, inspiration! What do you say, neighbor? Good loot, isn't it? I told you, you're drawing the wrong pictures. You'll never get anything from them, anything exceptional. And thanks for giving the pass back. I owe you one, as fun as that sounds."

"Am I really doing the wrong thing?" Boris thought when he returned to his room. "What did Colonel Petrenko say? That these broadcasts were useless, and people would forget them shortly after watching." What if he, Boris, was just wasting his life, and there wasn't much of it left now, that's for sure. He was forty, forty years old, and although the presenter this morning was saying something about the increasing life expectancy, it actually sounded like crap. Basil died at forty, so why wouldn't Boris do the same? His back constantly hurt, his limbs felt numb in the morning, his stomach periodically gave him pains after meals, and with every passing day he felt the gravity of life pressing on him harder and harder, like he pressed on an empty plastic bottle of tea drink before throwing it into a utilization bag. He stood in front of the window wallpaper and tried not to sink too deep into these heavy thoughts, but they overpowered him and gradually sucked him into the whirlpool of desperation. Boris tried to hook on some familiar things that used to comfort him, but there didn't seem to be any, and all his previous life was just a useless piece of nonsense, living for the sake of living, meaningless survival of a meaningless being, a hopeless struggle for nothing.

Boris sat down at the table wondering how not to make this day go down the drain, and suddenly remembered his neighbor's words about self-development. He might not be the wisest of men, but what prevents him from trying to improve? Especially today, when he's got absolutely nothing else to do.

"Katyusha, show me the list of inspirational and tranquilizing broadcasts," he commanded. "Free ones only"

"Three thousand four hundred and one broadcasts of level five found." responded the machine. "Load previews?"

"Yes."

The first hologram appeared above the machine. There was a middle-aged woman with long brown hair, sitting with her hands folded on the table. She looked straight into Boris's eyes and started speaking. The tone of her voice was very pleasant, like gentle sea waves crushing on the shore (Boris saw the sea once, in the army, when their division advanced to the north and spent two days at the seaside, eavesdropping the enemy's submarines).

"We all know that there are people who project confidence and draw other's attention at once. We always wonder how they manage to do it so effortlessly, as though they were born with it. The answer is – they practice assertive behavior. What is it, you might ask. If it will help, I can show you what I mean. Stand in front of the mirror. Yes, do it, right now. Look at yourself! Who is that person that you see? Do you trust them? Would you give them your last penny if they ask? The answer is 'no', as I can see. Then how do you expect others to trust you? Why would they listen to you at all? Do you want to know how to improve? How to become a better version of yourself? You've come to the right place. I will teach you because my job is to help the ones like you – lonely, lost, insecure. Buy a subscription for only 5,499 GKB a month, and soon you will see a different person in the mirror!"

"Money, money…" thought Boris. He liked the woman, but 5,499 was too much for him at the moment. He loaded another preview. It was helpfully called 'The secrets of money-making', and this time the presenter was a young man in a short-sleeved white shirt and a purple tie.

"Hey, guppies!" he said in a rather disparaging tone. "So, if you're watching this, you're probably wiped out. Completely ruined. Beggared. Impoverished. On queer street. Yeah, I know, I've been there, but as you've probably noticed, I'm a rich boy now. Look at me! I'm minted, made of money, rolling in it. You know, I've just ordered the latest communicator, which you will probably never be able to afford. It's perfect, believe me, and it cost me almost three million, but I swear, it's worth every penny spent on it. You probably think I'm boasting, but…"

"Yeah, I do think so," interrupted him Boris and suspended his braggy monologue.

The third broadcast began with a plangent melody and an image of deep blue sky above an icy mountain peak. The voice was a bit unnatural, with some hint of metallic intonations, and Boris guessed that it had been tuned, just the way he did it all the time with his own creations.

"Why can't you find a peace of mind in your everyday life? Why can't you love every bit of yourself, embrace into the dazzling light of your spotless mind and live consciously, concentrating on what really matters to you? Maybe you are overwhelmed with negative emotions, frustration and fear? Maybe you just don't realize how miserable your desires are, how pointless your struggle is in the face of eternity? Now it's time to go back to where you really belong – to the origins of your existence. These four practices will help you purify your thoughts and evolve your body, to awaken your hidden talents and fight the inner demons that prevent you from reaching the Enlightenment, which is the ultimate aspiration of every living being. Let us start with the first one. Relax. Feel every muscle of your body enfeeble, every string that tightens you to this world go loose, every unwanted thought vanish in the tranquility of nonexistence." Boris closed his eyes and leaned back, his chair giving a constrained creak under the weight of his body. "Now imagine yourself sliding down a mountain into a tender cloud of the softest snow. Experience this sensation of free-fall, with nothing to detain you, no strings attached, only this feeling of zero gravity. Let it overthrow your commotions."

Boris wasn't sure he was able to experience what the broadcaster was trying to compel him, but, without any doubt, he was under the influence of a very agreeable and relaxing sensation. His eyelids started to get heavy, and a wave of pleasant warmth covered him from head to toe. The music rang in his ears, as if coming from inside his mind, and even the old pain in his back seemed to ease, or at least to have become less annoying, and together with it, all the heavy thoughts that had pestered him earlier, dissolved in this bright tranquility, never to come back again.

The broadcaster continued hypnotizing him with the gentle melody, accompanied by soft mechanical voice.

"Do you feel the grace? Are you overjoyed by it? Catch this feeling and always keep it in your heart. Good. Now step two… Now step two… Now step two… Now…"

Boris forced himself to open his eyes and saw that the broadcast was frozen.

"Damn you! Damn you all! What the bloody heck is going on?" he shouted.

There was no reaction from the machine.

"Katyusha!" Boris's voice was hoarse with anger. "Resume the playback! Now!"

"Trying to resume…" Katyusha answered ignoring his frustration.

"Do it! Do it, you bleeding cursed device from hell!" Boris struck his fist against the table so outrageously that the broadcaster jumped in the air.

"Retrying…" said Katyusha indifferently. "Retrying failed. New complimentary device of data input, storing and processing found. Model: not found. Revision: not found. Contents: unknown. Reporting… Reporting failed."

On the other side of the city, an elderly man in glasses with thick lenses rushed to his computer and started checking something. "What the…?" he mumbled. "Did it just…? I should… God, yes, it did! It's working! It's unbelievable, but it *is* working!"

Of course, Boris didn't hear him and kept staring at his monitor.

"What do you mean new device? What's the matter with you, you stupid piece of tin?" he suddenly remembered that he'd already heard a message like this from Katyusha, but when was it? A long time ago, probably. Ten years or so, when… "Oh, my God, the card! The old memory card from the elephant's head! I couldn't pull it out, so I just left it there and completely forgot about it! It's still in the slot and that must be the problem!"

"Contents displayed on monitor," informed Katyusha. "Please check your settings."

Boris hesitated for a moment and then turned on the monitor of his calculating machine, ready to see something awful, something scary, something that would ruin his life immediately and irrevocably. The monitor was supposed to be used only to output data, which could not be transferred into holograms: 2D images, notes, pieces of programming code. Now it was blinking and trying to display something it had never displayed before. Line by line, page by page, until the whole bulk of information was loaded. Boris strained his eyes to make out what was on the screen. Some familiar symbols, which looked exactly like those he'd seen so many times in his book and often used to write a couple of lines of programming code when he couldn't find a suitable ready-made one in the database. Letters. He rubbed his eyes, but the letters didn't disappear. He struck his pen on the graphics, but they were still there, occupying the screen, looking at him stubbornly, as if they were the only owners of his device. Boris understood that something had gone wrong, and the only one to blame was himself, so incautious to have left the unknown and potentially malicious equipment in his working machine. His hands began to tremble, and he felt extremely scared, so scared that he couldn't think rationally and, instead, imagined the worst things that were bound to happen to him now. His calculating machine would certainly break down, and it would take him ages to get it working again. It might happen so that it would never go back to normal, and he'd have to buy a new one, but such huge sum of money was impossible for him in his current financial situation. During all these years he hadn't saved anything, just a couple of million GKB, which was enough to buy, maybe, a new drawing pen and the cheapest graphics tablet, not more than that. When the Ministry of Defense realized that his working tool had broken, they'd terminate the contract and he'd never get a new order from them. Finally, he'd have to apply for a manual labor position in a factory, or a distributional unit, but this prospect somehow didn't seem as bright now as it had seemed before. He was old and weak, and the job would kill him in no time. He hid his face in his hands and started shaking. Suddenly, Katyusha spoke again.

"Finished loading information. Device disconnected. Resume previous broadcast?"

Boris looked up. The letters were still in the screen, but the broadcaster was alive and ready to project the hologram.

"No," said Boris quietly. "Return to National Network."

After a small pause, he was returned to the First National Channel, which was airing some documentary about natural resorts of the Commonwealth state. The biggest lake, the highest mountain peak, the rarest flora and fauna – all of those were found in their beautiful country and belonged to its people. Boris turned to the screen, hoping that the letters would miraculously disappear, but they were still there and seemed to get brighter with every passing second. He had an awkward idea of calling Slavik for help, but then decided that it was the most inappropriate thing to do now. The neighbor would come, of course, and maybe he'd even seen some educational broadcast about how to fix crazy calculating machines, invaded by strange symbols from the past, but he'd surely get one up for Boris, and would go on remembering this embarrassing moment for ages. No, this was a task for a former sergeant of the provision unit, who used to decipher the most sophisticated codes and was assigned the most difficult programming jobs. Wouldn't he cope with these silly letters? Boris took out his book to reconcile the inscription. He ignored the hand-written note on the first page ('For Boris to learn to read. Your Grampy') and turned to the next one. So… The first letter in the monitor was known to him, it was "H", like in 'hike' or 'high'. The next one also looked familiar: 'e', for 'elephant'. Then followed double 'l', like in 'lobsters looked'.

"Hell?" Boris felt even more scared. "No, that's not it," he thought he could hear Lyudmila Ivanovna's voice. ("Borya, that's simple. It's round like a wheel and it sounds like "oooooooh. Say it after me.")

Suddenly the whole word made sense. 'Hello', as simple as that! The next word he could read easily because it was his name. 'Hello, Boris.' The stupid machine apparently considered him to be its acquaintance, otherwise why would it be fraternizing with him?

"Hello, Boris. It's your grandfather."

"What?!" Boris was absolutely blown away. "My grandfather?! Of course, it's you, old fart! Who else could have broken into my calculating machine and destroyed it with a single memory card hidden inside the head of my childhood toy? Are you happy now? Are the flames of hell hot enough to repay you for doing it to me? What do you want from me at all? Betray my motherland and become a foreign agent, just like you? No, asshole, I shall never do it! I'd rather die, right now, in front of this monitor, than follow in your footsteps! What are you trying to tell me from inside my calculating machine? I'd better not read it, just in case, but… It's only letters, anyway. What can happen if I go through a couple of pages?"

The first five lines were tough to Boris. The letters jumped on the screen, hid behind each other's backs, wriggled and bounced, and just wouldn't turn into words. But after he'd got used to their outlines, which he'd learned at the improvised lessons of Lyudmila Ivanovna in the Center of Patriotic Education, it all became easier and even fun.

"Hello, Boris, it's your grandfather, Vladimir Ivanovich Rogov. First of all, don't be scared. Your censorship isn't likely to reveal this message – our best programmer worked hard on it, believe me. It has the most sophisticated protection, and is disguised

as a piece of erroneous code, which is usually ignored by the security system. Well, this said, I'd better get down to business.

If you are reading this, it means that you've managed to behead Nastenka's elephant and get the radio-transmitting card. What is more, you somehow stuck it into your computer, or whatever they are called in your times. What is still more, it means that you've survived, that Uncle Gena had made it, as he'd promised, and you are a grown-up man now. How old are you, Borya? Twenty-five? Thirty? It all seems so unreal, because now you are six, you'll be seven only in five months, and right at this moment you're standing behind my door, asking me to let you in, so that we can watch Fidgy Freckles together, or read a book, or play with your toys. Sorry, Borya, I can't. I am writing something, something very important to me, to you, and to the rest of the country, and soon you will find out what it is. I'm sure you can read, even if no one else can. Don't ask me how, I just know it. And I know one more thing. You despise me now, you might even hate me, you think I'm the worst creature in this world. It's okay. I understand. I sometimes think so, too. I've probably broken your life and the lives of other people, but, in my defense, I had a damn good reason for it. I'll explain everything, but now I ask you to do me only one favor. Please, read this letter to the end and then decide for yourself what to do with it.

I'll start with history. No, not the twisted pieces of bullshit that you've been taught. The real and unchanged history. Read on, Boris, and do your best not to get lost in it..."

Chapter 5. The History

1

The Commonwealth State (formerly known as Slandaria, later as Crestland, and later as South Crestland) is a country, covering over 8 million square kilometers and occupying the northwest of the Elysian continent. The first reference to a human activity in this region dates back to 35,000 years, when a group of settlers from the north came across numerous deposits of natural resources in the area. Soon afterwards, other nomads were attracted by the riches of the region, and several major settlements were established within the modern borders of the country. In the early ages, it was one of the most densely populated areas, inhabited mostly by scattered barbarian tribes with no common governance or control, constantly fighting internecine wars with each other. Countless confrontations slowed down the development of the country, and lack of friendly contacts between the tribes contributed to its backlog from the rest of the world. However, in the Middle Ages, one of the local princes came forward and managed to conquer most of the territory, subdue the weaker leaders and destroy those who refused to surrender to him. Early written sources mention 'Seven Battles of Resistance', when 'blood mingled with sweat and tears, and soaked into the ground, where Hydra was lying deep and feeding itself on the grief and pain'.

The newborn country was named Slandaria, after the name of the Prince Slander, the Conqueror, and in fifty years after he took the throne, it turned into the cruelest authoritarian monarchy the world had ever seen, accompanied by mass executions and elimination of all dissent. Those fifty years were enough for the prince, who was already in his seventies, to strengthen the power within the country and to collect large troops of warriors to send them to conquer the nearby countries. Before being killed in one of the battles, he managed to move the borders further into the continent, but, within a couple of decades, his successors lost several important battles and were forced to leave the occupied territories and, eventually, to give up part of their own ones. The country was later dragged into more wars, but soon it learned to gain profit from it. It traded on its non-aggression towards the weaker countries, and it threatened the stronger ones with the weapon which became deadlier with every passing decade. It looked like it was finally able to take stable niche and rest on its laurels of unwon battles, but every epoch of stability gives birth to thinking, and some civil unrest started to form on its margins. The unrest resulted in some sort of revolution, which made the country from monarchy into republic. However, it didn't change much for the common people. The only difference was that now the dictator was not sitting on a throne but occupied a fairly comfortable chair in front of a group of speechless dummies called 'ministers'. Soon after the revolution, a major conflict broke out, splitting the state into two parts. One of the parts declared independence, refusing to report to the new government, and called itself North Crestland, while the other one – now South Crestland – threw all of its forces to reclaim its territories. For some reason, the reclaim never happened, and in about fifty years, South Crestland allied with two other geographical neighbors on very strange conditions, which resembled enslavement more than equitable union, and received a new name – the Commonwealth State.

Due to the State's large territory, its climatical and natural zones are varied, from humid continental areas to arctic colds. The characteristics of the soil are mostly unfavorable for its cultivation, but the vast reserves of natural resources provide the country with sufficient funds for prosperous existence. The Commonwealth State possesses almost 50% of the world's oil and gas deposits and one third of the continent's wood, which makes it its largest exporter. The country is washed by five seas, and another one, which cannot be found on any of the maps – the sea of blood shed on its territory. The population comprises 80 million people, 80 million of the unfortunate souls, who are bound to survive in this land of plenty, yet getting nothing of it for themselves. Rich country and poor country, the country which has always been coldly beautiful and mysteriously attractive for poets, artists and philosophers, the country with unique landscape and an oversensitively wounded soul. Let us cross the border and step inside.

Do you hear bombs and fire of guns? That's explainable. For the most part of its history, the Commonwealth State has been in war. It seems to be feeding on these wars, considering them part of its internal resources. When there were no outer enemies, the country started eating itself from inside, devastated by civil confrontations over its resources. However, later, the government understood how to keep its citizens occupied, by putting them in the conditions, when their only aspiration was to find a crust of bread to feed on. It was beneficial in two ways: firstly, they didn't have time to think of the surrounding injustice, and, secondly, they provided a nice free labor source, which was so easy to manage.

In spite of the severe living conditions, or, maybe, due to them, the State from time to time gave birth to strange people who didn't seem to belong to it. For them, those crusts of bread had no value at all, so working for the benefit of the country didn't make any sense. They were able to think further than tomorrow, even further than their own lives, and, more importantly, they were prepared to give away those lives of theirs for the sake of the future that they imagined for themselves. They foolishly thought that they alone would be able to stop this conveyor, transforming blood into wealth, make its mechanism choke with its own cruelty and ruthlessness. They were wrong, of course, because this machine was not designed by them, and it was far more complicated and durable than everything else in the country, and it would grind anything, becoming only stronger from it. But such was their role – to shed light, to give a hint of hope that things might be different, to keep the country floating and not let it sink into darkness forever. Their heads eventually rolled down the squares of the towns and cities, like they'd done hundreds of years before, and their blood was even redder and thicker, because it was a sacrifice to the god, which the State has created for itself – the god of greediness. This was how it has always been and how it will be for many more years because this god is deathless and will forever demand for new sacrifices. It will protect its ministers and provide them with the illusion of control and almightiness, but the illusion will dissolve, and their souls will burn in its jaws too. This order, once adopted, will be maintained throughout the centuries, and no one is going to change it, because life in the Commonwealth State has always implied sacrifice, and this sacrifice is to be made by common people – a desperate offering of those who have nothing else to give but themselves.

The new cycle began after one of the numerous wars, which the State had apparently won, but no one was sure what it had received in exchange of turning itself into ruins again. Indeed, the war brought only devastation and poverty to those who fought in it, and they desperately needed help, or at least its promise from the government. But the authorities were silent, too busy with their own problems. So people had to find a way to survive in this bitter post-war reality by themselves, not relying on any external mercy and charities. Fortunately, they had always been strong, tempered by the sufferings and hardships of their forefathers, and also, they'd been patient and obedient and preferred to humble themselves rather than demand for what they deserved. The shabby dugouts left from the times of war had been mended with all sorts of materials which could be found in hand, and had turned into low and dull homes, barely sufficient to sustain the bitter colds, which had settled in the country. These homes were the birthplace of the new generation – those, who hadn't seen war, but were aware of its consequences, who grew up stray and neglected, receiving no proper education and seeing no future, who were only able to fight for food with their peers, regarding it as their only way of survival. The new citizens were persistent and aggressive at times and would never give up on what they had been able to attain. They had their own authorities, who were living next to them, and not those who occupied the governmental buildings and unreachable civil offices. The point when the powers could have tried to establish order on its territory had been reached, and the only outcome of the situation for the government was that common people were out of their way and obeyed at least some of the most important laws. This was the funny time when the citizens and the State were preoccupied with one common business, as old as time – depredation.

Vladimir Ivanovich Rogov was born twenty years after the war, into a family of Ivan Ilyich Rogov, a hereditary logger, and Lilia Osipovna Lvova, a former teacher of arts. Volodya was the youngest of five sons, his mommy's pet, and he enjoyed all the advantages and disadvantages of having four elder brothers. His father was always busy at work because the wood was one of the most valuable things at that time, and the three of his eldest sons helped him at the sawmill. Another brother, Stepan, who was two years older than Volodya, had very poor health, and no one was sure he'd make it at least to his tenth birthday. Lilia Osipovna gave herself completely to her husband and sons, and, belonging to a noble family, she did her best to ensure the life of dignity to her close ones. She cleaned and washed the house, dressed and educated her children, and she did everything so smoothly and naturally, that it usually came unnoticed for the others. Ivan Ilyich was a good man too, at least that's what people said about him. He worked in all conditions, without giving himself a break, never complaining or sniveling. Being blessed by five sons, he demanded the same from them – work was put on their home altar, and work was prayed to in times of joy and sorrow.

They had a fairly prosperous household and could afford more than other people dreamed of. In his early years, Volodya and his sick brother stayed at home with their mother, who tried to give them as much education as possible before father took them to the sawmill. She herself had survived the hardest war and-post-war times and managed to retain the noble values of her family – honesty, faithfulness and generosity. That was what she taught her children: "Don't be afraid to go against everyone if you are sure you are right. Go on risking your life for the sake of your ideals – life without risk is nothing but a senseless existence. Be merciful: even in a sinner see a moment of greatness. Having a strong heart is worthier than having strong arms. Running from your pursuers means admitting you are wrong; always face your opponents – it will make them respect you and fight fair." Volodya listened to his mother open-mouthed, and although he was too young to understand all that she said, he was able to come to the most important conclusion in his life – being good is simple if you regard it as the only possible way of your existence. And he promised himself to be good no matter what because such was the will of his mother, whom he adored.

Lilia Osipovna could also play the piano, which she'd learnt from her grandmother, and, when she was in a suitable mood, she would sit down on an adjustable piano chair and play a penetrating melody, which was so comfortable to dream away to. Volodya would close his eyes and let his thoughts drift away to the notes of Passacaglia, and when its final chord died against the walls of the sitting room, he would look in his mother's eyes to make sure they both dreamt the same dream. But what fascinated Volodya even more was Lilia Osipovna's skills in visual arts. In the evenings, when Father and the three elder brothers hadn't come back from the mill yet, and all the housework had been done, they used to sit in front of the stove, and mum took a piece of charcoal and a paper.

"So, what do you want me to draw for you today?" she asked Volodya and Stepa. "A knight, or, maybe, a dragon?"

"A knight, mommy, please!" cried Volodya. "And make him strong and brave, will you?"

"Mom," said Stepa once. "Can you draw a bear?"

"A bear? Of course, I can! What do you want it to do? Sleep in its den? Gather mushrooms?"

"No, that's boring! Can it… Can it fly on a balloon? Pretend to be a cloud in the sky?"

They all laughed.

"Or…" Stepa rubbed his forehead like he always did when he was thinking hard. "I know! Ride a bike!"

"Bears don't ride bikes!" protested Volodya.

"They do! In circuses! Mum, please draw a bear, no, three bears on bikes!"

"Okay then, here we go…" Lilia Osipovna pressed the charcoal against the paper and drew two circles – a skeleton of the bike. The charcoal immediately made her long aristocratic fingers black, but she didn't seem to notice it. In ten minutes, the drawing was finished, and it looked so cute that Volodya regretted it was not his idea.

"Mommy," he said. "Can I add something?"

"Sure, honey, go ahead."

"I'd like…" he looked around. "I'd like a cat! A tabby, like our Barsik."

"On a bike, too?"

"Yes, but make it sit back to front!"

"And a wolf!" laughed Stepa.

"Next to the cat? Also on a bike?" Lilia Osipovna seemed to be enjoying the game as much as her sons.

"On a horse!" the brothers cried almost in chorus.

The ideas kept coming out from their imagination, and the drawing kept growing until the piece of paper finished. They looked at it once again, and then Lilia Osipovna folded it accurately and stuck it in the upper drawer of her cupboard.

"Why are you putting it away, mum?" Stepa asked.

"Yes, why?" repeated Volodya. "Can I keep it under my pillow, please?"

"Sorry, sweetheart, but I've just had an idea. I know a person… an old friend of mine. He lives in the town and writes books for children. Poems, mostly. Last time I saw him he was, well, not in the best shape and out of ideas. He was down and out, and I wished there was a way for me to help him. I guess I'll see him and give him the drawing next time I go to town. Maybe it will prove useful and he'll be able to make a nice book out of it. And then we'll read it together, deal?"

"Book…" Volodya looked at his mother in doubt. "Who needs books nowadays? Father said bookies don't make us stronger, only lazier."

Lilia Osipovna sighed.

"They do make us stronger," she said after a pause. "But not in the way your father thinks they should. He's right, people don't read much these days. But it hasn't always been like that. It's just that our country is… let's call it, unhealthy. It's ill, but, take it from me, Volodya, it will soon get better. And the healthier the country, the more books people read, that's for sure. I wish I had some children's books to read to you, but they were all lost in war. I'd managed to find some novels, biographies and philosophical works in the attic of my old house before your father sold it, and we bought this one. I keep them all here, in this cupboard. Maybe I'll read them to you when you grow up, or maybe you'll read them yourself. That's what I'm teaching you for, by the way."

When Volodya was eleven, Lilia Osipovna got very ill. Some doctors said it was typhoid, some called it tuberculosis, but, in any case, there was no cure for it at those times. She didn't want to see the priest, and she didn't want to say goodbye to her children because she thought it would make them sad. She just passed away one night, quietly in her bed, and that night Volodya, as the youngest one, was sent to one of his aunts who lived in the same village, and didn't come back until all the burial formalities had been settled down. When he entered his home, first thing he saw was a coffin lid, ornamented with pink and yellow flowers, leaning against the wall of the hallway, and a dozen of unknown people dressed in black, who were whispering something to each other and shaking their heads sympathetically. He knew that his mother was lying in the sitting-room, and he was expected to follow there to say his final goodbye, but instead he ran to his bedroom, threw himself on the bed and covered his head with his pillow. He cried so hard that it made him fall asleep, and no one disturbed him until next morning.

Lilia Osipovna didn't leave much after herself, only a dreamlike memento of the wise look in her eyes and a drawer of books, which she had treasured and protected from her husband's attempts to burn them in the stove.

After the death of his wife, Ivan Ilyich immediately stopped all his sons' education and sent Volodya and Stepa to the mill to join their brothers. It was a natural and indisputable decision, and no one could even think of disobeying it. However, quite soon, Ivan Ilyich realized that he was finding it difficult to do some of the jobs he'd easily done before, and the sawmill wasn't bringing in as much money as it used to. He gave it a thought, talked to people in the village and finally decided to sell his business to one of the local merchants who offered him a reasonable price for it. Next year, Ivan Ilyich moved to the capital, where he bought a four-bedroom apartment for the six of them, and in another four months, he opened a small family shop, selling tools and electrical equipment. Vladimir made sure that all his mother's books were carefully stored in a large chest, placed in the corner of the room which he shared with his brother Stepan, who was not much healthier now than he was in his childhood. He only regretted having left the piano in their old house, but his father was absolutely adamant about it.

"Don't be a fool, Vladimir," he said sharply. "People will laugh at us having these girlish toys in our flat. It's enough that you've cluttered up your room with those stupid bookies of yours."

Their new business went well, and gradually grew into a small family company where everyone was doing their part. Vladimir always got some easy and monotonous jobs like cleaning up the shop, arranging the goods or calling potential customers inside. He was always bored and wondered if all of his life would be wasted like that. Once, when he was about fifteen years old and stayed at home with a tiresome flu, he opened the chest with books and took one of them, just to see if he still remembered how to read. "The R-r-r-r... ep...-ub-lic," said the cover.

"The Republic?" wondered Vladimir. "Doesn't make any sense at all. Did Mother read it, too?"

His eyes were sore with fever, but he still managed to cope with five or six pages until his father returned from the shop. Next morning, Vladimir took the book again and by the evening he had finished half of it, not sure whether he understood what it was about. There were some hand-written notes on the margins, probably made by his mother or her father, who was said to be well-educated and impeccably-mannered. Vladimir felt that the book was not just a bunch of sheets of paper stitched together but it was closely related to his family and, consequently, to himself. When he was through with "The Republic", he took another book and read it in the evening when he was left alone in the shop in order to get everything prepared for the next day. Then he took the third one, and in about a year he found out that his small library had finished. Ivan Ilyich, upon seeing this weird passion of Volodya's, was a bit at a loss and first thing tried to ward him off it by threats and blandishments, but having faced unexpectedly strong resistance, he gave up and remembered that he had four more sons to teach life. Vladimir happily went to a flea market and spent his hard-earned money on ten more second-hand books, which were as cheap as dirt at those times. He didn't care about their contents much, he swallowed whatever was written there with gratitude and respect, and he always remembered his mother's words that "Books make us stronger."

Of course, it would be naïve to suppose that in those pages he found all the answers to the questions which he wasn't even able to formulate properly. But at least he could see the other side of life, the one, which was so different from what he had been used to. The world now started to look more complicated and more beckoning, and a simple "Life must be understood backward. But it must be lived forward" made him stay awake for the whole night and reflect on what had just been revealed to him. He thought about all those people who'd created this huge pool of wisdom, a well that now lay completely abandoned and discarded from the list of human values, and he started to look for more questions and, consequently, for more books. Eventually, he developed a sort of instinct which made him unmistakably tell good books from bad ones, and he read only those which he considered as good, which meant that they contained clues to his existence. By the time Vladimir Rogov was eighteen, he thought he'd finally come to a well-rounded picture of the universe and his position in it, and this picture enchanted him so much that he even distanced himself from his family and their business.

Ivan Ilyich, however, had another idea of his son's future. He opened two more shops in the outskirts of the city and was about to give control of one of them to his youngest offspring – Stepan and Vladimir. This was supposed to present them with a pretty nice start in life and teach them all the necessary skills of successful businessmen. Vladimir, in his turn, didn't want to continue his forefathers' way of life, but at the same time, he wasn't sure that he'd be able to invent something different for himself. At the flea market he talked to one of the book sellers – an old shabby-looking guy, who said that the best place for such poindexters was a university, which, for some reason, was still open in the capital. Vladimir thanked the bum for the brilliant idea and decided to apply. In the evening, he informed his father about his intentions. Ivan Ilyich listened to his son carefully, and when he finished, said that he'd have given him a damn good thrashing if he could, and he'd have done it much earlier had he known where those 'moronic bookies' would take him. "What you are about to do, young man, has no sense at all, believe me. I know life. I've been through the good times and the bad times, and the only thing that helped me stay afloat was work. Never have I read a single bookie, and never have I regretted it. Knowledge is for lazybones who don't know what they are given their hands for."

Nevertheless, he let Vladimir do it his way, on condition that he did it all on his own. Ivan Ilyich deprived his youngest son of all financial support and insisted on his moving to the university hostel after he was admitted. Vladimir agreed. His only desire at that time was to learn, and he didn't mind putting his familiar ties on the line. He had always been like that – a risky guy, a wildcatter, not able to find compromise or middle ground, a person of all or nothing. The world doesn't favor such people, and, naturally enough, it killed him in the end.

Vladimir made up his mind to take history as his major because it was the easiest subject at the entrance exams. He bought another pile of books related to the history of the Commonwealth State and started studying them, cramming, making notes, going deep into the details which seemed unclear or ambiguous. At those times, the events of the past hadn't been rewritten or changed, maybe only to a small extent, and it was still possible to trace some patterns, which the history had been following throughout its course. Vladimir was surprised at how cyclical it was, and the same things happened again and again, with different actors, but in the same decorations. It looked as if some external power was governing his country, and it had always turned the events the way it wanted to, leaving the people no chance for free choice. He wondered what it might be, and the more he thought about it, the more fascinated he became with the idea of making his country 'healthier', as his mother would have put it. In any case, the entrance exams were brilliantly passed, and right after his nineteenth birthday, Vladimir Ivanovich Rogov proudly walked into the room of the hostel of the State University of Economic Management.

However, his new life wasn't exactly like he had expected. Most of the lectures were boring and consisted of useless facts already known to him, and his course mates were, in large part, very dim, only trained to parrot what they'd heard from the old and weary professors, who could only stick to ready-made notes and ignored any questions that required meaningful answers. Rogov suddenly understood that most of the people in his country were like that, and that he'd never met anyone, apart from his mother and the bum in the flea market, of course, who was able to think out of the box, which at that time was called 'a TV-set'. Apart from that, Vladimir Ivanovich found himself completely out of money, and, quite reluctantly, took a cleaning job in a nearby grocery store. That was the first time he held the decision to leave his father's house doubtful, but anyway, it was too late to do anything about it. "I'll manage," he said to himself. "I still have my whole life ahead of me."

In his student years, Rogov proved himself to be a bright and hardworking young man, and after finishing the university, he was offered a position of a laboratory assistant of the Department of Applied Economics. It was very beneficial for him because this way he could continue working on his own articles and essays and, what is more, occupy the same hostel room and feed on the cheap lunches in the university canteen. He wrote about a dozen of articles, and several of them were even published in some unknown scientific magazines. He enjoyed writing – it brought him closer to all the great philosophers and dreamers he'd always admired, and he still enjoyed reading, getting himself deeper and deeper into the maze of cognition. Those few years were the happiest time of his life, and never again was he so close to becoming another enlightener of the masses. But the opportunity was foolishly missed as it always happens when one cannot read between the lines of their fate.

When Rogov was forced to leave the hostel and give way to first-year students, he moved to a rented room in a tiny flat and started saving for his own home. His articles didn't bring enough for him to be able to put aside any decent sum, so he found a teaching position in one of the state schools, which also implied opportunities for tutorship and other options for extra income. Vladimir Ivanovich loved teaching, and he loved children because he saw future in their eyes, so the job was very agreeable for him. In a couple of years, he was able to make his first deposit and moved to his own two-bedroom flat, which was conveniently located within walking distance from his university, where he still had a part-time job as a senior assistant.

Vladimir Ivanovich immediately started filling his new flat with books and other funny objects which he could find at the flea market. He even got a piano, untuned, with broken keys and smelling of rotten wood. He proudly placed it in the corner of one of the bedrooms, promising to himself that he'd learn to play it as soon as he had time. The only thing his home was missing was a lady's touch, and sometimes he thought that it would be nice to teach his own children. He was approaching his thirtieth birthday, but before sinking into family life, he wanted to achieve something significant in science. His doctoral dissertation was finished and successfully defended, which was a huge achievement for such a young scholar. Very soon, Vladimir Ivanovich, quite unexpectedly, was offered an office of the dean of his department, in place of the old one, whose age prevented him from performing his duties to the full. The new position naturally required full-time employment, so combining it with teaching was out of the question. Vladimir Ivanovich reflected carefully on his perspectives and finally opted for science. He wrote a letter of resignation to the school principal, who responded to this idea sorrowfully and even tried to convince him to stay, offering a bigger salary. But Rogov was as always, inexorable.

In two weeks' time, Vladimir Ivanovich was replaced by Sophia, a young girl of not more than 25, who had just finished a teacher's training college, and seemed to know nothing about pedagogics. It didn't worry Rogov much, and he was sure she'd cope because he himself also had to learn on the job. Next day, for the first time, he opened the door of the university's office with his own key, sat down at his own desk and started arranging all his paper swag on it. In the evening of the same day, he got a call from his successor – the young girl was weeping and complaining about her students, especially the senior schooler Semenov, who, for the whole lesson, had been cracking dirty jokes aimed at her provocatively short dress. Vladimir Ivanovich knew Semenov from his early ages, when his mother, having at least seven more children to attend to, ran around the school, trying to collect her numerous offspring, with the youngest of them tucked under her arms. He laughed, remembering it, and started to explain to the poor girl all the things that she should have been taught in her college. Next weekend, they met in the university park, and quite soon he found out that he was in love.

Their wedding ceremony was very modest and took place in their flat, too small to accommodate all the guests. Vladimir Ivanovich's father was happy to be invited and didn't seem to hold it against his son anymore. He even presented him with a decent sum of money – the most appropriate present for the young family. "Make sure not to waste it all on your bookies!" he said and grinned, punching his son on his shoulder. Two of his brothers had died, and the remaining two were also present at the party, together with Sophia's family and friends. They had a great time in spite of the fact that the food was poor, and the books were used as chairs, and the neighbors threatened to call the police if they didn't stop making so much noise. When the party was over and the flat was cleared from the remaining mess, the newlyweds started planning their future. They were both lucky to have accommodation and jobs, so everything seemed bright and beautiful, and there was absolutely nothing to worry about. At that time, Vladimir Ivanovich was working on another dissertation and apart from that continued publishing his articles, dreaming of prospectively issuing his own monography. One of these works, called 'On the importance of reforms in socio-economic development of a country', for some reason attracted the attention of the university management. Rogov was called to the science council, which recommended cancelling the article's publication due to the fact that it could be considered opposing and destabilizing. Vladimir Ivanovich answered that by no means was he trying to be objectionable to the current authorities, and his work was purely scientific and empirical, and, more importantly, it was a series and could not be simply removed from the publication. The Council insisted, but Rogov stood his ground.

Several days after the incident, Vladimir Ivanovich was arrested on charges of misappropriation of the university funds, which was such a ridiculous and artificial pretext that he at first considered it mockery. But it turned out to be quite serious, and even some of the witnesses were found who testified that he had spent a significant sum of money from the social assistance fund on stationery and equipment that he was using at home. The investigators also hinted on the possible background security checks of his wife's work and his father's business, and, moreover, digging deeper into Rogov's past life. Vladimir Ivanovich was outraged and prepared to fight for justice, but Sophia threatened him with divorce, and in the end, he gave up and destroyed all his current and earlier works. The Council recommended that he concentrated on the history of the neighboring states and their negative influence on the country, but he rejected and chose some other neutral topic for his dissertation. It was a hard compromise for Rogov, but when the wellbeing of his close people was at stake, he could not do otherwise. He planned to return to his previous studies at a more appropriate time, although he could hardly imagine when this time would finally come.

"There are crucial moments in every person's life story and in every country's history," he thought. "If I'm wise enough not to miss these moments, both of them, I'd make my own history and my own story. I just have to wait. Wait and be ready for it even if they happen in thirty more years."

Soon Vladimir Ivanovich was granted a position of a professor, and it thrilled him so much, that he completely forgot about his intentions. Like he read in one of his numerous books, "There is time in every person's life when comfort becomes more important than goodness."

Soon he had another business to preoccupy himself with, far from science, but more pleasant and even more important. He now had a child – a small person, wrapped in pink blanket, with a tiny turned-up nose and a misty-eyed gaze, the one that reminded him of his mother. He smiled and thought that he would definitely teach her to play the piano. He wanted to name his baby girl Lilia, but his wife considered it too old-fashioned, so they called her Alina, which was sort of similar, but sounded a great deal better. He was sure that now nothing would sabotage their fragile happiness, and gave up all his thoughts of crucial moments, and of changing the history, of writing new articles and issuing a monography – all of those had lost their significance for him and faded away, replaced by more pragmatic values of the new reality.

When their daughter turned five, Sophia started to behave strangely, and Vladimir Ivanovich didn't realize at once what the matter with her was. When he finally did, it was too late. His wife told him that Semenov, the former high schooler, who had never missed a chance to make a comment about her appearance, was now a handsome and well-proportioned young fellow, working quite successfully in the area of trade. They had accidentally met in the market, and then, also accidentally, at a bus stop, and, finally, in a nearby café. All those accidental meetings led to him proposing Sophia an alliance, which meant that she'd have to leave the family. She was about to accept it and asked her husband to make it quick and painless. Vladimir Ivanovich agreed, but only on condition that she left their daughter with him. Sophia had nothing against it because she wasn't sure that Alina and her new partner would get along. So they went apart, each getting what they wanted, and no one really dwelled much on it.

Life went on, full of everyday joys and sorrows. Alina grew up, Vladimir Ivanovich's head became whiter and balder, and soon he understood that there was no history, and no crucial moments, that his life was just one more birth and death, which would never make a difference to anyone except a few odd people scattered between those two events. There was also no more sense in books he'd been collecting for so many years, so he started selling them to those who were unwise enough to waste their time on such rubbish. He knew that he needed to save money for a decent dress for his daughter's prom night.

Ten years went by. Ten empty changes of seasons, which the professor only noticed from his daughter's growing up and by the baldness and whiteness of his temples. And another ten years would have passed, equally shallow and meaningless, if, one quite unremarkable evening, he hadn't been paid a visit by a young student of the Law department, who asked Vladimir Ivanovich to supervise his diploma work. The man was well-mannered and polite, and it looked like he was an impersonation of the crucial moment, which the professor had been waiting for so long. All Rogov's thoughts and memories came back to life, and he grabbed onto this young man, desperately hoping that his life might be of use to anyone, except for liquor manufacturers and the numerous cockroaches, which had comfortably settled in his untidy flat.

That was the time of complete stagnation in the State, and it seemed that the government was happy with it and wasn't going to make any effort to improve the situation. The power was divided between the authorities and half-criminal gangs, which controlled the territory and the rest of the citizens. The Constitution, the basic law of any state, initially designed to grant people at least a hint on security and protection, had been rewritten so many times that it turned into complete rubbish and could just as well be used as toilet paper. However, there were other laws – the laws of the streets, which hadn't been documented, but worked better than those issued by the State. 'Play it fair. Don't run the uniformed guys' errands. Don't give testimony. Make regular donations to the common fund. Respect the seniors and protect the weak' – those were the simple, yet effective concepts of survival at those times. Most of them were comprehensive and easy to follow, so the only thing left to be done was to spruce them up a little and implement into legal practice. That was what Sergey Anatolyevich Malinin did. He dreamed of freedom, and these laws of the street fitted perfectly into his dream because they were written by people themselves and reflected their own needs and desires. Probably that was the reason why so many of them followed their new leader, and even more joined him in the next years.

It seemed that after Malinin's victory the State entered a new age – the age of justice and equity, and common people started to enjoy all the benefits of the land where they had been born and grew up. They could finally speak freely, and they finally regained their long-forgotten values, suppressed for so many years. Science, arts and literature reemerged in the country, and books were printed again, not to burn them in the stove, but to exchange ideas with the others, even outside the country's borders. The necessity of war was reconsidered, and a sort of a peace agreement with North Crestland was signed, and although it implied certain losses for the State, the benefits of not having to tilt at windmills all the time overweighed them. Of course, it was only the beginning, and some other reformation projects were to be released in the following decades, so the future again looked positive.

Professor Rogov returned to his articles on political and socio-economic reforms, and this time his works were more mature and less emotional. He also documented all the process of this so-called 'revolution', which he had witnessed and had participated in, so that his notes could provide future generations with a first-hand outlook on the real situation. He completely immersed in his work, and he started reading books again, although it was difficult at times because there were three new people in his flat. Alina had married a talented and a bit gloomy doctor, Andrey Arsenyev, and in a year their first son was born, and soon a daughter followed. Rogov's grandson, Borya, had always been a charming little boy, who seldom cried or complained, and it was a great pleasure to take care of him and watch him grow. Vladimir Ivanovich was a good grandfather. He knew how to deal with children, being a grown-up child himself and enjoying all the activities that he used to engage in in those happy times when his own mother was alive.

But the Hydra, which pretended to be dead, was watching them from its hideout, licking its lips and longing for new prey. It took its time. Let these funny humans play democracy if they want. Let them think that they are free, let them enjoy their victory, which is really their first step to defeat. It will destroy them – all of them, and not only will it get back what it had so foolishly lost, but it will keep getting more and more, until they have nothing left. It will restore its power, and it will multiply its might until the very end of times. Of course, no one will be able to stop it, especially this young bunky dreamer, or the decrepit professor, whose only mission is to feed worms in the grave.

The first mention of Victor Vasilyevich Pravdin was made on the First National TV Channel in the beginning of March 2033. It was announced in the news that he'd been appointed Deputy Chief of Foreign Affairs Committee of the President's Administration. The news was very short and came unnoticed for most of the people, but not for the professor. Vladimir Ivanovich knew that Malinin would have never let an untested person into his circle, and Pravdin was surely not from their team. His face was too common, and his way of speaking too unnatural for it. After hearing the announcement, Rogov immediately dialed the President's number, but the former was too busy to give any explanations and just briefly said that there was absolutely nothing to worry about, and he was one hundred per cent confident in his action. This somehow didn't reassure the professor, and he continued watching for the new official with double attention. Pravdin's promotions were lightning-fast. In several months, he was already Director of Federal Security Service, and in another half a year received the position of the State Secretary of Defense. Rogov got restless and desperately tried to find out at least some tiny bits of information to shed a light on this mysterious personality, but all he came across were random interviews, in which Victor Vasilyevich dwelled on his past.

"I have always been a simple man with a simple life. I grew up in the poorest district of a provincial town, without heating, without running water, even without shops nearby. But we were always thankful for what we had. The times were tough, you know, and I made a great effort to finish secondary school. I had to work from the age of twelve, I guess, and it was donkey work, believe me. I could have done better at school, of course, if I hadn't had to go there after sleepless nights spent on unloading the trucks at a local farm. But I was taught not to complain and not to ask for anything, even if I was sure I deserved it. I know life from the inside, and I've seen it from the most unflattering perspective. It didn't ruin me, no, quite the contrary, it made me stronger. And now I am here to make our country stronger, too. Hand in hand with our President, whom I serve humbly and wholeheartedly. We work together to make it the best place in the world – for you, for me, for all of us."

The interviews smelled of good old propaganda, the one which had been making the professor sick only a couple of years ago. He called Malinin once again, but his answer was still the same:

"No need to worry, Vladimir Ivanovich. I know what I'm doing. Pravdin is our man." But the president's voice sounded weary and implausible, and Rogov understood that it was time to panic. He had a weird feeling that he was witnessing some strange dress-up game, when everything was not what it seemed, and just at the moment you thought you'd managed to figure something out, it changed and took another, more bizarre, shape. Soon after Pravdin, other officials started to emerge, whose biography was almost identical and whose interviews contained the same pre-written meaningless phrases. Finally, Vladimir Ivanovich realized that it was already too late. He insisted on meeting Malinin but was refused due to the President's tight schedule. He only managed to get a video-call late at night, and it looked like a mere lame excuse. Sergey was harsh and aggressive and told the professor to mind his own business and stay away from the things he didn't understand. He said something about the need for new people and new ideas, and they were cut off almost in the middle of the phrase. Vladimir Ivanovich was absolutely confused. He'd never seen his former student like this, and he even thought that it might have not been him. Maybe the Hydra had just spoken to him, showing its teeth for the first time.

With the emergence of Pravdin, the State started changing again, as if there was some invisible leech, sucking on it and slowly pulling out its life force. The borders were closed for the reason of some unknown virus, threatening to spread all over the country. Soon afterwards, the peace agreement with North Crestland was terminated, and military operation was re-announced. A large part of the country's young men was summoned for military exercises, so Rogov lost half of his students, and the other half quit themselves because educational grants were called off, and most of them couldn't afford to pay. Malinin was different, too. He only had enough energy to give orange-wedge smiles on the camera and take part in useless events and consultations. "President is helpless. Malinin's given up. The country needs a new leader," the newspapers copied each other's headlines, and the TV echoed happily. The country ended up in the same mess and mayhem which it had experienced all the previous years. The finality to this disgraceful situation was brought in the university park, and it became clear that the battle was lost. Lost completely, shamefully and with no hope on revenge. Vladimir Ivanovich now wanted only one thing – to get drunk and cross out all the previous six years from his life, or, better, wipe it off totally and start everything from the scratch, with burning his mother's books in the first place.

3

Rogov entered his flat early in the morning with two bottles of vodka popping out of his pockets and two toy elephants inside his bag. He wanted to crawl silently through the corridor, hoping that everyone was asleep, but he failed. Alina opened the door of her room, went out and closed it behind her back.

"Where have you been?" she demanded furiously. "I've spent the whole night trying to get through to you on the phone!"

"It was out of power," answered the professor calmly. "I stayed at the university with colleagues. We sort of chatted for a while…"

"At the university? That's crap! I know that the university is closed at night! I called the security post, and they said you'd left at nine, and no one had seen you after!"

"We were in the park…"

"The whole night? Under the rain? With whom? Are you drunk?" the questions kept on coming, and Vladimir Ivanovich was too exhausted to make up the answers.

"My colleagues and me…"

"What colleagues? Dad, you think I'm stupid? You think I don't understand what's going on? You were with *him*! I heard his speech, the whole country did, and I know what's on your mind! Don't you dare, father, don't you even think of it! I saw this Pravdin. He's a monster! Dad, they'll kill you. And they'll kill me, and Andrey, and the children. Think about it, dad! Don't do this to us, please!"

"I don't want to think now, Alina, I'm too tired. Let me go to bed, okay?"

"You're a total moron, Rogov. I hate you!" Alina looked at him through the tears of rage and helplessness.

Suddenly a snuffy whimpering came from behind the door, and she lowered her voice.

"That's it! You've woken the children up," she whispered. "Go to bed now, or go to hell, I don't care."

173

Vladimir Ivanovich sat on his bed and started changing his clothes, trying to brush up his thoughts a little. He opened his first bottle of vodka and was about to make a sip when he remembered something. His laptop was still in his bag, and there he had all his work – everything he'd written in the past three or four years. It was the real history, which would be very much uncalled for in the current situation, but hopefully crucial for the future, and he had to do something to it right now, before they break the door and confiscate his things. He opened his bag and took out the laptop and then went on rummaging through its contents. His keys, a packet of cigarettes, a couple of lollipops, workbooks and assignments of his students, which he was supposed to have checked ages ago, Borya's drawing… Where the heck was it? He finally felt a small rectangular object under his fingers and pulled it out. The memory card looked old and dirty, with all the small crumbs and tobacco pieces stuck to it, but it was the only one he had now. The professor inserted it into his computer and waited. "Work, please, please work!" he prayed. Finally, the file manager opened, and the card was recognized. Vladimir Ivanovich carefully selected all necessary files and started the copying process. It was supposed to take about two minutes, and while it was running, he could finally get his hands on the vodka.

"Grampeeee…" came from behind the door. It was Borya, who'd woken up and first thing went to check on his grandfather. "Grampy, are you there? Where've you been?"

"Nowhere, Borya, I'm sort of busy now, okay?"

"Okay…"

It was silent for a while, and Vladimir Ivanovich thought that his grandson had left. He grabbed the bottle again.

"Grampeee? Can I come in?"

"I said I'm busy, Boris. We'll play later, okay?"

"Okay… Can I show you something?"

"What? Not now, let me just…"

But it was too late. Borya's head was already in the room. Fortunately, the copying was finished, and Vladimir Ivanovich quickly ran the hard disk formatting.

"So, young man, what do you want?" Vladimir Ivanovich pretended to be arranging something on his table.

"I wanted to tell you something. And to show you my drawing," Borya was wearing nothing but his torn underpants with a picture of an anchor on the front, and holding a piece of paper.

"Go ahead then, chubs, tell me!"

"Yesterday mum was really angry. She didn't let us watch TV because there was this show on… I don't know, a sort of important speech or something. So we had to switch to the First National and wait for it, and before it they were showing people… women dancing, all dressed in white, and then a man in black came and seized one of them. It was boring, but mum said no Fidgy Freckles, and that's it. She said the dance was called 'The Lake of the Swans' and it was supposed to be beautiful, but to me it was really scary," Borya paused and looked at his grandfather.

"I see. And what happened next?" asked Vladimir Ivanovich.

"Then after the speech mum started crying, I don't know why, and Nastya cried too, and then mum… she called you on the phone, but you didn't answer, and they cried even more, both of them. I didn't cry because I'm a big boy. I tried to talk to mum, tell her it's going to be okay, but she pushed me and said we're all dead now. I didn't believe her, how can we be dead?" Borya gave his grandfather a disarmingly gullible and insecure stare, and Vladimir Ivanovich was suddenly overwhelmed with a wave of tenderness towards this little blue-eyed boy.

"Of course, we can't chubs. We're here, safe and sound, and no one is going to die, I promise."

"That's good because I was a bit scared when mum said that. So, you wanna know what happened next?"

"Sure!"

"Okay, so I switched on to Fidgy Freckles, and you know what? There was a new episode of Doctor Easemypain! You remember, the one who treats animals?"

"Yes, and who did he treat now?"

"I drew it for you, Grampy! I wanted you to watch the episode with me, but you weren't there. And I thought I'd draw it, so that you could see it too."

"Can I have a look?" Vladimir Ivanovich stretched his hand and took the drawing. "Oh, it so beautiful! What is it? Okay, let me guess… It's a… horse?"

"It's a butterfly, Grampy," said Boris with obvious resentment. "Actually, it's supposed to be a moth, but I thought I'd better make it a butterfly, 'coz I don't know how to draw moths. It was purple, but I don't have purple, so I colored it brown. That's why it may look a bit like a horse to you."

"And what was its problem? Why did it go… did it fly to Doctor Easemypain?"

"It burned its wings on the sun. It flew to the sun because it was so bright and warm but it came so close that its wings caught fire!"

"Oh, did they? How sad! Did Doctor Easemypain cure the poor moth?"

"He did. He made new wings from petals, and they were purple, too, just like the real ones. And then he stitched the petals to the moth's body. I guess it was painful, but the moth didn't cry or anything. And when he was finished, he said…" Borya made his voice lower to sound like a real doctor and continued. "I help you now, silly insect, but next time don't you come close to the sun, or it will… it will… BURN YOU WHOLE!!!" He shouted and made a scary face and then laughed at his own performance, urging his grandfather to do the same. Vladimir Ivanovich smiled, took Borya on his lap and patted him on his head.

"So, what do you think, Grampy? Do you like my drawing? See, here is the butterfly, and the sun, and its wings burning. And it's crying: 'Oh, I'm weak and I am sick, help me, someone, help me quick!' Do you think it'll fly to the sun again?"

"Maybe yes. Moths always fly to the light, you see. It sort of attracts them, and there's nothing they can do about it."

"And they really burn to ashes?"

"Well, some of them do."

"That's bad…"

"No, it isn't. I guess it's their life. Their destiny, so to speak."

"Their… what?"

"Fate… Never mind. Look what I've got for you, chubs," he took out one of the toy elephants and handed it to the kid.

"Grampy! Did you buy me an elephant?! A real elephant?" he was totally blown away.

"Well, it's not real, of course. You see, it's hard to get hold of a real elephant these days. But it can do something. Press on its head and see what happens."

Borya pressed, but nothing happened. He pressed again, but the animal refused to make even a slightest sound.

"Weird… I thought I checked it," Vladimir Ivanovich looked puzzled and distressed. "Oh, perhaps the other one… the one I bought for Nastenka…"

The other one worked perfectly. It sang a happy song two times and went silent, gaping at its new owner with curiosity and respect.

"Do you want to keep it? The good one, I mean."

"I don't know, Grampy," said Borya thoughtfully. "Nastya will be sad, and she'll start crying again. And anyway, I think I'll twist its head off and see what's wrong. Maybe I'll even mend it, I can fix all sorts of things, you know, because I'm… how's that called…?"

"Handy?"

"Yeah, that's it! So can I take the broken one?"

"If you want so, chubs. Look, I'm kind of tired. It's been a long day for me. I think, I'll take a little nap now, and, by the way, I can smell pancakes from the kitchen, so you'd better hurry before they're all eaten up."

"Okay, Grampy!"

"And don't forget to take the elephants and teach Nastya how to make hers sing!"

"I will! And you know what? I'll make another picture for you. I'll draw this sad man I saw on TV yesterday. Is he good?"

"Very good, chubs!"

"When I saw him, I had this name in my head… I'll call him Beetlefly, ok?"

"Beetlefly? Why?"

"Because he looked like that moth with burned wings. But he's not a moth, nor a butterfly, so let him be Beetlefly, so that Doctor Easemypain could come and mend him!" Borya laughed again, and skipped out of the room, waiving his drawing cheerfully.

After he had left, the professor took a generous gulp of vodka and started doing things. First of all, he hid the memory card with his work deep in his nightstand and made sure his laptop was clear.

After that, he took out one of his travelling trunks and put some things essentials there, in case of an unforeseen flee. Finally, he called the bank and froze all his accounts. He had some cash stored for a rainy day, so he could use it now, and later withdraw all his money from the bank and, probably, buy some precious metal on it. He knew that every change in state power was always accompanied by a collapse of the national currency, and he couldn't afford to lose any of it now. When all was done, he drank another glass, took a piece of some student's assignment and began to write on its back. The plan had to start somewhere, and first thing to do was to separate real officials from the images, which merely acted as a background, created information noise and dissipated people's attention. He remembered Malinin's last words: "Vladimir Ivanovich, look closely at their mouths. The models have artificial movements of lips, as if their faces are torn apart. Speech is a complicated process, which involves different groups of muscles, as well as eye expressions and emotions, which are hard to make plausible, even for an unsophisticated viewer. Mind the fact that models hardly ever appear on the screen in close up, and when they do, they are either silent, or their mouth is blocked by something – a mask, a microphone – anything. Their smile will also be unnatural." These were the former President's last words, and this was the last time Rogov saw him. Next day, when Malinin gave his final speech on TV, transferring his office to the interim Head of State, he was wearing a protective medical mask, which was later explained by the new virus he'd caught while travelling to the border with North Crestland. It looked like the President's eyes were painted above the mask, and they didn't have any human expression, apart from cold ruthless detachment.

By five o'clock in the evening, the professor had finished his vodka and was so drunk that he could hardly think. He closed the curtains so that the summer sun didn't disturb him and drifted off even without unmaking his bed. He dreamt of moths. and elephants, and an unknown beetlefly. While he was unconscious, Alina let inside the flat two military men dressed in civvies. They took the professor's computer 'for security reasons', but somehow didn't notice the piece of paper on his desk – a student's assignment, which, if flipped to the other side, contained the outlines of the newborn plan of resistance. War had begun.

Vladimir Ivanovich decided not to open the second bottle until his battle was won. He needed a clear head now – the clearer the better. He contacted his former associates – the ones he'd known from the times of Malinin's revolution. They responded very differently: some were reluctant and pessimistic, some preferred to wait and see "how Pravdin presents himself" but some were completely aware of the situation and realized that if they didn't act now, they would not have another chance later. There were about ten of them at first, but Rogov was sure that he could trust every person in his new team like he could trust himself. They started working on the list of officials, watching hundreds of TV broadcasts and putting a minus (model), a plus (real) and a question mark (not sure) in front of every name. 'Minuses' didn't bother Vladimir Ivanovich, 'question marks' could be left for later, and 'pluses' had to be considered in great detail and, eventually, destroyed. At the same time, Malinin's Team (a name they unanimously voted for at their first meeting) started mustering in new members, keeping in mind that they had to do it very thoroughly and meticulously because in the current situation anyone might turn out to be a traitor. In the first place, they were interested in those who were close to the government and to the army, but unhappy with Pravdin grabbing the power, and ready to retaliate.

Meanwhile, the situation in the country was getting more and more complicated. The election had been long since passed, and Pravdin had taken his rightful presidential position. All independent media were either closed or forced to change their course. Thousands of people were deprived of offices, and the ones who disagreed were proclaimed foreign agents, sent to prison for spreading false information and abusing people's trust. The new war with North Crestland and some of its allies was in full swing, and every day models of 'honest' presenters and influential analytics (also models, for most part) abducted public opinion from the citizens, devoured it and spit it back in their faces, digested by the stinky gastric juice of propaganda. Courtrooms were filled with new defendants and booked well in advance but still, they couldn't accommodate everyone. For this reason, some of the trials had to be held right inside penal colonies, behind the bars, and all the judges had the same face, which had nothing to do with the face of Themis.

Strangely enough, Malinin's Team was relatively safe for the time being. There were some odd detentions, and a few members were questioned by the police, but since there was no direct evidence of their involvement in extremist actions, they didn't receive any severe punishment. Rogov regarded it as a sign to move on and proceed with the final step – taking out the weapon. He already had a list of the real men of power – the people behind this masquerade, the ministers of the god of greediness, each of whom had to be destroyed completely, so that they never emerge again. Little did he know that this power was undestroyable, and he could just as well be fighting with the air, the sun, or the moon. This power was going to seize him too, of course, but not until it sucked out all his blood and poured it straight into the Hydra's mouth, which would swallow it and go on celebrating another victory of its humble servants. The god of greediness would be delighted this time, there was no doubt in that.

The professor had this odd, annoying habit of writing down all his actions and plans, and since his laptop had been confiscated, he had to use a desktop computer in one of the university's offices. It wasn't safe, however, and he was looking for an assistant who could take up an IT part of the Team's business. The person had to be as reliable as clockwork and able to keep secrets, and for quite a while Rogov couldn't come up with the right candidate. He thought and thought about it and suddenly remembered one of his former students – a young man in thick glasses whom he considered weird and a bit out of this world. The guy had already had two higher educations, one of which was in IT security and another one in radio electronics, and while studying history at Rogov's faculty, he was attending another course in computer networks. It seemed like he was learning for the sake of learning, and nothing interested him more than shoving another bulk of information into his head. His name was Konstantin, and when Rogov called him to hint on possible cooperation, he accepted the offer because it could provide him with an opportunity to put the knowledge into practice. Very soon Kostya proved to be a god damn genius in IT and technology. As someone from the Team said of him, he could program the sun to rise on the west, and find a needle in the haystack using nothing but his mobile phone. The professor was more than happy about it and entrusted him to assemble a new machine, which they could use in their headquarters. The computer had to be protected like a fortress, both from the inside and outside attacks, and Kostya started working on it in his measured and accurate manner, carefully selecting the hardware and then installing his self-designed software on it.

Everything looked perfect, and Vladimir Ivanovich was feeling lifted up, anticipating the coming collapse of the government. However, at one point, he was contacted by some Uncle Gena, a person from the army, who was strongly opposed to giving his real name and mentioning it even in their own records. He was the most secret member of Malinin's Team, and he had very good reasons for it. The army forces were being reformed at that time, with only the most reliable men admitted, and each of them would have been immediately executed at any sign of treachery. Uncle Gena didn't appear on any of the meetings of the Team, and hardly ever called them, only on business of extreme importance. So when Rogov received his call, he understood that it was something serious. Gena was brief.

"You'd better take precautions," he said. "There's a rumor going inside our ranks of a forthcoming revolution or something. You might have a rat inside your team. I don't think he's been able to get much so far, but he'll do it sooner or later if you don't stop him straight away."

The professor already knew it. Just about two weeks before the call, Konstantin had found a strange radio transmitting card in one of the slots of their new computer in the headquarters and had instantly reported it to the leaders. Since the computer had been assembled and configured by Konstantin quite recently, not much of the data could have leaked out, but the fact itself meant that the Hydra's tentacles had finally been able to reach Malinin's Team. They found the traitor eventually and stopped him, but who could be sure that he was the only one?

The situation started going out of control with every passing day. Referring to unprecedented threats to security, the government imposed a curfew from seven p.m. to seven a.m. and canceled all public events and gatherings. Then they stopped playing footsie with the opposition and adopted a number of laws, which was supposed to finalize the issue of freedom and justice in the country. Those who dared to say at least a word contradictory to the state doctrine, were immediately proclaimed extremists and foreign agents, which was actually their sentence of long-term imprisonment. The wheels of the law enforcement institutions were spinning at a breakneck speed, and a new devastating wave of arrests swept the country. At the same time, people started leaving Malinin's Team. Some of them were afraid to go to jail, others weren't sure that, being interrogated, they would not spill the beans and thus reveal the whole organization. In any case, they were all sorry, but their sorrow meant nothing to Vladimir Ivanovich, who knew that it would be impossible to find new associates under the current circumstances. Despite all those difficulties, he didn't want to give up. He kept on thinking about the ways to keep his unborn brainchild alive, and he did it over and over again, until his head was about to explode. His stayed up at nights, he hardly ate anything and literally looked like a rogue bear woken up in the middle of the winter.

The last gathering of the Team was the longest in its short history. They sat in a half-dark room in the same abandoned boiler house in the outskirts of the city and tried to be invisible there because there was a curfew, and everyone was supposed to stay at home. Needless to say, they were all scared to death. They had a decision to make, a plan which would mean their tactical retreat, but not a surrender. It was a hard move for the professor because the whole idea of retreat was not in his nature, and the plan was so bald and farfetched that it seemed almost impossible to fulfill. However, it was the only thing they could do, and every one of the remaining members of the Team took over a small piece of this plan, and they decided to put it into final action when the situation was at its worst.

"Kostya," said Vladimir Ivanovich, "switch it on when you get a message from Uncle Gena. It will say 'Grandfather arrived safe. Don't forget to water his flowers'. It will mean that I'm dead. It will mean that this is the only hope left."

In the morning, when the curfew was over, they all went their own way, agreeing never to meet again until they get the good or the bad news. Everyone knew what to do now, and that was supposed to keep them busy, distracted from what was going to inevitably happen to them. Their only aspiration at that moment was to have enough time to finish it. In a fortnight, Rogov got a signal from Kostya that the technical part was ready. Now it all had to be finalized right there, in the university park, where it had all begun. The professor wanted to do it himself, not entrusting this business to anyone else. Next day he sat at his desk for the whole afternoon and stared at the wall, trying to collect the last bits of common sense that he had left. He knew that he was being followed, and he had to act very cautiously not to fail the mission. Rogov left his home at about five o'clock, two hours before the curfew, and went to the nearest penny store with his old grocery bag. He put the bag with his mobile phone into a checkroom and resolutely entered the shop. Trying not to attract too much attention, Vladimir Ivanovich looked around and noticed his followers – one of them stood at the entrance, and another one started browsing something on the shelf. The professor filled his shopping basket with some unnecessary stuff and stood in line at the checkout. The stalkers were at their places – one inside the shop, and another one at the door. Rogov tried to look natural and took over an expression of extreme concentration. Then he suddenly put down his basket, took a small bar of chocolate from the counter, put it in his pocket and headed to the exit. As it was expected, the theft detector at the door went off, and the alarm sounded like music to the professor's ears. Two guards quickly turned up, pushing back the stalker at the door, took Rogov under his shoulders and conducted him to the security room.

"So, old faggot, you gonna pay or what?" inquired one of the guards in the usual manner of people in power.

"I'd like, sir, but I'm afraid I can't," responded Vladimir Ivanovich. "You see, it's for my grandson. I've lost my job at the university, so I'm sort of bankrupt. I thought this little sweet will cheer up my junior. Is it a problem?"

"A huge one!" nodded the second guard. "Do you think you can go on stealing things from shops only because you're old and dumb? Take out your money!"

"I told you, I've got no cash on me right now, sir," said Vladimir Ivanovich humbly.

"Okay then. Do you want the police to deal with it?"

"If you say so…"

The police were called, and Rogov insisted on drawing up a protocol before they issue a fine. He read everything carefully again and again, looking for grammar and spelling mistakes, and finally insisted on rewriting it.

"You missed three commas, spelled 'embezzlement' with one 'z', got the wrong address of the shop and, to top it all, never read me my Miranda rights. Protocols with mistakes, for your information, have no legal force. No, I won't sign it."

The protocol was finally written correctly and thrown in the professor's face. He only hoped that by the time he'd finished putting his signatures in the required fields, his followers would have gone, or at least would have lost his track. Finally, he took the ticket, which had to be paid in two weeks, and headed to the door.

"Where are you going, dumbass?" stopped him the guard. "The shop's closed, idiot! It's already half six, or you haven't heard of curfew?"

"So, what should I do now?"

"Squeeze your old dumb ass through the back door, of course. And make it quick before I call the cops again to arrest you for violating the regime!"

That was exactly what Rogov wanted. He had another thirty minutes to finish his plan and return home by seven. When the guard wasn't looking, he took an orange vest worn by supermarket internal staff and at the back door grabbed an empty box to make him look like a loader. With all these things, he quickly walked away, leaving behind his grocery bag in the checkroom locker with his mobile phone inside it, hopefully transmitting its location to the right people. Then he threw away the box and the vest in the nearest garbage container and ran towards the university park. The professor kept watching for his followers, but they weren't there. He couldn't believe how smoothly it all had gone, and, again, considered it a lucky omen.

Back at home, Vladimir Ivanovich kidnapped Nastya's elephant and spent another forty minutes with it, cursing his clumsy arthritic fingers, which couldn't even manage a needle. Then he invited his daughter for a walk to the hill near their house because it wasn't safe to discuss anything inside the flat. He told her everything about how he had spent the last thirteen months, ready to listen to all her cries and pleas, but being firm and cool. "It had to be done, sweetheart," he explained, "and it seems that it could only be done by me. I had no other choice." He told Alina to collect their emergency bags and keep them at hand and gave her a small piece of paper with a plan, developed by Uncle Gena. The plan had to be memorized, so that even woken up in the middle of the night she could easily remember and follow it. Provided they did exactly what Uncle Gena had told them, their family would be safe and in time forgotten, and they would be able to start a new life in North Crestland, where Uncle Gena had some close contacts.

Professor Rogov felt that he was ready to face anything that the State had in store for him. He had gone through denial, then he managed to cope with anger, after which bargaining and depression followed, and, finally, he came to the stage of acceptance, when the only thing he could do was wait and hope, and pray that they'd be merciful to the old man and kill him at once, without their usual tortures and harassment. However, nothing happened. Nothing at all. A month went by, and then another one, but no one broke into their flat shouting "Hands in the air!" Every morning Rogov woke up feeling that this might be his last day, but then evening came, and he went to bed wondering what the hell was going on. He hadn't heard from his colleagues from Malinin's Team, and even Kostya had disappeared and didn't answer the phone. Vladimir Ivanovich thought that the forces were just busy with something more important than himself – an old fool, a clown, who could not even make the most unpretentious audience laugh. Yes, he was a fool to believe the words of some mysterious Uncle Gena, who might just as well be a rat, too. He should have listened to his own heart, follow his own internal voice, his gut feeling, which had never failed him before. If only he hadn't let himself be led by the others, who, in their turn had been driven by fear and despair! They might be already celebrating their victory! However, he was wrong. Neither he, nor his Team had been left unattended.

One clammy November morning Professor Vladimir Ivanovich Rogov received a call on his secret phone.

"It's Gennadiy. They are coming. You have about twenty minutes or even less. Get your grandson ready. I'll be there too, but I'm too far away, so I might not make it on time. Tell him to wait for me. Get the others out – they'll receive their tickets at the station, as agreed."

He hangs up. Vladimir Ivanovich feels that he can't breathe, but somehow it doesn't bother him at all. He runs to his daughter's room and fortunately finds her and the kids there. He grabs her hand and throws her the emergency bags. Nastya cries. Borya looks at him with his big foggy eyes, and the TV plays a happy children's song: "We're happy all together, if we want, we'll make a ladder, it'll take us very high, we can even touch the sky."

"Allie, grab the bags and Nastya, quickly! There's no time for crying!" the professor's voice is hoarse and shaking. "Call Andrey to the hospital on your way, tell him to catch up with you at the station. No, Boris stays here, he'll be safer with our Team, I promise. He'll reunite with you in North Crestland in a couple of days. Go, go, go, they're coming!"

As the door closes behind them, Rogov turns to Boris, hugs him and speaks, speaks quickly, speaks right in his ear.

"Listen here, chubs, listen carefully. Soon there'll be men here, they might look scary, but try not to be afraid. We'll play a game called 'Who kills who first'. I'm sure they'll be the first to kill me, but remember, it's just a game. And you'll have to play with these men, too. The game will be called run-hide-and-seek. You'll have to run and hide, Borya, you hear me, run and hide, and those men will look for you, so do your best. Run as fast as you can, until Uncle Gena comes for you. When he comes – the game is over. Uncle Gena is good; he'll be with you… instead of me… Do you understand me? Wait, take these with you – your elephant and our favorite book. Look at them and listen to me, it's very important. Remember, Borya, please remember one thing. It all starts inside the elephant's head. Look in the radiator! The radiator, you hear me? And now I'm gonna tell you something else, something I'll never be able to say to you in person. I don't know what happens, what will come of you. But I hope, I really hope that one day in your long and happy life… (the door breaks open) … in your happy life… I'll find a way to come to you from the past… (there are four men in the corridor with sidearms in their hands) Go under the sofa, Borya, quick! I'll come to you from the past… ("Everybody down, hands behind your head!" Borya is under the sofa and can't hear his words). And I'll tell you that…"

Shot. And another one. And the final – terminal.

Chapter 6. Scattered memories

... that you've become a great artist, Boris."

"It is twenty-one thirty, and you are on the First National. Here is the last news report for today. Starting with tonight's headlines. President Pravdin, after long negotiations, signed an agreement, with…"

"Shut up!" Boris said it so loudly that he started at his own voice. "Shut up, please", he whispered, his hands at his mouth. But the broadcaster continued.

"President Pravdin, after long negotiations, signed an agreement, with the Secretary General of the Republic of Cobrain…"

The broadcaster didn't lie this time. There was really an agreement with the Republic of Cobrain, which required very long negotiations and meant a lot to both sides.

President Pravdin stood up from the long wooden table and walked to the exit, followed by a tall slender man with beady little rat eyes. They walked together in silence for a while, and then Pravdin inserted an automatic translator into his ear, and his companion did the same.

"So… When are we supposed to get the first tranche?" asked Pravdin.

"In three months," answered the tall man. "Or maybe even earlier. It depends on the situation in the…"

"Three months looks fine for me," interrupted him Pravdin. "You can start the delivery on the first of November. Now tell me, colleague. This… let us call it 'cargo'. How poisonous is it?"

"Poisonous!?" cried the man. "It's deadly! It's like… like a small nuclear explosion. I mustn't say that, but it'll be disastrous for the region where you're going to bury it, and not only for it. When the vapors condense in clouds, they'll sweep the country, causing illnesses and deaths, especially in young children. And even your so-called lockdown won't help."

"I know", answered Pravdin coldly.

"But still, you… What's your name, by the way?"

"Leonid. But please call me Victor. I've already got used to it in these… let me see… five years already."

"So, Victor, are you not afraid to stay here? Your land is becoming a nuclear polygon, a 'ticking bomb' if I may put it like this."

"Well, that's part of my job. It was in my contract. I'll have to play Pravdin for at least two more years, and then I'll give this place to another lucky man. I already have a nice little nest egg, in the south, where I'll spend the rest of my life. The climate here is literally killing me. Giving me backaches an all these colds. Do you know how Pravdin the fourth died, by the way?"

"No… How?"

"Well, then I'd better not spare it to you. I can only say that he was too persistent. Didn't want to make a clean break. Killed by his own stubbornness in the end of the day. The idea is that you mustn't stay in this country for too long. It's toxic. and when I say 'toxic', I mean something way more dangerous than just radiation, colleague."

"But what about your people? Are you prepared to lose them?"

"My people? Oh, you mean, citizens? Let me answer your question by posing another one. What do *you* think about it? How do *you* feel now when you've just signed a contract that will turn dozens of acres of land into a nuclear waste site? Do you like the way your signature looks on the death warrant of those whom you call 'my people'?"

"I think it's none of my business," The Secretary General of the Republic of Cobrain said quietly.

"It's none of mine either," answered Pravdin. "Actually, it's not so bad, so, please, don't feel too guilty about it. The citizens - they're resilient, like cockroaches. They will survive dozens of such 'cargos'. They already have, in case you didn't know."

"How did you manage it? They seem to eat what they're given, even if it's slop!"

"Manage? Me? I didn't manage anything. It's pure luck – slavish people on the land of treasures. They're just born with obedience, I believe."

"All of them?"

"Ninety-nine point nine per cent. Approximately."

"And the remaining tenth of the precent?"

"It's insignificant. And, anyway, they get their injection of slavery sooner or later. We don't really bother with them nowadays. So, back to business. I strongly recommend you ensure that we get the tranche not later than in three months. Otherwise, we'll be forced to give this location, this polygon, to a more interested party. I still have a pending agreement with Pearland, as a matter of fact," Pravdin gave his companion an eloquent stare and cleared his throat. The thin man nodded and looked away.

"And now to the situation in North Crestland," announced the broadcaster. "The latest events show that the country is still not ready for any negotiations with the Commonwealth State. Instead of accepting our terms, or offering its own way out of crisis, it keeps slinging mud on our land and its people, both literary and figuratively. The latest findings on the liberated territories prove that not less than twenty terrorist attacks were planned on our major cities. Our reporter Rudolph Chaika on the situation on the border…"

Boris covered his ears not to listen to the shrill voice of the presenter. Grandfather wrote that he was planning to smuggle his family to North Crestland and keep them safe there. What if they are still alive? He remembered how eager he was to go to war and fight with the Crestlanders, and he was horrified at the thought that he might have fought with his kith and kin. "We're not even pawns in their big game," he thought. "We're nothing. Rubbish. A shallow pool of mud."

Now he could remember it all. That clammy November morning, mum didn't go for a walk with his sister and himself because both of them had runny noses. Dad was at work, as usual, and grandfather didn't want to play, so he just sat on the floor and watched cartoons. He even remembered that song, coming from TV – it played in his head the whole day afterwards: "We're happy all together, if we want, we'll make a ladder, it'll take us very high, we can even touch the sky," and then the horror-stricken look in his mother's eyes, and the crying of his little sister. He remembered all the three shots, and how he ran headlong outside, away from his dead Grampy. He had to stay in a police station for the rest of the day, where he was placed in a tiny windowless room with only a gray table and a lonely hard chair as furniture. He sat on the chair and looked at the wall. It was painted blue, but it was not the blue of the sky, but rather the blue of death, and fear, and loss. He put is arms on the table and is head on top of them because he was finding it hard to hold it straight. When he was about to close is eyes, the door opened, and a woman in police uniform entered the room.

"So, you're Rogov's grandson?" she asked.

Borya was drowsy and didn't feel like speaking, but he lifted his head and nodded because he was afraid of the woman's uniform.

"You don't wanna talk to me?" she looked him in the eye and it was impossible to tell whether she was sorry for him or was going to interrogate him. "Well, maybe you want to draw? Here, I've brought you some paper and a pencil. You can draw anything, okay?"

Borya shook his head. The woman placed a sheet of paper and a black pencil in front of him and bent to catch his look. Then she walked away, and he heard the key turning in the lock. He took the paper. One side of it was clear, and on the opposite side there were some words, two signatures at the bottom and a big blue stamp. The pencil was very sharp and made a nice thin line, which somehow made Borya feel better. He knew what to draw and it took him about fifteen minutes to finish. It was Doctor Easemypain stitching back the wings to the poor moth. The moth was lying on the ground with its eyes open and its left leg twisted in a strange and unnatural way. Easemypain was holding a long needle, which actually looked like a gun, and he was pointing it right at the moth. But it didn't scare Boris at all. He knew that Doctor was kind and sympathetic, and he always helped the poor and the sick, so he'd find a way to make everything right again.

In about an hour the key clanged in the lock, and the same woman entered the room. She saw the drawing and took it, but then she frowned and put it back on the table again.

"Look," she said in a very low voice. "I'm sorry about what happened to you family and your grandfather. And I see that you are a big and brave boy! That's good, but, you know, big boys also cry sometimes. So, if you want to cry, it's okay, I won't tell anyone. I have a son just your age, so I know what I'm talking about. Can I keep your picture? Will you give it to me?"

Borya sighed. He didn't want to cry, and he didn't want to give his Doctor Easemypain to this scary woman, but he knew he'd better not argue with her in this place where she was the boss. She folded the drawing and put it in her pocket. "Report on the interrogation of the suspect, Nadezhda Vasilievna Komissarova," was written on the opposite side.

The woman went away and never came back. No one else did, and no one gave Borya anything to eat, and he felt that he desperately wanted to pee, but he was afraid to knock at the locked door and ask to go to out. Finally, in the evening, Uncle Gena arrived, gave him a bottle of water and a packet of peanuts, and after Borya had finished them, he accompanied him to the toilet. Then Uncle Gena took Borya by the hand and led him out of the police station. They walked a couple of blocks to the car. The city was silent because of the curfew, and they didn't say a word to each other, only the sound of their footsteps echoed against the asphalt, wet from recent rain. Borya didn't know how long they were driving, time was now something out of his perception, but finally the car stopped, and they got out. He saw a three-floor building with dark windows and his lips started to tremble. Uncle Gena looked at him without any sign of sympathy, still holding his hand tight.

"If they ask you about your family, tell them you don't remember. Got it?"

Borya didn't answer.

"I said, got it?" repeated Uncle Gena and squeezed his shoulder. There was no effect. "Say it, kid! I don't remember!"

"I wanna go home…"

"This is your home for now, okay? And don't fool around with me here! Repeat after me: I… don't… remember. That's easy!"

"Where's mummy?"

"She's ok. And your father, and your sister, they're all fine. But from now on, you don't remember them, or you'll end up like your grandfather. And I'll end up like him, too."

Borya finally burst in tears.

"Stop it!" Uncle Gena gave him a jolt. "You'll be ok, if you just listen to me! I! Don't! Remember! Say it! Now!"

"I don't… remember…"

"Good. Now if anyone in this world – even me – asks you about your folks, you must answer as I've taught you. So, where's your family?"

"Is Grampy dead?"

"Where is your family!"

"I don't remember…"

"Perfect. We're almost there now. When you're inside, there'll be this woman, Lyudmila Ivanovna. Try to stick to her – she'll help when she can. I'll leave you here so that they don't see us together. Just a precaution. Ring this bell and they'll open eventually. There will be a security guard at the entrance, tell him who you are, and he'll call the supervisor. Oh, I almost forgot. Here's your book and your… toy. Take them, with you, although I'm sure they'll be confiscated. So… It won't be a pleasure cruise for you, kid, not at all, but, hopefully, it'll make you stronger, fitter for what awaits you in the future. I'll catch up with you later, kid, much later, so please try to make it through the next ten years or so. And you have to be as good as your grandfather said you are. You're part of Malinin's Team, after all. Shouldn't have said that, I guess…You can go now, Boris Arsenyev. I've done everything I could for the time being. For you, and for… Never mind. So, are you sure you don't remember your family?"

"I don't… I guess…"

"Go then. Good luck. Good goddamn luck to you!"

Eventually, they opened. And there was this woman, who first took away his things, but then stuck the book under his pillow, and he was lying there, in the dormitory, surrounded by identical shortly cut heads, but still all alone, trying to close his eyes and dissolve in the stinky enveloping darkness.

"The National Network will be disabled from 22:00 until 6:00", said the broadcaster. "Please make sure your home is safe. Have a pleasant night rest. Informing citizen Boris Arsenyev, internal number 152-AH1021, that today's identification procedure has been missed. To avoid penalty, make sure it is undergone tomorrow. According to the regulations, only two absences from the procedure a month are allowed."

2

Boris didn't know how much of his grandfather's message was left and he wasn't sure whether he'd be able to finish reading it in the morning, after the electricity is turned on. He remembered that he hadn't received his grocery set, and wondered if Slava had kept it for him or thrown it away, which was more like is neighbor. Boris thought about the message. It was obvious that the main information was in the second part, and it would be another eye-opener for him, maybe even more than what he'd read today. With these heavy thoughts he could barely sleep. He forced his eyes to close and lay still for a very long time, and when he was just about to pass out, he felt a punch from inside, and all his sleepiness was gone. It happened two or three times, before, at last, his body surrendered and was able to relax. Although his overloaded mind couldn't produce any dreams, he slept restlessly, tossing and turning under his dusty blanket.

When Katyusha woke him up at six o'clock, he switched on his calculating machine at once to see if the letters were still there. They were, and they looked at him invitingly from the screen, but he decided to take his time and have a snack first. He even thought he might not read it at all and just try to live with the information he'd got so far, but he was also curious to find out the ending of the story. So, in this case, the best option was to take a little break, and nothing made waiting as enjoyable as food did. There was no movement in his neighbors' room, which was a good sign, and he quietly sneaked into the bathroom, and then crawled to the kitchen. His grocery set number three was on the table, obligingly collected by Slavik, and only upon seeing it, Boris realized how hungry he was. He opened the bag and started chewing on turnip chips with third-category bread, classified as standard. Luckily, there was a pot of fresh water saved from yesterday evening, and the stove was turned on, so he made himself a nice hot omlette from powder and a delicious cup of coffee from condensed coffee drink. Breakfast wasn't bad at all, although, as usual, Boris got an annoying heavy pain in his solar plexus while his stomach was trying to digest the food.

There was no water to wash the dishes with, so he just threw them into the sink and started putting the remains of the grocery set back into the bag, imagining that today he'd be able to combine them with the new delivery and have a double dinner in the evening. While doing this, Boris noted to himself that it had been quite a while since he'd last seen dried fruit in the package. Probably Yegor Semenovich's apple trees had finally been destroyed, or just stopped producing fruit for this unholy land and its people. Yegor Semenovich himself had long been dead now, and Juliana Pavlovna had left life even earlier. She was a staunch woman and never complained, until one day she simply couldn't make herself get out of bed.

It was in the summer of 2065, and everything went as usual, until one day the old lady didn't come out for an identification procedure. Yegor Semenovich stood in the kitchen all alone, confused and very frightened, like a small child who had lost a parent in a department store.

"Old girl," he explained, "she's unwell, I think. Says, her legs are numb. Is it something to worry about?"

"No, no," Boris tried to reassure his neighbor. "Such things happen at her age. Might be the weather or the pressure. Let her rest and see how she feels tomorrow."

But the next day nothing changed. Yegor Semenovich seemed even more worried and depressed.

"It's never happened before," he shrugged his shoulders. "Maybe I should call the self-aid?"

"That sounds sane", answered Boris, although he wasn't sure it would help. He went to the neighbors' room to see if things were as bad as Yegor Semenovich said they were.

Juliana Pavlovna was lying in bed under a light synthetical blanket, and although it was quite hot, she was shaking like a leaf.

"Basil is that you?" she said in a feeble voice. "Sit down, sonny, I want to tell you something."

"I'm Boris, Ma'am," he wasn't sure he should have said that, and he wasn't sure he should sit down.

"Oh, how stupid of me," the old woman gave a faint apologetic smile, "to forget my own son's name. Come, dear, come closer, let me have a look at you."

Boris looked at Yegor Semenovich questioningly but received no definite answer. Juliana Pavlovna didn't seem to take any notice her husband. She continued.

"It wasn't an easy life for me, sonny, and you probably know it. But I enjoyed every single moment of it because I knew I won't be given another one. And I wouldn't have been so happy if not for you, for my dear family. I remember every little thing that happened to me, and now it's all even clearer in my head: our little flat in the suburbs, our dog, Tresor, and how happily he ran in our 'dacha', the war, the first wave of virus, which killed him as well as other animals, and small children. Our temporary home in the north, and then the new wave of virus and numerous terrorist attacks, bombings, poisonings, chemical weapon. Our moving here, the lockdown, another war, the famine, the cold, the grief. And it was all so quick and scary that I sometimes thought – why? Why was I to spend my only life surviving, being afraid, losing what I cherished most of all? Who or what has done it to me, and who gave them the right to dispose of my fate? But then I thought I should be grateful for having you by my side. My family. My close people. I thank you for all that you've done…" she closed her eyes sunk into her thoughts.

Boris gave Yegor Semenovich another stare and walked to the door. They both stood in the corridor and didn't know what to say.

"So, have you called the self-aid?" asked Boris, trying to make his voice sound as natural as possible.

"They promised to come in the evening."

"Let's wait for what they say. I've heard that now doctors have a cure for almost anything. I'm sure they'll give her a pill or an injection, and she'll be just fine."

Yegor Semenovich nodded dejectedly and went back to his room.

The self-aid didn't come until next morning, and Juliana Pavlovna was almost unconscious by that time.

"Attention please," informed the front door speaker. "Self-aid visiting in process. All present in the premises, please stand back three meters from the door. Warning: according to the Order of the Government Committee of Migration Control, all unauthorized attempts to leave the premises during the unblocking will be suppressed. The door will be unblocked for ten seconds. Starting the countdown. Nine…" The door opened and a short nimble man, aged thirty to fifty, stepped inside. He was holding a shabby leather case with the emblem of a snake spitting venom into a medical vial. "Doctor Easemypain," thought Boris and smiled, because seeing someone who reminded him of his childhood hero made him believe that the situation was under control.

"So…" Doctor Easemypain looked around. "Where?"

"Well, I guess…" mumbled Yegor Semenovich pierced by the eyes of the doctor.

"Is that you who need help?"

"No, my wife… Juliana, so to say… Mikhailova… Pavlovna, I mean."

"Take me to her, then."

Boris wanted to withdraw and tried to quietly retreat in his room or in the kitchen, but the old man looked at him with puppy dog eyes, and he reluctantly followed the doctor. Old girl was lying in bed, her wrinkled fingers holding tight to the thin blanket, and her breath was coming out if her scratchy throat with frightening crackles. The doctor opened his case and took out an automatic health registrator.

"Can you help her stand up?" he asked Boris and Yegor Semenovich

After several unsuccessful attempts to make Juliana Pavlovna stand up or at least sit down, they gave up.

"Okay," said the doctor and gave a cough of annoyance. "Do you think she can hear me?"

Yegor Semenovich shrugged his shoulders.

"Madam! Take a deep breath and try not to move," he pointed the health registrator at Juliana Pavlovna and switched it on. The machine made a beeping noise and started scanning.

"Object: female person. Approximate age: 75. Body structure: regular, proportional. Breathing: relaxed, controlled. No crepitations in lungs detected. Continuing scanning… Heart rate slowed down, with signs of sinus bradycardia. Abdominal organs with foci of inflammation. Free fluid in the pelvis and the abdominal found. Soft tissues with numerous calcifications. Foci of inflammation found in the tibial bones of both legs. Scanning finished."

The doctor put the registrator away and rubbed his hands.

"It's all pretty clear to me," he turned to Yegor Semenovich. "Nothing much to worry about, believe me. The woman will outlast us all. So, these are my recommendations. First, give her enough water to drink. Secondly, make sure she gets plenty of rest. Thirdly, I'll make you a prescription of supportive capsules. If everything goes well, you'll get them with tomorrow's delivery. Questions?"

"Thank you very much, doctor," Yegor Semenovich gasped with relief.

However, Juliana Pavlovna never got the prescribed supportive capsules. She died that night in her sleep, still holding tight to her thin blanket. She might have probably seen Basil before death, and their 'dacha', and the apple trees in full bloom. Yegor Semenovich sat in the kitchen, squeezing an empty aluminum spoon and looking even older and extremely miserable. Boris doubted whether he should disturb him now, but finally decided at least to offer some semblance of consolation.

"Yegor Semenovich, maybe you want a drink? I still have about half the bottle left."

"No, soldier, I don't feel like drinking. It'll get stuck in my throat, I'm sure."

"Do you want to sit in my room?"

"In your room? Okay… Let's sit…"

In Boris's room, Yegor Semenovich got himself seated on the sofa with his head sunk so low upon his chest that it seemed not to belong to him. Boris noticed that he still had his empty spoon in his hand and wondered if he was going to spend the rest of his life with it. After a while, Yegor Semenovich lifted his head and spoke.

"We were almost half a century together, old girl and me. She did everything and never said a word of complaint. How am I supposed to carry on now?" he asked Boris as though his question was not a rhetorical one.

"Yegor Semenovich, just try to calm down a bit. You should wait and let the whole thing go, and you'll see that everything will be fine. I went through it too, and look at me, I'm more than okay now."

"I've not much to live either," stammered the old man. "I'll let them bury her and then I'll go there, too. To the grave, I mean."

"Don't say that! You're completely healthy, and I heard that life expectancy nowadays is increasing. You're in no pain at the moment, so you'll live another ten, twenty or thirty years, I promise!"

"My soul's in pain. Have you heard of it? We think there's nothing inside us, only flesh and bones, but it's there, our soul, I mean. It lives deep inside each one of us – sometimes it rejoices, and sometimes it hurts. Mine hurts now, and when Basil died, it did, too. Well, something like this, soldier, something like this…"

"Yegor Semenovich, do you want to watch the news? Or a show on First National?" Boris had a feeling that his neighbor was going to cry, and he was afraid he'd not be able to do anything about it.

"What do I care about the show! Or the news!" Yegor Semenovich slapped his hand on the sofa, making it spit with dust and musty smell.

"Or, maybe, can I read to you? You know, I have a book, it's nice and funny."

"A book? Where did you get it from? You're not old enough to be able to read, are you?"

"I can! Not too fast, but I can. Do you want me to show it to you?"

Boris took the 'Cock-the-Roach' from under his pillow and handed it to the old man. Yegor Semenovich turned it in his hands and opened it at the front page.

"Your grandfather," he read. "Grandfather, it says. Will you tell me?"

"I told you I don't remember him at all. I was too small when he died."

"Were you sad about it?"

"No, I don't think so. Not much, anyway. He wasn't too fond of me, you know. And he worked all the time, so we hardly ever saw him."

"And your parents? You said they were killed by terrorists?"

"I don't remember this, too. I think, there was an attack. It happened shortly after the Glorious Election, I was six back then. Those terrorists, they just went mad. They kept killing the civilians in their own flats because they wanted to revenge the Destabilizer."

"True," confirmed Yegor Semenovich. "That's how it was."

"So, when they broke into our flat, I managed to escape. I could run quickly, but they almost got me. I was on a hill near the house, and I was scared, and I stood there and cried 'Help me, Pravdin! Save me!' And just at that very moment there was a brave soldier of the National Army, and he killed all the terrorists, every one of them. And the most dangerous terrorist, the scariest one, was shot first, and I saw it with my own eyes. His body was lying there, his leg was twisted, and his eyes were still open, and I will never forget how he looked at me. It was like he wanted to destroy everything around there with that look, and especially me. I'm glad

Pravdin killed him and keeps killing all of them right at the moment they pop up on our territory."

"Serves them right!" Yegor Semenovich nodded approvingly.

Boris went on pulling out of his memory some odd colorful patches, trying to sew them together in a quilt. He tried and tried, but somehow, they didn't match, and the quilt fell apart, so he kept on remembering, although he knew that his neighbor wasn't a good listener at the moment.

"A good terrorist is a dead terrorist, like they say," he concluded finally and looked at Yegor Semenovich.

"Dead, you say," he pronounced slowly. "Like my old girl. So she's dead too. Gotten cold already… Take your book, soldier, I know it. Used to read it to Basil when he was small. He laughed at some elephant and a hedgehog, or whatever…"

"Basil!" Boris smiled. "Yegor Semenovich, let me show you something."

There were still some minutes until the electricity shutdown, so he quickly turned on his calculating machine and commanded it to display the very first image on it, which he'd made upon Juliana Pavlovna's request. She'd asked him to delete it, but he disobeyed, and now he was happy he'd left it in the memory. There was this sparkling snowy hill, and Basil with his mother were standing there, holding hands and looking at each other. Yegor Semenovich stared at the monitor.

"Who's that?" he wondered.

"It's Basil. And your wife. She asked me to make it, as though they were together again."

"No, it's not Basil. He was shorter and kind of stronger. But the old girl looks like herself here. So, there they are now, standing together, hand in hand, on the hill… I like it, the drawing, I mean. It has soul, remember, I told you? You have soul, too, that's what I think. Now, where will they bury her, I wonder? You know what, soldier, pour me a glass. But make it nice and strong, so that it gets straight to my bones."

Boris made a drink for Yegor Semenovich and himself, and they sat in his room until the electricity was turned off, and then, when it got dark, the old man collapsed on the sofa and passed out. Boris didn't want to disturb him and stayed up all night, sitting on his uncomfortable chair, looking at the dead monitor.

Juliana Pavlovna's body was utilized in 48 hours, and after the utilization brigade had left, they finished Boris's bottle of alcohol. Days began to fly, one after another, and at first it was strange not to have a third person in their home. The memory of her, her spirit, remained in the room, and in the kitchen, and Boris could sometimes swear he heard the familiar rattling of pots and pans on the cooker. But then it happened more and more rarely, until, finally, the old lady rested in peace and left them forever. They never played cards anymore because games for two were boring, and they hardly ever spoke about the past because it now belonged to Yegor Semenovich only, and he didn't feel like sharing it with a strange person. Their daily routines changed a bit, too. Boris did all the cooking, but the washing up was often skipped, and they both cleaned the floors now and then. Yegor Semenovich gradually started to cheer up. The first sign of his recovery was that his broadcaster started working again, airing good old news reports and analytical programs. Soon Boris again heard the neighbor's apt remarks on the situation in the country, his cursing of bad guys, his wishing death to North Crestlanders, who wouldn't lay their weapon and surrender to the might of the merciful president.

"Don't they understand that he'd squeeze them like chickens if he wanted?" he shook his fist at the broadcaster. "They have to be grateful, yes, grateful for being alive to this point! Are you with me, old g…" he habitually looked on his left, where Juliana Pavlovna's armchair was standing empty, covered with her thin synthetical blanket.

They got used to this life, and Boris eventually understood that his neighbor would be his only family. He didn't regret it much, he was now too old even for internal matching, and all his life was concentrated on drawing holograms for the Ministry of Defense and for himself once in a while. He could still get a route list two times a month to go out and embrace into the quietness of his home town, and now that he had a lot of drawing tools, he could picture its beauty better than when he was a kid with a handful of broken pencils. Soon he had a cozy collection of landscapes of his own, but there was no one to show them to. The orders from the Ministry of Defense came in regularly, every three or four days, and most of them were of the same type and didn't present any challenge at all. Boris made them automatically, programming the holograms, selecting the right colors and sounds, choosing the proper background and special effects. He was happy working, and even though it was so monotonous, now it was the only thing that made his life worthy. He woke up every morning waiting for a new order, and if he didn't receive it, the whole day went in vain.

But everything comes to the end. In about a year after Juliana Pavlovna's death, Yegor Semenovich came up to Boris with a worried expression on his face. He tilted his head on the left and pointed to a small bump on his neck. Boris felt it, and it was hard like a pea under his fingers.

"Maybe it's foreign agents' microchip? Or a poison capsule?" supposed the old man. "Maybe they inserted it when I was sleeping?"

"Maybe…" Boris wasn't sure but he had no other ideas.

Soon there was another tumor on the other side of the neck, and then another one under the armpit. Boris called the self-aid, and this time Doctor Easemypain was replaced by a woman, not much younger than her patient. She scanned Yegor Semenovich's body and after getting the results, confirmed their assumption that it was a poison capsule, and that it had now spread all over the patient's body, so there was basically nothing to be done with it. However, the doctor prescribed some pills, which arrived in a couple of days, but they didn't make Yegor Semenovich feel any better. He stayed in bed almost all the time, very weak and apathetic, and even the broadcaster didn't interest him at all. Boris had no other options than to nurse his neighbor: change his sweaty linen, feed him with pearl barley porridge, sit beside his bed and listen to his shallow respiration. The tumors were now countless, and some of them were really huge and scary, which made Boris sick at times, although he tried not to show it to the dying man.

Yegor Semenovich passed away in the afternoon, when Boris stepped out to the kitchen for a moment to get him a drink of water. When he came back to the room, the neighbor was already lifeless. Boris stood there with the glass, looking at the breathless body, which he had already taken into his heart, and a crushing flashback hit him so hard that he almost dropped the water. *"You have to run and hide, Borya, you hear me, run and hide…"*

If only he had been able to run. Run and hide from the injustice of this world, where he had been losing every single thing, every single person whom he considered dear. Why was he, himself, still alive, why didn't he follow his family, his fellow comrades, his neighbors? Why was this world, which he'd been so thoroughly putting together all this time, always slipping through his fingers, leaving him nothing but emptiness and grief? And what was he supposed to do now? Report his death to the Self-aid and call the utilization service, of course. It is so plain and obvious – someone is dead, their body should be utilized in 48 hours, their grocery sets are cancelled, and their broadcaster returned to Ministry of Mass Communications. But what about their soul, which Yegor Semenovich was talking about? Is there a special drone, which would carry it to a suitable burial site? Boris knew that there wasn't, and it made him bitter with grief.

In the evening, the food drones delivered two sets number three, which meant that they hadn't received the notice from the Self-aid, and Boris wondered what he should do with Yegor Semenovich's ration. It would be wasteful to leave it there, in the provision point window, or just throw it away, so he decided to take it into his room and wait. Maybe he'd be required to send it back with the next food drones or pay for it and rightfully consume it the following day. Boris made himself a dinner out of his own set and took the other one to his room. There, he put it on the table and set in front of his calculating machine, brooding and intense. Then he loaded his collection of drawings and scrolled to the first one, the one with Juliana Pavlovna and Basil. He took his pen and quickly added another silhouette – an old man in white shirt and sweatpants. They stood on the hill, all the three of them, and the sparkling snow glowed at their feet. "Now they are together," thought Boris and closed the image.

Two weeks after the utilization of Yegor Semenovich body, Boris's broadcaster cheerfully announced that soon he would have other neighbors. "Attention, please. In the next 72 hours, the adjoining premises will be taken by new residents. Please make sure that the room is free from superfluous items and be ready for the unblocking of your entrance door. Warning: according to the Order of the Government Committee of Migration Control, all unauthorized attempts to leave the premises during the unblocking will be suppressed. Wishing you a pleasant joint residence."

At first, Boris was really upset about it because he felt like being all by himself for a while, at least until the memories about Yegor Semenovich became less painful. But then he thought that it might not be as bad as it seemed: rooms were usually given to young families with small children, and he might get a pleasant company to brighten up his life. Boris was sure he'd enjoy spending time with a junior, and they'd find a lot of things in common. He thought he'd finally have someone to read his book to, and maybe he'd even have enough courage to show them his holograms. He still remembered some of the cartoons, which he'd seen on 'Fidgy Freckles', and was more than happy to discuss the braveness of Fabio from Ninja Cats and the devotedness of Doctor Easemypain.

In the evening, Boris started to 'make sure that the room is free from superfluous items.' He collected all the rubbish, dusted the remaining furniture and even thought about washing the floor, but finally decided that it would be too much, considering that he didn't know his future neighbors at all. However, if he had known them, he wouldn't have made even a slightest effort to please the little devils. He'd probably have limited himself to releasing a herd of cockroaches into their room, or preparing a poison capsule, preferably the most lethal and excruciating – the one that would have been perfect for the morons. Boris woke up from his memories.

3

He was there, in 2070, sitting at the kitchen table, munching his yesterday's breakfast. Funny how the food reminded him of good old times, so contrasting to what he was facing now. The flat was still quiet, and he guessed that his neighbors were away – probably they'd received their second monthly permission to go outside and were walking along the empty streets "of this godforsaken city and look for… what's it called? Ah, inspiration!"

After breakfast, Boris checked his mail to see if there was a new order. There was one, and he could easily figure out what it was about. It was the end of September, and, as usual, the country was getting ready for the Day of National Election. For the second time during the year, everyone could go outside without a route list and walk to the voting poles, where they were supposed to elect a President for following twelve months. Boris liked this day or at least he used to like it before, and going outside was always an unforgettable experience for him. The city was breathing with life. Everything was so joyful and festive, no one stopped you to check your biometry, and you could get lost in the crowd and become part of it, an invisible, yet so important cog in this machine. In top of that, in the end of the day, when the votes had been counted and the name of the new President was announced, they displayed a fantastic broadcast with lots of fireworks and balloons released from special locations. It looked so breathtaking even as a hologram, and Boris could hardly imagine what it would be like to watch it in real life. Starting from the beginning of September, the election was the only topic discussed in the country – broadcasters threw out hundreds of pompous slogans, presenters jumped out of their pants in competition who overshouts who, and even Pools of Ideological Interchange, which, for most part, were nearly dead with no new messages posted, bloomed with enthusiastic thirty-second mantras praising the State. The order received this morning contained the same newsbreak – the election, of course.

Boris was afraid that the letters in the screen wouldn't let him do his work properly, but he quickly figured out that when he opened something on the screen, the message disappeared, but as soon as the current program was closed, it appeared again. He wondered how he'd be able to get rid of it when he finished reading, but decided to think about it later, when he was done with his broadcast. He needed a push to boost his productivity, but just at the moment he pronounced the word 'inspiration' in his head, the door signal beeped and the broadcaster announced that "all unauthorized attempts to leave the premises during the unblocking will be suppressed." Boris heard the door opening and some unusual bustle in the corridor, which sounded like clatter of metal and friction of rubber against the floor. He felt extremely curious and even forgot about the broadcast and indifferently walked out of his room, pretending to be heading to the toilet. The corridor was dark, but he could still see his neighbors in the company of a strange object made of metal, which smelled of rust and landfill.

"Hello there, my beautiful neighbor!" declaimed Slavik cheerfully. "So glad to meet you in this surly minotaur maze! I was worried about you when you didn't receive your grocery set. I thought you were ill after my caramel sticks, so I didn't dare to disturb you. Come along now, I need your help with this object."

"What's that? Where did you get it from, Slava?" Boris tried to look casual, but his eyes revealed the opposite.

"Don't you see, my ass – ahem – astute friend? It's a bike! The bears' vehicle. But, in the absence of the latter, it can just as well belong to you. I suppose if they saw such a handsome lad on this little essence of speed, they'd be delighted to accept you in their company. So, do you think you can fix it?"

"Well, it looks quite feasible to me. But where did you find it?"

"In a deserted junkyard, of course. Those places are full of treasures designated for the privileged ones. You do remember my third level of access, don't you? The poor thing was lying there, in the middle of the rubbish, lonely and abandoned, and it reminded me of someone. I'm sure you know him too. Let me think… Oh, yes, of you, of course! So, do you take it?"

First thing Boris cleaned all the dirt and rust from the bike, and then started studying its mechanism. He figured out that most of the details were in their places, and the missing ones could be replaced by what he had in hand. The more he studied it, the more he remembered about it, and soon he was completely sure he had one of those in his childhood.

In September 2035 just after Pravdin's Glorious Election, grandfather bought him a bike, as he'd promised earlier. Boris was five back then, and the bike had only two wheels, so his mother looked at it skeptically and finally made her verdict, calling it 'a killing machine and 'a damn torture device'. She asked Boris's dad to put it away somewhere in the closet for the next couple of years until their son is old enough to ride it. Grampy disagreed and said that he himself could do it even earlier, and boys must be brought up in a less patronizing way. "Must they?" asked his mum sarcastically. "Then I'm happy you didn't have a son. You'd kill him right in the cradle, that's for sure."

For some time, the grandfather and the grandson walked around the closet in circles and finally came up with a genius plan. When dad left for work and mum took Nastya for a walk, they made it a look like they were absorbed in watching Fidgy Freckles and waited for the door to close. When it did, Grampy took out his screwdriver and started to adjust the bike. In half an hour, Boris tried to make his first ride on the 'killing machine' along the corridor, which was about five meters long, but even that was enough for him to fall down and quite painfully hit his elbow on the wall. The next attempts were also unsuccessful. Grandfather sighed and put the bike back in the closet. Boris didn't like the idea at all, but he also didn't want to upset his Grampy, so he persistently continued the training, and soon it became easier and less scary for him. In a week, he seemed to have tamed the bike, and Grampy said he was ready for a big ride. However, they had to wait for a couple of days for it to stop raining, and then for another couple of days when they could finally get chance to go out alone, just the two of them.

"Are you ready, fighter?" asked Vladimir Ivanovich one morning, when mother took Nastya to the doctor, and father departed to work.

"Yes, sir Grampy!"

"Let's go then."

On their way to the suitable riding place, Vladimir Ivanovich talked to Borya warmly and encouragingly because he felt that his grandson was extremely nervous about the whole thing.

"You know what they say, chubs? They say that if you learn to ride a bike, at any time of your life, you'll never forget it. Imagine, you're grown up, a good man, a brilliant artist, and, on top of that, you're a cycling champion! What is more, you'll be able to go anywhere on it – to a different town, or just to a shop to get some stuff for home. Riding a bike absolutely essential, especially nowadays, when you can't trust public transport anymore. Just imagine how much freedom it will give you!"

"Grampy, and what if you're dead by the time I grow up? I know people die sometimes. Mum told me about it."

"Well, they do, chubs, but they go on living in the memories of their close ones. I want you to remember me, Borya. When you're grown up and you decide to get yourself a bike, you'll think of me, okay?"

"And what if I don't?"

"It's not a problem. You'll remember me even if you think you don't. That's how our memory works. It never deletes anything, it just keeps it hidden, waiting for the chance to get it revealed. Do you see what I mean?"

"I dunno. I just don't want you to die. And my memory isn't so good. I always forget to wash my hands before meals and blow my nose before bed."

"It's okay, chubs. Don't worry about it."

It was much harder to ride along the street, and Borya instantly broke to a sweat, despite of quite chilly weather. He was nervous, but he knew that fighters don't show their fear, so he continued pedaling, while Grampy was running behind and holding the bike.

"Am I doing good, Grampy?"

"You're doing perfect, young man!"

"Are you still behind me?"

"I am! All the time! Don't stop!"

Of course, neither Borya, nor his grandfather noticed a stone lying on the way, and of course the bike flew at it at full speed, and of course, the accident was inevitable. A frightful red spot was spreading on Borya's pant leg, his eyes began to water with pain, and the bike was lying beside him, rolling both of its wheels like mad. Grampy quickly ran to the poor frightened kid.

"Borya, my dear, are you hurt? Forgive me, forgive the old idiot, will you? We'll go home now and wash everything away! You'll be ok, I swear!"

"I'm fine, Grampy," Borya's voice was weak, and his lower lip was red with blood coming from a bite, which he'd made while falling. He felt the salty taste and suddenly broke down in tears, the helpless, bitter tears of a little boy who couldn't cope with the wave of pain coming from the world of adults. Vladimir Ivanovich held his grandson against his chest and squeezed him tight, as though he wanted to absorb all his pain and hurt. "Yes, I am the only one to blame in everything," he mumbled hysterically. "The boy just isn't ready, and I kept on insisting, kept on pushing him onto this dangerous road, against his will and consent. Who do I think I am? A wise instructor? An all-knowing parent? No, I'm just an old fool, who made his own grandson cry! My own grandson!"

On their way home Vladimir Ivanovich and Boris hoped that Alina and Nastya hadn't come back from the doctor, but, as luck would have it, they were there. Upon seeing her son's swollen lip and injured knee, and, on top of it, the crippled bike, Alina popped out her eyes, gave a cry and rushed to the kitchen to get some bandages and 'Zelenka' solution. She treated Borya's wounds, still lamenting, and then turned on Fidgy Freckles, seated him and his sister on the sofa and went to go confront her father. They talked about something, but Borya could only make out 'murderer', 'stubborn old jerk' and 'brain-dead donkey'. All the other words he didn't know or wasn't supposed to know at that time. When the fight was over, he heard the front door slam, which meant that Grampy was gone. When he came back, he gave Borya and Nastya an ice cream and sat down on the sofa with a guilty look on his old face.

"There-there, chubs," he muttered, "such things happen to everyone. The idea is to be able to stop at the right time."

To Borya's relief, the bike was never seen again. Until the end of September 2070. Of course, it was not the one that he remembered from his childhood, but it worked the same way, so it was easy to figure out how to make it suitable for riding again. Despite the pending broadcast, Boris spent another two or three hours tightening the screws and unbending the shriveled details. In the end, he greased everything with machine oil that he was using for smoothing up the cooler of his calculating machine and thought that it was time to give it a try. He rolled the bike in the corridor and hauled up his body on the squeaky saddle. Slavik heard the noise and went out.

"Did you manage to get it going?" he asked.

"Not sure, but it looks as if it's not going to break in the next five minutes."

"Good. Very good. Do it, handsome! Show all the bears who the real King of the Wheels is!"

Boris smiled. Of course, he will show it to them. He'd fallen down that time, with his granddad, but now he's strong and skilled, a former soldier, the best runner in the orphanage. He pushed off his back foot and rolled two meters along the corridor. The next thing he could feel was a strike of pain in his elbow, accompanied by Slavik's applause.

"Marvelous! Absolutely genial! Ladies and Gentlemen, we have a winner here!"

"It's impossible!" cried Boris. "I don't know how it's supposed to work!"

"Give it to me, my dear friend. I'll try it but promise not to laugh if I… if I can make it."

Slavik made it. At least he could go through the whole corridor, and even turn to the kitchen, where Angie was eating her set number one.

"Not rocket science at all." he concluded. "I guess, Bobby Boy, you just don't have balance inside you. You're all fragmented, disparate, shattered. Even this soulless thing feels it, and it won't submit to you until you become a better man. Fight your inner demons, Bob, sorry to sound trivial."

"I don't remember asking for a psychological consultation." Boris said, boiling with rage.

"It comes as a compliment," smiled his neighbor. "Completely free and totally amicable. I guess I'll put it in the closet, so in case you want to have a ride, you'll know where to find it."

4

Very good, Boris. Now you know the history, but it's only half of the story. Please, read on, and you will soon find out the rest of it

Remember I told you about the last meeting of Malinin's team? It was the longest and the most difficult one, and we were all scared to death because we knew that we were about to lose everything. I tried to gather everyone, although not everyone was brave enough to come, but every single person present was a real hero. Yes, we might have looked like a gaggle of lunatic witches in that dark room, but we were heroes, the last ones left on this land, and we were ready to go all the way, although we were fully aware of where it would lead us.

Vladimir Ivanovich stood at the window and looked outside at the dead city. It was a curfew, and everything was dark and silent, but the silence cried in their ears louder than any words.

"My dear little friends," spoke the darkness, and a pair of green animal eyes stared from the depth of nowhere. "How lovely to see you all gathered here, how lovely to smell your fear and insecurity. Let me indulge myself on it for a moment, while you're wallowing in your own foolishness. Let me look at you for the last time, before you get yourself forever immersed in history that you are so desperately trying to make."

No one heard these words, but everyone felt a cold breath of horror on the back of their heads.

"Let me start, then," said the professor finally. "We all know that the rat in our team has been captured and destroyed. However, Uncle Gena informed me that there may be other traitors, so we all must be very careful. We don't know exactly what information they have now, and I hope it's not much, but I can't be sure. We have to decide what to do straight away."

Nadezhda Vasilievna Komissarova, a strict woman aged forty-five to forty-seven, with masculine features and a short haircut, the professor's most valued member of the team, was sitting upright, playing with a pen with her long dry fingers. Vladimir Ivanovich had known her for at least ten years, and he sometimes thought that, had he been younger, he'd definitely have fallen for her, and who knows where it would have taken him. She hardly ever smiled at all and when she spoke, every word of hers had a worth of a hundred of those said by the others. Her short hair was almost wholly black, with a touch of silver on the temples, and her eyes had an indefinite yellow-to-green color, and it seemed at times that two copper fish were looking at you from the depths of troubled water.

When the professor spoke, Nadezhda Vasilievna didn't look up, but kept staring at a piece of paper with some of her previously made doodles. Rogov considered it as endorsement and continued.

"I suggest that we act right now. According to my calculations, we have enough people and arms for the beginning of the operation. Later, I hope some of the internal army forces will join the rebellion, at least that's what Uncle Gena told me."

"He didn't tell it to you," said Nadezhda Vasilievna quietly, still looking down. "He only hinted at the fact that there might be those who would consent to negotiations. And that doesn't mean anything to us, well, at least in the current situation."

"That means a lot!" thundered Vladimir Ivanovich. "The people! They still remember the times of Malinin! They will follow us, and those who won't, will be destroyed at once, so that they don't spread the virus of totalitarianism on our land! On the land that we've won for ourselves with these very hands!"

"Vladimir," Nadezhda Vasilievna's voice was still calm, but Rogov felt a metallic note ringing through her tone, "you seem to have gone off the rails recently. Do you understand what is really going on now? Do you understand that everyone in this room can be dead at any moment? We are the last hope of this land, we are the last barrier between the power and the people, and we can't jump to such snap decisions only because you want us to do it! We can't go out now, with our hayforks against their tanks!"

"This is exactly what I understand," the professor stood in front of her and looked directly in her yellow-to-green fishy eyes. "If we don't do it now, we never will."

"No, my dear Rogov," hissed Nadezhda Vasilievna. "We won't act now. I won't let you waste our lives like that. But why am I the only one who disagrees? Let us ask the rest. What do you think, comrades?"

But everyone was silent. Maybe they were just afraid to say anything at the heat of the moment, or maybe they hadn't made up their minds whether they were prepared to die for nothing. Rogov breathed heavily.

"Do you know…" he tried to catch his breath. "Have you ever heard that life without risk is nothing but a senseless existence? Are you all just a bunch of scared children screaming at the sight of Baba Yaga in a kindergarten amateur play?"

"I've heard what they say about risking your life," Nadezhda Vasilievna spoke for everyone again. "But someone also said, 'I would never die for my beliefs because I might be wrong'. Now will you try to think rationally, or shall we continue playing quotes until they come and shoot us all?"

The professor sat back on his chair and scanned the surrounding people as if in hope to find support at least in some of them.

"So…" he asked. "Are there no other options? It means that we either give up and lay down our weapon now, or take the fight and die heroes, for the sake of the following generations?"

Nadezhda Vasilievna calmed down a bit.

"I don't believe in dying for the sake. We're old enough to understand that death is the end. No following generations will remember us as long as we don't appeal to them now."

"But the State! The new State machine! It must have some weaknesses, some vulnerability that we could use. It can't be invincible, no, I don't believe it!" the professor looked like a child trying to persuade his parents to buy him a coveted toy.

One of the people stood out of the darkness. It was Mikhail, a member of the new President's PR team, who was supposed to monitor all changes in the governmental policy.

"Vladimir Ivanovich," he spoke, "what about the document I sent you the other day?"

"What was that?" Rogov looked at him blankly. "I don't remember getting anything from you."

"It's the information about the Delta-Center. I think I've told you. It's top-secret, and it was almost impossible for me to make a copy of it… But I managed and I sent it to our protected database, just like Konstantin told me to."

"So, tell it to all of us, Mikhail," Nadezhda Vasilievna nodded approvingly. "And Vladimir Ivanovich will listen, won't you, professor?"

"The Delta-Center System is a major means of control of the country's infrastructure. Let me explain," Mikhail took a sheet of paper and placed it in the middle of the table so that everyone could see. "It consists of three major levels. Level One is called Communication Level and it controls everything that people see in indoor and outdoor media. TV-sets will soon be forcibly replaced by 3-D devices, which will broadcast holographic images created by special propagandistic units. Billboards, systems of emergency notification, radio – everything will be connected to Level One. It's almost ready to be implemented, and our PR department has full access to it," he made a pause to clear his throat.

"Go on!" commanded Nadezhda Vasilievna.

"Level Two is extended to the city infrastructure. It seems that it will control all doors of the living premises so that they can't be opened without special permission. Automatic patrolling and goods delivery devices will be introduced where possible, which will enable them to watch for every single person in the country. Special machines will detect the violators and destroy them right on the spot."

"That can't be true! It means we'll all be under their scrutiny!" Vladimir Ivanovich looked terrified and desperate.

"Not "we", professor. Well, hopefully, we'll see it too, but Level Two will be implemented only in ten to fifteen years. Its structure is already clear, but it will require lots of work – replacing the old systems, installing the sensors, making them available in every flat and house. And some of the people will be relocated, especially from hard-to-reach areas, to enable even more control of them. It can't be done quickly, believe me. And, finally, Level Three. It controls all the military power in the State. It's still under development, and only about ten per cent of it has been documented so far, so I don't know how it's supposed to work. However, what we have now on Level One and Level Two can help us immensely."

"But how? What can we do with it?" asked Vladimir Ivanovich.

"Basically, if we hack it, we'll be able to have control over the whole country. Not more and not less."

"It's impossible! You said something about five to ten years! We don't have this time! We might be dead tomorrow!"

"Calm down, professor," interrupted him Nadezhda Vasilievna. "If it's not us, there can be someone else. And we will give this person the key. Will we, comrades?"

"Well," said Konstantin, who could program the sun to go down in the west, "it is possible to hack any system…"

"See?" Nadezhda Vasilievna smiled triumphantly.

"On condition it's up and running. If it isn't, I'm afraid, I'm powerless."

"Maybe you can at least have a look at the documentation?" metallic notes were heard in her voice again.

Kostya shrugged his shoulders.

"Well, if you give me… about two hours, or a little more, I might give it a try."

He went to the neighboring room where they had their computer. The others remained sitting at the large round table – the kingless knights without hope and beyond reproach.

"So, what do you think of it?" Vladimir Ivanovich's voice faded in silence.

"Of what?" asked Nadezhda Vasilievna.

"Of the whole situation. Of its outcome. Is it what you expected when we started?"

"Yes, I supposed something of the kind. If you want to win, you must be ready to lose. It's always a double-edged sword."

"Will they really kill us?"

"Eventually, yes. One doesn't need a fortune-teller to say it. But you're thinking in the wrong direction, comrade. Death doesn't always mean defeat. Sometimes it's the beginning of a new fight. I'm sure there'll be someone better, stronger, more successful than all of us. We'll pass the baton to them – to the future, professor."

Rogov sighed and hid his face in his hands. The room breathed out his desperation.

Kostya came out in two and a half hours, when everyone had already started to lose their nerve. He was holding a piece of paper written within and without, which he put in the middle of the round table, like Mikhail had previously done.

"It looks insane to me," he said hesitantly, "but it's the only thing I could invent."

"Please, Kostya…" whispered Nadezhda Vasilievna.

"Well, we all know about the three levels of the Delta-Center. We need access at least to the second one, which can enable us to take control of some crucial elements, and maybe, eventually, even get us to Level Three. However, what we have now and what we can put our hands on, is the first level, which is almost ready and can be hacked. But, it's only the top layer and can't give us any significant benefit. So, my idea is to get to Level Two through Level One, which can act as a gateway, as a loophole, so to speak. Are you all with me?"

"We're fine," ensured him Nadezhda Vasilievna.

"At the moment I can make a device, a sort of memory card, which will ping the Level One servers. They are well-protected, so the only way to hack them is to wait until they are depreciated and exchanged for the new ones. The new servers will automatically canvass all available devices and connect them to themselves. Our card will disguise as a friendly transmitter and connect to the system as such, so that it could hitch a ride on the network and act as part of it. As soon as it is done, it will steal the access codes to Level Two and record them. You see, Level One and Level Two are closely interconnected. This means that Level Two information transmitting devices, which are called 'broadcasters' in the documentation, are supposed to receive signals from Level Two machines, called 'drones' and 'registrators'. When my device gets the passwords, it must be inserted in a computer of a member of our Team. It should be done manually, of course. Then it will start pinging for Level Two servers and trying to receive their access codes. For security reasons, they are changed every twenty-four hours, and this process makes the servers vulnerable and possible for hacking. When my device retrieves the codes, it will give access to Level Two to the owner. It can be any computer, actually, it must only be equipped with a universal hub to insert my card in, and it will do all the job by itself. I don't know what happens next and it's not my responsibility, but I'll write all the technical instructions for the one who gets the card. It shouldn't be difficult, but it's desirable that the person has some computer skills and is able to write a simple code, or at least to copy and paste mine. And… this is it, basically. Now, your questions, please."

"Okay," said Nadezhda Vasilievna. "First question. How long will it take to get Level One passwords? Will Level Two network be fully implemented by that time?"

"As I could make it from the documentation, the servers' replacement is supposed to take place every fifteen years".

"Good. It means that your device will have to work continuously for fifteen years from now? How is it possible?"

"That was a tricky part. No battery will last for more than a year, even if it is connected to a renewable power source. I suggest we use the city's electricity network: a streetlight, traffic lights, public phone booth, something like that."

"A phone booth in the university park!" said Vladimir Ivanovich.

"Yes, that could work," answered Kostya. "Of course, I will provide my device with a UPS in case of power shortcuts, and I will keep monitoring its condition. What else?"

"How will this person, the one who will put it all into action, know that the codes are on the card? How can we inform him about it?"

"I've thought of it, too. Well, we need another device, which he will keep with himself, in his computer. It will connect to the one in the park, and as soon as the password codes are there, it will alert that guy."

"How are these two things going to be connected? Mobile network?"

"No, it's too risky. We need something more reliable. Radio signal, for example."

"You mean, we'll have to install a radio transmitter in someone's computer? But that's impossible!" argued Vladimir Ivanovich.

"It's more than possible. What if I tell you that it has already been done once?"

"By whom?"

"Our traitor. I informed you about him even before Uncle Gena did. I knew it because I found a card in our computer, which was intended to collect our data and transmit it to them via radio waves. I saved the card, of course, because it looked quite amusing to me. It can help us now."

"But it has to remain in the computer all the time! All fifteen years! We might not have a chance to contact this person and ask him to be careful with it."

"I'll make it difficult to take out. A small nick on one side will be enough to make it sit there forever. Well, unless he wants to disassemble his machine, but I hope he won't do it. I just hope. He'll have to use a special tool to withdraw it, which will come with the second card from the park."

"Are you sure computers will have the same slots in ten years?"

"No. I'm not sure of anything. But I don't think they'll make any major changes in personal machines. They have more important things to do."

"Okay," Nadezhda Vasilievna looked at those present in the room. "Kostya's plan does sound insane, but it's the only one we have now, and I think we should all thank him for giving us this hope."

The room responded with applause, and she gave a slight nod to show she was with them.

"What I'd like to discuss now," she spoke when the applause finished, "is who will do it. Who will be our successor, the one to take the baton from us? Any ideas? Kostya, maybe you?"

"Me?" Kostya shook his head. "No-no-no, I'm a technical specialist. I can assemble, program and service the device. But I'm not a fighter. I don't have enough guts for it. And, anyway, in fifteen years I will be too old for this sort of adventure."

"Agreed. Who else?"

"Well, if we speak of fifteen years, this person should be fairly young now. Twenty, or less. Maybe even ten," said Yuriy, a PhD in economics, Rogov's colleague. "My son is eighteen, but he's not in good health, I must admit. Of course, we hope for the better, but we can't be sure…"

"I have no children," said Nadezhda Vasilievna.

"May I?" it was the voice of Lyudmila Ivanovna, a former Chair of the University Child rights institute of the Faculty of Social Sciences, whose daughter had died in prison for supporting liberal views. "In our orphanage… where I work now, there are kids of different ages. Some of them are quite bright, and I can make sure that the chosen one will receive all that he needs. I will do anything to revenge my little girl!"

"We know it, my dear," answered Nadezhda Vasilievna warmly. "But we can't trust this thing to an unknown child from the orphanage, no offence. However, your help in working with juniors will be invaluable. Maybe someone else has an idea? Vladimir Ivanovich, what about you?"

Rogov sat quietly. He wanted to open his mouth, but some invisible force didn't let him utter a word. Everyone looked at him, and he dropped his gaze to the table. His face was gray and even more wrinkled, and his hands lay moveless in front of him, like two dead birds.

"Vladimir Ivanovich, we're all waiting. Weren't you the one who was ready to 'act now or never'?"

"My grandson," he said resignedly. "He'll be seven this January. He's a smart little boy, and he learns quickly. People say he'll be a captain one day."

"Isn't he too young?"

"He might be, and we might postpone our plan for five more years, until he is at least twenty-seven. But he's my only little hope. Just mine, so I'm not sure I can do this to him. To share him with the rest of you…"

Chapter 7. Catharsis

I am a historian, Boris, and I've read a very old chronicle of one of the first major wars on our land. It's called 'The Song of the Seven Battles of Resistance' and it goes like this:

Inside the land, beneath the Hell
The Hydra lies inside its den.
It sleeps in its unholy shrine,
But then its eyes begin to shine.
For blood and sorrow does it crave,
To bury in its gloomy grave.
Beware, stranger, not to wake
This creature up, for it can take
Your pain, your blood, your holy soul,
So run before you hear it growl.

The Hydra is still here, Boris, and we made it completely pissed off, so now it's longing for a rematch. It has already destroyed us, and our death is just a question of time. You may ask why we couldn't escape, run away from this place before it's too late. The answer is plain and obvious – because there's no escape from them. They will keep hunting us down until each and every one of us is destroyed. But more importantly, we don't have the right to quit. We must be here, with our people, on our land, and here shall we be buried and find our peace in this very ground, under this very sun.

We couldn't stop the Hydra at our time, and it must be enjoying its complete permissiveness at the moment. It will become madder and more violent, and I can hardly imagine what atrocities you will have to face. The information about the Delta-Center makes me think that you'll be placed in an unprecedented jail, a prison, which will cover all the country, and you'll be serving your sentence for the crime that you hadn't committed. No, it is not your fault that you are suffering now. The only person to blame is me and my being so shortsighted. The crime is mine, and I fully accept it, so if you hate me, if you can't forgive me for it, you have all the reasons to feel this way. But you can make it all right again. You can do better than an old fool who thought himself to be a savior of the humanity.

Now, Boris, to the main point. If you have received this message, it means that the Level One servers were replaced, and Kostya's device is now ready to be used. We can already call it our first victory, and what happens next depends entirely on you. I've placed all the instructions at the end of this message, so read them carefully before you take the card out. You will have all the information that you need. But first of all, you need to get to the university park, where our main device is hidden. Do your best to get out of the flat, I know it's hard at your times, but you must find a way to do it. Don't waste your time because the access codes to Level One network are changed every seven days, so you must be really quick. Go to the park and find an old telephone booth (the satellite coordinates are in this document, too). It is about 150 meters from the main entrance, under a large oak tree. It may have been knocked off already, but some remains of it will still be visible. There, just under the support stand, you'll find a hermetic safe box, connected to an electricity cable. You'll need an access code to open it, which is 451F. Get the card out and don't forget to take the pliers, which Kostya put there. Go back home and withdraw the radio card from your device using the pliers, and then insert the one from the park into the slot, just like you did before. You'll see a pop-up window, where you'll have to confirm that your device is now part of Level One network. In the command line enter the program code from this message. If it displays a mistake, you'll have to use your brain and adjust it, but Kostya said he knew the characteristics of your operating system, so the code is very likely to work in it. Press 'Enter'. Now, in less than twenty-four hours, your device will be able to control all Level Two equipment of the State. Act quickly – the intrusion will soon be detected. Follow our instructions exactly, at least in the beginning of the operation. They've been written by our best specialists, and they can't fail you now. Also, in this message, you will find a list of people, who, at our time, were our main rivals. Trace them, or their ancestors, and destroy them. You'll manage, I'm sure.

And, finally, listen to this. I don't know if I'm doing the right thing or just messing it all up. All I know is that freedom is easier to retain than to regain. It seems to me that we have lost our freedom, your freedom, Boris. But I guess there is always a hope, and in our situation even the faintest hope is enough to keep us going. And now

"My grandfather," thought Boris. "I have a grandfather again."

He understood even less now. Grandfather, Hydra, a pile of half-crazed revolutionists cherishing some old-fashioned values, which they called 'freedom', 'equality' and 'justice', who were prepared to die for them, and, most evidently, they eventually did. They were mad, of course, but they were not evil. Lyudmila Ivanovna, Colonel Petrenko, and unknown Kostya – they all seemed characters of a fairy-tale, which was told to him in the childhood, but has received a new meaning now. And what is he supposed to do? He, Boris Arsenyev, a traitor's grandson, a hapless soldier and a mediocre artist? Whatever he is, he's not an opportunist, nor is he a fool to follow the instructions of someone who once failed it all completely and irrevocably. Why at all did his grandfather imagine that the State needs to be saved? Why couldn't he just be happy with what he had, and he had much more than they are all having now. How can anyone be condemned to be free when all their life implies imprisonment? And it's not the State's fault that everyone needs chains, and it's not the State which puts them on our wrists. One thing that is clear at the moment is that the State needs Boris's broadcasts and that's what he'll do now. Grandfather can wait. Anyway, he's been waiting for almost thirty-five years, so a couple of more days will not make much difference.

Boris commanded Katyusha to open and reproduce the message with the text of the order.

"Starting playback. Subject: informational broadcast to increase people's awareness of the importance of the forthcoming election and urge them to take an active part in it. Purpose: to inform the citizens on the current political situation in the Commonwealth State and the background historical events that made it possible. Places of the broadcast demonstration: social institutions, military units, outdoor information stands, hospitals and mental homes. Payment: one hundred fifty thousand GKB. The text: Dear citizens of the Commonwealth State! You all know that very soon we'll be celebrating the most important day in the political, cultural and economic life of our beautiful and prosperous country. Year after year, generation after generation, we've been moving towards the bright and cloudless future, which is becoming closer with every Election Day. From the first vote in 2036 and up to the current 2070, you've been making the right choices, the ones which you considered to be the best for yourselves and for your children. This is why the State is delighted to trust this choice to you again and again, and it asks for your opinion every year. Some of you will vote for the first time in your life, and you might feel anxious about it. There is absolutely nothing to worry about. Please remember: the State is here to guide you, to tell you where to go and what to say in order to make your voice heard. Look at this opportunity as a great honor given to you by those who protect you and care for you. But our present would be impossible without the past, so now, let us have a look at how it all began.

Our State has always been strong and able to defend its borders and its citizens. Not a single terrorist, not a single foreign agent could destroy the peace that it has maintained throughout centuries. But at one point, in early 2033, the power was seized by an evil and mean man who wanted only one thing – to command and to destroy. We will not call his name here because evil has no definite name, but most of our elderly viewers can remember those times, when they suffered from his vicious acts. He was not alone. Thousands of foreign agents and corrupt Commonwealthers crept from their hideouts and supported him, which made his victory possible. We call them the Black Plague now, because evil is infectious, and it spreads like a disease among those who aren't strong enough to resist it. However, our country is rich in courageous fighters and honest citizens, who, in their turn, could not stand being impaired so outrageously. During the next two years, every single day, people went to the streets to fight the cause of the Destabilization, they cried out for the lunatic President to stop his malicious rule, but their voices of indignation were brutally stifled by him. Finally, he sold all the riches of our land to those who financed him from abroad, to our eternal enemies, so dishonored and malice that they didn't even mind to steal from the poorest. The starving children were crying while their starving fathers were desperate to earn a penny to feed them and to keep their ruined houses warm. Others were engaged in wars with the rest of the world, together with North Crestland, Bottland, Turialia and Meaglecan. But the people couldn't suffer forever. They chose another leader, who was there to guide them through those hard times, to the end of the tunnel, where they could see the light. This leader was young and full of power, and his name is now known to everyone – Victor Vasilyevich Pravdin. They gathered around him, like chickens gather around their mother hen, and he accepted them – poor, hopeless and confused, and together they were strong and united, and nothing could stop them now. The new army went to fight those who tried to challenge their future. The fights were fierce, but the army stood firm. Finally, the battle was won, and it was a glorious victory of the good versus the evil. We are all part of his Team now – Pravdin's invincible Team of those who want our land to continue being prosperous and generous. This is what the Day of National Election symbolizes – the unity of the people and the State, the end of the bloody regime and the return to decent life.

You all know that our President has justified the hopes of every citizen of the State. He provided them with comfortable accommodation, which can sustain any terrorist attack, explosion or virus outbreak. In this accommodation every citizen can receive adequate food, medicine, clothes and basic necessities. All the supplies are delivered by high-tech drones and distributed on automatic service lines, which means that people do not have to bother themselves with grueling work and have more time for personal development. The President has been able to form outstanding army forces, which can detect and destroy any terrorist, any foreign agent who tries to break our country's borders. Pravdin works hard every day and night for our country and for the people who gave their votes for him. This is why it is crucial for our President to know that every one of you is still with him, that you support and trust him like you did thirty-four years ago. He wants to see all of you in the streets of your towns and cities – happy, prosperous and determined to go with him hand in hand. On this solemn occasion he opens the doors of your houses and guarantees each one of you that you will be safe under his supervision.

You have to do just one thing: in the designated time, according to the approved schedule, come to your voting pole and pronounce the name of whom you elect to be the President for the next year. If, for any reason, you won't be able to do this in person, you must leave a request on the National Portal, and special drones will deliver voting equipment to your home. All the information from the voting poles will be collected and processed in real time, and at half past nine, thirty minutes before the electricity shutdown, you will all know the name of the next President. Afterwards, we will broadcast a show with fireworks display and inflating machines will release five hundred thousand balloons into the air. This breathtaking show will express our government's gratitude to all citizens for being so committed to the ideals of pluralism, freedom, peace and democracy, the ones that have always been promoted by our President and his Party of National Unity. We remind you, that last year, and all the previous years, one hundred per cent of the votes proudly went to Victor Vasilyevich Pravdin. We don't have any doubts that this year will not be an exception. Good luck, dear citizens, and may the truth be with you! End of the text."

"Bullshit!" swore Boris through his teeth. "Running off at the mouth! Lies, lies and lies – that's what I can call it!"

He sat in front of the broadcaster, overwhelmed with rage and helplessness. How could they be so bald-faced in deceiving their own people? How could people be so naïve to believe this hoax? And how did it happen that he might be the only person in the country who knows the truth? Will he keep it to himself? Will he let this bunch of liars get away with it like they've been doing all these thirty-six years? No, he won't let them. He'll be the one to tear the country's eyes open so that everyone could see the real State, the real Pravdin and the real history. Freedom or not, he will give people another chance, just one little chance, maybe the last one for them. He might be a bad artist, a clumsy cyclist or a gloomy hermit, but he is not a liar.

"I am the only free man in this prisonous state," he thought. "And I'll follow the dictates of my conscience. I will kill Pravdin. He might be a model, a 3-D image, but I will kill him just because I can! I swear it on the memory of my grandfather, Vladimir Ivanovich Rogov, I will be your last day, Mister President! You'd better run and hide, like I did when you tried to kill me, run and hide, you deceitful scoundrel, because I am coming for you!"

Boris pronounced these words in his head and laughed at his own might. The laugh should have sounded triumphal and sinister at the same time, but just at this moment the door opened and Slavik entered the room, spoiling all the mise-en-scène.

"And what is this demonic laughter supposed to mean?" he asked. "The drones are to arrive in less than thirty minutes. I know you are aware of it, but just thought of calling in and reminding you of the coming dinner. You always fancy a snack, don't you? So, another broadcast you're working on, neighbor? What is it? One more tank? Or a military rabbit?"

"Worse than that," Boris gave a sad smile. "Motivation for the National Election Day."

"You can't be serious! You'd never stoop so low, would you?"

"I wouldn't. But I feel that if it goes on like this, I'll end up making tutorials of pearl-barley cooking."

"Sad but true, my friend. And we can't resist it. You know, there's a rule in any work of art. There must always be the one who suffers: the creator, the hero, or the reader. Your reader is clear to me, he hardly has enough intellect to suffer. The hero isn't good for it either, so the choice is obvious – it's you, the creator. You must carry this burden of suffering for all of us and finally spew your jingle forth from your mouth and be rewarded your thirty pieces of silver for it. This is our life, darling, at least that's what's been reported to me about it. You want a hand?"

"Yeah, thanks!" Boris was more than happy. "I'm sure we'll work something out together."

"So, play the companion text, and better do it quickly because I have lots of pending orders as well. Decent orders, mind you."

Slavik listened to the text with his eyes half-closed, as if trying to grab ahold to "what's it called? Ah, inspiration!" At the most important moments he closed his eyes completely and nodded, which was supposed to say "yes, that's just what I imagined". When the playback finished, he sat quietly for some time, looking at the window wallpaper, and then turned to Boris.

"May I ask you something, my dear colleague?" he said thoughtfully. "Like an artist would ask an artist. Who are you going to vote for?"

“Are there any options?”

“There are plenty of them, even if some of us are too blind to see.” Slavik smiled philosophically. “However, we’re off the topic. So, my idea is to create both a conflict and a catharsis. The conflict is obvious: two presidents fighting for the throne. One is bad and the other one is good, and it doesn’t really matter who is who. The election is a catharsis, so we should present it as an event of ultimate liberation, the quintessence of the power of the State. Are you still with me, Michelangelo?”

“Sure.”

“In order to come to a catharsis, your reader must suffer. And the worst, the primal fear of any rational person is the fear of death. So, let us depict the evil President as a horrible imminent threat to all the simple, not to say narrow-minded, citizens. We’ll place him a bit on top of the others, so that there’s an illusion of attack, of destruction, of total annihilation. To scare the shit out of them, if I put it in the literal language. Agreed?”

“No,” answered Boris coldly.

“Why?”

“Because I disagree.”

“Oh, that counts. But may I just clarify with what? With the threat, or with the catharsis, or with the way I’m sitting, maybe?”

“With the whole thing. It wasn’t like that at all. There was no threat. There was no evil president.”

“And do you mind me asking where you’ve received this information from? Level One broadcasts or a little birdie told it to you? Or maybe even the bears?”

“Stop joking about the bears, you sound so retarded when you do it!”

“Ah, now you don’t like my jokes! Say a better one if you’re so witty!”

“There’s no time for jokes. I must… I must work.”

“Work, then! Expose them all to the real thing!”

“I can’t…”

“Well, in this case just do what I tell you!”

“I can’t do this either,” Boris whispered.

“And since when have you developed such interest in politics? I’ve never noticed anything of the kind in you,” Slava asked sarcastically.

"Aren't you into politics yourself?"

"No, of course not, and you can shoot me straight away if I ever am. Politics is the shittiest shit in our world. It's food for dumbass livestock, not able to produce any mental effort with their rotten brain. They're waiting for someone to tell them what's right and what's wrong, for a shepherd to draw this line for them. And the shepherds are often even more stupid than their flock, and all they are capable of doing is declaring pompous stamps and slogans, so pathetic and shallow that they will hardly fool a child. Politics is an attempt to divide this world into black and white, but there is no black or white, and it's not the world's fault. It's the fault of those who are trying to disassemble it with their clumsy paws, making it all even more messy and confusing. You don't believe me when I call politics 'shit'? Just let me prove it to you. Shit makes everything it touches shit, doesn't it? Now, add politics to anything, what do you get? Add it to art and you get politics. Add it to science – politics again. Add politics to economy, religion, human relationship, fashion, pearl barley cooking – you still get bleeding politics! Isn't it typical? Now, will you draw the evil President downcast by the good one and close the subject?"

Slava breathed heavily and looked derailed by his own eloquence.

"Sorry, mate, but I won't."

"You won't? And who in the whole world is asking for your consent? The one who sent you this order, maybe? The darn Ministry of Defense when they signed the contract with you, leaving you destined to draw stupid tanks and soulless jingles for the rest of your life? Wake up, Boris, it's 2070, and your personal opinion doesn't cost a penny. If it's not you, then someone else will make this broadcast, and he'll make it better and quicklier than you. It won't be me, of course. I prefer to deal with other subjects and leave politics to rams. But, as an exception, I will accept your viewpoint and let you proceed with drawing your Pravdin in the tank or whatever you have on your mind. But remember, it was me who brought you the bike, and read about the bears to you, and maybe this will make you feel at least a little bit sorry for being so obstinate."

Slavik left, slamming the door resentfully. Boris thought for a while and decided that when he gains control over the city communications, first thing he'll turn on the water supply in their flat and flush his neighbor in the toilet, after using it in its intended application. If only the neighboring room had been granted to someone else, or at least ripped by a swarm of ubiquitous cockroaches.

2

This time Slava seemed to take a serious offence. During the identification procedure in the kitchen, he tried not to look at Boris and assiduously demonstrated to the drones the retina of his furious eyes. Boris, however, was in high spirits and even felt like singing. "On the road paved with clouds…" Where did that come from? Of course, it was the toy elephant's song – the one it sang when you pressed the button on its head!

On the road paved with clouds
I am walking stiff and proud
And my little shiny eyes
Look directly at the skies.

When I step into the mud,
You can hear my loud thud!
With my tusks used in their might,
I can take on any fight!

Fight! Fight! Fight!

Boris wasn't sure that the last three words were initially in the song, but they fitted perfectly into his current mood, so he repeated them several times and looked at his neighbor victoriously. Slava gave a contentious snort and demonstratively threw his set number one on the table, which was supposed to mean that he wasn't going to consume it. Then he hugged Angie tenderly and drew her inside their room. Boris didn't care. He was happy to receive a free set number two from the President as a celebration of the coming National Election Day and felt a pack of instant noodles in it. Now, it was something. Not the same old pearl-barley, which made his stomach sick, but a decent dish, an olive branch for the winner. Boris

227

turned on the cooker and put a pot of water on the burner. When it began to boil, he emptied the contents of the instant noodles bag into his blue plate, that he'd inherited from Juliana Pavlovna, and added a packet of spices, which he found inside. It looked perfect. The water momentarily became bright-orange, and the smell of artificial meat tickled his nostrils invitingly.

While Boris was gorging on the noodles, he thought of his further action plan. The moment was perfect, and he'd be a complete idiot to miss it. The doors would open in three days for the election, so he wouldn't even have to think of an excuse to get a route list to leave his flat. Had it been any other time of the year, he could make use of his monthly permission to go out, but two weeks before the Election Day and two weeks after it, they stopped approving the passes except for urgent cases. It was assumed that people would satisfy their communication needs during the mass open-air events. So, for the time being, the Election Day was the only way for Boris to get to the university park. He'd been there in his childhood, with his grandfather, but he could only remember the smell of pine needles and moist ground, from which endless trunks of centenary oaks were making their way to the freedom of the radiant bottomless sky.

For the rest of the evening, Boris sat in his room and made sketches for his final broadcast. He didn't need inspiration for it, he already felt inspired and uplifted, so he just kept playing with his drawing pen and staring at the monitor, and thinking, thinking, thinking… His thoughts finally drifted him to his grandfather. He imagined the old, baffled professor writing this message to the emptiness of the future, with only one per cent chance that it would be received by the addressee. Anything could have happened to the elephant, or to the card in its head, or to the device in the park, or even to Boris himself. It was so weird to realize that he was the most important link between the past and the future, the truth and the lies, the freedom and the prison. But why did it take them so long to replace the servers? According to his grandfather's calculations, it should have been done ten years ago, the year he'd been transferred to reserve, but nothing actually happened at that time. Or maybe it did, but the device couldn't detect it? And now they needed this upgrade, just before the Election Day, to make sure the system was still able to control everyone in the country – all those people who would go out into the streets and condemn themselves to another year in prison. And why was it called election at all? It was a sort of a roll call, a check-up to see if they were all there, ready to voluntarily stay in their cells for hundreds of years more and being thankful for small mercies that the government threw them from time to time. The more lips pronounce the name, the more real it becomes and the more difficult it will be for the people to reject it from their minds. The name, which was their lock, their curse, the way to completely destroy their identity. All the voices wrested from their throats would go directly into the brand-new servers, which would eat and digest them and then, as the apotheosis of this farce, throw them out with vomit of fireworks and colorful farts of balloons.

"This is disgusting," thought Boris. "So utterly wrong and unfair. But what can I do? How can I fight it all alone?"

He decided that he'd study his grandfather's instructions carefully tomorrow and see if the plan is feasible at all. Now it was time to draw his final hologram, and he took the pen again and made a few more sketches. But the hour was already late, and his hand was shaking, and he suddenly felt exhausted and sleepy. The broadcaster was playing a concert with simple earwormish songs, performed by intensely cheerful singers, all of the same type, with the same faces, which you forgot right after they disappeared. Boris yawned, lay down on the sofa and fell asleep at once, although there was still more than an hour until the electricity shutdown. He didn't even wake up when his neighbor's head appeared in the doorway, and he went on sleeping when a shadow sat down on his chair right in front of the monitor, which was still turned on and, behind the sketches, that he'd made for his broadcast, displayed something, which was not intended to be seen by the prying eyes of a stranger. When Katyusha said goodbye for the day and the lights went off, the shadow stood up and left the room quietly, on tiptoes, which was, however, an unnecessary precaution, since the snoring coming from Boris's mouth meant that it would take not less than a gunshot to wake him up.

The deadline for the broadcast, which Boris thought would be a final chord in his career of a mediocre artist, was this afternoon, so he had no time to waste now. He poured himself a glass of cold condensed coffee drink and started organizing the sketches from yesterday evening. First of all, he had to choose the background. He tried dark-blue, then pale gray, then khaki-brown, and finally opted for scarlet red with flashes of white. On the background, he placed Sergey Anatolyevich Malinin, just the way he imagined him from his grandfather's message – tall and thin, with a pointed pale face, sharp-nosed and big-eyed. He was standing on a pedestal, holding a national flag, which looked like a heavy burden in his feeble hands. The ex-President waved the flag haphazardly, as if urging for others to join him and help him with it, and some schematic figures climbed up the hill and approached him, but as they did so, the background became even redder, and a tiny black spot appeared on the horizon. As the spot grew larger, it started to take a form of the person everyone was supposed to know – Victor Vasilyevich Pravdin. The perspective changed, and now Pravdin was looking at them from above – the technique prompted by odious Slavik, which turned out to be very effective. On the sight of Pravdin, Malinin slouched even more and dropped the flag, which fell on the nacreous snow. When he bended to pick it up, Pravdin made a leap towards him and put his foot on Malinin's back, nailing him into the earth. The background turned to purple-red, and soon Malinin's weak body was completely absorbed by it, and the schematic people seemed to have forgotten all about him, mesmerized by the grandeur of their new idol. They kept on creeping up the hill, longing for his attention, and soon all the landscape was filled with their insect-like bodies.

Just at that moment, Pravdin stretched his hand, grabbed the flag, which emerged from nowhere, and held it high, like an axe, ready to strike anyone who stood out from the crowd. His lips opened in a peculiar way, so that his face seemed to be cut apart, appealing everyone into submission. One by one, people started falling on their knees, bowing to the President in unreserved surrender, and Pravdin's figure grew up and turned to the viewer, so that his face took over all the visible space, eating up even the background, which, by that moment had become almost black. The face stayed there for a while, hypnotizing the viewers with its sharply edged smile, and then it was replaced by the symbols of the Commonwealth State – the coat of arms with two snakes, biting on each other's tails, and the snow-white flag with a red star in the top right corner. "Good luck, dear citizens, and may the truth be with you!"

Boris didn't know whether his creation would be approved or rejected, but it was the only one he was capable of drawing now. He played it once again, added some final touches and in the next communication interval sent it to the client.

"Nice and neat," he thought. "Now let us get to a more important business. After lunch, of course."

He hoped that there wouldn't be any more orders to distract him from studying his grandfather's team's instructions because he didn't have much time left. The doors were to be opened in two days, so he had to think of every step he'd make, take every precaution, consider every detail of the operation. He had no right to make a mistake, not this time, anyway. The neighbors were discussing something in their room, and Boris quietly made his way to the kitchen to get something to eat. He didn't feel like cooking and made himself an ugly sandwich with standard bread, butter spread, and spices left from yesterday's instant noodles. It was almost two o'clock, and he had about three hours to read the message before the food drones arrived.

First of all, he checked the satellite coordinates of the device from the park and memorized them. Then he calculated that it would take him about twenty minutes to get there on foot, which seemed OK, and, considering twenty minutes for the way back, he'd even have enough time to go to the voting pole and say something offensive into it. Then he checked the list of people, who, in granddad's times, were closely associated with Pravdin. Some of the names sounded familiar – Boris was sure he'd heard them on the broadcaster, and it meant that their bloody dynasties were still there, at the trough of power.

"And what if someone of Malinin's Team is still alive?" he thought. "Hiding somewhere safe and waiting for a sign to resurrect the past. And my family? If everything went well, my sister must be thirty-five or thirty-six now, and I don't even remember what she looked like. I'd definitely not recognize her if I saw her walking by… Is North Crestland a good place for them to live? Did it accept them, the citizens of the Commonwealth State, its eternal rival? I must do my best to find their traces, too bad that Colonel Petrenko died and didn't leave me a clue. He probably didn't want to live through another period of changes, and releasing me, thought that his mission was over, and he could finally retire to reserve forever."

The next section of the document was the information about the Delta-Center system. It was not a full set of documentation, but just a brief description, written by the team's technical specialist, Konstantin. Boris was surprised at how wisely it had all been designed. He was sure that the best minds of the country had been working hard for years to create a state-of-the-art tool that, instead of serving people, would forevermore become their nightmare. The system could have just as well been used for treating, educating and even entertaining people, it just needed a few adjustments.

"I'll do it," Boris said to himself. "I didn't spend all these years in the provision unit for nothing."

When he finished reading the documentation, he started going through his grandfather's instructions. The first hour of the operation was crucial. His calculating machine would be connected directly to the operational console, which would let him disable most of the stationery and mobile self-registrators and then lock all the premises that could be locked. At this point, the intrusion would be detected, so he had to direct all of the most powerful combat machines to the governmental buildings and other important objects, having preliminarily blocked and deelectrified them. All the broadcasters in the country would start airing a special message, which would be a sign to Malinin's Team members, if any of them were still alive. The code word was 'Beetlefly', and as soon as they heard it, they'd know everything was going according to the plan. The Team would know what to do and how to contact him. Boris also thought of using Pools of Ideological Interchange, which, without being censored, would provide a good communication channel. At some point, food drones, would have to be restarted and continue the delivery of pre-packaged food sets, so that locked and frightened people at least wouldn't be starving.

Was the whole thing possible at all? Professor Rogov had an idea that all these years had made the authorities relaxed and less vigilant, so it would be possible to take them off-guard, like they'd done fifty years ago, with Malinin. Doubtlessly, the state had reserve resources for such occasions, but they were not sufficient for a real fight. Their location could also be identified through the Delta-Center, and it wouldn't take long to disarm them too.

Boris's next task was to gather as many people to support him as he could. Access to Level One database would provide him with the details of all citizens, and there he could find former members of Malinin's Team or those who had taken sides with it at any point of its existence. This time a public communication channel could not be used because some of them might still be afraid to reveal themselves. Boris had to think of a sort of personal contact, at least with some of them, and eventually get more and more people to join him. There had to be those who had got tired of staying in all these years and would want to stretch their legs by going out and shooting at whoever comes their way. With proper guidance, such people would provide a core of the new wave of resistance. Next step was to divide the capital and all major cities into zones, and each of the zones was to be controlled by drones and military machines in order to keep those people in tune with his intentions. Boris had to make sure that the old infrastructure is still capable of supporting all citizens' basic needs, and the broadcasters would continue airing the right ideas until it is clear to everyone that the new power is of no threat to them. Simultaneously, they could start, one by one, destroying everyone associated with Pravdin and the State. No negotiations were to be held with them, just complete and merciless annihilation. By that time, the interim government would have taken enough functions to proclaim itself the new leading power. It would include only the most faithful and ideological members, who would be fully aware of the responsibility they were assigned.

"Boris, our experience has showed that weak people, dreamers and idealists should not be admitted to power. They are only good for buzzing around, making white noise and creating ineffective turbulence in the masses. Only the bold, the madmen, the hotheads can take real action, Boris. Only a firm hand, an absolute and unquestionable authority, only resolve, determination and full-hearted commitment, combined with brutal force and intransigence, can set this world in motion. It might seem another side of totalitarianism, but, believe me, it isn't. It's not violence for the sake of violence, which always leads to nothing, but an indispensable means to achieve noble objectives, which we've set for ourselves. It is important not to wallow in power, but to make it an instrument of sustainable growth and improvement," his grandfather admonished him.

All this reasoning made Boris's head spin, and he was
desperately trying to calm down and think rationally, but he
couldn't. "Okay, just let me leave it as it is for now," he thought.
"I'll start it and then, probably, it will be easier. Anyway, there must
be someone left who will be on my side, one head is good, two is
better. I've always been able to think quick under pressure and
granddad told me that a person's beat qualities are revealed in
stressful conditions, so I'll manage." He checked the National
Information Portal and happily found out that his interval of going
out was from 14:00 till 17:00. This time they were being generous
and granted him three hours instead of two, and these three hours
were perfect. When he got home, at five, he'd have enough time to
install the device and get it working before the electricity shutdown,
and, hopefully, he'd have access to Level Two by next morning. The
new day would start, and the country, for the first time in God knows
how many years, would wake up not to the usual "It's six o'clock in
the Commonwealth State and here is the news," but to a message
which would make them all jump out of their beds. Funny how they
didn't know about it now. However, Boris did, and it made his knees
weak.

3

The night before the Day of National Election Boris could
hardly sleep. He knew he had a long day ahead of him, but it seemed
that his eyelids were stuck and couldn't close properly. He got up
several times and walked to the window to watch the images on the
wallpaper change at regular intervals. He counted in his mind the
time of the intervals, and it was always sixty-four seconds, but the
last one was sixty-eight, and it made him absolutely frustrated. Then
he sat back on his sofa, opened his book and tried to read it in the
dark.

Then one morning through the dew
Hopped and skipped a Kangaroo.
When he saw great Cock-the-Roach
Loud he shouted with reproach:
"Goodness! Do you think he's strong?

Ha! Ha! Ha!
Think again, for you are wrong!
Ha! Ha! Ha!
Cock-the-Roach! Cock-the-Roach...
He's nothing but a brown cockroach!
That's the horrid midget's name –
If you obey him, you're to blame!
Haven't you got claw and paw,
Fangs to tear and bite?
How could you bow down before
Such a tiny mite?"
But the Hippos now felt bad,
So they whispered:
"Are you mad?
Go away! Don't make a fuss,
You will make things worse for us!"

At about three a.m., Boris could finally doze off. He didn't
dream of anything definite, and all he could make out of the images
scattered in his brain, was the faces of the people he'd met at
different periods of his life. His parents; his crying little sister in the
paws of a huge elephant; his old neighbors singing the anthem of the
Commonwealth State in front of their broadcaster; Colonel Petrenko
in Yegor Semenovich's white shirt, pointing his service pistol at his
temple; Lyudmila Ivanovna with the head of a kangaroo; Olga with
marshmallow lips; Slava and Angie on a bike – these characters
were coming together and then falling apart like he was looking into
a kaleidoscope, getting a new pattern with its every turn. They tried
to speak to Boris, but all he could hear was some hooting in the
background, which at first sounded like a huge machine gaining
momentum, but soon the hoot merged into one word, pronounced
distinctly and overbearingly: "Go… Go. Go!". And then Boris saw
his grandfather, alive, but with an unnaturally twisted leg, and he ran
towards him to find comfort and consolation in his arms once again,
but suddenly something made him stop. His grandfather's eyes
didn't belong to him. They were motionless and didn't express
anything apart from cruel revulsion. Boris kept looking into them,
hypnotized by terror, and then he suddenly understood whose eyes
they were. They belonged to Victor Vasilyevich Pravdin. He tossed

in his bed, dropped his blanket and woke up. He felt the elephant under his pillow and took it in his hands, but the toy's eyes were alarming too. "They just don't believe in me," thought Boris and woke up completely. The darkness didn't say a word this time. It was watching him and preparing for its final feast.

Katyusha had already turned on and was greeting the citizens warmly and cheerfully, reminding them of the big day that had just started. "The National Election Day is finally here! Today, millions of people…" "Will become free…" continued Boris for the machine and started making his preparations. He packed his satnav, his old army shovel, a screwdriver just in case, all carefully placed in his backpack. He wondered if it would attract the patrols' attention, but then remembered that people sometimes carried bags with them, although he never understood what for. After packing, Boris went to the kitchen. He had to grab something to eat because he wasn't sure he'd have this opportunity later. The food drones were going to arrive earlier today, so that the identification procedure would not be missed, and Boris decided to save some of the food for the future. He went to the kitchen the same way as he'd done ten years ago, on the first morning in his new flat. It seemed that it all had happened to someone else, to someone who had only a distant resemblance to what he was like now. Sergeant Arsenyev. Wounded soldier. Criminal bastard. Orphaned boy. This flat had taken over all of him, made him old and overweight, and he thought that he'd move somewhere else as soon as everything is settled down.

Quite unexpectedly, in the kitchen he found Slava sitting on a badger-legged stool, his keen eyes cast in the direction of a fly, making uneven circles under the ceiling.

"When's your exodus?" he asked without any attempt to be polite.

"At two. Yours?"

"Three. You know what these highly esteemed gentlemen did? They separated me and Angie. Her time out starts at eleven. She's getting ready now, and I don't want to disturb her, so I am sitting here, thinking."

"Of what?"

"Nothing. My life. My catharsis. Where're you gonna go, anyway?"

"Just for a stroll. I'll make use of my vote and then just stretch my legs a bit. How's the weather out there?"

"What does it matter?"

"You're right. It doesn't. And you? What are you going to do with your fragment of freedom? Go to the landfill to get yourself another bike?"

"A tank, maybe."

"Sounds like a plan. You might even be lucky enough to find a submarine."

"No, not my cup of tea. I'd still prefer a catharsis."

"You might be lucky enough to find it too."

"Who knows. These things can appear at any moment without warning and against our wishes. That's why you have to be alert at all times."

Boris sat on another badger-legged stool waiting for the food drones. He didn't care what they would bring, he just needed to distract himself from his heavy thoughts. The water was boiling on the stove, the wallpaper was showing a peaceable landscape of a stream in the mountains, Slava was sitting on his shaky stool, and everything seemed usual and ordinary, just the way it was a week or a year ago. But it wasn't, and Boris suddenly felt the long-forgotten pain in his spine, which could be his wound, or his heart just as well. He kept voicing his grandfather's instructions in his mind, like a prayer, and inserted "It'll be okay" now and then instead of "Amen." He looked at his wrist timer. Two hours and twenty-eight minutes to go. He'll be okay.

At 13:59 Boris was standing at his front door and checking for a thousandth time the contents of his backpack. His micropass was in his pocket just waiting to be swiped against the lock to grant him his well-earned permission to go out. "This micropass is authorized to exit the premises. Door will be unblocked for ten seconds. Starting the countdown. Nine... eight…" Boris waited until it said "five" and pushed the door open. He got a familiar feeling of deep panic terror he had every time he went into the corridor. It all rooted from the day when his grandfather died, and he was playing 'run-and-hide' with armed to the teeth soldiers of the National army. He'd enjoyed running ever since because it once saved his life, and he thought that he might run now, too, so that the panic attack couldn't seize him. However, it was just the heat of the moment, and he walked down the stairs, like a normal obedient citizen. Only the strange things in his backpack could hint on his real intentions.

The weather was okay. Not too good because the sky was autumn-gray and unwelcomingly scowl, but at least it wasn't raining, and the wind wasn't strong enough to sneak under his buttoned-up coat. The air smelled of rotten leaves and burning garbage. Boris could hear some subdued music coming from the distance, which indicated the location of the voting poles, and he wondered if he could avoid going there and get straight to the university park. Unfortunate for him, he couldn't because there was only one road from his house in this direction, so he started walking slowly on the cracked asphalt, which seemed soft and tenacious under his feet. In a couple of minutes, he heard familiar humming above his head and rose his eyes to see a patrolling drone, which froze for a second and then flew away in the direction of the voting space. "Hello to you too," thought Boris, watching the machine's silhouette dissolve in the distance. "Was it a salute to your future commander?"

As he was approaching the square, the street was getting busier. People were coming out of blocks of flats, identical to his, and moving towards the place, appointed to them from above, where they would happily give away another year of their worthless lives to the refurbished image of nonexistent President. Boris tried not to look in their faces because he suddenly felt a deep disgust for being part of them. "We are happy all together," he tried to convince himself. "If we want, we'll make a ladder. It will take us… Take us… Stupid goddamn song, why does it sound so wrong?!" But the words of his song were soon absorbed by another one, which he also knew by heart.

Victor Pravdin is our heart and soul!
Brave and strong, he has the only goal
Take the country to its finest hour,
And he'll do whatever in his power!

Victor Pravdin never makes mistakes,
Never rests and never takes a break,
He's our only true and dear friend,
And our friendship's never bound to end.

The singer, a young boy of twelve or so, finished his song and bowed to the audience. Everyone clapped their hands as he went off stage, and the loudspeakers behind his back turned on and started playing a piece of music, which sounded somewhat familiar to Boris. The music was followed by the usual mechanical voice.

"Dear citizens of the Commonwealth State! You all know that we are now celebrating the most important day in the political, cultural and economic life of our beautiful and prosperous country…"

"Stop! Wait-wait-wait… Isn't it my broadcast? The hill, and Malinin with the flag… No, it wasn't meant to be like this, turn it off, now! I don't want to take part in this orgy!"

A volunteer ran towards Boris, smiled at him and slipped something in his hand. Boris looked down and saw a flyer card with a hologram of Pravdin's face in front of the national flag.

"May this day stay in your memory for as long as possible!" declaimed the volunteer and smiled widely.

"Erm… thanks," Boris returned the smile and squeezed the card in his fist.

"Please, if you have any questions, feel free to ask me, or anyone of us. We are here to help and to guide you!"

"I know. I will, I promise"

"Have a great time then, citizen, and may the truth be with you!"

Boris felt that his lips were stiff because he couldn't get rid of the wide unnatural smile that had frozen them. He turned his back on the volunteer and almost ran across the square. "It's a nightmare", he said to himself. "I'll wake up and I'll be in the army barrack, or in the Center of Patriotic Education, or at home with my family. I must only endure for a little while, and it will be gone! Please, mommy, I want to watch Fidgy Freckles! Please turn off this scary show!"

"Your attention, please! President Victor Vasilyevich Pravdin speaking!" announced the loudspeakers on the stage. Boris was almost knocked down by the first chords of the national anthem and pulled his head into his shoulders, prepared to hear the familiar voice.

"Dear compatriots! Dear fellow citizens of the Commonwealth State! To start with, I want to thank you all for your courage, for your fearlessness and unconditional support of the policy of the Party of National Unity. I am delighted to see all of you here in the streets of your hometowns, not put off by the threat of terrorist attacks and evil tricks of foreign agents. We all know what you are here for, and, once again, let me express my personal gratitude for your consciousness and responsible attitude to the future of our State. It was a hard year. We have faced colossal challenges in almost all spheres of our life, but nothing could break our victorious spirit. We were gratefully greeting each coming day and not even for a moment thought of giving in to our enemies, even though they keep changing their tactics all the time and develop more and more sophisticated weapons aimed at our sovereign State, aimed at you, my fellow citizens. Their plans failed under our onslaught, but they didn't surrender. They keep assaulting on our independence and on our lives, trying to scare us with bioweapon and toxic releases, promoting the most barbaric and untraditional values through their foreign agents. But, my dear friends, they are bound to fail again and again until they are finally destroyed by the power of the truth, which we represent..."

"Will you knock it off!" whispered Boris. "For God's sake! Stop making an idiot out of yourself and me! We both know that this war will never end, as long as you are in power!"

"Apart from the glorious victories, we have made hundreds of breakthroughs in industry, economy, social security. Our plants and factories constantly produce all the goods necessary for prosperous existence. Thousands of kilometers of roads have been built, hundreds of new machines have been produced, and, consequently, millions of people can enjoy all the benefits of being proud citizens of the Commonwealth State... And now, let me give you this promise, a word of a simple honest man, your humble servant. Very soon you will be able to walk the streets freely, like you are doing today, to look into the sky without fear of bombings, but to admire its beauty, which is cast on every citizen of our great and invincible State!"

"Let me promise the same," Boris thought. "But, to my deepest regret, you, Victor Vasilyevich, will not be there to see it," the sound of the national anthem was a perfect accompaniment to his words, and Boris cheered up a little.

When the speech was over, he continued making his way through the celebrating people, picturing in mind the map from his satnav. His grandfather had probably been using the same road all the years, turning gradually from an inspired professor into a cynical and somewhat cruel revolutionist. The crowd was becoming thicker with every hundred meters, and soon Boris almost had to elbow his way out of it, fearing that he was getting short of time. People were walking on the sidewalk and on the cracked road, many of them carrying flags and balloons, talking to each other, smiling at the volunteers, enjoying the autumn chill and the atmosphere of holistic exhilaration.

"Are they really so happy?" Boris wondered to himself. "Are these their real emotions or are they all just feeling what they were told to feel? If an outdoor screen suddenly started compelling them to cry and grieve, would they obey? Do they have anything left that really belongs to them and is not a product of the state propaganda? Will freedom make them really happy? Are they still capable of making choices – right choices, wrong choices, it doesn't matter as long as they are made by themselves? Maybe they just want to continue their snailish life, eating the same food, doing the same job, electing the same President year after year? Maybe this point of balance, which I am going to shift, is the only possible way of their existence, and I will only send them into chaos and destruction? Can anyone tell me? Please, can anyone tell me what to do?" Boris looked into the faces around him, but couldn't find the answers, so he continued walking until he saw the outlines of the fence surrounding the university park.

As he was approaching his point of destination, he noticed that, to his relief, the crowd started to disperse. A few citizens were strolling down the street, and Boris decided to wait until they go away to enter the park unnoticed. However, there was one figure that seemed to be stuck in front of the gate and didn't want to move. Boris waited. The figure waited, too, and then suddenly started walking in his direction. Boris almost dropped his liver and made a few steps back, but then decided that it would attract even more attention, so he stood still, pretending to be lost and trying to find his way. The figure belonged to an elderly woman, who, in spite of her age, was very upright and moved graciously and with unusual dignity. However, something in the way she put her feet on the ground, one after the other, seemed unnatural, as if she was walking on stilts. Boris felt that she was going to speak to him, and so she did, as soon as she came close enough for a conversation.

"Well, hello there, young man!" her eyes were pale green with streaks of yellow and looked blindish. She looked extremely old, ruined by age, and her body was trembling and shaking, so it was unclear how she had been able to walk at all. "Might you be Boris by any chance?"

Boris started as if he was whipped by her words.

"Am I Boris?" he repeated the question. "No, no, ma'am, I'm not Boris. No, I'm definitely not!"

"Okay-okay, not-Boris, I understand. Nothing to get so agitated about. Can I, maybe, introduce myself, then? I'm not-Nadezhda, nor… wait, what am I? Fedorovna? Konstantinovna? Vasilievna? Never mind. I lost myself some thirty years ago. So, it doesn't really matter who I am. But what really matters is why I am here. And you? What are you doing off the grid of the celebration? Something called you, young man, not-Boris, just like something called me, didn't it?"

"I'm sort of lost, I guess."

"So am I. Lost. You know what? Can I tell you? They deleted my memory. Took me to a horrible place and tortured me until I broke down completely. Do you see it?" she lifted her hands and Boris saw that the fingers on both of them were crooked and bended, and some missed their first phalanges. "They made me speak, and I told them everything. I don't remember what it was exactly, but they were happy, and, in return, they wiped off my memory. I think I asked them to kill me, but that was too much of a favor, so they threw me out in the street after nine years behind the bars and laughed at me while I was walking away on my broken legs. Did I tell you they broke them, too? And my ribs, so I find it hard to breathe, especially at night. But that doesn't matter. Why did I come here, you ask? I come every year, twice a year to be exact, for Boris… or for Vladimir… let me think… no, I'm sure it's Boris. Pity you're not him. But it's okay, I'll come here again and again, until I finally die. I might even die here, if I'm lucky enough. Do you think I'm mad? Come on, talk to me! There's nothing wrong in talking, is there? Tell me that everything will be fine, and I'll meet Boris, or Vladimir, or… what was his name?"

"Sorry ma'am," Boris wanted to hug the woman because she looked like a Good Witch of the South from one of the fairy tales his mother used to read to him. He wanted to tell her everything, but he couldn't say a word. "Sorry, ma'am, but I must go. I haven't voted yet, and my time out finishes soon."

"Sure. Go if you have to. That's what you've got your legs for, I guess. I'll go now too. See you when I see you, then?"

The woman walked away slowly on her pogo-sticked legs, and Boris waited for her to disappear so that he could sneak into the park. The road was empty at last, so he took a deep breath and made his final step towards the gate, but then stopped straight away. Something was not as it was supposed to be, but he didn't realize at once what it was. Only after a few seconds he saw a lock on the iron door and a diode flashing red, which didn't mean anything but the fact that the park was inaccessible. Boris knew that some places of the city had been permanently closed, at least for citizens with passes of the first level, and even if he had a route list, granting him the permission to go in, his pass just wouldn't work. As simple as that. He stood at the gate and wasn't sure what he should feel now – disappointment or relief. Perhaps he could at least try to climb over the fence, but it didn't look like a good idea because it might have been energized or fitted with an intrusion detection system. And even if it wasn't, Boris was just too clumsy and unfit for such a leap. There had to be another way to get inside, maybe some hidden door or a tunnel, made by his granddad – he should have foreseen such an obstacle. Or, maybe, it was an omen. The fate itself was trying to prevent him from this step, and he had no other choice as to obey it and just walk away with nothing.

It was a hard decision to make, and Boris stood there in hesitation, wondering how long it will take the drones to notice a strange citizen in front of the locked gate. His thoughts were answered within a moment. There it was – a noise behind his back, which sounded weird, but, at the same time, he was sure he'd heard it before. His nerves were going up on adrenaline, and every small thing could ruin his mind completely. His limbs momentarily stiffened, frozen by his own paranoia, and he couldn't even make himself look back, while the annoying chirping was getting louder and louder, and becoming more and more threatening. It could be anything – a patrolling drone, or a self-registrator, or a random citizen looking for his voting pole. But when Boris picked himself up and looked around, he understood at once that it was none of the above. It was Slavik. On a bike. His neighbor was sweating and out of breath, and his tousled curly hair was stuck to his forehead, which made him look like a funny little animal escaping from a predator.

"Erm… Slava?" Boris tried to sound natural. "I didn't expect to see you here. Did you… Did you want to get inside the park for some… what's it called? Ah, inspiration! Just like me? Well, I'm sorry to say, but it's locked. You know, some of the city locations are always…"

"Bears went on a hike a-riding on a bike…" declaimed Slava. "Listen, Boris, have you ever wondered what kind of hike it was? And what was this idea, which made the bears abandon their lairs, leave their comfort zone and saddle those bikes, the craziest means of transport in the world, so unnatural to them? Maybe they'd received a message from someone? A message from the past? From their grandfather, perhaps?"

"Slava, what are you talking about? I don't understand! What grandfather? What message? Are you mad?" Boris was almost crying.

"Your grandfather, my dear friend. Vladimir Ivanovich Rogov. 1968 – 2036. A traitor. A foreign agent. A murderer. I katyushed him. It was hard but I came across an old database of the enemies of the state, under the third level of access, and there he was, classified as one of the ideologists of the Black Plague and a former colleague of the Destabilizer, the Bad President, as you might know. Tough guy. Murky business. Just the way I like it."

"Slava… How did you know it? Did you hack my calculating machine?" Boris understood that there was no use in denying the obvious and just wanted to play for time and think of some way out. Maybe, run away, or pretend to be dead. Anyway, he hadn't done anything wrong so far, and a little message on his machine wouldn't probably provide enough ground for the forces to liquidate him.

"Well, to begin with, there was no need to hack your device. You sleep so soundly that I could fully enjoy my bedtime reading without being disturbed. So, where were we? Ah, the bears…"

"I never thought you'd be so mean! How could you, Slava?"

"Sorry, Bob, I didn't want to. It's just that you were acting so strange that day, remember? When we had this argument about politics. You seemed to know something that I didn't, and it was like a blow to my ego. I had to find it out, you see? Had to reveal your secret. I didn't have enough time to finish reading it that night, so I came back today, the moment the door closed behind you. I wasn't sure whether you'd do what your grandfather had told you, thought you'd not have enough guts for it. But I still decided to come here in case I was wrong about you. I was, Boris, and I'm sorry for that."

"It's ok. Now, let's go. I haven't voted yet, have you?"

"Nope. I'll do it now."

"There's no pole here, mate, don't be ridiculous. Let's go back to the square. And leave your bike here before it attracts the drones' attention."

"Are you giving up so easily? What about the revolution? What about your grandfather? Too bad he wasn't my granddad, really."

"It doesn't matter who is whose grandfather! The park is locked! This is it! Full stop! End of the story!"

"And what if I tell you that it isn't?"

"What do you mean?"

"I've got something for you, Bobby-boy. Something you've forgotten about. Something that is called a micropass of the third level of access. I got one for my small job for an important person, remember?"

"Will it work?"

"For this location, yes. I have a month's route list, which covers this area as well, so there won't be any problem."

"You sure?"

"Absolutely."

"And will you open it for me?"

"Why wouldn't I? That's what I'm here for, anyway."

"I thought you were going to report me…"

"Report you? Yeah, I might seem mean, sneaking into your room and reading the message. But I'm not a killer, Boris. Catharsis doesn't work like this. It's meant to be self-purification, not self- or anyone else's destruction. Do you understand the difference?"

Slava looked at Boris questioningly.

"I do," answered Boris shortly.

"I said I was going to vote now. I vote for you, Boris."

Slava went into his pocket to find his micropass, but suddenly felt something there and smiled.

"Look what I've got." he said, pulling out the card with Pravdin's hologram. "The bastard caught me and pawned it on to me without even asking whether I want it or not!"

"I've got the same." Boris grinned and demonstrated his trophy. "What are we going to do with them? Let's maybe throw them away, shall we?"

"Not until we finish the business. I'd happily tear it in pieces and toss them right into their faces."

"I thought you were out of politics."

"I am. I just like beautiful gestures. Victory must be beautiful, or it will lose its charm. You'll make it a beautiful victory, Boris, I'm sure," Slava gave him a strange stare, and for the first time ever since he'd known his neighbor, Boris noticed a hint of respect in his eyes. He looked away.

"So, here's my pass. I'll swipe it and you'll go inside."

"Will you go with me?" Boris desperately hoped that he'd say yes.

"I guess I'll be more useful here, watching your back. I haven't seen any patrols in this area, only the drones, and it makes me feel uncomfortable. There must be someone to watch us and they might be doing it surreptitiously, from some hiding places. Or maybe I'm paranoid, but it doesn't mean that we mustn't be cautious."

"Okay. It'll take me about fifteen minutes or so. I'll meet you here, and we'll go away with the card. And put your bike away somewhere, it can be a trigger for the watchers."

"I'll drop it in this ditch over there. I might even come for it later; it's become sort of dear to me."

"Right. Let's do it."

Slava took out his micropass.

"Hey, Boris. Tell me one thing before it all begins."

"What?"

"Your book. How did it end? Were the bears and all those freaky beasts consumed by the cockroach? Did they surrender?"

"No, mate, of course not. It's a children's book, remember? Such things always have a happy end. I liked the ending, so I learned it by heart, and I still remember it. Listen.

Suddenly a wee bird flew
From the woods dark green and blue,
Flitting fast as any arrow,
Such a perky little sparrow!
"Cheep-peep-peep!
A-cheep-a-peep!"
How he nips! Oh, what a cheek!
For the cockroach in his beak
Dies without a single squeak.
His long ginger whiskers are hidden from view.
That giant, the tyrant has now got his due!

They had a celebration afterwards. With dances that ended up in the moon falling on the earth. They had to nail it back on the sky, which was a hard job, but they were still happy to do it together. So, what do you say, Slava? Will you help me mount the moon back to where it belongs when we finish with the Cockroach?"

Slava didn't answer. He quickly swiped the micropass against the lock. "This micropass is authorized to enter the premises. Door will be unblocked for ten seconds. Starting the countdown. Nine... eight…" Boris waited until it said "four" and pushed the door open.

"Wait," Slava squeezed his arm. "Take the pass with you."

"Why?"

"To open the door from inside. Take it! Just in case I'm not here when you come back."

"Why? What are you…?"

There was no time to argue, so Boris grabbed the pass and on the last second entered the park.

4

Slava was left alone outside the gate and looked around. There was nothing suspicious, so he took his bike and rolled it towards the ditch. It fitted perfectly and was almost invisible for the one who didn't know that it was there. He came back to the gate and looked at his wrist timer. It was not more than five minutes since his neighbor had gone inside, so he had only about ten minutes to wait. He leaned on the gate and started whistling.

"Excuse me, citizen!" The voice came out of nowhere, and it might have been only in his head, but it immediately made his back sweat.

"Is there any problem?" continued the voice.

He could finally see his interlocutor. From a small path on the right, a figure in white and blue volunteer uniform was approaching him, and he could swear that even from a distance he could see a smile on its face, and the smile scared him even more than the words.

"No," Slava cleared his throat. "No problem. Just taking a rest after a long walk."

"Have you voted yet?" asked the volunteer cheerfully.

"No… Yes… I'm in doubt, actually."

"Really? What sort of doubt? Do you need any help?" the volunteer gave him a sympathetic look.

"No, I'm fine. You'd better go – someone else might be needing your help right now."

"May I have your name and internal number, citizen?" the tone of the volunteer's voice changed.

"What for?" there were about eight minutes left until Boris was to come out, so he had to think quick.

"We had information that a third-level access card has just been used on this door." the mask started to flow off the volunteer's face, and Slava could see his eyes now – the eyes of a patrolling security man. "Do you know anything about it?"

"No, I…"

The man pointed his biometrical analyzer at him.

248

"Are you Vyacheslav Lebedev, internal number 343-AT2917?"

"Do you want my autograph? I usually try to avoid publicity, so why should I make an exception for someone like you?"

"Can you be more specific? I repeat: are you Vyacheslav Lebedev, internal number 343-AT2917?"

"I was him in the morning, I suppose. If nothing has changed, I might still be him."

"Very funny. Why did you use the micropass?"

"To see if it works."

"Where's the micropass? I'm confiscating it in the name of the law!"

"I threw it away"

"Where?"

"It must be somewhere on the ground. I'm sure you have all the necessary equipment to track it"

"You are not supposed to have this level of access. Who gave it to you?"

"That's none of your business!" four minutes to go. Think quicker, Slava!

"How do you speak to an authority?"

"You? Authority? Well, let me tell something to you. Your power is nothing! A piece of paper that can be torn and trampled into the ground! I'll show it to you, and then you can arrest me, liquidate me, or do whatever you want!" Slava took out his flyer with Pravdin's hologram, burst it into four accurate pieces and threw them into the face of the volunteer. He instantly felt a cold hit of electroshock, and his hands went numb, and then the other one went on his legs, and, finally, a blow on his head, which made him see stars and floaters. "That's not the catharsis I was looking for," the last thought swept his mind. "But it's not too bad. There are still three minutes left for him to go out."

Almost at the same time, on the other side of the city, an elderly man in thick glasses jumped on his chair.

"I can't believe it!" he cried. "The device! My device! It's been taken out! He… He did it, Liza! The grandson, the son of a bitch managed to get inside! Liza, come here, quick! You'll never believe what I'm going to tell you!"

Liza, a fat tidy woman in a chic dressing gown rushed into the room.

"Kostya, what's going on? Are you okay? Is it your heart again? Self-aid…" she babbled, looking at her husband alarmingly.

"I'm fine, Liza, that's not the point! I was keeping something back all these thirty-four years. A secret, which could kill both of us. But now I can tell you. Listen up, Liza, and listen good. There was this guy… No, let me start from the beginning… I was young and I knew a lot. I could even program the sun to rise on the west, well, at least that's what they said about me. And then I met this team, these people who needed my skills, and together we did something insane, something that was not supposed to work, but it did! It happened just a minute ago! No, let me start again. In 2034, just after the Glorious Election, I was contacted by this professor…" Liza listened to her husband and thought that it was the first time in their life together when she'd seen him like that – inspired and full of childish excitement. She was worried about his weak heart but didn't dare to say a word not to make him even more anxious.

Boris didn't go out of the park until after another seven or eight minutes, and he felt that he was awfully late. He opened the door with the micropass and looked around for his neighbor.

"Slava?" he called quietly. "Stop hiding, it's time to go! I've got it!"

There was no answer. Boris didn't want to listen to his worst thoughts and stood there, searching for the familiar silhouette with tousled curly hair, but all he could find was some white spots on the ground, which he at first couldn't identify. He bent to take one in his hand, but before he did it, he knew what it was. On one of them was half of Pravdin's hologram, which looked at him triumphantly with its iridescent eye.

"Slava…" Boris's hands trembled and he dropped the paper, so that Pravdin's face was stuck in mud. "You said you'd do it after the victory. Why, Slava? Who was this beautiful gesture for? Me?"

He understood now. Everything was so plain and obvious, but he refused to believe. He felt a vice-like grip squeezing his heart and an immediate urge to run away from this surreal place, which had just destroyed his supporter, who could have later become one of his close companions. They must have detected the door opening, and they might have done it when he'd opened it to go out, so he had to escape as quickly as possible, before they send another patrol. Boris remembered about the bike and peeked into the ditch. It was lying there, as if waiting for him, and although it didn't look reliable enough, he was sure it would sustain a short ride to the landfill on the edge of the square, where he'd bury it for the rest of its life. In any case, Slava didn't need it anymore. Boris pulled the bike out with his sweaty hands and realized how heavy it was, heavier than it had been in the flat. *"You know what they say, chubs? They say that if you learn to ride a bike at any time of your life, you'll never forget it."* – "I know, Grampy. My memory isn't so good, but it never deletes anything, it just keeps it hidden, waiting for the chance to get it revealed. The time is now, Grampy. The time is now, so let's do it. Look at me, Grampy. A good man. A brilliant artist. And a cycling champion! How does it go?"

Bears went to the hike
A-riding on a bike.
Then came Tom-the-Cat,
Back-to-front he sat.
Spry mosquitoes drifted by
In a big balloon on high.
Lobsters looked like shrimps
On a dog that limps.
Wolves were mounted on a horse.
Lions drove in cars, of course.
Hares in pairs
Crammed in a tram.
Toad rode on a broom...
What a merry bunch!
Gingernuts they munch.

"Am I doing good, Grampy?"
"You're doing perfect, young man!"
"Are you still behind me?"
"I am! All the time! Don't stop!"
Boris reached the landfill in less than ten minutes, and even managed to make it without falling over or being noticed by a patrol or a self-registrator He got off his bike and carefully placed it on top of a heap of garbage, like a dying animal that he had to say goodbye

to. Slava's micropass went there too, to wait eternally for his owner
– his well-deserved reward for doing a small business for a big man.
"You'll be okay, both of you," thought Boris. "I promise." It was
only half three, so he didn't need to hurry anymore. People were still
walking along the street, most of them going in the direction of the
square with the voting poles and the entertainment, from which
Boris heard the familiar "Victor Pravdin is our heart and soul" song,
performed by the same young boy. It meant that soon there would be
President's speech, then they'd show his broadcast, and then the loop
will start again. Volunteers were ubiquitously digging around, and
their white and blue uniform vividly diluted the plain outfit of
common citizens.

"Victor Pravdin dragged the state from hell!" the boy almost
screamed the words, and it was clear that he was already deadly tired
and wanted to go home. Boris didn't know what he was sicker of –
the song, the singer, or the whole situation, but he started pushing
the crowd more intensely in order to get to the road, leading to his
house.

"Good afternoon, dear citizen!" a volunteer came out of the
blue. "Have you voted yet?"

"No, I was just going to," answered Boris automatically.

"Do you know the location of your voting pole?"

"Yes, thank you. I'll go there right now."

"Oh, let me come with you. I know how difficult it might be
to make such an important step."

"No, don't bother with me, I'm fine. I know everything, I do
it every year, believe me!"

"Bother? It's my job to direct the lost citizens and to make
sure they do the right thing. What's your internal number?"

"It's… wait, what do you need it for?" Boris felt anxious and
alarmed, which obviously reflected in his voice.

"To find your voting pole, of course! You surely know that
each pole can take in a restricted number of votes. So, what is it?"

"152-AH1021"

"Let me check…" the volunteer looked something up in his
mobile information machine. "Oh, yes, it's on the left. Here, let me
show you."

They both walked a couple of hundred meters in silence until they came to the opposite edge of the square, where Boris saw a pole, white and blue, as usual, with a green diode flashing on top.

"Here we are, citizen!" the volunteer gave him an encouraging nod. "Off you go then!"

"Thanks a lot. I really appreciate it."

"You'll thank me after you've made your vote!"

"Are you going to…"

"No, of course not. We ensure the secrecy of the ballot, so I'm not going to disturb you. I'll just stand by and see if you do everything correctly. I'll close my ears when you say the name, of course."

Boris walked the plank to the pole. He turned around to see another encouraging smile of the volunteer and then swiped his micropass against the slot and said his name and internal number. The volunteer was still watching him, his ears demonstratively closed with his hands in white gloves. Boris opened his mouth. The diode blinked at him, and a mechanical voice confirmed that the vote had been cast.

"On behalf of the President, let me express our gratitude for your responsible attitude to your civic duty." said the volunteer pompously. "Now, you can enjoy the celebration, and don't forget to watch the fireworks on your broadcaster later in the evening!"

Boris nodded and rushed through the crowd. People were laughing and cheering to the sound of the National Anthem, which meant that Pravdin's speech was over, and everyone was saturated with the fluids of pride and joy that it had given them. Boris looked in their faces. Happy faces, inspired faces, faces filled with overwhelming inclusion. "They *are* happy," he thought. "Even if it's not their real emotions, even if it was compelled by the broadcasters, they don't know it, and, therefore, it's genuine. More genuine than anything else in this world," he stopped in horror and astonishment. Victor Pravdin looked at him from the screen with his shrewd, close-set eyes and smiled with his unnaturally sharp mouth.

"How on earth did you manage to do it?" asked Boris, and Pravdin's eyes became alive.

"It is very simple," he answered. "I just gave people what they wanted and in return took what they didn't need."

"But you can't deprive them of their freedom!" protested Boris. "We are all born with it, and no one can take it away from us!"

"You are right, citizen Arsenyev. What's your internal number? Never mind. You're still right. One can't deprive people of what they don't have."

"But I have it, my freedom! And I feel it inside me, right now!"

"No, you don't, believe me, my dear friend."

"I am not a friend of yours!"

"Yes, you are. You are my friend, like everyone in this square, in this city and in this country. My close and most valued friends."

"No, I can't be friends with those whom I hate!"

"Really?" Pravdin made a disappointed face. "I'm sure you didn't mean to say this. Remember, citizen Arsenyev, when you were fifteen. We sat on a beautiful green hill, and I told you stories from my life. I told you about this funny incident with a very important person whom I had to convince to take sides with us. Remember, I gave him a handful of our earth? The most precious thing that I could give to anyone. Your memory isn't so good, but you still remember, don't you? And that's when we made friends. Friends forever, citizen Arsenyev. You know it – every time you look at my face you know we'll always be together."

Boris sunk his head, and Pravdin continued.

"You might be experiencing some sort of agitation or even anxiety, but, believe me, it's nothing but fresh air. They say it can do weird things to those who spend most of their time inside. Freedom? No, my friend. I don't need your freedom; it doesn't cost a penny. I'm interested in more pragmatic issues. So, dear citizen Arsenyev, my friendly advice to you is to go back home before your time out finishes. Or you might see or feel something else. Something inexistent, I mean."

"Are you threatening me?" Boris was shaking with indignation. "Do you think I'm afraid of you?"

"My dearest friend, I can't think. I'm just a hologram, remember? An image created on a calculating machine, just like the one you have in your room. No, I don't need you to be afraid of me.

Fear is a destructive emotion. I don't even need you to love me. It will be enough if you just believe in me."

"I don't believe in you, then!"

"You don't? What a pity! Just let me clarify one thing, will you? Who exactly don't you believe in? This one?" Pravdin's face changed into an old man's with wrinkles and small slanted eyes. "Or this?" it changed again and became younger, thinner and paler. "Or maybe this?" this time it had sharp features and a long, crooked nose. "Would you like me to go on? Do you still think you're talking to Pravdin? Which of us, may I ask? The first, the second, or maybe the fifth one? No, my friend, you are talking to the power itself. We can take as many forms as is needed to keep you believing, and you won't even notice the change. And now listen to this. No one, not a single person in this country, will be able to stop us. Not even your grandfather with his little idiotic bookies, not even this pathetic dreamer, whose name I've already forgotten, not even you, who gave in to this system thirty-four years ago! You are with us, citizen Arsenyev, and you are us, and now stop messing with what you don't understand and go back to your cell! Now, I said!"

Boris closed his ears with his hands and squinted. "I will do it. I will do it. I will do it," he whispered to himself.

"You ok, lad?" Boris gave a start. He knew that voice from somewhere. "Lost something?"

"I'm fine, just thinking…" he answered and looked up. "Hey, do I know you?"

"You probably do, mate. Ev'ryone knows Joseph from the plant!"

"Oh, Joseph! I remember!" Boris cried. "You're the… the cat guy! I met you here ten years ago, when I… doesn't matter. I'm so happy to see a familiar face!"

"Oh, mate, no way, 'how you doin'?" Joseph seemed to have recognized him too. "You're… what's your name… Boris! Boris the Conqueror! So, what's up, Boris? 'ow's life treatin' ya?"

"Can't complain, mate, and you?"

"I ain't seen you bleedin' donkeys years! Class, I'm glad everything's working out for you. Still drawing pictures?"

"Kind of… And you?"

"Nah, I'm still here. Livin', workin'… Just sort of grafting in the factory. The pay's okay, the boss is a bloody wonker, though, but it is what it is at the end of the day, innit?"

"Yeah, you're right, mate. We don't choose our life, do we?"

"No, no, it all keeps a roof o'er our 'eads. Anyways, you 'aven't changed your mind about my offer? It's still valid, and I've got a nice place at the polygon. You know, working with the waste and stuff. Not an easy one, but you look like a tough fellow, so you'll manage."

"Oh, I don't know. It's not the best moment to make such important decisions…"

"Of course, no problem. You don't 'ave to decide now. 'ere, take my internal number. Lemme put it into your broadie."

Boris took out his device.

"Okay Katyusha, store the number," he commanded.

"It's Joseph Beglow, 862-BC2253."

"Thanks mate. How's your cat, by the way?" Boris didn't want to end the conversation, although he was aware of the time.

"That daft ball of fat, you mean?" Joseph smiled widely. "Oh, 'e's fine, don't worry about the bastard. Still catches the fattest rats in the borough. I take 'im out ev'ry mornin' before work and then 'e comes back for the night. Sleeps on my bed, doesn't 'e!"

"That's good. Say hi to him from me, then."

"I will. So, care for a walk around the place?"

"Sorry, Joseph, I must be going now, I only have about thirty minutes left. Next time, maybe?"

"Sure. You know 'ow to find me. Message me up in any case, ok? Just for a chat."

"I will. Thanks for… everything."

"No problem, mate, we're friends, anyway. A team, let's call it."

"Sorry? What team?" Boris stiffened.

"Boris and Joseph. Stand-up guys. Keep safe, lad!"

Joseph walked away, and Boris shrugged his shoulders. His paranoia was killing him, and he kept seeing things and signs that wouldn't have meant anything in his normal condition. He had to hurry up, as it was already twenty to seven.

Boris entered the flat, his head spinning from all the events of the day and walked slowly into his room to get some solitude and time to think. He opened his backpack and took out the card that he'd retrieved from the park. It was just the same size as the one in his calculating machine, so it wouldn't take much of an effort to insert it there. But first he needed to withdraw the old one, which meant saying goodbye to his grandfather's message. The tool for this operation was there – a pair of pliers with red handles and rusty tips. Boris carefully hooked the card and pulled it out of the slot. Then he placed it on the table, just beside the one from the park, and looked at both objects, trying to keep his thoughts together. It was time to act. He took the pliers and held them in his hand for some time.

"Slava?" he heard Angie's voice from the corridor. "Are you here? Boris, where's Slava? His time out was from three till five, and he promised to come at half four. It's almost five o'clock now, and he…"

Boris pretended not to hear. He quickly grabbed the second card and put the pliers' tip on one of its edges. Then he pushed the tip into the plastic until it broke off. The small black piece fell on the table, followed by another one, and one more, until the card became so small that it was difficult to hold it between his fingers. He broke off one last piece and took the other card – the one which had been waiting in his calculating machine for ten years. It was a bit harder to break, and his fingers got scratched from the sharp plastic, and some of the scratches started to bleed. Angie was crying in the neighboring room, and the broadcaster was playing another patriotic song about the battles won and the rewards to be received. Soon they would show a firework display, and then five thousand balloons would fly into the dark sky and vanish there, like they had every year, ever since he could remember. Somewhere, far away, Slava's body was dissolving in a self-liquidator, somewhere, even further, Angie was speaking to emergency services with her voice trembling from tears, and somewhere, very close, stood his grandfather, Vladimir

Ivanovich Rogov, stretching his hands towards him as though he was trying either to hug, or to stop him.

"You're late, professor," said Boris calmly and solemnly. "You're awfully late. Both cards are damaged now, broken to pieces, so that they'd never be able to break anyone's life anymore. Isn't it what you expected? Did you ever think that your foreign agent's tricks would work on me? Me, Boris Arsenyev, internal number 152-AH1021, proud citizen of the Commonwealth State? You were wrong. You were always wrong, but you were too weak and stubborn to admit it. You went on ruining your life, my life, the lives of everyone that you came across, even Slavik's, whom you'd never met, but you just wouldn't stop. And fortunately, I am here to stop you. I did it even earlier, this evening, when I was at the voting pole. You know what I said? You do, of course you do, you were there, behind me, all the time. But I still want you to listen to it once again. I, citizen Boris Arsenyev, internal number 152-AH1021, give my vote to Victor Vasilyevich Pravdin, my close friend. Yes, I said it, and the people who went past me, smiled at me like no one had ever smiled at me before, not in the army, nor in the Center of Patriotic Education. Or did you want to deprive me of it, too? Of this faceless, yet so close crowd that has been my home ever since I lost my family? No, Vladimir Ivanovich, you failed again. You are a loser, professor, not an almighty arbiter of the universal fate, not a wise mentor, but an average loser, millions of which are scattered all over the world, buried in their own ignorance and insanity. And I don't hate you anymore. I don't despise you. I have no more feelings towards you, and, I guess it's my own catharsis, as Slava would have put it. Purification through suffering. So, goodbye, Vladmir Ivanovich and I hope that you won't disturb me anymore. For my part, I promise to forget you completely, and my memory isn't so good, as you probably know. Goodbye, Vladimir Ivanovich, and may you find your utopia in the hell you are burning in!"

It was nine o'clock on the day of the National Election 2070. Boris was sitting in front of his calculating machine and tearing the last page from his book.

What a fuss the Beasts are making!
From the lake the Moon they're raking.
They must nail it up on high
In its place to light the sky!

Then he took his toy elephant and tore off its head. He placed
the debris of both cards inside the artificial cotton so that they were
hardly visible, and then put what was left from the toy inside a
utilization bag. The bits of the book went there too, and the pliers
with red handles and rusty tips. He sealed the bag and kicked it in
the corner of his room. In two weeks', time he'd be able to get a
permission to go out, and he'll throw the bag somewhere –
somewhere safe, so that no one could find it. The broadcaster
announced the last communication interval for the day, and suddenly
he had an idea.

"Katyusha, find the number of Joseph Beglow."

"One entry found in memory. Joseph Beglow, internal
number 862-BC2253."

"Record the message for Joseph Beglow, internal number
862-BC2253. Start of the message. Joseph, I thought about your
offer at the polygon, and I am ready to accept it. Please let me know
what is required from me. Waiting for your answer. Your teammate,
Boris Arsenyev. End of message."

The darkness licked its lips while its belly was digesting what
was left from Boris, and a pair of green animal eyes blinked and then
closed again. The darkness, the god of greediness, was happy with
its new sacrifice.

"Very satisfying," it spoke. "Just the right way to present a
gift to the god. Not that I had any doubts in him, no, but I was
curious how long he'd last. And he lasted long. Not too long, though,
but considering the given circumstances, he was good. I might
change my mind later, but for now I'd call him one of my best
sacrifices. Why him? Not his grandfather, nor President Malinin, nor
hundreds of others, whose names I've already forgotten? Well, I

don't know. Perhaps, it's because he did it all himself. Self-purification is always better than the one which comes from the outside. Can you imagine? I didn't even need to kill him in order to eat him whole. Will there be more of them? Of course, there will. Because every time someone dares to stand out and to raise their head, it is only to put it on my altar. On the altar of the god of greediness. It's always been like that, and I'm getting bored of it, I guess, but this guy made me laugh. We'll see to it that he gets the best place on the polygon, among the select toxic waste. We'll make sure he receives what he deserves, ain't we? 'ey, I said ain't we? I'm talkin' to you, ya daft ball of fat! You sleepin' or what?" a pair of green animal eyes opened lazily, stared from the darkness for a while and then closed again.

Epilogue. 2070

Next morning, on the other side of the city, an elderly man in thick glasses, who used to be able to program the sun to rise on the west, was still sitting on his chair looking at his broadcaster expectantly. The National Election Day was over, and everything was as usual – the news was on, and the presenter was cursing the Black Plague using the same words as he had used ten or twenty years ago. Liza quietly came into the room and put her hand on his shoulder.

"Kostya, are you okay? Have you been sitting here for the whole night?"

"I can't afford to sleep, Liza. It might happen at any moment," he said sharply, but his voice was weak, and his eyes were watering, and seeing him like this was extremely unsettling for his wife.

"What can happen, Kostya?" she asked.

"The freedom…"

"You have a bad heart, dear. You shouldn't be so careless about it."

"I *have* a heart, Liza, and it wants to be free. I cannot miss this moment, and it's almost now, according to my calculations."

"What moment, Kostya? What are you talking about? I don't understand. Freedom? What do you know about it?"

"I know everything. All these years I've been thinking… Waiting… Making plans…"

"So, realize them! No need to wait for someone to set you free!"

"I can't."

"Why? What prevents you?"

Kostya looked at his wife as if she was speaking in another language.

"What prevents me?" he repeated. "Everything. All this…" He made an indefinite sign with his hand, circling the room.

"What? The walls? The ceiling? The furniture?"

"No, Liza! The micropasses, the drones, this red diode, after all!"

"Really? Do you really think that should they all disappear, you'll become a free man at once? Even if you do, what will change for you, Kostya? Will you go outside? With you high pressure and your weak heart? Your swollen legs? You'll tumble and fall at the first crossroads, and other free people will walk past, or step on you just because they are free to do it! Kostya, we've always lived like this. We don't know any other life, and we can't be sure whether changing the order of things would be good for us. What if this freedom is not our fate? What if it's not a blessing, but a curse, making us fully responsible for the choices we make – right or wrong – all the infinite choices that are now so generously made for us from above? Are you prepared to take full liability for your own life? Do you think these choices will make you a better man? Stop being ridiculous, Kostya, you've always been so cold-hearted and reasonable. Have you taken your supportive capsules, by the way? Forgotten again, haven't you? Now, let's go to the bedroom. You'll lie down, and I'll make you a nice glass of tea drink. Oh, do you hear it? Yes, 'Time to Think' is on!"

And off they went, hand in hand, slowly, through the corridor and past the locked front door, which blinked at them approvingly with its little red diode-eye. Millions of other diodes flashed in sync, and they shone so brightly that if you take a closer look, you can even see them now. If you look even closer, you are likely to see faces in these flashes, and some vague figures standing on the hill in the middle of the nuclear waste site, which, for some strange reason, is called the Commonwealth State. And there they are standing now, keeping this state together with their own hands and their own lives, and a little white balloon is still trying to make its way into the sky above them. And although it doesn't matter to anyone, maybe it is worth saying goodbye to them before they disappear forever in the nacreous snow.

Sergey Anatolyevich Malinin, the Destabilizer; 12.05.2000 – 10.08.2035

Vladimir Ivanovich Rogov, a traitor and a foreign agent; 23.11.1968 – 19.11.2036

Gennadiy 'Uncle Gena' Petrenko, internal number 031-BBL1984, colonel; 03.07.2003 – 23.04.2060

Vyacheslav Lebedev, internal number 343-AT2917, an inspiration seeker, 28.12.2039 – 01.10.2070

Nadezhda Vasilievna Komissarova, a broken-handed lady, 27.10.1990 – 13.10.2070

Boris Arsenyev, internal number 152-AH1021, an artist; 07.01.2029 – 23.04.2072